Praise for
Love & Conductivity

"A gorgeous literary historical novel that will transport readers to post-WWI America with sumptuous period details, beautifully crafted imagery, and a swoon-worthy romance that's the stuff of dreams and yet feels oh-so real. Nieto has magicked a story that is perfectly of its time and ours, as every page rings with echoes that resonate today. I was swept away by the emotional depth of this slow-burn love story, and its conclusion left me teary-eyed and tingling with the best kind of goosebumps."

—Erin Lindsay McCabe, *USA Today* bestselling author of *I Shall Be Near To You*

"*Love & Conductivity* by Erin Nieto is a beautifully written tale that captures the elegance of a bygone era with lyrical prose and emotional depth. Nieto's masterful storytelling blends romance and adventure with a touch of whimsy, creating a narrative that feels both timeless and refreshingly original. Her vivid descriptions and nuanced characters draw readers into Eleanor Morgan's world, making every moment resonate. A celebration of dreams, love, and self-discovery, this historical romance is as enchanting as it is heartfelt."

—Dianne C. Braley, author of *The Summer Before*, winner of the 2024 NYC Big Book Award

"*Love & Conductivity* is a refreshing work of historical fiction. Based on real-life letters, readers will dive heart first into this unforgettable romance that's both sigh worthy and sweet. It's been a long time since I've come across a story that's so smart and endearing. Erin Nieto is definitely an author to watch!"

—Brandy Vallance, author of
The Covered Deep & *Within the Veil*

"*Love & Conductivity* evokes a bygone era in full color through tender prose and elegant description. Nieto deftly executes the epistolary format to illuminate the tension of dreams bigger than the space allotted to them, the power of words to transcend convention, and the electric warmth of a love that seeks not to change but to simply be embraced. A wonderful read."

—Rachel Stone, author of *The Blue Iris*

"From its opening lines, *Love and Conductivity* reveals that, while the historical setting of 1917 may be familiar, the language used to describe the war's events sparks unexpectedly thought-provoking considerations from its vivid opening lines. . . .
"This reference, with its intriguing capture of a home front which harbors a countenance of uncertainty similar to Schrödinger's cat, promises a story that eschews the traditionally staid approaches to World War I history, creating a more vivid perspective than readers might anticipate.

"This, in turn, strengthens a powerful saga of separation, friendship, and love which is cemented by Erin Nieto's attention to different devices to capture the shifting tides of these times. This includes letters such as the ones written in 1921 between Thomas Erwin Phipps (a student of chemistry in Berkeley) and teacher Eleanor Morgan. Eleanor longs for adventure in her staid life, finding it in an unexpected meeting of minds with a lieutenant on his way home after the Armistice.

"Their brief encounter grows love slowly, over time and the miles, but Eleanor must first overcome her innate tendency to reject the adventure she so desires before she can take the kinds of risks that lead to more intimate connections. "Nieto creates a forceful story of self-discovery and coupling against the backdrop of changing times. Her ability to inject history with a gripping 'you are here' feel of immediacy through psychological and social depth lends the story a revealing tone that is at once poetic and intimate. . . .

"Readers seeking a vivid, slowly-evolving romance in which life events buffet Eleanor and her beau, yet create serendipitous moments of growth and discovery, will find *Love and Conductivity* exceptionally vivid and thought-provoking.

"Libraries will want to highly recommend *Love and Conductivity* to book clubs seeking blends of romance and history that point to many possible discussion topics about social mores, love, and the kinds of risk-taking that result in truly effective changes, whether they take place on a personal or a social level."

—D. Donovan, senior reviewer, *Midwest Book Review*

"*Love & Conductivity* is a cozy story about two souls that brushed each other and instantly knew where they belonged. Even though life took them to opposite ends of the country, they closed the distance one letter at a time, fighting against societal norms to find their way back to each other. This lovely novel pulled every single emotion out of me: hope, anger, frustration, longing, fear, apprehension, joy. It had me in tears more times than I can count. It touched my heart, made me cry tears of joy, and I think it will stay with me for a very long time. I think thousands of others will adore it just as much as I did."

—Lydia Pilot, actor

"Inspired by real historical correspondence, Erin Nieto has crafted a charming epistolary romance that is at times playful and tender. A heartfelt and heartwarming love story!"

—Jessica Brockmole, internationally bestselling author of *Letters from Skye*

Love and Conductivity
by Erin Nieto

© Copyright 2025 Erin Nieto

ISBN 979-8-88824-602-3

All rights reserved. No part of this publication may be reproduced, stored in a retrieval system, or transmitted in any form or by any means—electronic, mechanical, photocopy, recording, or any other—except for brief quotations in printed reviews, without the prior written permission of the author.

This is a work of fiction. All the characters in this book are fictitious, and any resemblance to actual persons, living or dead, is purely coincidental. The names, incidents, dialogue, and opinions expressed are products of the author's imagination and are not to be construed as real.

Edited by Miranda Dillon
Cover design by Catherine Herold

Published by

◢ köehlerbooks™

3705 Shore Drive
Virginia Beach, VA 23455
800-435-4811
www.koehlerbooks.com

LOVE AND CONDUCTIVITY

ERIN NIETO

VIRGINIA BEACH
CAPE CHARLES

For my family.

Your encouragement, love, and support made this all possible.

I love you.

CHAPTER I

> The course of true love
> Never did run smooth
> —William Shakespeare, *A Midsummer Night's Dream*

IN 1917, THE men went away and were replaced with photographs. At the Brandenburg Boarding House, which rented rooms to women of the Oklahoma University faculty, they all had someone swept away by the draft: brothers, husbands, sons, lovers, all now smiling back from their framed perches, where they both existed, and didn't.

Eleanor Morgan was a transplant from North Carolina and, at twenty-three, had long been accustomed to separation from her older brother, Lawrence. But it had never occurred to her to display his photo. Until, that is, she became consumed by the fear that the separation could become permanent. So there he sat, atop the bureau where she could see his dark, curly hair and the tilt of his wide, frog-like grin, which, to Eleanor, implied he'd rather be reading Elizabethan broadsides than training at officer's camp in Texas.

Next to Lawrence's photo stood Erwin's, who was the younger brother of Helen Phipps, with whom she shared a room. Helen was a professor of Spanish and a seasoned woman of thirty-six. She'd been born in Turkey and had traveled the world.

In Erwin's snapshot, taken in the garden of their home in Austin, he wore a boater hat and bow tie, eyes squinting to slits from the glare of the sun, or discomfort, or both. His worry look, Helen called it. With both Lawrence and Erwin called to duty, somehow, she and Helen felt that if they spoke about the boys in the presence of their photographs, they would remain safe. They dubbed their ritual the Brotherly Adoration Society.

Eleanor had first come to Oklahoma in Lawrence's wake after he'd accepted a position in the English department. She was to finish her graduate studies and then consider living her own adventurous dream: to live by the sea and write, as far from North Carolina as possible. But the war had come and upended it all, unexpectedly elevating her into Lawrence's teaching position. And amid the unrelenting tide of chaos that year, Eleanor and Helen had found a bond that felt like kinship, lit by a spirit of compassion.

"He says he expects to be sent to a school of artillery in France," Helen said, her slender frame stretched across her narrow bed as she read Erwin's latest letter, sent from Camp Jackson in South Carolina. He was a natural-born scientist, Helen had told her, fascinated with nature and drawn to the more dangerous aspects of chemistry—volatile substances and powerful forces.

"Artillery," Helen repeated, glancing at Erwin's photograph, then quickly away, a shadow of grief crossing her face. "I could just cry at the irony of it all." She folded the letter back into its envelope. "But never mind *that*." She looked over to Eleanor, who sat in their little rocking chair. "He won't be killed in the trenches of France."

"Certainly not," came Eleanor's response.

Helen smiled once more. "He will come back. And then he will find a way to convert base metals to gold."

Eleanor laughed and rocked. She thought often of Erwin's return, forming a picture in her mind colored by all she knew of the alchemists of yore. "And Lawrence will become the world's next Shakespeare," she said.

And then, one October afternoon, Eleanor found Helen in stunned silence at their shared desk, a telegram on the floor beside her reading simply, "Erwin dead."

A scent of burning leaves hung in the air, Helen's gaze locked with anguish on Erwin's photograph on the bureau. Eleanor felt the stinging impossibility of this occurrence. Erwin was here with them just as he had been all year long, the worry look still occupying his face.

Eleanor had never seen Helen drop her composure. She seemed instead to slip into a groove she already knew. Incredibly painful yet familiar. This is what you do when someone you love dies.

Helen called the newspaper, bought a ticket home to Austin, and solemnly announced to the Brandenburgs that she would return in a week's time. In silence, Eleanor helped her pack, handing her Erwin's photo from the dresser, leaving Lawrence to hold his post alone. Helen placed it between two layers of clothes and closed her suitcase, and they cried together.

```
The Daily Transcript
Norman, Oklahoma
Friday, October 11, 1918


MISS PHIPPS'S BROTHER DIES IN SERVICE

Miss Helen Phipps of the Department of
Spanish at the University received a
message from her sister Miss Peggy Phipps
of Austin, Texas, yesterday, stating that
```

```
her brother, Thomas Erwin Phipps had been
killed in service. The telegram was very
brief and did not tell the date Mr. Phipps
was killed or the manner of the death.

Before entering the service, Mr. Phipps was
professor of chemistry at the University
of Texas. He had formerly received an
MA degree and had a distinction for
accomplishment in his line of work. He was
considered a man with a brilliant future.
```

Eleanor read aloud from the newspaper, her voice breaking at the last sentence. Helen was typically the one to read to the breakfast table at the Brandenburg house; her measured manner of speaking could dull the sharp edges of even the most horrific news reports, allowing the women to take in the day's information and get on with their lives. But Helen was gone, and Eleanor found herself, in the face of her sorrow, unequal to the task. There was a terrible finality about it, reading Erwin's death in print. That any man so alive could be blown out like a match. A silence fell across the room as Eleanor laid the newspaper back on the table and tried to regain her self-possession. Helen would be arriving at her home today, she reassured herself, to the comfort of her family.

Mrs. Brandenburg broke the silence. "Such a pity," she said. "Helen adored him."

Eleanor's thoughts flashed on one of the stories Helen loved to tell about Erwin as a small child, gone missing one morning from their new, sprawling farm property in Tennessee; she and Peggy searched for him frantically amid the pastures and timber, Helen calling out until her voice nearly gave way, fear rising with each passing minute. And then she happened upon him, finally, under a willow tree at the bank of a small pond beyond their land, carefully studying every little thing within his reach—the flowers and rocks and insects—blissfully unaware of any sense of danger whatsoever. He'd simply wandered off, she said, enraptured by nature.

And Eleanor could see from Helen's face when she told that story that this was the essence of the Erwin that she loved. And Eleanor had thought that this was the very thing she longed for in life as well: to wander off and indulge her own curiosity about the world. And that here was a man she might be able to talk to, as she talked to Lawrence.

But now, it would never be. And she must press on. She had to muster the fortitude to carry on with her responsibilities. And that morning, it meant her work with the Food Administration, preaching "the gospel of the clean plate," as Hoover called it, so more resources could be sent to the men overseas.

The telephone in the front hall began to trill, and with a scrape of her chair, Mrs. Brandenburg rose to answer it.

Mrs. Dungan, the piano teacher, retrieved the newspaper from the table and scanned it, her eyes alighting on one of the advertisements. "Now they're urging us to begin our *Christmas shopping*," she said. "Can you believe it? Begin your shopping very early, it says, so as not to clog the nation's war business!"

"That doesn't sound very merry," said Miss Green, an instructor of economics. "I suppose they'll suggest next that we all gift each other war bonds."

An air of amusement returned to the table as Mrs. Brandenburg reemerged with an expression of shock. "That was Reverend Phipps."

Eleanor seized with alarm for fear that Helen, too, had met with some unfortunate fate.

"He's just received word from the major in charge of Erwin's battery," she said. "His death report was made *in error*. He was terribly stricken with Spanish influenza, but the major says he's now expected to make a full recovery."

Eleanor launched to her feet immediately, propelled by a burst of sweetness and light in her heart. Her grief transformed to joy at the news, realizing that Helen would be regaled with this same happy news upon her arrival home. That she, in turn, would come back to Norman and reinstate Erwin's photograph next to Lawrence on the bureau. And this would all be another story to tell someday.

"Oh, how wonderful! I'll call up the newspaper," she said as her mind eagerly formed the words of the conversation.

```
The Daily Transcript
Norman, Oklahoma
Monday, October 14, 1918


MISS PHIPPS' BROTHER NOT DEAD, AS REPORTED

The report of the death of Thomas Erwin
Phipps, brother of Miss Helen Phipps of
the University faculty, was unfounded,
according to word received in Norman
Saturday. Mr. Phipps was said to have
been killed at Camp Jackson, SC, but
the facts are that he was critically ill
with influenza and is now improving. Miss
Phipps went to her home in Austin, Texas,
upon receiving the first message.
```

CHAPTER II

```
WESTERN UNION TELEGRAM
Received at: NORMAN OK
1918 DEC 15 AM 9 45
To: MISS HELEN PHIPPS


DEPARTING MUSKOGEE. ARRIVING NORMAN AT
1: 50 PM CAN INTERRUPT YOU FOR 6HRS AND
RETURN FOR NIGHT TRAIN THROUGH TO HOME


YR BRO ERWIN
```

ERWIN SENT THE telegram and bid goodbye to his older brother, Foster, with a boyish cuff to the ear as he did. When he boarded the train bound for Austin, he became possessed by a thrilling sense of starting over. The war had ended, and the world he left behind and was coming back to was both familiar and unfamiliar. Foster was now a father, with a home of his own, a respectable position as an assistant US attorney, and a neatly trimmed mustache. At twenty-three, Erwin could only wonder what the future now held for him.

In 1917, when the draft had come calling, he'd just been accepted into Berkeley's doctoral program of physical chemistry. His plans were to settle in California and finish the program as a scientist. But the war had upended all of that. His dreams of research and invention were replaced with foot drills and cannoneer rolls, and here he was a year later, a lieutenant but not yet a scientist. He was eager to resume that life but apprehensive over whether it still existed.

The more boisterous of the uniformed men in the train car banded together, singing, "There's a long, long trail a-windin, Into the land of my dreams, Where the nightingales are singing, And a white moon beams."

The long winding road they had all apprehended for themselves not so long ago had seemed immeasurable, with only the reflection of hope in those songs to sustain them. And now, however improbably, the train lurched each of them, finally, to the trail's end. Erwin joined in the song that had become so familiar, his voice booming like it hadn't back when he enlisted: "There's a long, long night of waiting. Until my dreams all come true; Till the day when I'll be going down, That long, long trail with you."

He hadn't seen Helen for nearly two years. And he knew that if he didn't see her today, another two years could well pass before he had the chance again. If the previous months and years had taught him anything, it was that people could disappear in the blink of an eye. And then there *were* no more chances. In a different reality, just inches away, it seemed, he was being returned home to Austin, not among the singing soldiers clutching their discharge papers but in a wooden box in the baggage car.

As much as he foolishly wanted it, he knew there would be no easy picking up of life where he'd left off, as if the war had never happened. It was easier to imagine himself a Rip Van Winkle, the world to which he returned a blank slate. Foster had not been carried off by the war. And as grateful as Erwin was for that, he had been taken by surprise at feeling a yearning, a pang of jealousy, for the start Foster had made. For his lovely home, which rang with the laughter and joy of a brand-new life. Erwin had been afforded a second lease on his, and he could thrill at such novel possibilities were it not for the debilitating regret he felt at having caused his family the pain of his death report. He felt he needed to make amends to Helen before he could press forward and truly clean his slate.

As the train's wheels screeched to a halt at Norman, Erwin nudged his way through the car to the vestibule and searched the faces of those gathered on the station platform. He leaned over the rail, jockeying for position among the jumble of fellow soldiers, hurriedly glancing around until he spotted her at the back of the crowd, bespectacled and clutching tightly to her hat: Helen. He waved high, his heart filling with euphoric gratitude.

"Sis!" He leaped from the vestibule to the platform, pushing through the crowd.

"Erwin! My dear!" she exclaimed and opened her arms wide. "What a lovely, lovely surprise." She tightly embraced him, and amid the scent of rosewater and the warmth of her body, he realized how long he had missed such basic human contact. A lump rose in his throat. He made up his mind to say something right away. To tell her how sorry he was for bringing her pain, for amplifying her duty to the rest of the family again. "Sis," he started.

Helen pulled back, a gaze instantly familiar, maternal. "You're back from the dead," she said in a wry manner and sent up a hand to smooth his forehead.

Erwin let out a huge breath and laughed. He knew then that he didn't need to apologize, that just like that, they'd communicated all.

Helen walked him through the campus, on a whirlwind tour of the University, and then to the Brandenburg house, where, she said, she wanted to introduce him to her "Norman family."

"And you've arrived just in time," she said with facetious air as they approached the front porch. "We're having tea to celebrate Mrs. Dungan, the teacher of piano. She gave an extraordinary performance in Oklahoma City yesterday."

Erwin stopped. He hated tea parties. And he didn't want to sign up for an evening of polite chattering. He'd endured a lot over the previous year, but still, *anything* but that.

"Oh, for Pete's sake, Helen. Isn't there some kind of loophole to exempt me? I'm neither properly dressed nor prepared for such a thing."

"Tea parties are eternal, dear brother." Helen pulled at his arm. "Even after one comes back from the dead, even after war and pestilence."

Erwin shot her a look.

"Well, whether you think so or not, they're good for us," she said decidedly. "They force us out of ourselves and into the lives of others. We need that."

"Isn't that what books are for?" he muttered. He didn't expect an answer, and she didn't give one.

They were alike in so many ways, but this is where they had always differed. Society was a place where she could forget life's cares and feel rewarded and energized. Erwin believed that a good, long hike through nature could achieve the same effect without all the accordant fuss. If anything, being in society produced the opposite effect—exhausting him. Being so focused on surfaces, nobody could see each other anyway, and that put him on the defensive. *Tea battles*, he'd come to call them.

"And in regard to your uniform," she continued. "'*Good humor may be said to be one of the very best articles of dress one can wear.*'"

Thackeray. Erwin shook his head and started walking again. Helen had already put him in the best humor he'd enjoyed in a long time. And he was the one interrupting her life, after all. He would put up no more resistance. For her, he would subject himself to the tea battle.

"Just please don't tell me there'll be singing," he said.

"Well! One can never be sure of that." Helen suppressed a grin. "The singing mood can strike at any time." They approached the door. "In any event," she said, "you can meet Eleanor. She hates tea parties too."

Erwin's heart gave a little lurch. He was keen to meet Eleanor, who Helen had often mentioned in her letters. *Eleanor is a marvel*, Helen had written, *well-read, adventurous, and perfectly sympathetic.*

And with that, Helen entered the house, announcing his arrival as if it were some formal gala. "Ladies and gentlemen, my brother, Thomas Erwin Phipps!" She bid him forward. "An unexpected arrival, but then he always did like a reaction!"

Erwin entered. "That's Lieutenant Phipps, Sis."

Helen laughingly saluted, and the assembled group in the house's front hall stood and moved toward them in greeting. A merry fire danced in the grate; vases of white lilies graced the tabletops. Helen rattled through names as Erwin shook hands: Miss Brower, Miss Bell, Miss Johnson, Mrs. Mackay—he forgot them instantly, wondering only which one of them was Eleanor. Finally, they came to Mrs. Dungan, an effervescent woman of small stature with big, round eyes and salt-and-pepper hair. She took Erwin's hand with hers, clasping them together.

"I'm sorry to have invaded during your tea," Erwin said.

"Nonsense, dear boy," she said and released her grasp. "The war is ended! It's the best cause for celebration."

She took to a nearby piano and began to play and sing, "Gee! What a wonderful time we'll have when the boys come home. The flags will fly and the bands will play. We'll all turn out with a smile so gay. And ev'ry one shouting, 'hip hip hooray' when the boys come home."

"Hip hip hooray!" the assembled guests shouted as Mrs. Dungan played. Erwin shot Helen another look. As grand a gesture as it was for them to join in the song for his benefit, he was wholly embarrassed by the attention. And it was just the kind of surface-level treatment he'd wanted to avoid—arriving here not as Helen's brother, someone to know on his terms, but instead as a uniformed representative of the wave of soldiers arriving home. He'd been cheered at enough throughout his journey. He began to consider a retreat.

At the sound of the commotion, however, an attractive young woman with loosely curled, cropped auburn hair descended the stairs, appearing to wonder what all the fuss had been about.

"Eleanor," Helen said, reaching for Erwin's arm. "Look who's here!"

His heart leaped up again to hear her name, and Eleanor's eyes grew wide and flashed recognition. She quickened her steps to the landing. "Well, well, Lieutenant Erwin Phipps, I believe," she said. "This *is* quite a surprise. You didn't realize you would end up having tea in your honor, now did you?" She smiled sweetly. She wore a plain white blouse with a smart collar and a long, pleated skirt. Far less ornamentation than other guests, yet far more radiant. A line by Tennyson floated into his mind: *wearing all that weight of learning, lightly, like a flower.* Perhaps he would have a comrade here after all—a quite lovelier one than he'd imagined.

"It's unfortunate to have to be rehabilitated back into the ways of society so quickly," he said. "It's quite a shock to the system."

She nodded in agreement and extended her hand. "Pleasure to meet you."

He took her hand, pale, soft, and delicate, and as their eyes met, he felt a spark of something quite unexpected. It wasn't just that her gaze was sympathetic, but her face held an expression that felt clearly familiar, as though she *knew* him.

In any proper first greeting, a man oughtn't to hold a woman's hand for longer than three seconds—this he knew—yet at least five had passed before Helen cleared her throat decidedly, startling him back to the moment.

"Well," Helen said, and he broke his gaze, leaving him more than a little abashed.

Mrs. Dungan's performance the previous night in Oklahoma City, it turned out, had featured an operetta of childhood songs—"Mother Goose" and the like—which she replayed on this occasion as a game of Going to Jerusalem. The three Brandenburg children joined in, singing and laughing, as the adults romped around the room, scrambling for chairs at the stop of each song.

And amid the excitement of the silly game, Erwin's spirit rose. Between the demands of family, scholarship, and military service, he'd been "in harness" for years. Throwing off the yoke in this unexpected way made him feel lighter. And all the more that *he* wanted to live, rise, and have his chance at joy. Perhaps with a laughing playmate, he thought, as he watched Eleanor, the winner of the final chair of the game. And her eyes gleamed with the hilarity of the moment, reflecting his own; against the odds, they were the ones having the most fun at a tea party.

Seizing on the return of his lighthearted, jocular self, he leaped in to suggest the next game to the Brandenburg children. "Do you think," he asked the three, "that if we tried together, we could lift a person using just two fingers?"

"No!" said the youngest, a small blond girl Helen had introduced as Winifred.

"Oh, I bet we can," Erwin said. "How about if Helen helps us?"

"Yes, let's try!" The oldest boy, Jack, shrieked in delight. "Miss Morgan! We could lift *you*! Please, let us lift you!"

Eleanor's face flushed with surprise. "Oh well," she stammered and looked to Helen, who gave a lighthearted shrug to communicate that she knew the game.

Eleanor's eyes set in wry amusement. "Well, I suppose I oughtn't to be a sore winner," she said. "And only because of that, Mr. Phipps, I agree to the experiment." Their eyes met, and he felt another spark, with a current of tenderness, drawing him in with its magnetic pull.

"You're gracious in your victory, Miss Morgan," he said smilingly.

Once she was positioned, lying across two chairs as best she could, Erwin, the Brandenburg children, and Helen stood around her. He and Helen, at opposite shoulders, would ensure her safety.

"Now," he said. "Forefingers underneath. Close your eyes." He felt the softness of Eleanor's blouse, the warmth of her arm beyond the material, the movement of her rising breath.

"What holds us to the earth?" he asked the children. "It's the force of gravity, isn't it?"

"Yes!"

"Then I'm going to count to three," he said. "And while I do that, you blow away all of the gravity from Eleanor, and then she'll be light as a feather."

"One . . ." The children blew onto her legs, arms, and torso. "Two . . ." Eleanor's blouse fluttered. "Three!"

They hoisted her up slowly, with an ease that brought astonishment and delight. Erwin's body filled with warmth as he regarded her, her eyes closed with a serene expression. Unexpectedly, his thoughts reached home. He was seized with a longing to stay, unbroken, with this warmth and this sight, in this moment of perfect joy, free from the weight and demands of transiency. He felt nearly as though the house around them had disappeared, becoming instead a sunlit meadow, and he had stumbled upon the perfect sight of the season's first wild rose, perfectly formed and flushed with color underneath a still blue sky.

Eleanor was lifted nearly up to Winifred's shoulders before the distribution of their combined mortal strength buckled. Winifred, unable to lift any higher, let fall her right leg, and Eleanor immediately tumbled toward Erwin with a shriek. Snapping out of his daze, he kicked away one of the chairs and freed his hands to catch her, which he did—barely—with them both in an awkward heap on the floor, her cheek pressed tightly to his. Dropped back rudely into time and space, back to the world of moving bodies and gravity, he'd broken the spell.

"Are you hurt?" he asked, helping her up.

"No. It's—I'm—fine," she stammered and smoothed her skirt.

"Now Miss Greene!" Jack cried, the rest of the gang chiming in, "You next! Let's try again!"

The jest flashed on. So many things Erwin wanted to say to Eleanor at that moment, but his mind could not form the words. That her presence energized him, and he wanted to know her. That, in her weightlessness, he had gone a hundred miles away and stayed a hundred years.

Eleanor made her way toward the hearth. Erwin and the children had just finished levitating Miss Greene without incident, and Eleanor had nearly recuperated from the exhilaration and embarrassment she'd felt upon her tumble into his arms, the press of his cheek to hers, the frantic rattle of her heart.

The children lobbied Erwin for another round, but he declined. Spotting Eleanor in the room, he joined her at the fireside. He wasn't quite conventionally handsome, but he was handsome—a combination of vivacity and intelligence, a kind of earthy grace that had not shown in his photograph. And in his uniform, he was devastating.

"I'm sorry about the tumble," he said. "I'm afraid I was too caught up in the experiment."

Eleanor sat in a nearby armchair. "No harm done. I'd say your hypothesis still holds up."

This seemed to please him, and he pulled the footstool over to sit beside her. "Well, this tea party isn't nearly as bad as I expected," he said.

"They never are, of course. And yet we dread them just the same."

"Oh, I don't know, sometimes they *really* are awful."

They laughed and leaned toward each other.

"Are you from here in Oklahoma?" he asked.

"No, North Carolina. Goldsboro, more particularly."

"I've just come through Asheville. Was Goldsboro nearby?"

"Not quite. Goldsboro is farther south and east. Our main distinction is having been one of General Sherman's last stops on his march to the sea."

"Aha," he said. "And will *you* be marching back to the sea for the Christmas holiday?"

Eleanor smiled. "Not this winter. I'm afraid my war work with the Food Administration is still too heavy," she said.

"A Hooverite!"

"Wheatless and meatless to save Democracy!" she saluted playfully.

"Democracy saved," he said with a disarming earnestness. His evenness and wit did indeed remind her of Lawrence.

"And I'm occupied also in my suffrage circle," Eleanor pressed on, surprising herself by wanting to share with him what she felt about this remarkable thing happening across the country. "Now that Oklahoma's gone and done the right thing, we have to get as many women registered to vote as possible."

"And a suffragist!" He nudged her warmly and advanced his inquiry. "What do your politicians in North Carolina think about suffrage? Do you think they'll follow Oklahoma's lead?"

And with Erwin, Eleanor felt like a knot inside her had been untied. Somehow, she'd known all along that she *would* feel this way if they should ever meet. She felt that she liked him—that she could continue to like him very much.

They talked on at length as the tea party went on around them, making their way through politics and on to poetry by the time Helen reappeared with a pot of hot chocolate.

"Care for a cup?" Helen asked.

"I would never turn down your hot chocolate, Sis," Erwin said. "Helen used to make up a pot every weekend back when I was still in primary school. She picked up the specialty on her travels in Mexico."

"Luckily for us, she carries on the tradition here," Eleanor said.

"Lucky you indeed," Erwin said. "I dreamed of this stuff when I was back in the barracks."

Helen poured two cups and placed them on the hearth to cool. "And for another of our home traditions." She handed Erwin a small wooden box. He smiled.

"Eleanor, have you seen this one?" Erwin asked.

"I'm not sure. What is it?"

"Driftwood powder," Helen said.

"What do you do with it?"

"Just watch." Erwin's grin spread to his ears. "Gather round! Come look!" he called to the children. Winifred slipped onto Eleanor's lap, and when the guests assembled around the hearth, Erwin stood and opened the box.

"Sis, have you got an incantation?" he asked Helen.

"Naturally," she said. "In the spirit of the evening, *Cross Patch, draw the latch, sit by the fire and spin; Take a cup, and drink it up, Then call your neighbors in.*"

As Helen spoke, Erwin sprinkled a handful of the powder onto the blazing logs. And when Helen's little rhyme stopped, as if by magic, color leaped out from the flames: flickers of violet and blue and deep green.

A collective sigh raced around the room. Winifred sat straight with wonder.

"Fire fairies!" she said and reached up to lace her arms around Eleanor's neck.

Erwin carefully explained the chemistry involved in the trick; the "driftwood" was from planks of old whaling brigs, he said, which absorbed deposits of the chemical interaction between the metals of the boat's construction and the salts of the seawater. And it was this interaction, he said, that caused the changes in the fire's color.

Eleanor sat, looking up at Erwin. She was enchanted. He couldn't have known he had already carved out territory inside her heart, even before his arrival. And as he spoke, detailing this alchemistic mixture of fact and something like poetry, he filled that territory so fully that Eleanor felt a magnetic charge. He caught her eye as she looked at him across the hearth. He gave her a private smile, and she blushed, which set her body trembling despite the flames' heat. And she realized it must be the thing she had never felt before: love. Deep, electric, intoxicating love.

After the party, they were alone for a few minutes. Mrs. Dungan returned to the piano as the ladies cleaned up, and Helen had retreated upstairs to fetch her coat. She was to walk Erwin back to the station.

"Perhaps we'll bump into each other again?" Erwin said.

"Possibly," Eleanor said. "But I'm afraid I'll be redundant here as soon as my brother returns to his position." She held out her hand, which Erwin took and held in both of his, studying it.

"And then what will your next plan be?"

"Something daring and glorious, I hope. Scaling Mount Everest, perhaps?" she kidded, but something about Erwin's presence made her feel that brave.

"I have every confidence in you."

"Thank you," she said, a flush rising as he gazed at her hand.

"That's a lovely ring," he said of the gold filigree band set with an opal, which Lawrence had given her for her eighteenth birthday. "Size six, looks like?"

Eleanor could not speak. She felt a quiver run through her again. She could only smile with lips that trembled once more, feeling that if she spoke, Erwin might hear the quiver in her voice. But she wouldn't betray herself; she couldn't fall in love. Not now, not with her life of adventure still ahead.

Helen reemerged with her coat.

"I wish—" Erwin said, while Eleanor said, "Goodbye." And she paused, wanting intently to know what he had been about to say. He flustered, saying only, "I wish I weren't going."

"So do I," Eleanor said, laughing, but she knew it had to be so. And then, despite herself, she could think only of all the things she still wanted to tell him and wanted him to tell her. And when he moved away from her, she felt a keen sense of loss. She buoyed this by drifting her thoughts to the lines of Keats.

Then I felt like some watcher of the skies,

When a new planet swims into his ken.

CHAPTER III

Norman, Oklahoma

May, 1919

ELEANOR SAT IN front of the fire at the boarding house; it would be her last at the Brandenburg's hearth. The weather didn't require it; the late spring days had already taken on the feel of summer. But the wind was so fierce that it was unwise to attempt an outdoor fire, and Eleanor had to burn papers to lighten her load; she would be going home to North Carolina.

She sorted the stack to burn and read Erwin's New Year greeting for the last time.

December 30th, 1918
Austin, Tex.

Dear Miss Morgan,
  Happy New Year! May 1919 bring you much daring and glory.

Sincerely yours,

Thomas E. Phipps

She swallowed hard, feeling only a sinking inside where there had once been delight. She folded the card back into its envelope, letting herself recall once more the euphoria she felt at first receiving it, punctuated by a particularly cold and lonely holiday season. Aside from the Brandenburgs, she had been alone in the house with only Miss Johnson, whose fiancé had just returned from war duty. And even amid their merriment, she'd felt an acute sense of distance and longing. And so the arrival of Erwin's letter seemed a gift to her soul at the very moment she wished most for one. She reread the response she'd made to his card, immediately, that day.

January 2, 1919
Norman, Okla.

My dear Mr. Phipps,
   Happy New Year yourself! I was glad to get your card. You should have been here to watch the old year out with us. We had almost as much fun as the evening that you were here—though our hearts failed us, along with the heat, so as early as ten o'clock, we had to resign the living room to a certain injured-looking couple who didn't mind the cold. Considerate of us, wasn't it?

Sincerely,

Eleanor Morgan

Heat rose in her cheeks as she read it. It was so forward. What had she been thinking? And how close she was to sending it before she found, upon Miss Green's arrival the following day, that he'd also sent her a nearly identical New Year greeting. *May 1919 raise you to new heights!* hers said. Miss Green, with whom Eleanor was certain Erwin had exchanged barely a few words! And he signed the card "Thomas E. Phipps" after he'd been introduced as "Erwin," which suggested to her that he hadn't been soliciting a response anyway. It was all such folly in retrospect. She held both card and response together for a moment in her hand and then tossed them both into the fire. Though a tiny part of her still thought—*perhaps*—not that she was destroying them, but sending them to the fire fairies, in the hopes that they'd grant her a wish: that she could somehow have one more moment with him, someday, just as they were that December night.

ACT ONE

We say love is blind, and the figure of Cupid is drawn with a bandage around his eyes. Blind—yes, because he does not see what he does not like; but the sharpest-sighted hunter in the universe is Love, for finding what he seeks, and only that.

—Ralph Waldo Emerson

Friday, February 13, 1920, Goldsboro, North Carolina

CRITICAL TIMES FOR CONFIRMED BACHELORS.

Today is a Friday, the thirteenth day of the month, and it will merge into tomorrow, which is St. Valentine's Day, and withal, it is leap year.

There seems no possible escape. Seldom does the calendar so contort itself to bring all these things together so near. It is fate, undeniable.

Those who have refused to pursue will be pursued with all the chances of the chase against them. And unwooed women, having been girded about by conventions that denied them the privilege of selection, may fare forth, armed with the unusual combination of Friday and thirteen, red with the spirit of the Patron of Love, and pursue such men their hearts desire.

The fates are with them.

CHAPTER IV

Goldsboro, North Carolina

February 14, 1920

At the apex of Miss Georgia Freeman's Valentine's Day party, seven red, heart-shaped cards fluttered through the air. From each card hung a long ribbon of gold, which had, until the previous moment, been dangling from her parlor ceiling.

Miss Freeman shuffled through the room, decorated with vases of pink and white larkspur, past her blindfolded party guests, gathering the cards from the floor. She put on her reading glasses to inspect them, looking for the lone card emblazoned with a silver arrow.

"Aha!" she exclaimed upon finding it and traced the card's ribbon to the hand that grasped the other end. Eleanor felt the tug.

"Eleanor has won the prize heart!"

Eleanor's chest tingled. A thought of Erwin came to her unbidden, but she shooed it away. She removed her blindfold. "Oh, stuff and nonsense," she said.

"But it's not, my dear. It's fate!" said Miss Freeman, holding up her card for all to see. Eleanor's fingers grasped the other end, and the half dozen remaining gold ribbons attached to non-arrowed hearts were clutched by the remaining members of their old XYZ society club.

"Alice, I think even *we* didn't expect that, did we?" Miss Freeman added teasingly to her niece, over her spectacles, gray hair wound tight in a top bun. She handed the card to Eleanor.

"Well, then there must be something she's not telling us," Alice said. She was a brunette with an upturned nose who never missed an opportunity to play at romance novels.

Eleanor's ears prickled. The only thing she wasn't telling was how ridiculous it felt to continue playing silly parlor games now that they were grown and the world had been through a war.

"No. Of course there isn't," she said.

"Now, don't be so sure." Alice narrowed her eyes. "What if this is a sign? Did the postman deliver you any mysterious missives today? A declaration from a cowboy back in Oklahoma, perhaps?"

Eleanor had heard the postman's whistle and observed as Papa retrieved the mail from the door. As he often did in his gruff manner, he had stuffed the letters into his vest pocket, likely oblivious of the day, certainly oblivious of her. She never could quite figure out a good approach to Papa. And so she didn't try.

"No." Eleanor looked at her red paper heart. "This day has been all backward from the start. Otherwise, I'd be standing before my poetry class reading Keats, not accidentally winning Sarah's prize heart." She looked up toward Sarah, a pretty, popular blond who, everyone suspected, would be engaged soon to her longtime beau.

"Well," said Sarah. "You're *not* teaching Keats today. That's the fun of it! Don't you see? And now, you're fated to be married!"

"Isn't it just delicious?" Alice chimed in.

Eleanor felt rattled and slightly nauseous by this unwanted attention paid to her love life—and lack thereof. But with education and war work behind most of them, her old girlfriends seemed intent now on charting their courses toward marriage. And that was simply not a card in Eleanor's deck. She was plagued instead by a longing for something *else*, something *more*.

"I'm sorry to put one over on Providence, ladies, but Julia Allen and I are going to a mountaintop in Scotland to live by the sea and write," Eleanor said.

"Julia?" Alice started. "I've just gotten a letter from her, but she didn't mention that. She was telling me all about her new beau out there in the West. She sounds delirious about him!"

A sense of treason welled in Eleanor at the sudden notion that this plan would never work out. That Julia just wasn't telling her so. Surely there was a letter for her waiting back home, sending her the same news, she reassured herself. She cleared her throat.

"Is that so?" Eleanor said.

"Oh! I know," said Alice, mind moving swiftly. "Paul Best. Didn't you take a shine to him? He could be the one. And he's returned to Goldsboro to practice law, did you know?" She ribbed Eleanor.

The color rose in Eleanor's cheeks, a little abashed that it had shown. There *had* been a time Paul Best was what made her heart go pitter pat. Until that fateful day on Neuse Lake, when he shamed her for blurting out her dream that she might one day explore the Arctic Sea.

"That," Eleanor said, without hesitation, "would *not* be a glorious adventure."

So eager had she been to cast off just this kind of prying, she'd lost all pretense. She briefly considered backtracking so as not to appear so harsh about Paul, but fearing it would only encourage Alice, she let it hang in the air between them.

Better that than to reveal the name of the only man whose arrow had ever truly pierced her heart, the man by whom she was so keenly able to judge Paul Best as inferior. She simply couldn't love a man like Paul when she knew there to be men like Erwin in the world.

"Well, well, then it must be Harrison," Alice pressed. "He is quite the adventurous type. Soon to return from London, I hear."

Harrison Summerlin. A lifelong fixture at the same gatherings and an old school friend of Lawrence's. The good, Methodist boy that Papa would want her to marry, except he often wasn't so good. Her heart went heavy, then, with the notion there might be something fatal in her propensity of nature if she could be satisfied with nothing but adventure. Because for now, there seemed to be nothing of it on her horizon.

Miss Freeman approached and patted Eleanor gently on the arm. "Only time will tell, my dear," she said with a solemn air.

Eleanor bristled but mustered a smile and made a motion toward the door. "Thank you, Miss Freeman, for hosting this lovely party, but I must go. I'm due back in Raleigh tomorrow, and Mama's expecting me home for supper."

"Just a moment, dear," Miss Freeman said. "Let me get Mrs. Darden to walk with you."

Consternation rose in her that, as an unmarried woman, she was no longer sanctioned to move about the streets with the same freedoms she'd enjoyed as a child. She missed her life in Oklahoma for many reasons, not least among them that it had been a place where a woman could go about without consideration for propriety.

"No, thank you, it's quite unnecessary. I'm fine alone." She spoke firmly, shoved the prize heart into her skirt pocket, and set off down William Street.

The house smelled of freshly baked cornbread when she arrived home, and a pair of white tapered candles sat on the dining table, which was laid over with a dainty checkered cloth.

Humming a little tune, Mama placed a porcelain vase of sweet pea blossoms in the center of the table. "The season's first," she said with a smile. Mama doted on her garden and was known throughout Goldsboro for the beauty of her flowers. The intense fragrance of the sweet peas brought back the summers of Eleanor's childhood in one breath—a venturesome girl dotted with sweat from her playful romps and dabbed with dirt from digging alongside Mama; those were the happiest times.

"The table looks beautiful, Mama."

"Thank you, Eleanor. Could you fetch the blue and white china? Then we'll just about be ready."

She nodded and retrieved the short stack of plates from the china closet. Mama brought them back after Papa's missionary stint in Japan. They were painted over with pictures of shichifukujin—the Seven gods of Fortune—sailing on their treasure ship. Eleanor was just three years old when they returned to North Carolina, but throughout her girlhood, she'd delighted at the stories Mama would tell of the gods when they set the table with these plates, wondering about her own luck of being born to such adventure. She felt it was her inheritance.

Mama brought out a basket of the still-warm cornbread with a jar of the summer's blackberry jam and retrieved a big bowl of her famous fried chicken from the icebox. She'd made a tremendous batch as a special treat the night before for the roomers of the house who let Lawrence's old bedroom. Eleanor set the table, feeling much more centered now than she had at Miss Freeman's party, the slight nausea having given way to hunger.

"Alex*an*der," Mama called in the direction of the living room, where Papa sat in his chair in front of the fire. "Come to supper."

Eleanor took her seat, and Papa ambled to the table, newspaper still in hand. If he noticed the dainty setting of it, he made no mention. He sat and, in the manner of someone being in a different room entirely, shook open his paper and continued to read.

And Eleanor knew, from bitter experience, what it signaled: no talking—unless, of course, *he* decided to speak. So they ate silently, with only the sounds of delicate crunching and the slip and touch of the silver.

They were alone at the table. Absent was Lawrence, home from the war and studying for a year at Harvard, and Clara and Neuel, children of a wife early lost to Papa. Clara had a family of her own, and no one ever saw Neuel, not anymore.

An accustomed ache grew in Eleanor's chest as she registered Mama's disappointment, the frown lines that had grown deeper with the years. She looked down at her plate at the lone female god of Fortune, Benzaiten. The goddess of love and wisdom, she had saved her people by marrying the sea dragon who had terrorized them, thereby neutralizing his threat.

Papa put his paper down and reached to fill his plate with food. His fingers met with a drumstick. "Cold chicken?" he said with irritation. "Something wrong with the stove?"

Mama remained silent. If only she would look at Papa and say something disarming. But she looked at her plate. Eleanor always hoped Mama was just ignoring him when she went silent, but she knew Mama was internalizing and fretting. If only he could appreciate her kindness, they could have some semblance of happiness. And Mama was swayed too much by her love of home, pouring her marital dissatisfaction into creating order and beauty rather than standing up for herself. Possessing a more intractable disposition, Eleanor spoke up.

"I like it cold," she said brightly. "It makes me think of a summer picnic. And the table looks beautiful this evening." This she repeated for Papa's benefit.

"Easy for you to say," Papa scoffed. "You don't *have* a husband to cook for."

And thank goodness for that. She would be self-guided and escape this fate, despite whatever the stupid prize heart was supposed to mean.

"I only mean to say that for me, a supper like this is a great treat," she said. "The kind that I miss most when I'm away, and I don't often get the chance of a satisfying meal."

"That hardship is one you brought upon yourself, dear girl. No one is making you go out in the world, battling among strangers," he said with stinging nonchalance, sure in his dogma.

The point was never to be settled. Eleanor had grown extra layers of skin to protect her against injury from these darts of Papa's, but her stomach churned as she watched the painful expression rise on Mama's face. She'd tried to help but had somehow made things worse. Papa tossed his napkin on the table, stood, and returned to his fireside chair for his usual postprandial nap, draping his vest over the footstool—the vest into which he had pocketed the day's mail.

Eleanor now realized that a letter from Julia may be squirreled away in that pocket. She eyed his vest, heart in her throat, and helped Mama clean up the kitchen, washing, drying, and replacing, removing all of the elements of her thoughtfully curated Valentine's supper.

Later, amid the rolling thunder of Papa's snoring and the heat of the flames in the hearth, Eleanor fished out the stack of letters from his vest, heart racing. She'd never resorted to such a drastic measure. She flipped through them in the fire's glow, immediately finding Valentine cards for Mama from Aunt Minnie and Cousin May. Just the thing to reinstate some joy in her day. Eleanor tucked them under her arm. She continued shuffling through what was likely days of mail, looking for Julia's rounded lettering that she knew so well when she discovered a letter in an unfamiliar masculine hand with her name on it. Only this wasn't from Julia. The return address was across the entire continent, in Berkeley, California.

Her heart leaped up momentarily at the possibility of who the sender might be, but then she coolly tucked the envelope alongside the others under her arm. It most certainly was not a Valentine—having been sent and lost in Papa's pocket for days—and had nothing to do with the silly, superstitious prize heart. She returned the remaining letters to Papa's vest and looked quickly about for Mama. Not finding her, she spirited the letters into a nearby volume of Tennyson's poetry and retreated with the book to her room upstairs.

First, she let her disappointment at Julia's lack of communication and burgeoning romance wash over her. She was tired of having her hopes dashed. Scottish mountaintop idyll may have been just a fancy to Julia all along, but for Eleanor, it had become a dear plan. She wasn't sure she could bear one more such disappointment before all possibility of a truly adventurous life was squelched and a North Carolina high school poetry teacher became all she *was*, her two years in Oklahoma the sole adventurous interlude, if it could even be considered that much.

She removed the curious letter from the book, studying its neatly formed hand. Erwin. She recalled with a flush a letter he sent to Helen in the months following his visit when he had first arrived in Berkeley for his doctoral work. How Helen's face lit up at the sight of the envelope's contents: poppies like she'd never seen before, even at their home in Austin, vibrant red-gold, nearly the size of her hand.

"Such a dear," Helen said, beaming as she showed them to Eleanor and flanking Erwin's bureau-top photo with them. Oh, how that sight had inflamed her own wanderlust, imagining the sunny mountainsides covered in this flaming beauty, the perfect sympathy of Erwin's company, which she'd known that lovely December night. Her heart rose once more with the memory, which now mingled with hope.

And then she promptly scolded herself for being swept away. It was positively silly to daydream that he might care after all this time, with all this distance now between them, that he'd even cared at all. And with a forlorn sigh, in this spirit, she opened the letter.

February 6, 1920
Berkeley, Cal.

Dear Miss Morgan,
  How are you going to know that I had a New Year wish all ready to send you—but couldn't learn your address in time—unless I write and tell you so? I hope you'll play like it's New Year now.
  You remember about the geese in the rhyme, don't you? "One flew east, and one flew west." History seems to be repeating itself in our cases. The main difference is that the goose that flew east was going home, while the one going west got farther away all the time. Apparently, some geese have a better sense of direction than others.
  Please, if you have time, write and tell me how you are and whether or not you favor Mr. Hoover for our next president. I don't mean to limit you to these topics, but I suggest them in a selfish way as things of great interest to me. And perchance you don't have time, I shall not bother you with such again.

  "Fare thee well, and if for ever,
  Still for ever, fare thee well"

With very best wishes, I am,
Sincerely yours,

Thomas E. Phipps

Erwin, she tingled; though he'd again folded that name back down into his middle initial, it was *him*. She set the letter on her desk, and for a moment, time bent backward. Once more, she saw Erwin's face in all its expressions, not just the worry look immortalized in Helen's photograph. That likeness had not captured the gaiety that sparkled in his eyes, the character and intelligence in his face.

She'd always thought herself prepared to meet unexpected turns in her life calmly and assuredly, but her emotions that night had been so unexpected and so strong that they'd quite frightened her, making her feel almost a stranger to herself. And the union with Erwin was so fleeting that she'd since convinced herself she'd at least partly imagined it. Yet here she sat, the embers still aglow in her heart; the wonderful harmony of those moments reflected back to her through the arrival of this poetic New Year wish. And it had found its way to her on Valentine's, of all days, fanning the embers once more into a low, bright flame. He did care. And it all seemed so comical and gay that she felt as if a fire fairy had touched her with her wand.

She heard the creak of footsteps on the stairs and the whisper of starched skirts down the hall. In a fluster, guided by a strange instinct, she hid Erwin's letter in her desk drawer. Mama entered the room with a short pile of newly laundered blouses from the line downstairs.

"You really ought to have a new pair of shoes, Eleanor," she said. "There's only so much I can do with the polish, and your soles are getting so thin."

"Thank you. I will," Eleanor said. But new shoes didn't count. Every penny funneled into her hopes for travel and further education. She would wear them as long as they *had* soles. She fingered the Tennyson and watched Mama put the blouses away in her cedar chest.

"I hope Papa didn't ruffle your feathers too much," Mama said. "I don't think he realizes you're returning to Raleigh tomorrow, and I didn't much feel like reminding him. You know how he disapproves of travel on Sundays. He might've been a little kinder if he was aware."

But that was exactly Papa: scathing in his judgment and

unaccountable in his actions. She brought out the letters from Minnie and May. "Valentines for you, Mama."

"Oh!" She took them, hugged them to her chest, and then flashed a bewildered look.

"In Papa's vest."

"Of course. Thank you, dear." She dropped them into her apron pocket. "He would have passed them along to me in time. But I do love to get cards on Valentine's Day."

Eleanor imagined Mama leaving them in that pocket until she could have a proper rest, savoring them at her leisure, using them to bridge a river of loneliness left from the nearly emptied house of children. And even when the house was full, it had not been easygoing.

Before they married and set sail for Japan, Mama was employed to look after Clara and Neuel for Papa, then a widower from a prominent Goldsboro family. This fact was scandal enough to the keepers of the very old North Carolina family trees on both sides of the Exum-Morgan equation. And Papa, knowing that their budding romance would introduce a devastating controversy, arranged for the position in Yokohama. What particular skeletons they were fleeing from, Eleanor never knew. But eight years on the other side of the world seemed to be time enough for the fault lines to mend and for them to return with two of their own children and settle into respectable, if unhappy, lives. But beneath the familiar order of the world that Eleanor grew into lay another forever waiting, it seemed, to tear it in two.

And yet Mama strove, despite the hardships, to hide the ugliness of life from her and Lawrence, to provide a home and a life filled with beauty and lofty ideals. She generously spread before them a world of literature, music, histories, possibilities, fairies, and ghosts. And under her constant love and care, they'd grown into thoughtful, sincere adults, but Papa had the power to mar everyone's happiness so.

"Papa just wants to see you settled, dear," Mama said, as though reading her thoughts.

"Yes, he's made himself very clear on that. But I don't want to see myself settled." She paused and thought. "You haven't intercepted a letter for me from Julia, have you?"

"No, dear, I haven't," Mama said. "But Mrs. Allen wrote to the Flower Club that Julia is expected to be engaged soon."

"Oh," said Eleanor. "Well, there it is, then." She pressed her lips together. She was on her own.

"For the record, I'm proud of the life my little girl is choosing for herself." Mama smiled and sent an arm around Eleanor's waist, pulling her close. "I know that you're called to go forth into the world, and I, for one, am glad of it." Kind, sweet, generous Mama. Her love and support were Eleanor's lucky charms; if only she could provide the same to her.

Mama patted the curl of ribbon in Eleanor's skirt pocket. "What's this, dear?"

"Oh! I nearly forgot. It seems I was the winner of the prize heart at Alice's party." She removed the red card from her pocket, revealing its silver arrow to Mama. She laughed anew at the folly of it. "Wouldn't *that* just suit Papa!"

Eleanor had thought, earlier, to throw it in the wastebasket at the first opportunity, but instead, now thinking of Erwin again, she displayed the card against the lamp on her bureau. "Perhaps I can use it in my defense, for a time," she said.

Mama turned away, growing suddenly earnest at the sight of the heart-shaped card. "I have to say, I do worry that your brother has spoiled you," she said after a moment.

"What do you mean?"

"You and Lawrence are so companionable," she said, her gentle hands smoothing the pleats of her apron, unknowingly using the very same word Eleanor had thought describing her feelings with Erwin. "Always have been. And as wonderful as that is, I hope you also realize you may not find someone as special as him, dear."

"Yes, Mama, I know," she said, glancing from the silver arrow to the desk drawer concealing Erwin's letter. How uncommon it really was to find intellectual companionship and perfect sympathy. If she didn't realize the rarity of it before, she knew it now. And how slender the thread of chance that brought them together. How wide the distance keeping them apart.

After Mama retired for the evening, Eleanor approached the drawer and rested her hand on its handle, nearly afraid to look for fear the letter had been part of some wild hallucination. The Tennyson remained open on her desk, the spine worn from repeated reading. Her eyes fixed on an underlined passage her heart knew well: *Love took up the glass of Time, and turn'd it in his glowing hands; Every moment, lightly shaken, ran itself in golden sands.*

With a shudder of electricity through her body, she remembered that evening in Norman. The moment of their parting, in which Erwin had held her hand with such care and delicacy, turning it slowly, gazing at it and at her, as Mrs. Dungan played a Chopin polonaise in the background.

She opened the drawer and found his letter still there. Did she remember the geese in the rhyme, he'd asked. Eleanor thought with tenderness of the musical game that brought them together in spirit and laughter for the first time, the alchemy of that mysterious transformation in her heart. *I will never forget it.* She drew a leaf of her stationery from the same drawer and sat down to write.

Feb 14, 1920
Dear Erwin,

She stopped, considering her choices soberly, and crossed it out. Her enthusiasm mustn't show too much. "Erwin" was what his family called him, and he hadn't signed his letter that way. And the significance of this particular day was too charged. She slowly untangled herself from the ecstasy of the moment and drew a fresh leaf. Little by little, touch by touch. And someday, perhaps *after* she'd had some adventures, he might come to return her feelings for him.

Feb 16, 1920
Goldsboro, N.C.

Dear Mr. Phipps,

Your New Year's greetings reached me on the fourteenth of February, a more interesting date than January first, after all.

The school in which I am now teaching poetry has been closed for weeks on account of influenza. The epidemic is worse than last year, with a greater number of cases and more distress among the poor. Not having had the flu last year or this, I feel as if I have been cheated out of a universal human experience; everyone can discourse about sinking spells, palpitations, and hair coming out, and I am left out of the conversation. The implication is that I have the fragile constitution of a Missouri mule. I shall be glad to go back and begin work.

You are finding your study interesting, I hope? Your sister used to tell me what you were doing, and I envied you beyond measure. California has always had a golden sound to the Southerner with wanderlust; you won't tell me its enchantment is only that of distance, will you?

I was very glad to get your note. Well, it's a long time before another New Year's, but there's Easter or the Fourth of July down the road.

Sincerely,

Eleanor Morgan

CHAPTER V

Berkeley, California

ONCE AGAIN, THE joint of heated glass melted as it let in air, marking Erwin's fifth failed attempt to fuse two glass tubes together. An impulse toward impatience began to simmer inside, tightening his ribs. This was supposed to be an elementary exercise.

He'd been at Berkeley for nearly a year doing chemical research. At the very least, he had expected to finish his degree work in two years, certainly well on his way after the first year. On his family's dime, Erwin had intended to show that he was putting the investment to good use. He could capitalize on the opportunity afforded him and return home for the holidays with a breakthrough to report; perhaps, he sometimes thought heroically, one that would ensure his future stability and allow him to offer support in return. This was of the utmost importance in his mind. But so far, that wasn't the case.

Instead, his chief accomplishment had come in the form of a lab accident during the Christmas holiday. Ammonia under pressure had gassed him and left him unconscious on the lab floor. After he was revived and admitted into the infirmary, he was left, over the ensuing holidays, to grapple with the specter of his own emptiness.

When he'd met Eleanor, he'd felt—what? Not just alive but the glimmer of something much larger. Untethered. With depth and texture. A landscape, a tree, a valley. Something that called directly to his heart. He'd held himself back, a little stunned and unbelieving. This wasn't for him.

He thought of this often in the lab. If he was honest, he was thinking of it when the ammonia gassed him. He'd let himself get good and mad at his inability to generate a consistent electric current in the liquid sodium. He was despondent that that lovely December night was all there was to be for this feeling of far-reaching awe, which now seemed so distant and cold. Maybe, he'd thought, if he could just work a miracle in the lab, some breakthrough that could establish him in the field, his path might find a way back to her. He would not be bound by these dispiriting ties any longer.

But after the accident, he'd lost a good deal of the optimism necessary for him to continue to try, to resume his work with ammonia to develop his beautiful blue aqueous solutions of sodium at the heart of his research that had caused him such injury.

His lab mate, Roy, goaded him back to the lab to take up glassblowing for a while instead. It was just the trick for him when he was in the slough of despond, he'd said, and now he didn't have to wait for old man Hollister to produce inferior versions of his apparatus designs. A rare win-win.

Erwin understood Roy's efforts, appreciated them, even, but despite it, his lack of progress, even with glassblowing, was pushing him further into despair. He fingered the ruined connection of his previous effort, the glass now cool and smooth. He began to imagine other things that he could have done in his studies, things he could still do.

"How long can you continue to fail before you develop the

hypothesis that *you* are the problem?" he said.

"Don't let the whims of inanimate matter get the best of you, Phipps," Roy said. "You can be sure it'll always keep on trying."

He had reached the familiar point where his thoughts urged him toward recklessness. He had to get a foothold this time. Roy came around to Erwin's side of the bench.

"You blew it too thin," he proclaimed. "Try again. Let it shrink under its weight, cool off, while you keep the rotation going."

Erwin knew this, at least in theory. But at each attempt, he had ended up either with a hole or a pronounced lump in the joint, with only a handful of seconds to get it right.

"Easy for you to say," Erwin said.

"Keep your hand even, keep trying, and you'll get there." Roy shrugged and resumed his spot at the opposite lab bench. "Just picture old Hollister's face when he learns that you're able to make your own apparatus, *thank you very much*, and you don't have to subject yourself to his peevishness anymore."

Erwin couldn't help but smile at the image of the lab's surly mechanician. "Ah, now that gives me hope for the future!" He turned off the blast lamp and reached for two more Pyrex tubes, but as soon as his grin straightened, his resolve disappeared, despair creeping in once again. Blow glass tube A, then blow glass tube B, then try to fuse them again, and lose them both once more. Keep hoping. And keep failing. *Keep trying: the chemist's mantra.*

He placed the glass tubing back on the bench. What he most needed now was at least a little success—the feeling that he could unravel some of nature's tangles, *be* a scientist. But, at nearly twenty-five—an entire quarter century old—and without a lick of scientific discovery to show for it, he began to feel quite earnestly as though he would never get there. That, after all, the field of chemistry would never provide him the recognition, the stability, he craved.

It didn't help either that Roy was both younger and much farther along in his degree work. As easy as it would be to lay it to the war, he and Roy had served alongside each other. And here they both were: one advancing quickly, and one mired down in mud.

Erwin closed his eyes and stretched out on his chair.

Roy contemplated the scene. "Want to go throw some sodium into the pond?" he asked. They'd done this a few times to relieve the strain of the long days in the lab—watching the yellow ball of flame speed about the water's surface. As thrilling as the experience was, it now left him cold. The magic of science was slipping away from him.

"No."

"How about some supper?"

Erwin's stomach growled.

"Yes," he said. Sustenance. Fuel.

They walked home from the lab through drizzling rain to their bachelor apartment on Haste Street. Roy talked animatedly about a new idea that they'd recently hatched together, around the creation of a new kind of refrigeration unit, one that could operate on a kerosene flame—an idea that had sparked Erwin's imagination—but now he just didn't feel equal to the discussion. His inner world felt just as cold and colorless as the landscape they traversed, and the air castles that Roy was speaking of hovered somewhere above the clouds, where he couldn't see. He felt as though this was all there was, all there would ever be. And it wasn't enough.

And so he arrived home, resolved to eat and sleep and hope for a better day tomorrow, one in which he at least felt like he could try to try again.

In the mailbox, Erwin found a letter awaiting him from North Carolina. A miniature sun rose in his heart at the sight of it, one whose rays he had not felt for over a year: Eleanor Morgan. The fog lifted, and his wits returned. The future might be looking up after all.

CHAPTER VI

Goldsboro, North Carolina

HATLESS ON EASTER weekend, Eleanor stood alongside Alice among a gathering crowd awaiting the spring carnival's welcome parade. To be in the open again was a balm to her soul. She closed her eyes and tipped her face to the warming sun as they waited. All of Goldsboro now seemed to conspire in pairing her off. On her weekends at home, she had taken to declining all offers of parties, luncheons, teas, and the like, which had become a front to the service of introducing or suggesting possible future husbands. And after the long months of being corralled indoors, Eleanor was eager for the arrival of outdoor entertainment.

"Here they come!" she heard Alice say.

She opened her eyes and adjusted her sight down the parade route, looking for the procession. Seeing nothing, she turned back toward Alice, who was facing the opposite direction. Two figures in the jumble waved back across Ash Street. Eleanor recognized them as Edgar and Harrison Summerlin, but before she could form the words to ask Alice whether she was expecting the brothers to join their outing, they'd already dashed across the street.

Edgar tipped his hat and offered a sly smile. "Hello, Alice, were you miserable without us?" he said. He was a stouter version of the slim youngster Eleanor had known in school.

Harrison came up behind him, taller, with the same dark hair and deeply set eyes. Otherwise, he seemed a different person, with a new set of clothes and mustache.

"Well, well. Eleanor Morgan," he said.

Eleanor's neck stiffened. She was unpleasantly reminded of Harrison's name being floated during the grilling she received over the prize heart at the Valentine's Day party. And now she was trapped. But, of course, Alice had invited the brothers to join. It was Alice's way. But she betrayed none of the annoyance she felt at their appearance; as part of her Southern fabric, her default demeanor was always to set those around her at ease.

"Hello, Harrison. Back from London, I understand?" she said.

Alice cut in, "He was an attaché for the court of St. James," her tone telegraphing that this was a very impressive fact.

"Guilty," Harrison said, his gaze fixed on the parade route. "How is Lawrence?"

"Very well, thank you. Presently a professor of English at Oklahoma University, but he is studying for a year at Harvard."

"Did he serve?"

"Yes. At the Officer's Training Camp in Texas."

"Good man. Does he ever get back this way?"

"On occasion," Eleanor said, though she hadn't seen him since she left Oklahoma nearly a year ago. "During the war, I was there at Oklahoma in his absence," Eleanor continued. "You see, I—"

"Oh! Here they come!" Harrison interrupted her upon seeing the first of the fair's parade beginning: a trio of ladies dressed in white with long black hair riding chariots of gold. Their appearance coincided with a gust of air from the south, carrying a jolly tune from the steam calliope that rolled along behind them. Eleanor's heart leaped up at the excitement of the spectacle, burying the fleeting irritation she'd felt at having her words cut off.

"I haven't been to a parade since the Victory March!" Harrison said, waving his hat down the parade route. His face revealed a youthful exuberance, one that reminded Eleanor of all those long-ago afternoons spent playing "baseball" in the yards of Goldsboro, using dead tennis balls and sticks. Harrison had the distinction of being an accomplished base stealer.

"And how was life in London, Mr. Summerlin?" asked Alice.

"You don't have to 'Mr.' me, Alice," he said.

"I meant it merely to make note of your breathtaking rise," she kidded.

The wind gusted again, blowing several hats into the air. The sun slipped behind a darkened cloud.

"Are you staying on in Goldsboro or going back?" Alice asked him.

"Going. Wherever it is I'm detailed next. I spent some time at the embassy in Wales before London. I'd fancy returning there as well."

Wales. Eleanor tingled at the sound of it.

A blue platform rolled by with a young woman atop in a long green swimsuit and a cascade of brown curls, like an exotic flower. *The Diving Venus*, read a brightly colored banner above her head. "See her dive from a height of one hundred feet into shallow water!" barked a man through his megaphone. The Diving Venus smiled and waved to the crowd.

"Oh! Eleanor's going to Scotland," Alice blurted. "Isn't that so?"

Eleanor flushed. "I hope to," she said after a pause. "Julia Allen and I, for a long time, have been planning to set sail." Ever since their walks through Stony Creek, picking bluebells, when she had planted in Julia's imagination the image of the bluebell's cousin, far off in the Scottish highlands, waiting to be discovered.

"Ah, Europe's gone silly these days with American girls making fools of themselves," said Harrison, bringing Eleanor rudely back to the moment to wonder what behavior in his mind could possibly classify them categorically as fools and whether he was insinuating that she would be a fool too, if she went.

"It's a pity you can't get into the Foreign Service," he went on, unaware of her vexation. "They don't take women."

The flush of embarrassment gave way to indignation. As if she needed reminding of the things that she *couldn't* do. Just because a man is educated and well-traveled doesn't mean he has a license to speak so condescendingly. Erwin would never speak so.

A troupe of Arabian horses pulled the final platform, upon which sat a caged lioness, roaring at the crack of the lion tamer's whip, who walked alongside, dressed in safari gear.

"Ha HA!" Harrison said at the sight of it, waving his hat again. The sky darkened.

As the parade finished, the gates to the fairgrounds opened to the crowd, punctuated by a crack of thunder and a sudden shower. Dashing through the gates, the group sought refuge in one of the fair's attractions, the "King's Castle." They scurried up its narrow stairs into a darkened entryway painted over to look like stone. Once through its swinging doors, darkness enveloped them all until the flash of a devil's head sent Alice shrieking off down the passage, pushing Edgar ahead of her. Harrison and Eleanor laughed at her foolish display, cutting the tension, and they made their way forward. At the end of the passageway, a picture of King Solomon opened on the wall, and as it did, the floor began to shake underneath them, forcing Eleanor to fall awkwardly in Harrison's direction.

"Oh!" She lurched against him, quite against her will. It was like falling against a tree; he may as well have been made of wood. Harrison caught her in a series of clumsy movements, one with a hand momentarily on her breast. Eleanor was mortified; she wished they hadn't sought shelter in this place—wished, even, that Alice hadn't invited her in the first place. She already knew, however awkwardly, what it had felt like to fall into the arms of a gentleman. And Harrison was no gentleman.

Past the shaking floor, they had sight of the exit across one more passageway.

"Ladies first," Harrison said, bidding her forward once more. "I'll bring up the rear."

Eleanor made her way determinedly toward it, resolved to stand in the rain if need be. As she did, a blast of wind shot up from a grate on the floor, blowing her long skirt toward her waist. Harrison laughed. And Eleanor shrieked and ran, overcome with the embarrassment.

"Perhaps we might go downtown instead? See a picture?" Alice said as they reassembled under a nearby tent, the dirt of the fairgrounds pooling into mud.

Eleanor avoided eye contact with Harrison. She could feel the weight of his gaze on her and did not care to identify the expression that went with it. But the opportunity of seeing a picture appealed to her, if only, perhaps, she did not have to sit next to Harrison.

"I have been wanting to see the new film dramatization of *Evangeline* at the Opera House," she offered.

Harrison moaned. "*Longfellow*, so old-fashioned," he said.

"*Timeless*, I'd say," she fired back with as much politeness as she could muster.

"So sayeth you." He waved with his hands, as if shooing away the thought. "Quite the sentimentalist then, are you? The English are crazy over this Sherwood Anderson. Have you heard of him? Perhaps you could be converted."

Having come, finally, to the point of exasperation, Eleanor forgot her Southern fabric. "I am a teacher of literature and poetry now," she said curtly, *which you'd know if you'd asked*, "and I find that Anderson's style is often like my own students: at times, he shows . . . difficulty handling his material. He, and perhaps the English as well, have a lot to learn yet."

"Ouch," Harrison said, comically rubbing his jaw like she'd hit him. Eleanor wasn't sure what reaction she expected, but it certainly wasn't the open, broad smile that he offered in return. He seemed to find her displeasure amusing.

The ladies bid goodbye to the Summerlin brothers at the end of Ash Street and walked together toward home.

Alice could hardly contain her glee. "Oh, Eleanor, think of the life of adventure you could have with him!" she said. "International society, earls, dukes . . . surely he's your prize heart, remember?"

Eleanor's stomach lurched. "Oh, my dear, sweet friend. I am not now, nor have I ever been, fond of Harrison Summerlin."

"Oh, give it some time," Alice teased. "All the greatest love stories start with the principals disliking each other."

Eleanor scoffed and waved her off. Alice was playing at romance novels again, and Eleanor didn't want to give air to the notion there could be a love story here for her.

"He's much changed, don't you think?" said Alice. "I hear he's met the *king*."

"He doesn't seem much changed to me," Eleanor said, glancing over her shoulder. Still king of stealing bases, she thought.

Eleanor boarded the train back to Raleigh on Monday morning, skipping her chance at seeing *Evangeline*. Harrison had dampened her enthusiasm about staying longer in Goldsboro, and Alice's words left her feeling slightly nauseous. The best option seemed to be escape.

She often knew people on the train, allowing her to pass the hours of travel in friendly distraction, but she was unpleasantly surprised to find no familiar faces among her fellow travelers on the platform. Most women looked to be college girls, heading back to their studies after Easter weekend, just as she had done in the not-so-distant past.

As soon as she stepped into the train car, she heard a shrill female voice from behind. "Porter, *porter*! Is there *no* Pullman car to be found on this train?"

Without so much as a glance, Eleanor recognized the voice of Miss Powers, longtime teacher of homemaking at Raleigh and all-around busybody. With a slight dread, Eleanor quickly shuffled to the car's rear, hoping to avoid Miss Powers, leaving her alone beneath a flowerlike electric lamp to her own disagreeable thoughts. She was disappointed in Alice, first and foremost. Her weekend might've been pleasant were it not for her ridiculous efforts at matchmaking. Although Alice *had* been right about love stories, those tales also carried the opinion that women don't know their own minds or have the circumstances of a large family fortune to lose. Eleanor knew her mind. She knew such a match would bring abiding unhappiness. And for better or worse, she had no fortune to lose. If she were to accept love into her life, it would have to be a love that lifted her up and stoked her fire inside rather than one that tamped it down.

Alice's lexicon of romance novels just didn't include anything suiting. And even Eleanor's was lacking; Dorothea in *Middlemarch*, yes, but only if Mr. Causabon could have met her passionate nature. George in *A Room with a View*, yes, but only if Miss Honeychurch were not so stunted by society's demands. All love stories seemed to play against what she would accept into her life. *I am Dorothea, and Erwin is George,* she thought fleetingly. Warmth built inside her at the thought, but as quickly as the feeling arose, she pushed it away. No. She knew her own mind, after all, and wanted her own adventure instead.

Listening to the girls around her, she rested her thoughts on her college years. A time when her head had been full of possibilities as to what fate was preparing for her far off in the darkness, the future still benevolently veiled. How shocked younger Eleanor would be to learn that five years hence, she would be aboard this same car, her fancies for an adventurous life turning out to be something of a dud. But at least she had an income to save up and keep hoping. At least she wasn't in a position where she had to accept a man like Harrison into her life to have her shot at travels. But a solitary existence on a mountaintop, just as any adventure he could offer, no matter how thrilling or glamorous, would ring hollow without true camaraderie. And there seemed to be no way she and Harrison could ever understand each other. And what is love without intellectual companionship?

As the train lurched to a halt at the Clayton station, her thoughts flew back to Erwin. How well, by contrast, they'd instinctively understood each other, how charged that made her feel.

The passengers began to shuffle at the stop, and a voice sounded across the stopped car. "Why, Miss *Morgan*!"

Eleanor put her thoughts on hold; Miss Powers had rooted her out. She proceeded down the aisle, approached the seat opposite her, plopped down, and smoothed her matronly frock.

"Good morning, Miss Powers," Eleanor said, ever polite.

"Just the person I'd hoped to see today." Miss Powers expressed a forced smile at Eleanor, who, to the best of her knowledge, had never witnessed a genuine smile from her. "Oh, but how I despise train travel!" she said. "All the smoke and dirt. I'm only thankful that the journey is a short one. Remind me again where your people are from?"

"Goldsboro."

"Ah! Of course. You must be thankful, too, to be so close by." Miss Powers adjusted her spectacles. She paused, regarding Eleanor, her plump face drawn, lips pressed into a fine line. Her voice took a strident tone.

"Miss Morgan, I've become aware that you recently took your students to see a rather vulgar performance by some sort of . . . wandering poet?"

Eleanor bristled at her choice of words but sat straight, hoping to politely defuse the situation.

"Yes, Miss Powers. Vachel Lindsay," she said. "It coincided with an upcoming unit on modern poetry. I thought it useful to—"

With a flash of disdain, Miss Powers interrupted. "Miss Morgan," she said. "Are you aware of the meeting next week between our superintendent and the state board regarding the creation of a unified vision of education?"

"No, Miss Powers, I wasn't." Eleanor leaned back into her seat. It just wouldn't do to convince her of the merits of her actions. It never had, and Miss Powers, with her seniority and standing, exerted too much authority over her. Much as she wanted, she couldn't risk her income by standing up on principle.

Miss Powell softened her tone. "While we do encourage individual initiative, you see, we must never forget that our influence must be in harmony with the life and teachings of a good home. And I'm afraid there's no room for such tawdry entertainment. Please, strike this *Modern Poetry* from your lesson plan."

Eleanor knew of no fable in which the mouse rebuked the lion to any effect, but faced with the supremacy of Miss Powers's unreasonable demand, she took a fiendish delight in wondering what poet might fit with her particular educational vision. Were they not all radical in some way? She had been a little shocked at Mr. Lindsay's performance—that had rather seemed to be the point of it—but that shouldn't mean that she narrow her students' thoughts by avoiding it. What is poetry intended for but the expansion of ideas? That which relates to what might be rather than what has been?

"Yes, I see," said Eleanor. "I apologize for my indiscretion. Perhaps, though, I might trouble you to suggest an alternate course of study? I wouldn't want to further upset the board."

Miss Powers's eyes narrowed. "Well," she said, straightening. "I suppose I hadn't quite considered . . . well, we revered John Milton in the home of my girlhood."

"Ah! Yes—*Paradise Lost* is a sublime example," Eleanor said. "The height of what a fully mature epic poem can be."

"Indeed it is."

"Did you know, in Milton's years at Cambridge, his poems were quite antagonistic? He was quite the radical at first."

Miss Powers looked bewildered. Eleanor continued, fully poised. "If I teach Milton, perhaps I should avoid mention of this early material?"

"Oh dear," Miss Powers started. "I shouldn't think that *Milton* would present a conflict." A burst of laughter arose among college girls in another section of the car.

Eleanor was satisfied that she'd made her point. And she didn't care to teach Milton. "I suppose one can't go wrong with the sentimentalists of the last century," she said, leaving an intentional vagueness upon which she might hatch her new course.

Miss Powers appeared relieved. "Yes. That will do," she said. "I trust your change will please the superintendent as well and aid him in his decisions regarding contract renewal next school year." The thin, pious smile returned.

This veiled threat was not lost on Eleanor, who now keenly wished she'd remained in Goldsboro. There seemed no escape after all.

―※―

Upon Eleanor's return to her rooming house, she was unhappily resolved to spend the rest of the day reconfiguring her lesson plan.

On the parlor table, she retrieved the letters that had arrived in her absence: one from Mr. Carpenter, a former college instructor of hers at Raleigh, and another from Erwin. An Easter missive. She felt a quickening inside, and wanting to savor this buoyant feeling, she set it aside, first opening Mr. Carpenter's letter:

April 1, 1920
Columbus, Mississippi

Dear Miss Morgan,
 I understand, via the alumni news, that you are teaching at Raleigh High School.

I am presently heading up the English Department at Mississippi State College for Women and on the search for gifted instructors to improve the offerings here.

I believe that you'd be just the one to teach our American Literature course. If you'd consider the change, I'd like to offer you a position for the upcoming year.

Sincerely,

L. G. Carpenter

Eleanor knew Mr. Carpenter to be rather impish, but she couldn't believe he would go so far as to send this letter as an April Fool's trick. She'd grown uncertain she'd ever have the opportunity to teach at the college level again, and here it was. Certainly, she'd just dreamed this. And yet another letter, this one from the man she had just been dreaming of?

April 2, 1920
Berkeley, Cal.

Dear Miss Morgan,

I regretted not being an Irishman so I could celebrate the seventeenth of last month and not have to wait until Easter to write you again.

Several of us Chemikers here at the house have organized a Gesellschaft recently, but you'd never guess what the object of the organization is. It has nothing whatsoever to do with Germany either. We have meetings every Sunday afternoon, when we go for long walks in the hills in the back of the University looking for steep slopes suitable for gazelling.

This consists of a series of gazelle-like leaps which

jar the spinal column to its foundations but which are exceedingly exciting. There are other interesting things about Gesellschaft meetings too. The California poppies are in their glory now, and it is a rare sight to see a whole hillside orange from top to toe. The last time, we lost our way because of a heavy fog that came in while we were still deep in the hills. Then there is poison oak too, which all gazelles dread.

So you see, there's a thistle for every rose.

Is it springtime in North Carolina too? Perhaps you have something more gorgeous than poppies on your hills. And if you haven't, you can make up for that, I suppose, by using more gorgeous words than I have. Please write and let me know.

Sincerely,

Thomas E. Phipps

All at once, Eleanor felt uplifted, her mind full of sights and sounds and tender emotion. He couldn't have known he was telling her exactly what she had dreamed about when Helen flanked his photograph with the poppies he'd sent her in Norman. And now he'd brought her there himself: to a mountainside covered in them, lost in the fog with Erwin and his cadre of friends, becoming once more possessed by the lure of California. To think that just this brief flight of fancy was already more of an adventure than anything she might have imagined with Harrison.

An affectionate warmth spread in her chest. How strikingly different Erwin was from Harrison, how much more closely their sensibilities ran together. There was something else in the difference too, searching for the right notion to capture what Erwin made her feel. *Confidence*, she settled on the word. Erwin gave her confidence. Harrison did not. Maybe, at least where Erwin was concerned, she was wrong in separating love and adventure; maybe she *could* have both—if only they could somehow find their way back to each other.

Her internal Ms. Prudence intruded on the moment, bringing her back down to Earth. *Take control of your feelings before they take control of you. Special observances* only *until you've reached the familiar aspect. A lady mustn't be forward by responding too quickly.*

Eleanor considered this dogma and consulted her calendar. Ascension, May 13? Interesting metaphor, but the context is too religious. Memorial Day, May 30? Maybe, but entirely too far away. If she decided to accept Mr. Carpenter's offer, she'd be making arrangements to move from Raleigh by then. Out of holiday observances from which to choose, Eleanor settled on one Ms. Prudence would never endorse: April 19, the start of the Revolution, the "shot heard round the world." The great poets would approve. What words had we for the observance but Emerson's and Longfellow's? She would take that confidence that Erwin had given her, she decided, and fashion it into poetic justice. She would shoot her arrow. She would not defer to Ms. Prudence; she had confidence. The confidence that Erwin was the prize heart.

Ms. Prudence whispered, *Cupid had two arrows, one golden and one leaden.* But Eleanor paid no heed.

April 19, 1920
Raleigh, N.C.

Dear Mr. Phipps,
  This is the nineteenth of April, and I'm thinking I'll fire a letter half round the world. Nothing if not apropos. Listen, you chemist, and you shall hear an anguishing, languishing story, I fear. You see, I've missed my calling.

Alas, I should have been a poet.

Your account of University life makes me hungrier than ever for the time, I mean the lucre, to come when I can go on and study. Most of all, I want a year of refuge from the autocracy of the public schools and, what is worse, the cant of teachers. In college, that doesn't oppress one, but in the schools of North Carolina, it becomes intolerable. And so I'm trying to screw my courage to the borrowing point for a year at Columbia, perhaps, or Radcliffe.

But really, you haven't all the poetry in California. We've had the profound honor of a visit from Vachel Lindsay. If you ever have the opportunity to hear him, you do *want to miss it. He raves about the "musical pattern" of his verse and chants his creations like an outraged steam calliope. Music? It's jazz. Jazz flatters it; it's a bray and a squeak and a squawk and a swear. And he "chants" with his body bent backward like a jack-knife half open. He keeps his eyes shut, afraid their fine frenzy would terrify the audience, perhaps, and he hasn't any eyelashes. I enjoyed him, you notice. But I have a right to be sore; how will I teach Longfellow against such? However, I felt better when I found one of my boys doing a rich burlesque of the recital. Maybe Mr. Lindsay didn't do much harm after all.*

Gazelling sounds most interesting. I remember you sent your sister some poppies in a letter last year; the country must be glorious. But I won't exchange with you my pale little anemones and bluebells and rare, sweet jasmine. It's curious how no matter where you are, it is always the home flowers you want.

It was strange how your sister and I—she hailing from Turkey and I from Japan—should have come together in

Oklahoma, wasn't it? Is there any way I can persuade Helen to write to me? I don't want her to forget me a bit.

And what do you think of our staid, conservative, ladylike old Carolina's sudden interest in suffrage? I'm afraid it means only that the politicians recognize the inevitable.

I enjoyed your Easter letter, even if it did just escape being written on the first of April. You must admit that I did well to think up April the nineteenth.

Sincerely,

Eleanor

She lifted her pen, leaving only her first name on the page, considering whether to write out her last name or leave it as an initial, "M." Hadn't they already achieved the familiar aspect? Then she would be the first to do away with formalities. She'd capitulated to Ms. Prudence long enough. She set the pen down and folded the paper, emboldened. For Erwin, and Erwin only, she would risk her heart to Ms. Romance. As to the Mississippi offer, she decided, holding Mr. Carpenter's letter in her other hand, she would respond with questions about the position. And then let fate decide: to whoever responded first, she would clear a pathway in her life. One way love, come what may; the other, adventure.

CHAPTER VII

Raleigh, North Carolina

Sail fast, sail fast,
Ark of my hopes, Ark of my dreams;
Sweep lordly o'er the drowned past,
Fly glittering through the sun's strange beams;
Sail fast, sail fast.
—Sidney Lanier

AS WAS HER custom, on the final day of poetry class at Raleigh High School, Eleanor compiled a reading list for her students, carefully written out on the blackboard.

"For each poet whose works we have read this year, a wealth of additional poets are awaiting your discovery," she said. "Robert Burns suggests Sir Walter Scott, William Blake suggests Robert Louis Stevenson, Longfellow suggests Ralph Waldo Emerson, and if *Vachel Lindsay* struck your fancy"—she gave the class a wry smile as several giggles broke out—"then Carl Sandburg would be well worth your time. The sea of poetry is vast indeed, and I encourage you to let loose your lines and go explore it."

Eleanor was no longer fettered by Miss Powers's judgment; she had two weeks previously accepted Mr. Carpenter's offer of the Mississippi position and submitted her resignation at Raleigh.

The promise of a new adventure, the anticipation of putting some much-needed distance between herself and North Carolina, rang sweet. But her disappointment at not receiving a response from Erwin after what she now feared was a risky and too-forward letter sat heavy in her heart, a ballast to her elation. After the initial rush of sending it, she sat in great anticipation of the postman's whistle for more than a week, propped at the breakfast table with her heart on tiptoe, earnestly wishing for the delivery of Erwin's letter ahead of Mr. Carpenter's, one that matched her own daring tone, which would telegraph to her that he was indeed answering her heart's call. She'd tracked the calendar too—looking for dates he might use as an excuse to write, if he still cared to do so. But even Memorial Day had come and gone, and now, fully four weeks after she had received Mr. Carpenter's lengthy description of the position and, in turn, written her letter of acceptance, she'd received no word at all from Erwin.

His silence was a puzzle, one she tried to reconcile in her mind during any idle moment. Why would he have sent such thoughtful proofs of remembrance and yet not written the one letter she was expecting? Or at least interpret, from its tone, from the date she had chosen to write upon—of historical significance, of which there was surely for every day of the calendar—that she was inviting him to do away with the ponderous convention of waiting for a holiday observance. Perhaps he didn't quite care as much as she wished, and he was waiting until the Fourth of July, after all, to respond. But by then, she would be gone. Then disappointment gave way to fear that he might've met with an accident or fallen ill, recalling his near-fatal brush with influenza that caused Helen such a shock all that time ago.

She distracted herself from these sorrowful musings as best she could by building the anticipation of her new "deep South" adventure in Mississippi, pouring her efforts into creating the final unit for her class, one very close to her heart: Southern poetry. She'd long found magic and musicality in the words of the Southern poets, and in sharing them with her students, she, in a short time, began to shore up her despair and instead develop a delicious sense of providence around her new plan.

There seemed to be a touch of fate in it, as Mr. Carpenter's class in Raleigh had been pivotal for her. "You can say anything you want in poetry," Mr. Carpenter had said with a flashing smile, his introduction, on the first day. And the idea had seized her imagination. There seemed a rightness that she would now be teaching under his direction. She would still be making eighteen a week, a starvation wage, really, but she would be *free*.

As her classroom emptied of students for the last time, she delighted at the hugs and kind words she received from many of those who'd become dear to her, coloring the hardships of the school year with nostalgic pleasure. They filed past her out the door—until just one remained behind. Walter Hawk was seventeen, taller than Eleanor by several inches and fully two years older than most of her students. He had presented her the most taxing challenges over the course of the school year. The Hawk family was well known in her neighborhood for their open-air quarrels, and Walter had often attempted the same tactics in her classroom.

"Miss Morgan," Walter started, eyes fixed on the floor, the volume of his voice uncharacteristically low. "I sure am sorry I ever bothered you."

His words were tender, and Eleanor felt no desire for reproach. She knew Walter to have difficulties at home, and she had always felt sympathy for him. While his homelife was the explosive kind, hers was just a quieter type of the same despair.

"I think about that Wordsworth poem a lot," Walter said. "The one about finding your inward eye? About being happy by yourself?"

"'I Wandered Lonely as a Cloud,'" Eleanor said, softening her tone to match his.

"That's the one. That helped me in some hard times this year. Gave me something nice to think about instead. Your class . . . it was my favorite. Thank you, Miss Morgan." And with that, he drew her in for a big hug, a strong scent of tobacco clinging to his clothes. Then, just as quickly, he flashed out the door, leaving Eleanor wordless, without the opportunity to tell him that the same poem had also helped her over the years, that she'd memorized it ages ago and often used it as a touchstone. She never could pass a patch of daffodils without reciting it in her heart. But to learn that this private joy of hers had been transferred to the one student in her class who perhaps needed it the most—this felt like a triumph. She recalled those difficult days when she had been forced to eject a quarrelsome Walter from her class, only to have him march up and down the hall, fussing at the top of his voice until his vocal cords seemed to have sufficient exercise for the day, how trying those times had been. But learning that she had helped him, even though it often felt like the opposite, set her heart aglow.

This is my calling, she assured herself, proceeding to her rooming house. She'd worked hard in the past to convince herself of it, and now, for the first time in a long time, it felt true. Finally, there rose before her a vision of a future to which she could look forward confidently. She would bury her disappointments—her extinguished fancies, Erwin's lack of response. She would go home to Goldsboro with the conviction that the path she was following was true, and then she *would* have the adventure she craved. She would bring the beauty of words to show to the girls in Mississippi, to share, to wonder at, together.

She checked the parlor table on her way into the house, finding a letter. Her heart leaped to see her name in a masculine scrawl . . . only to drop when she realized it was *not* Erwin's familiar hand but some other, and then, when she saw the return address, all her hope turned to a terrible dread—it was from Harrison, inviting her to accompany him to see the Belgian Veterans Band, scheduled to play on Monday at the Chautauqua in Goldsboro on her return. "If that prospect does not tickle your fancy," he wrote, "the film *A Virtuous Vamp* will be showing at the Acme Theater." Eleanor couldn't help but appreciate the little dark humor, but she also felt that it highlighted the abyss between them; if he suggested something like that, he was either kidding or misunderstood her completely, and she couldn't discern which it was.

What keeps him trying? she wondered. It certainly wasn't her. She'd done nothing but maintain a cool politeness with him. The letter filled her with new dread, and her head ached. It was as if Harrison was intent on shining a spotlight on that hollow space she felt inside, between the person she was and the person she felt she was supposed to be. She would rather he left her alone entirely, and her arrival during Chautauqua meant a new round of difficulties with Papa.

She knew from experience that the round of inevitable sermons from traveling preachers would stir Papa to a new frenzy, causing him to double down on his prejudices. And this usually resulted in lashing out—suddenly accusing her of spending her life in sin, imagining that she cavorted with men and danced and played cards, which the Evangelists decried and which Eleanor did not, in fact, do. Except, of course, the occasional dance, but that didn't count with her—she would stop it entirely if it was simply a matter of not dancing to win Papa's approval. Already, she felt like she could do no good when she was at home. Now she dreaded what her presence would do for both her and Mama, that it would be just another cross for Mama to bear.

CHAPTER VIII

Berkeley, California

SODIUM HAD LONG held an irresistible beauty for Erwin. In its aqueous form, it was a deep, indigo blue, and along with potassium, it stood as the only aqueous chemical solution that conducted electricity. He spent many hours contemplating what powers might be concealed within this element. In many ways, sodium's draw and his hope to unlock its secrets had delivered all the thrills of a chase. But in the end, it required infinite planning and infinite patience.

Professor Lewis squinted as he sat among the assembled faculty of the Chemistry Department, his gaze fixed on a diagram of Erwin's proposed apparatus, a snakelike circulatory system of airtight capillaries, reservoirs, stoppers, and electrodes.

"It is a question of stability, is it not?" Prof. Lewis asked. "Is creating conductivity in sodium *stable* enough to get a reliable measure?"

Erwin, standing next to the diagram, mustered his will and cleared his throat. "No. It has been my aim to increase stability," he said. "If you recall, I began my research by experimenting with high concentrations of sodium, hoping to offset the persistent fading caused by a secondary reaction with the solvent."

That had proved to be, well . . . explosive. His mind returned to that black moment in the infirmary when he'd lost all hope, emptying Pandora's box, fearing the entirety of his scientific career had reached a dead end. He let his thoughts rest there for a few seconds and travel to his breast pocket, which contained Eleanor's two letters. Erwin had long drawn fortitude from words—beginning in his youth with his father's fiery sermons, continuing through a fascination with the bravado of Lord Byron, often read aloud hearthside with zeal by his brothers. In adulthood, he continued to strive to find the words to bolster his spirit. The words that allowed him to get out of the way, let things pass, be changed. Words into willpower. Lead to gold. Poetry, he believed, was the only true form of alchemy.

And so, from his receipt of the first of Eleanor's letters in February, they'd had a curious effect; his outlook improved significantly, and his will strengthened. He reentered his research with a new, hopeful determination. In scientific terms, the prospect of her friendship lowered his activation energy—the indecision each reaction faces before committing to its path. In other words, she had become his catalyst.

"When I took up my research a second time," he continued, "I found that low concentrations of sodium helped to create the stability necessary for measurement. It is still susceptible to fading, however, and the entire process is much slower. But at these low concentrations, I intend to find out whether the conductivity can reach a constant value"—Erwin pointed to his design of the glass rod stirrer—"if the solution is continuously stirred."

Even though he had laid it out in black and white, standing as confidently as he could in front of the panel, there was still something of the wild goose chase in it. He knew, but he didn't dare say as much.

The faculty members shuffled at the long table, the air in the room growing heavier. At length, they questioned him about the uncertainties in his design—how the stirrer was to be powered, how it was to be supported, how he might modify the design to account for unforeseen difficulties, whether he was aware that Dr. Kraus, an early pioneer of this research in aqueous solutions of sodium, was conducting his own research along these same lines.

Erwin's heart fluttered particularly at this last line of questioning. He knew it to be true; no matter how innovative he was in his research, it remained a race—for the laurels associated with being the first to this finish line. He presupposed that this factor could be a significant stumbling block for the faculty. Why support his research when they knew it was being carried out by a far more prominent figure? And he would be forced to start over. Try, fail, repeat.

Erwin slowed his breath as they shuffled in their seats again, the silence agonizing.

"Mr. Phipps, are there other aspects of this work with aqueous solutions that interest you? One in which you might lead the way?" asked Dr. Lewis. "It's awfully daunting to have to compete for the same result with Dr. Kraus himself."

He thought again of the letters in his breast pocket, of Eleanor. *Try.*

"I'm afraid not, Dr. Lewis," he replied. "The apprehension is understandable under the circumstances, but I believe very much in the importance of this work in gathering our body of knowledge about how these substances operate."

"Very well, then. Any further questioning from the faculty?" asked Dr. Lewis.

"Yes," said Dr. Carver, a big stoop-shouldered man with specs down on the end of his nose, who had a perpetual look of just having thought of something funny and not knowing whether to spring it or not. "This is all good and well, but what's it for?"

"Pardon?"

"If the conductivity in sodium is successfully measured, how may this knowledge be used? In industry? In energy?"

Shorthand, Erwin knew, for how it could be profitable. He bristled.

"I get your meaning, and forgive me, but I am merely a research scientist. I tend not to focus so clearly on the applications."

Dr. Lewis again surveyed the faculty. Dust particles illuminated in the sunlight, streaming through the windows. The silence deepened. The longer it lasted, the more he felt its weight; his future seemed to hang in the balance.

Dr. Lewis spoke up. "As for myself, Mr. Phipps, I'm impressed with your diligence and attention to detail," he said. "Taking up the mantle again after an accident such as yours reveals much about your character going forward. I am intrigued by your design and will be eager to learn of your progress as you proceed. Consider your research plan approved."

Erwin felt buoyant. He'd taken a risk for what his heart wanted, and his wishes were granted. He would proceed, finally, toward the target he'd willed for himself.

"Thank you, Dr. Lewis. Gentlemen," he said and shook their hands with great relief.

"Good luck, Mr. Phipps," said Dr. Lewis. "I hope your summer is pleasant and productive."

Erwin wanted to celebrate, but he'd never felt quite so alone. Until that moment, he had been so pressed with study—devoting every spare minute toward gearing up for his presentation—that he hadn't allowed himself the luxury of thought beyond it. He exited the doors of the building to a quiet street, the campus nearly empty. It was the week after Memorial Day, and most students had already concluded their affairs and gone home. Even Roy was gone—having completed his degree and moved to Chicago. His bachelor apartment was empty.

The bells of the Campanile tower began to play, wrapping him in a pang of homesickness. He felt completely untethered, but at the same moment, his heart hungered for companionship, someone with whom to share his happiness. Helen had proposed visiting him in Berkeley at the end of the summer, but it would be a long, lonely stretch until then.

He sat on a courtyard bench, took Eleanor's latest letter out of his pocket, and read it again, allowing himself to savor it. His thoughts dwelled on this lovely friendship in a way he hadn't quite let himself since receiving it. He tried to imagine her going about her day in North Carolina, wondering what she would make of Berkeley. It was time to respond. More than that, time to test that strong connection he'd felt—still felt whenever he read her words. He longed for that sense of lightning that passed through him that night and not to have to rely on such ponderous written and social conventions. He needed to be, once more, in her orbit.

Buoyed by his progress, Erwin decided he would take another risk: in writing to Eleanor, he would invite her to visit Berkeley at the same time as Helen. That way, there wouldn't be anything untoward about his invitation or her coming; she would be in Helen's company. After all, she had said, "Your account of University life makes me hungrier than ever for the time, I mean the lucre, to come when I can go on and study."

And then, "Is there any way I can persuade Helen to write to me? I don't want her to forget me a bit."

And if there were sparks again and Eleanor just happened to decide to take up study here, well, that would be just about the most promising thing he could think of.

CHAPTER IX

Raleigh, North Carolina

June 2, 1920
Berkeley, Cal.

Dear Miss Morgan,
 I have something to celebrate today that can't be found in any school history as yet, namely, the passing of an oral preliminary exam in Physical Chemistry, which came off yesterday morning in the presence of the assembled faculty of the College of Chemistry. Gentle reader, have you ever been through the Third Degree? If not, you can't imagine even faintly how it feels to have a dozen profs of high degree flatten you out mentally and then dance gleefully upon the cold remains. And to better appreciate the situation, you will recall that I am much more fluent a listener than a speaker.
 After twenty rounds, I got the decision on points. I then

painted the town red, that is to say I went to Oakland and saw a movie, bought myself a new pocketknife, and ate ham and eggs for supper. Wasn't that rash?

Pobrecita! I don't wonder why you should want a year of study after a year on the educational rock pile. I wish the English department here might be strong enough to attract you away from the east. Isn't it, really? I have persuaded my sis to come out for a few weeks at the end of the summer to see me and the University and Frisco and California. She is preparing to go north and east to study commerce, foreign trade, etc. (This being the latest bee to crawl into her bonnet). California is admittedly weak in this department, or she would spend the next year here with me. The fall session begins about the end of August. During her visit. I wish you might be here then too.

Your warning regarding Mr. Lindsay was very timely. I shudder to think how narrowly I escaped. I think I could draw a picture of him with your very vivid description— and the English, I hear, are hog-wild about him. Maybe it's their sly way of denying that any literary good can ever come out of America.

Juneteenth comes before the Fourth of July, I believe, but isn't there something important to celebrate before the 'teenth'? I will leave it to your ingenuity.

Yours sincerely,

TE Phipps

Eleanor sat in her rocking chair, pitching it back and forth as she read. She was to leave Raleigh the following day, and a wave of relief had passed through her at the appearance of Erwin's letter—the silence was broken. Maybe he still cared.

She was glad of his choice to share his accomplishments. Her heart celebrated with him. But was he inviting her to come to Berkeley, to take up study there? If so, at this point, it would be an impossibility. And even if it weren't, what was he really asking? It was simply too late for her to find out. Fate had already decided, and she had committed herself to another path.

And after the daring, forward tone of her previous letter, she was disappointed that they still seemed to be Miss Morgan and Mr. Phipps to each other. Hadn't she signed her last letter "Eleanor"? And yet, he seemed not to have noticed. She longed, at the very least, to *be* Eleanor to him and to call him Erwin. But that benchmark of formality remained unmoved. Her internal Ms. Prudence intervened to scold her: *Never take a man into your heart until he comes all the way. Romance shouldn't be a literary analysis; you shouldn't have to excavate for affection.*

She wished she didn't care for him so. If she didn't and things had unfolded differently, it might have been possible to hatch out this little adventure with Helen. But she did, and as such, she just couldn't come to him in this way—without a dearer assurance, to believe that it's real, not simply another free-floating fancy to be punctured.

So, as far as their friendship growing into something more, she would just be better off not hoping. It probably wasn't real, anyway, this fancy of companionship with Erwin. Just as her fancy of Scotland with Julia. And the more she thought along these lines, the more she tried to fashion her thoughts toward a far more sober response, rereading his letter once more: *Isn't there something important to celebrate before the 'teenth? I will leave it to your ingenuity.*

Her ingenuity. She wondered if what she fancied as a growing friendship had only occurred due to "her ingenuity" all along. In her first letter to him, she had tried to find some way to tell him that his letters would be welcomed if he cared to write, taking the calculated risk of being forward in this manner to let him know that he didn't have to wait until the next New Year, that he ought to write sooner if he cared to. And on Easter, he had given her the confidence to write so.

She wouldn't have the furtherance of their conversation left to *her* ingenuity. Ms. Prudence nodded approvingly. *Indeed*, Eleanor thought, *this is a sign*. He hadn't intended to start a correspondence with her. He'd only sent along a belated New Year wish out of politeness, just as he had the year before, and now he was just being considerate in the correspondence, only minimally keeping it up. It was clear to her now: she ought to let him stop writing. Ms. Romance had held far too much sway over her these past months; all that magic she had once felt was just another figment of her overactive imagination.

She packed and left Raleigh without penning a response.

CHAPTER X

Goldsboro, North Carolina

PAPA WAS WAITING for her at the train station. He had done so only once before, back in her college years, during Mama's health scare, so her thoughts went dark upon her first notice of him on the platform after the train had stopped. Charged with alarm, she made her way to the vestibule as quickly as she could.

"Papa?" she shouted.

He spotted her and began his approach, a toothy grin atop a long white beard. There was something definitively jolly about him.

"Welcome home," he said.

Eleanor blinked in bewilderment and stepped down to meet him.

"Well, *thank* you," she said. "Is Mama all right?"

"Just fine."

Eleanor exhaled.

Papa called to the porter, instructing him to deposit her trunk next to his motorcycle.

"I've attached the sidecar for you," he said, still smiling.

Eleanor could not remember the last time she'd seen her father in such good humor. And she was still very nearly a child when she last rode in his sidecar. She scrunched into the seat with the trunk at her feet.

"Chautauqua started this week," he said. "Best it's been in years, everyone is saying." The motorcycle chugged to life.

The Chautauqua. Of course.

He raised his voice over the rumble of the engine. "Which evening is it, then, that the Summerlin boy invited you for?"

In an instant, she understood. She'd been a little surprised at the arrival of Harrison's letter but had settled on the easy assumption that Alice provided him her Raleigh address and hadn't given the matter any further thought. Now, she realized, maybe it wasn't Alice.

"Wednesday," she replied. "But I hadn't thought to accept his invitation."

Eleanor knew that she was making a cardinal mistake in saying so because it carried the likelihood of disrupting Papa's good mood. Although it had been a long time since she had seen Papa happy, there were rules to be followed. Papa was happy, so everyone had to be happy. Anything less was a personal rebuke.

He didn't speak for the rest of the five-block journey. The motorcycle came to a stop in front of their house, and Papa removed his goggles. He was no longer smiling.

"Why haven't you responded yet?" he asked calmly, gaze forward, still seated on the motorcycle.

What could she say that would cause the least disturbance? That she'd been busy? She felt the familiar sense of walking on eggshells. No. Her timeworn tactic of treading as lightly as possible wouldn't do in this case. She must get to the direct truth of the matter.

"I hadn't thought to accept because I don't want to encourage him in his attentions. Harrison is a fine young man, but I have no particular interest in him."

That *fine young man* bit was an appeasement; she knew she could never say to Papa what she really thought of Harrison.

"'Fine young man' is right, Eleanor," he said. "He came calling weeks ago to inquire as to your summer plans. You frankly couldn't do better, and by some divine providence, he's interested in you." Papa lifted himself off the motorcycle with an exasperated huff. He regarded her with serious eyes. "Go to Chautauqua with him, Eleanor. Accept him. Please," he said in the same matter-of-fact tone he'd always used when directing her life in the opposite way she wanted it.

This prompted Eleanor to rebel. If nothing else, she had to stand her ground. She wouldn't let such a capitulation punctuate her return home.

"Papa, I am a grown woman now. I can make these sorts of choices for myself."

Gruffly, Papa lifted out her trunk. "Come back to live in my house, did you?"

Eleanor felt the thrum of her pulse.

"I'm starting a position in the English Department at Mississippi State College for Women in two months," she said. She hadn't shared this news with Papa, and it was clear from the mildly stricken reaction in his eyes that Mama hadn't found a way to tell him. She felt a quiver in her stomach.

He was possessed by an unnatural stillness. "Will you never learn?" he muttered finally and walked with her trunk toward the front gate. "Kate!" he shouted impatiently to Mama, huffing up the stairs toward the door.

So much for her warm welcome home. Already, her presence would create strife for Mama. Perhaps it would just be easier on all of them if she accepted Harrison's invitation. To smooth things out for Mama's sake, at the very least. She would be gone in two months anyway, far away from Goldsboro, she thought, surveying her old block. Far away from this life.

She stopped herself. She'd already come this far, and it wasn't her responsibility to backtrack, to make herself smaller to suit Papa. She wasn't a child, and she wouldn't allow him to treat her as such.

She removed herself from the sidecar and made her way inside.

To mend things with Papa required an apology on her part, Eleanor knew. But there wasn't anything to apologize for. And so they fell into a hostile kind of silence. For Eleanor, this arrangement suited her fine; she took to reading novels on the front porch while Papa went determinedly back and forth to Chautauqua without so much as a glance in her direction. Eleanor entreated Mama not to fret about it but knew it couldn't be helped.

Alice and the rest of the XYZ club had recently taken up mah-jongg. They included Eleanor when they needed a fourth player but were so transfixed by the new game that, at least temporarily, Alice had subsided her matchmaking habits. If Eleanor could just coast through another six weeks in this fashion, maintaining this kind of détente with the forces of opposition in Goldsboro, she would mark it an astonishing success. Come August, she would move to Mississippi, find a new boarding arrangement, and kick off her life of adventure.

Because she had stationed herself on the porch, she could intercept the mail and, for once, keep up with her correspondence while she was at home. Lawrence, having spent the past year studying at Harvard, wrote, *I'm sorry I have neglected you, but examinations were threatening, and there was only one way known to me to prepare for them, and that is by constant repetition. How else could I decide why Shakespeare killed Falstaff, where Spenser got his dragon, or whether the ducking stool was, even before it ducked, a basket or a utensil for domestic or private use? Try it.*

Eleanor wrote back, *Your letter found me on the front porch alternating my readings between the* Atlantic Monthly *and Sinclair Lewis's* Main Street, *while inside Mama has taken it upon herself to put a new coat of calcimine on the walls of the old dining room and refuses any assistance. Papa is, as usual, either at Chautauqua or in his armchair, with the* Daily Argus *and his favorite yarns. I suppose that puts me under Lucifer's feet in the house of Pride, speaking of Spenser's dragons.*

She wrote more letters to Julia, her cousin May, and, most importantly, Helen. The flight of fancy she'd had with Erwin unintendedly disrupted her friendship with Helen for quite a long period of time, much to her remorse. Eleanor cherished Helen and, remembering that she had a summer birthday, took the occasion to fill her in on all the salient details of the year that had elapsed since she left Norman.

But when she returned home after mailing Helen's letter, she found Papa sitting on the porch, in her usual spot.

"Papa?" It was the first word she'd spoken to him in two weeks.

He looked vacant, somehow, as if all emotion had been smoothed out. "Please sit, dear girl." His tone was much softer than she'd expected.

Eleanor sat, pulse thrumming with uncertainty.

They sat in silence for a moment; then Papa cleared his throat.

"Remember when you were set on joining the Navy during the war? You wanted to serve your country and see the world, you said."

"Yes."

"And I prevented it. Do you recall why?"

"Yes."

Another moment's silence.

"Harrison Summerlin is to be detailed to the Department of State in Washington, DC," he said.

"Oh." She couldn't manage to make any other comment on the matter; she didn't see a relation between those two things.

"You want adventure, Eleanor, but you need protection. And I only want your safety. The way I see it," Papa said, "with Harrison, you'd have both. With him, you would be able to serve your country.

See the world. Just as you've longed to do. It's an ideal opportunity."

The notion of traveling the world had never seemed quite so unpalatable.

"I can tell you," he went on, "that a position in diplomacy is greatly enhanced by having a spouse. I saw it time and again in my work. So you see Harrison's predicament: As a bachelor, it becomes rather a closed society."

"Harrison's predicament?" she repeated. "You're moving very swiftly. What have you been hatching out?"

"He'd like to call on you, Eleanor, and I've given my blessing for him to do so. I just hope that you can set pride aside and see the advantages in it. For both of you."

Eleanor blinked. "Papa, I don't care for Harrison. Not in that way."

"You needn't," Papa said, stood up, and removed himself from the porch.

Eleanor's chest tightened. Of all the young women actively seeking husbands in Goldsboro, why had Harrison settled on her? She who would be least suited to him? It was as if the forces at play in Goldsboro saw her as a character in some book, like her fate could be altered at their whim, not a real person in the world with reasons for wanting the things she wanted, with her own depths in which to take pleasures and solace. This, more than anything, angered her. She could never be the kind of wife prevailed upon to grease the social wheels of Harrison's diplomatic career. Her vexation reaching a peak, she would have to confront Papa. But she was keenly aware that she had to take a measured approach.

She entered the house, the entryway threshold squeaking under her feet. Papa was settling back into his chair.

"Harrison deserves to be with someone who loves him," she said.

"Plenty of people already do, Eleanor. His family, the community," Papa easily countered. "Love needn't be part of the equation. But you may come to love him in time. After you've warmed to the position."

She felt she would cast her fate to the wind by standing her ground, but she wouldn't be put through this hurtful exercise. She had to end this ridiculous escapade.

"Papa, I will not marry Harrison."

A momentary flutter of pain broke across his face, and he clenched his jaw against it.

"I just can't understand what's wrong with you, Eleanor. Harrison is the perfect suitor for you, and if he isn't up to snuff, you must be in league with the devil."

The following morning, a little earlier than usual, Eleanor was urged awake by a soft tapping on her bedroom door.

"Eleanor, dear," came Mama's voice softly.

With puffy eyes, Mama told her that one of the boarder's sisters, Miss Beckford, was soon to arrive in Goldsboro and needed a room to let. And Papa had settled last night on renting out Eleanor's room.

Unfortunately, familial expulsion was nothing new in the Morgan house. Eleanor's brother, Neuel, twelve years older, had been a saint in Papa's eyes until he made the wrong choice of who to marry. And in turn, Papa had ejected him seven years previously. His absence remained an open wound for them all. Because of it, she came to imagine her expulsion as a kind of inevitability, if she ever pushed too far in whatever Papa deemed to be the wrong direction. And now here, apparently, it was.

Mama knew Eleanor was better off elsewhere, so they packed her things again. "Papa's convinced himself that you will come to a bad end," Mama told her. "But I know you'll prove him wrong."

Her words were a small comfort but could not turn the rising tide of anguish at being replaced in her family home. And ire at Papa, for whom faith was a cornerstone in life, but somehow he could not extend the simplest of faiths to her. Eleanor pared down her possessions to what she could carry to Mississippi. A roaring backyard fire was a greedy receptacle for everything she left behind, save some books and childhood keepsakes in Mama's possession.

She reserved a little compartment in her trunk for her treasures and packed Erwin's letters away in it, bundled with a bit of lavender, as a reminder that life can be beautiful. She threw the prize heart, which had stood its place against the lamp atop her bureau, into the fire, feeling a satisfaction at watching it blacken and disappear into the flames, the silly prophesy along with it.

CHAPTER XI

Austin, Texas

ERWIN SAT WITH his two brothers on the wide veranda of his family home, the breeze of the afternoon cutting the stifling heat of the mid-July air. Peggy, his eldest sibling, had at last been successful in her attempts to extract Foster from his busy lawyer's life in Muskogee, and he visited Austin for the first time since Mama's death nearly five years previously. In turn, Erwin jumped at the chance to have all five siblings together again, his days in Berkeley having become unbearably lonely, his invitation to Eleanor without response, and he was left to wonder why. From the end of the block, the postman's whistle sounded, and Erwin watched his approach along the opposite side of San Jacinto Boulevard in the shadow of the state Capitol building.

As was Papa's custom, he read aloud from the newspaper about all the political outrage of the day. They had already banded together in pummeling Harding over the artifice of his new "front porch" campaign. They settled the European policies—areas where they agreed perfectly, so disagreement was the expected next course. Erwin readied himself for a customary go-round with Foster and his younger brother, Kent, over what he considered their unfortunate prejudices.

"Just listen to this," Papa said over the clatter of a streetcar rumbling by. "A former suffrage leader in Los Angeles urges Tennessee *not* to support ratification of the amendment."

"Former suffragette! Ha! Now, doesn't that beat all?" Kent said, throwing down the gauntlet, stretching his length down the porch stairs with his elbow propped at the top, a familiar pose of his younger self. Erwin's muscles tightened. Tennessee was the last holdout, the remaining obstacle to a Constitutional amendment to give women the national right to vote.

Papa continued, "She regrets her former activity. Suffrage, she says, coarsens and cheapens women."

"HA," Foster said, echoing Kent. He sat on the opposite side of the stairs and rocked on a creaking board. "Just like I've always said, give 'em enough rope, and they'll hang themselves!"

Erwin had attended the Democratic Convention as an usher the previous month in San Francisco. He was stirred by the speeches of the women delegates, injecting new hope into the future of political discourse. He thought of Eleanor and women who've been so long in the trenches to fashion such a victorious development. His brothers' reactions to the mere notion of suffrage seemed old-fashioned and wrongheaded. *Here we go*, he thought. He composed his retort, sidestepping Kent to get to the front gate. The postman handed him a bundle of letters.

Peggy emerged from the front door. "I'll take that mail, Erwin," she called and held out her hand. "Helen's putting the last touches on the cake."

He absently flipped through the letters as he walked back toward the porch. But when he saw Eleanor's handwriting among them, he stopped dead in his tracks. For a fraction of a second, the world around him dropped away, and the fireworks show he'd seen ten days previously from the hills of Berkeley went off again in his heart. Eleanor had found him—here!—and sent a Bastille Day greeting, answering his secret longing. But when he looked more closely, he could see the addressee of her letter: Helen. He sobered quickly. A birthday card. He coursed with jealousy. How thoughtful of her.

Peggy stretched out her hand further, but Erwin hesitated. Even if it wasn't addressed to him, he didn't want to give over Eleanor's letter, not yet. He burned with curiosity over whether it contained anything about his invitation.

Papa went back to reading. "She says since suffrage has been granted, there has been an alarming increase in immorality, divorce, and murder in California."

"*Who* says?" Peggy asked with an incredulous look.

"A reformed suffragette," Foster said, affecting a lilt in his voice.

Peggy grimaced, then waved him off. "Oh, *please.*"

Erwin stood still, one ear on the conversation unfolding around him, while his thoughts remained on Eleanor. He yearned to see his name on her letter, feel anew that sense of—what?—electricity that the prospect of her friendship brought to his heart.

"*Erwin,*" Peggy said, bringing him back to the moment. "The mail. And then set these menfolk straight about morality in California."

With a masked reluctance to let Eleanor's missive out of his hands, he finally ascended the steps and handed the letters to Peggy.

Foster sat straight on the steps and donned his lawyer's tone. "Don't you see, Sis? You women are so close to having your suffrage amendment, you can probably taste it. All you need are just a handful of votes to ratify it, and now you've got your leaders changing their minds and turning against the cause."

"My money's on the liquor lobby," Papa muttered. "I wager they set up their campaign to reform this girl, and it worked—in bold print."

"Doesn't matter if they did," said Foster. "Because the *real* problem here is the variability of women." He looked gamely toward Erwin. "One day, they're leading the march, and the next, they're against what they used to stand for. There's no rightful place in politics for that."

Peggy's eyes narrowed into a flinty stare. "Morality *is* the issue, Fos," she said. "This 'reformed suffragette,' as you call her, wants to make you think that California's going to pot because *women have won the right to vote there*. But one person's opinion, bought or not, is hardly a survey of the entire state of California." She let out a disgusted "hmph!" and stormed back inside the house, letters in hand.

Foster chuckled, stretching back out on the stairs. "See what I mean? Variable as the shade," he said. Then he sang in an operatic voice, "*La donna è mobile. Qual piuma al vento.*"

Kent chuckled, and Papa lowered his paper to shake his head disapprovingly at Foster. Erwin heard Helen's and Peggy's voices through the house's open windows and considered the striking contradiction with the little air from Rigoletto that Foster had just sung. *Fickle as feathers in the wind? Hardly*, he thought. He'd always looked up to his sisters.

"I'll do one better than Peggy," Erwin said, turning his sights on Foster. "You're wrong, *and* you ought to know better than that. Suffrage hasn't harmed morality in California one bit. It's just as immoral as it's always been."

"Oh, keep your shirt on. I'm just striking a little spark from her steel," Foster said dismissively. But Erwin's ire had already built up, thinking about the strength of the women around him. Their struggle just to get this far.

Erwin pressed on. "For a man who is supposed to have a legal and judicious mind," he said, "it's a shame that you would fall in with that silly propaganda about the variableness of women. You're only being foolish in repeating it."

"Yeah, Fos," Kent said teasingly. Foster looked up at him with a smirk.

"I *was* just being foolish, Erwin," Foster said. "Now you've gone and grown tragic about a little thing."

"It's not a little thing to Peggy. Serves her right to push back."

"Well," Papa chimed in. "I'd say this girl in California is right about one thing—politics *is* coarse and cheap. And for that, I just can't see a woman's place in it."

Another streetcar rumbled by. Erwin bristled; he couldn't just let the matter rest with that.

"Listen," he started again, putting on a more conciliatory tone. "Take Helen. The most stolid of the Phippses, wouldn't you say? Who can always stop and reason sanely and carefully about worrisome things—something I wager all men have often been incapable of. Wouldn't politics be better for women like her?"

"Who?" Helen popped her bespectacled face out of the door. "Now that you gentlemen have settled the question of suffrage, let's have some cake, shall we?"

Strawberry shortcake was Helen's summertime specialty, one that filled Erwin with childlike glee. The men took their places at the dining table as Peggy topped the layers of sponge cake, berries, and cream with little pink candles to celebrate Helen's thirty-eighth birthday.

Helen had always been more aunt than sister to Erwin, looking after him, guiding him. She was well-educated and well-traveled, yet her professional life had gone in fits and starts—there always seemed to be obligations at home that tore her away at critical junctures. She'd borne the brunt of family ups and downs, and Erwin felt a deep regret that she'd been held back in her wishes. And now, Helen was using some of her wages from Oklahoma to pay for his tuition at Berkeley while she could only dream of returning to her education.

Peggy struck a match to light the candles. "Make a wish, Sis," she said.

Helen closed her eyes for a long moment and blew them out. They all clapped on cue.

"What'd you wish for?" Kent asked.

"She can't tell. It won't come true!" Peggy reached for the knife to slice the cake.

"Oh, Peggy, it's just a wish. There's always at least a fifty-fifty chance it won't come true," Helen said. "I wished for the fortitude—and finances—to go and study in New York."

Erwin's chest expanded. "You'll surely have it, Sis," he said, vowing to do everything he could to help her. He didn't want life to pass her by and considered it his duty to help her take her place in the world. *How very much*, he thought, *we owe to Helen and can never repay.*

After the celebration and the strawberry shortcake's reduction to crumbs, Helen and Peggy cleared the dining table.

"Speaking of suffragists, Erwin," Helen said, "I've just had a card from Eleanor Morgan." She lifted a stack of plates from the table and went to the kitchen. The fireworks went off again, just to hear her name spoken aloud. He collected the cake stand and server from the table and followed her. "You remember Eleanor, don't you?" she asked.

"Yes, of course! How is Miss Morgan?" He set the dish down by the sink as casually as he could and smiled in a bid for Helen to tell him something about the card's contents. Anything at all. He was clamorous to know whether she had mentioned his invitation to Berkeley. Helen filled the wash basin with soapy water. She looked over her shoulder, sunshine breaking across her face.

"That was a lovely evening we had in Norman together, wasn't it? I shall remember it always," she said. "Eleanor is one of the loveliest and most interesting friends I have ever had."

To continue the conversation, Erwin grabbed a dish towel and assumed a drying position. He had a vision—a playful Eleanor dancing and skipping along to Mrs. Dungan's little Mother Goose operetta, her light, melodic laugh in the air.

"Yes," he said, "I remember it fondly too."

"But now she's taken on a new position at a women's college in

Mississippi. So she'll at least be closer by than North Carolina. I can only hope that our paths cross again."

Erwin's heart dropped. Eleanor hadn't mentioned anything to him about Mississippi. Now he wondered whether his letter had arrived at Raleigh too late, and she was already gone.

"Now you get out of here, Sis," said Peggy, butting in between the two of them. "You already baked your cake. I'm not gonna let you wash these dishes. Erwin and I will finish."

Helen acquiesced and went to join Papa, who'd reassumed his position on the front porch swing. Peggy submerged the drinking glasses into the soapy bin.

"Speaking of familiar people," she said, "I heard that Thornton Read has returned to the Chem Department as a professor. You remember Thornton, don't you?"

Erwin did, but he'd much rather remain preoccupied with thoughts of Eleanor than listen to Peggy gleefully continue with her brief of all the latest Austin gossip. But he nodded and dried the dishes as she regaled him with tales—some of long-lost Austin cohorts, some of names that he bore no remembrance of nor attachment to. His thoughts, again, were elsewhere—in Norman, one singing December night.

Peggy stopped talking and looked to him expectantly for some response, probably, to whatever she'd just said. But he hadn't been paying close attention.

"You sure are in a good mood, Sis," he said instead. "Glad to see those anti-suffragists didn't get you down."

"I'm just so happy when we're all together." Peggy looked out the kitchen window, and her smile faded into a shadowed expression. "Everything will be so much harder when you all go away again. Papa will go back to being his usual irritable self, and Kent is keen on getting oil work down in Tampico. I do so miss Mama."

He sent an arm around Peggy. "We all do," he said softly, then, adopting Mama's particular Tennessee accent, said, "*My dear little girlie*," which she had always called Helen and Peggy, even as fully grown women.

Mama had fallen sick in October 1915. At first, with her accustomed autumn cold and neuralgia, she removed herself from her household duties of meal preparation, boarder management, and letter writing. She turned instead to her handiwork while Helen took over in her stead. Waiting for the illness to pass, she crocheted a dresser scarf.

It was November then, and Mama became weaker instead of stronger. Erwin took time away from his studies to help Helen with kitchen cleanup and with Kent in his studies. Together, they wrote optimistic letters to Peggy, who was teaching in Port Arthur, assuring her that Mama would soon be on the road back to health and not to worry—they had everything covered. Mama asked for her great-grandmother's quilt to be brought out of the cedar chest, and on the milder days, she sat outside with it in the garden.

By December, Mama's efforts to speak had grown spare. Her face carried the same serene features they always had, but thin and sallow. To everyone's astonishment, she ripped up the quilt and began re-carding the wool, telling him in shallow breaths about her memories of Tennessee, her simple happiness there, and how she wished the same for him. Helen wrote to Peggy to say she might want to come home. She wrote the same to Foster, up in Muskogee.

By Mama's last week on Earth, she couldn't get out of bed, but she ensured they all knew she was content. To be lifted from life's cares, to be called home. But this met with a flat refusal to accept the notion. Mama always got better. They spoke instead of a time that she'd be sitting among the poppies in their garden and going to town with Mrs. Faut to buy brand-new wool. Mama listened and smiled and asked them to sing "Faith of Our Fathers." She closed her eyes on Tuesday, December 14, and by the time they woke up on Wednesday, she was gone.

It was Papa who told them, Papa who'd been the fretful one

throughout Mama's illness. Erwin's heart was heavy with disbelief. She was only fifty-eight. She was supposed to get stronger, to come back to life to make them all happy again. But she hadn't.

Erwin, Helen, and Foster grew quiet and pensive. Their shared instinct seemed to be an inward retreat. Peggy, however, was stricken with grief and wept inconsolably. Kent left and didn't return until the next day.

They buried her on Saturday. And afterward, they were thrown into darkness, as if the sun had been blotted out, distant from each other. Every day, they went together to the cemetery, Helen reminding them that though this was where Mama's body lay, she also lived in their hearts, in their memories, woven into the very fibers of their being.

Peggy, however, continued to be plagued by bouts of grief and despair. *Mama was my source of hope and cheer*, she'd say, *and now she's gone. You told me she would get better*, she'd say, bursting into tears at the sight of the half re-carded wool of the tattered quilt.

Erwin tried to be patient with her. Mama would have wanted that. But Helen had taken over Mama's duties without hesitation and had cared for Mama and all of them in her stead without complaint. They did their level best, and still, she died. It was already unfair without Peggy casting aspersions, as if her pain held sway over theirs.

Peggy washed the last dish and handed it to Erwin. "Somehow, I'm still struggling through the dark," she said, but her tone was good-natured as if she had recognized and accepted this state of being. She wiped her eyes. "Well, brother, let's join this merry bunch of fools on the porch, shall we?"

With a little clatter, Erwin put away the last of the dishes and turned to follow Peggy. On the breakfast table, he saw Eleanor's opened letter and stopped.

How he longed to chase that same happiness they'd had that December night, watching fireworks in the hearth or the kind of warmth he'd felt when Mama was alive and the family was all together, singing in front of the fire into the future, some fine day with his own family. With Eleanor. He grappled with the notion that she'd slipped away from him when he wished so earnestly for her to be closer. But once more, they were instead getting farther away from each other. The idea that he'd lost her arose in him like a physical pain. He couldn't just let her go. He would sneak a look at her return address, he decided, and test the connection again.

CHAPTER XII

Mississippi State College for Women
Columbus, Mississippi

IRMA HINES WAS a willowy junior of eighteen from Jackson, made taller still by the heels she wore each day. They made a dull click as she approached Eleanor's desk after class.

"Miss *Morgan*," she said in her honeyed tone, drawing out the two syllables of Eleanor's last name. She had her latest assignment in hand, which had been freckled over with red ink.

"You say here that I shouldn't get so personal in my argument, but it was Governor Russell who got personal in his speech. Not I."

"Not *me*," Eleanor corrected. "And Miss Hines, the assignment only required you to listen for clichéd speech patterns around you. It was not intended as a vehicle for voicing your displeasure with the college's most esteemed board member."

Eleanor gathered up her books and papers. At the close of each class day, she walked a few of her students to their dormitory as part of the college's regulated system of chaperonage.

"Then I suppose you favor his decision to limit our dances and impose a stricter curfew?" Irma asked, one manicured hand resting on her hip, the other hugging a stack of books to her chest.

"No, I don't favor it." She favored not losing her job immediately by getting in political crosshairs, so she halted her commentary there.

"That's right." Irma nodded curtly. "If you want *me* to stop dancing, Governor, you're going to have to cut off my feet, just like in that fairy story."

Lucy Whittaker, another junior from Jackson, with long dark hair piled on the top of her head and light blue eyes, took her place in the group. "So you dance too, Miss Morgan?" she asked.

"I only mean to say I approve of dancing," Eleanor said. "And if you would like to form an effective argument with Mr. Russell, I recommend you don't make it so personal to *him*."

Eleanor and her group of three exited the classroom, beginning their walk through the warm and musky late October air, to Hastings Hall, the girl's dormitory, a block down from the Carpenter house, where Eleanor had her room.

"Auntie Morgan," said Irma, "can we first go to the PO today? I have letters to post." As soon as they were out of the classroom, Irma always took up her family associations and had early on deemed Eleanor the maiden aunt of the bunch. She found it endearing, if a little jarring.

"I have letters to post too," chimed Elizabeth Byrne, a small-framed, bespectacled freshman from Greenville.

"Miss Byrne," said Eleanor. "Did you forget to turn in the last assignment? I don't think I saw yours."

Elizabeth reddened. "I'm sorry, Auntie Morgan," she said. "I didn't have the time."

Irma guffawed. "Didn't have the time? Sister Elizabeth, you have to do better than *that*."

It was a well-accepted truth that time was a natural resource of Columbus, a place beyond all haste, a forgotten bead from a broken string. "They call Columbus the Sleeping Beauty," Mr. Carpenter had said, as he gave her a tour in his automobile after she'd first arrived, making note of the various old plantation homes, ostentatious even by old Carolina standards. It looked to Eleanor that perhaps Columbus had gone to sleep around 1864, content to stretch its antebellum dreams as far into the future as possible.

"I'll expect the assignment tomorrow, Miss Byrne," Eleanor said.

Eleanor led her charges toward Main Street, in the direction of the post office. Truth was, Eleanor needed their chaperonage as much as they needed hers (which, she believed in her own mind, was *not at all*), but Columbus required it for unmarried women who endeavored to be thought of as ladies. And a lady simply never walked alone on the streets of Columbus, not since the first streets were laid down, and not for any reason, even something as simple as going to the post office. And Eleanor needed to settle the question of her own mail service.

Since her arrival in July, she'd received only sporadic letters from home, even from family and friends equipped with Mr. Carpenter's street address. And even so, each one suggested another letter that had gone missing. After visiting the basement mailroom at the college, she'd intercepted a stack that had inexplicably been forwarded to Mr. Carpenter's office. In Goldsboro, she was accustomed to having all her letters forwarded, but not here.

At first, this lack of identity in Columbus had been freeing. Back home, everyone knew her business and had opinions about it. Here, she felt that she was remaking her life, free of the kind of expectations she felt in Goldsboro. She hadn't known anyone at all other than Mr. Carpenter when she arrived, and he was a person who thought highly enough of her to offer her a position in the first place.

It also came as a relief to her soul after the difficulty of her last weeks in Goldsboro. The tragedy of it had scared and saddened her, but Mr. Carpenter was kind enough to offer her a room in his family home, and here in Columbus, she was the object of no one's scorn, gossip, or unwanted attentions. She was happy being a nobody.

But she came to realize that Mississippi would fast develop its own identity for her, one she found nearly unrecognizable—neither suiting nor flattering; like a fun-house version of the reflection she hoped she displayed, sheathed in a veneer of difference. And she was surprised to find she missed being part of the fabric of a place. That she longed for contact with someone who *knew* her.

"Hello, Mrs. Carpenter," said the postmistress as Eleanor approached the window. Irma ribbed her from behind.

"I'm sorry, but you're mistaken," said Eleanor. "I'm not Mrs. Carpenter."

This had become a common mistake, quite an embarrassing one; although Mr. Carpenter was in his forties, his wife, Edna, was the same age as Eleanor, also a former student of his, and remarkably similar in appearance. Slight variations of the same type, in build, coloring, and facial features.

The postmistress narrowed her eyes. "Oh my. I am sorry, ma'am. You look just like her! Well, now you're up close, I can see that you aren't. You must be one of the college girls? How can I help you?"

She felt an odd mix of annoyance and delight at being taken for a student. "I'm an *instructor*, yes," she said over Irma's giggles. "The fact is, I room at the Carpenter house and have had trouble getting my letters consistently."

"I was unaware that the Carpenters had any roomers." The postmistress went quiet, her eyes still narrowed, grappling at the odd incongruity of having mistaken Mrs. Carpenter's roomer for Mrs. Carpenter, how two women in one house could look so similar.

After a moment, her eyes flashed. "Oh! Then this must be for you." She turned on her heel to retrieve a bundle from a cubby behind her. "Are you," she read from the top of the bundle, "Eleanor Morgan?"

"The very same." Seeing a bundle of mail with her name and

being recognized sent a wave of relief and thrill to Eleanor.

"Say, are you the same Eleanor Morgan that's from North Carolina?"

Eleanor's heart lurched into her throat. "Yes."

The postmistress disappeared momentarily and reappeared with a second, larger bundle. "Well then, that solves this mystery too," she said, handing over both bundles. "We've had these accumulating in the dead letter stacks for weeks. Apparently not one of our clerks knew where the girl from Goldsboro was staying. We do our best, Miss Morgan, but I do suggest you take yourself out a box here at the PO, if you're hoping for your mails to regulate themselves. Next!"

Eleanor stepped aside and blinked with wonder at the letters. There must have been two dozen. She joined Elizabeth and Lucy, who'd posted their letters, and Elizabeth now sat with her notebook open, eager to share some phrasing she'd been jotting down amid the comings and goings of people. Eleanor, filled to the brim with joy, flipped through letters while she listened.

"How about these: 'Slow as molasses. Hold your horses,'" read Elizabeth.

Eleanor's spirit continued to rise at the sight of the handwriting of friends and family that she had heretofore seemed to have lost contact with: Julia, Alice, Lawrence, Cousin May.

"Knock on wood. Heart's content." Elizabeth pushed up her glasses and looked at Eleanor. "Am I doing it right?"

Eleanor froze. Her eyes welled at the sudden sight of Erwin's handwriting among the letters. It was addressed to her at the college. She looked back at Elizabeth but couldn't speak. He'd found her again. Against all probability, he'd really *actually* found her again.

"Yes," Eleanor sputtered finally. "Yes, my dear Miss Byrne, you're doing it just right." And she hugged her right there in the post office.

"Okay, what'd I miss?" said Irma, approaching the others.

Eleanor tried to straighten her face to avoid any interrogation. "I've finally settled the confusion over my mails," she said. "I have a big stack from home that had gone to the dead letter pile. I'm very happy to see them, after all these weeks."

"I thought maybe you'd gotten a letter from a *man*." Irma grinned.

"Miss Whittaker," Eleanor said, changing the subject as she led them out of the post office, "I wonder if you'd like me to show you this little dance we used to do in Oklahoma together. It's called 'moon-shines.'"

Although it was just a one-block journey from the college gates to the Carpenter house, Eleanor didn't care for the lightness in her step to result in any questioning among the porch sitters of Third Street—she'd already been ribbed quite enough by her girls. So she slowed her pace, hugging the bundles of letters to her chest, letting her mind rest on thoughts of Erwin, which she simply hadn't allowed herself to do since leaving Raleigh.

The sun was lowering in the sky, and the heat of the afternoon gave way to a crisp early evening breeze. Autumn had arrived, touching the dogwood trees with scarlet and the oak trees with gold. And Eleanor's heart was charged with anticipation at receiving his letter, but there was also a strain of trepidation; why had he chosen to seek her out again? What did he mean to convey? And although she kept on with her slowed pace, she was seized with a desire to steal upstairs to the privacy of her little room so she might find out. But as she approached the Carpenter house, she could see that Mr. Carpenter was outside on the porch with little Mary, his four-year-old daughter.

Mary spotted her and tripped down the porch steps, her big gray eyes sparkling. "Eleanor's home!"

"Well, hello there," Eleanor said. She couldn't help but smile. Mary was such a dear little girl.

"Greetings," said Mr. Carpenter. "We've been ejected from the house while Edna gets Sonny down to sleep."

Privacy was a precious commodity at the Carpenter house. "I see." Eleanor swallowed her disappointment and sat on the porch swing with her stack of books, the bundles of letters resting atop.

"Do you need the throat-weller again, Colorie?" Mary said to the rag doll in her arms, dressed in red and yellow flannel.

"Colorie has the croup," she said to Eleanor, by way of explanation.

"Ah," said Eleanor. "No singing for her today." She set the stack next to her on the swing.

Mary held her doll close and rocked her with pride.

Eleanor glanced over to Mr. Carpenter, who was staring at the letters. He was a distinguished man with sandy hair, his profile strong and rigid. The girls had all been a little in love with Mr. Carpenter.

"I've just come from the post office," she said. "And the postmistress mistook me for Edna! Can you imagine? And now apparently the only way I can regulate my mails is by taking out a box there."

Mr. Carpenter regarded her with an unreadable expression that made Eleanor suddenly uncomfortable. "Those are from all your beaux back home, I suppose?" he jested and took up his pipe.

The heat rose in her cheeks, and she stole a glance at Erwin's letter atop the stack, feeling her heart flutter at the sight of it, longing for the moment when she could read it freely.

"Nothing of the kind, Mr. Carpenter."

"Good thing." He softened. "I seem to have developed an unfortunate habit of losing my best instructors to their faraway lovers and the shining of their black inks." He let fly a large puff of smoke.

Eleanor had heard the story of her predecessor, Miss Sparks, now Mrs. Badger, who Mr. Carpenter had booted at the first rumor of her engagement. Mary swiped at the pipe smoke above her head.

"Let's go for a stroll, Colorie." Mary proceeded to put her doll in a miniature buggy and pushed off down the front walk.

"It doesn't help that Columbus can be such a strange and *lonely* place, to the outsider," said Mr. Carpenter. "I've been here for six years now, and I still feel an outsider oftener than I'd like. Are you finding it so?"

Where she might have denied herself the expression, Eleanor felt a sense of relief at his words of sympathy, releasing her from the scaffold of pretense.

"At times I barely recognize myself here," she said.

A formation of geese flew overhead.

"I'm afraid I know what you mean," he said warmly, and she felt a comforting alliance with him—a small bond of foreignness—until he solemnly added, "I so often wish there were more men here to *rub minds* with."

His words dealt Eleanor an unpleasant surprise, but she did not swerve from her politeness. Judging from his earnest expression, she could see he'd intended no insult to her, but regardless she felt the barbs of his words puncture something delicate inside her.

"And we at least hoped to travel, Edna and I," he continued, "but then little Mary came along and quite spoiled that for us."

Mary pushed her doll buggy along the street. Eleanor felt a creeping uneasiness. How could the arrival of such a dear child possibly have a spoiling effect? More and more, adventure seemed the exclusive territory of the unmarried.

Edna's tired face emerged from the screen door. "The coast is clear. He's down," she said, motioning them inside.

Mr. Carpenter called to Mary and stood to reenter the house, leaving Eleanor with the privacy she craved but also with a rather sobering thought. Here was a learned man, one who had inspired her toward poetry, encouraging her to use it to "eat the world," as Emerson originally put it, and one who, until this moment, she assumed had *seen* her—recognized her intellect and courted her as an instructor because of it. A mind of her own, fit for rubbing. But now, she'd been made to realize, he thought less of her than she imagined. And she thought less of him.

As the evening darkened around her and the windows of Third Street illuminated, her longing for camaraderie grew stronger. Against the lamplight, she saw neighbors playing cards, standing in doorways, or coming out into the evening. The tinkle of a piano. No one noticed her perched, unmoving, on the porch swing. She felt, looking out into the half light of the evening, untethered, as if she could float away, should she choose to let go. Even here in academia, on what she intended to be an adventure, where she expected to find the ballast of respect that she had been fighting for, she felt as though she didn't belong. She ached for sympathetic company—someone who cared for her, to hold her hand and tell her to bear up, that all is well and would eventually be even better.

She picked up Erwin's letter, her mind now pressed with the image of his letters bundled up in the compartment of her trunk she'd reserved for her treasures, where they had remained these last four months, a secret joy, another extinguished fancy. To reopen that compartment would reopen the sense of loss she had felt, and so she hadn't. But now, here was another letter. Would opening it only invite heartbreak back into her life? She was having her adventure, as much as she was able, here and now. And she was better off, she was quite sure, for having it unmixed with any notion of romantic love.

But Erwin was one of the few people who had both recognized and honored who she was. That he found her here meant he wanted to continue the conversation, and she could now be assured of his friendship. What she needed, most of all, was a friend. Not a beau, not a new fancy, a friend.

She held the letter in her hand, her thumb tracing the neat, tall loops of his handwriting. Its postmark was dated October 12. Columbus Day. She smiled at this clever touch of his, her heart rising again at the promise of his affection, but she stopped herself at the sensation: *No*, she would not attach any fancy to this correspondence. And that was that. But her heart needed this friendship.

She opened the letter.

ACT TWO

Over the monstrous, shambling sea
Over the Caliban sea,
Bright Ariel-cloud, thou lingerest.
Oh wait, oh wait, in the warm red West, —
Thy Prospero I'll be.
—Sidney Lanier

CHAPTER XIII

October 12, 1920
Berkeley, Cal.

Dear Miss Morgan,

You didn't send a Juneteenth answer to my last missive. As I remember, it was an unusually poor letter and undeserving of an answer, or perhaps it died and was taken to the dead letter office. I sent it to your Raleigh address, from which Sister tells me you have been moved for some time.

A lot of unusual things have happened to me since then. I was an usher at the Democratic Convention and listened with bated breath while the eighty-odd women delegates made eighty-odd seconding speeches for the various nominees.

I was glad to see your state stand with mine for McAdoo in support of the suffrage amendment. (Are you enjoying this political hash, or shall I serve the next course? It's your own fault, though, for being such an ardent suffragist).

After McAdoo and I were steamrollered so gloriously at the convention, I went back to Austin for a couple of weeks. There, I found my brother from Oklahoma already on the scene. Helen and I left Austin early in August, and she spent a month here in Berkeley with me. So there you have my travelogue (?!) for the last three months. And now I am back in my ordinary role of greasy grind and pale student, burning the midnight Mazda. I am having a good deal of trouble getting back to serious work again after eating angel food cake, manicuring my fingernails regularly, and doing other such effeminate things consequent to Sis's stay here.

I have wondered often about what the future can hold in store for a crazy old state that just won't let the women vote. You will notice that a few thousand miles of space makes one very bold. California, I never refer to as crazy or old, as I don't like bricks hurled in my direction.

From April to October is a hiatus, I think. Please write me soon. "Pretty please."

Sincerely,

Thomas E. Phipps

October 30, 1920
Columbus, Miss.

Dear Mr. Phipps,

Uncle Sam seems to have a special grudge at me somehow; he just won't let me write to the Phipps family with any sort of comfort. Even this newest letter from you was missent; it had been traveling more than two weeks. However, if the mails and your nomadic habits and my scatter-brainedness permit, I'll hope for more success this time.

Your summer sounds very interesting; mine was a slumberous affair, made up of a front porch, a bit of embroidery, a novel or so, and small-town talk. I suppress all such details as rolls and pies and cakes—devil's food is my kind.

Mississippi has so far been most accommodating. Just now, some of my students are forming a club and have hit upon the original idea of making their club a family—with all the proper mothers and fathers and brothers and sisters—and they have asked me to be their maiden aunt! How the once youthful have aged.

But the four-year-old mistress of the house I live in consoles me. She came up to my room last night and asked me as soberly, "Don't you want a job? I'd like to get you to take care of my rag doll while I eat supper." So I 'reckon' I'm provided for against age and infirmity; when I can no longer be a teacher or a maiden aunt, I can protect Mary Carpenter's rag dolls.

How does your work go on? Is the degree not far off?

With best wishes,

Eleanor Morgan

P.S. Don't by any chance write to me at the college, please, because I'll never get it. Box 467 is sure.

November 25, 1920
Berkeley, Cal.

Dear Miss Morgan,

Your letter came at a time when I sorely needed for something cheerful to happen to me. Imagine me, if you can, dragging my weary length home from San Francisco at 1 a.m. on the morning of November 3, where I had just come to the bitter realization that Harding was elected, and civilization was headed straight for Scylla and Charybdis (at the same time, apparently). I had just decided, as I got off the train, to adopt the modified Mark Anthony pose: "My heart is in the grave . . . and I must pause . . ."

In this sad state of mind, I read your letter and testify cheerfully to the fact that it enabled me almost immediately to pull one foot out of the Slough of Despond. At any rate, my mental attitude became less tragic, and before going to sleep, I had reached the point of telling this unthankful country she would have to muddle through the rest of the Slough by herself. From this last attitude, the passing of three weeks hasn't changed me greatly. Possibly another letter from you will be needed before I become entirely optimistic about the future of America.

I have a few things to be thankful for though. We got three days holiday for Thanksgiving, which, along with Armistice Day, enabled me to be free of freshmen long enough to catch up a little with my own work. My thesis problem has been of such a nature that I haven't learned any chemistry but only glassblowing in construction with it. If I fail as a chemist, I suppose I can easily turn my hand to glassblowing, which, by the way, might also be more remunerative.

Just now, one of the local dramatic circles is staging some of Ibsen's dramas. I saw A Doll's House *a few years ago and wasn't greatly pleased, but maybe Ibsen deserves* a better trial than I've given him. Things theatrical are at floodtide, but your sober chemist lets all this go by while he gazes intently into a test tube, trying to see a dollar at the bottom.

Unfortunately for me, there's no four-year-old mistress at this house where I stay. That's where you have the best of me. I've always thought that the prettiest sight in the world was a little girl just four years old—and her solicitude for her doll's welfare. When they get past five, though, from then on, a rag doll is made out of rags, and the glamour is gone, so big girls aren't nearly as interesting generally. But I'm reminded by the witty Frenchman that all general statements are false, including this one. So in the future, I will promise to try and steer clear of false generalities.

Please write me another long letter soon.

Sincerely,

Thomas E. Phipps

December 10, 1920
Columbus, Miss.

Dear Mr. Phipps,

Ibsen and A Doll's House, you don't like? You would except for the ending, wouldn't you? You don't really object very, very strongly to dolls becoming women? However, I think, too, that the ending is wrong; it may be artistic, but it isn't true. Nora should have stayed with her job. You know it was a man who wrote the play; no woman would have made that unthinkable ending. [Beware the *feminist!]*

And you don't like disillusioned ladies of five, who know that rag dolls are rag dolls? Well this is what does happen: when they're three times five, they learn that, even if rag dolls are rag dolls, the world holds other treasures; when they're four times five, they see how wonderful it is that a rag doll is a rag doll, and when they're five times five, they admit that rag dolls are rags, but they believe that in the far off event of time, these rags may be evolved into exquisite French darlings that have real hair and can go to sleep. Years and years and years from now, I'll tell you what they know when they're six times five.

Escape, interpretation, hope—that's all I know so far. You see, the election didn't leave me very jubilant either. The far-off is farther off than we thought. But I don't despair. You don't either really, do you?

Merry, merry Christmas to you and the glassblowers.

Sincerely,

Eleanor Morgan

CHAPTER XIV

Columbus, Mississippi

ELEANOR DID NOT go home for the holidays. And despite Mama's entreaties to consider it, Eleanor had her pride. Her room was Miss Beckford's now. Not since the war had she skipped being home for Christmas, but between the expense of the trip and the indignity of being made to sleep on the parlor divan, she told Mama it would be impossible.

Her one consolation was that the empty college afforded her the opportunity to develop a friendship with Elise, another odd duck who had arrived at the English department from New York City, of all places. She'd come to Columbus for a year to teach, to "take a rest," as she put it. The last thing she wanted to do now, Elise explained, was go back north.

On this, they developed an easy bond, made stronger still by the discovery that Elise, too, had grown up playing at books. She had a large family that amused each other by acting out adventure stories and Shakespeare's plays.

On New Year's Eve, in front of the fire at the otherwise-empty Carpenter house, Elise told her about New York. Moving there had been her adventurous goal for a long time, she said, but she found it all rather maddening, disorienting. And expensive. It is too much, all the time. And one cannot simply close it like a book at the end of an evening and put the light out. It just goes on and on. She rather valued slowness and comfort, she'd come to realize. If New York taught her anything, it was that. She meant to find those things at MSCW. And if she went back to her family home in Massachusetts, she said, they'd never let her leave again. They all had ideas about what she should be doing, and profession played no part: marry this person, take care of that older relative, be a chaperone, and have children. That never ends either.

Eleanor nodded in perfect recognition.

Elise suggested that Eleanor try a summer course at Barnard College, and they would be able to travel to New York together. Six weeks in the summer would be time enough, Elise said, to experience the Big Apple. And so, a delicious new opportunity presented itself. And for once, both the timing and expense could be managed.

The old year passed, with the cheering effect of a fire, the spark of a new idea, and good companionship.

January 1, 1921
Berkeley, Cal.

Dear Miss Morgan,

As our nomadic habits seem to be at least provisionally quelled, this round of New Year's wish may stand a chance of arriving to you in timely fashion, and to see that it doesn't end up stuck to the bottom of a mail bag somewhere, I send also a little calendar featuring the Campanile tower, stationed near the front entrance to the campus. At 307 feet tall, I would expect it to make a fine chaperone to this letter.

I've spent the holidays here in California while much of the family is gathered in Austin. I'm sorry I didn't know your North Carolina address more accurately, or I would have chimed in with a Christmas wish when they were seasonable.

I've been doing quite a bit of light reading at nights during my holidays after the day's laboratory work. I've read Christopher Morley's The Haunted Bookshop *and George Eliot's* Middlemarch. *I thought I'd start a new sentence here so as not to have H. G. Wells in the same breath with these others, but I admit tearfully that I was beguiled into reading parts of* Twelve Stories and a Dream.

Morley, I enjoyed thoroughly. I have just one serious objection to him: he tried to poke Walt Whitman down my throat, and this makes me so perfectly furious under all circumstances.

I'm sorry if my letter has degenerated into a poor book review, but I've thought of little else this week. I go on a regular book spree whenever the pressure of daily toil is relieved for a short while. I suppose if Helen were here, she would give me a good "wigging" and take me to some tea battle for diversion and health's sake.

Please accept my heartiest wishes for a Happy New Year.

Sincerely,

TE Phipps

January 16, 1921
Columbus, Miss.

Dear Mr. Phipps,
  The calendar you sent me is beautiful, and I'm very glad to have it. I do appreciate your thinking of me, but

did you mean to make me envious three hundred and sixty-five days this year? Because the entrance to this little college is rather different, you may imagine. There isn't much classic dignity here. The chapel is a turreted, gabled, and spired red brick monstrosity with tiny, slim windows that go up and up and up forever, one narrow red, blue, green, orange, or purple pane after the other, looking as if a steamroller had struck the balloon stand at a country fair; you know the horrible, awful kind of colored glass. And most of the other buildings are tacked onto this one by covered ways, solariums or porches, a series of afterthoughts. There really is one fairly respectable dormitory, however, and one good building, Music Hall, comparatively a jewel.

I never can see why all the poetry should be locked up in books, why a woman who appreciates Keats can fail to appreciate the fact that her house might be the more beautiful for a little care, or why another, my dear Cousin Margaret, for instance, who knows all about tone color and can draw music from the hearts of us who only wish we could play, can forget that she mustn't wear a red hat with a pink blouse. I wish these girls could see something beautiful before they leave college.

But I shan't be envious quite all this year. At least six weeks of it, I'm going to New York, to be at Barnard College. Summer school is just the leavings, and New York in summer must be not altogether heaven, but the scraps of Barnard and New York will be glorious to me as these wonderful buildings here are to the MSCW girls.

You tantalize me with your reading—it's such a nice way to be tantalized though. Sometimes I wish I had done as you have, kept literature only for my pleasure instead of making it my work and pleasure. Thank you for the phrase "book spree." I'm trying to intoxicate myself. I'm on a book spree all the time, except for when I'm toiling through the Great American Desert of theme papers. There is so much reading that I ought to have done, and haven't, that I'm always ashamed of myself. Wonder if I'll ever be able to hold up my head? Recently, I've been reading Meredith. He couldn't possibly let a woman act with ordinary intelligence, could he? And not often even a man.

Thank you very much for the calendar; I like it.

Sincerely,

Eleanor Morgan

February 14, 1921
Berkeley, Cal.

Dear Miss Morgan,

Today is the 13th, but rather than get this letter lost by dating it so, I am calling it the 14th. As spring comes on apace, I find myself so deep in work and so far from the goal that I have scarcely stopped for meals and Sundays. If you don't mind advice, here's some: don't ever—ever—put yourself in the way of taking a higher degree in an experimental science.

To illustrate, some wags about the department here have formulated a General Law of Nature, which we believe to be the most comprehensive of so-called laws. It is known as the Law of the Perversity of Inanimate Matter and may be stated thus: "Nature always makes it hard for man in the easiest way" (easiest for Nature, of course). Some of the everyday corollaries are "Bread always falls buttered-side down," "It never rains, but it pours," etc. (The student, as an exercise, may think up others). Though most people have never reduced it to words, they tacitly assume its truth on all occasions, and as you know, all great truths are embedded deep in man's consciousness, and only wait for some Newton or Galileo or Avogadro to state them tersely and simply. The Law of Perversity has been working overtime in all my attempts at research, and I speak very earnestly on the subject.

It is my turn now to take on the greenish hue of envy, if you are really to see New York so soon. I hardly know what my next move will be when (or if) I finish here. This school doesn't pretend to fit men for industrial work, only academic; nevertheless, I have decided that I will try to get into some kind of industrial research work in the east and only fall back on teaching as a last resort. I have myself experienced the very great danger of flopping down into a little academic mold somewhere and "setting" there like a flock of concrete, which, to be removed, must be blasted out. But the dean warns me that industrial work is becoming increasingly difficult to find, so I may teach, after all.

I had the opportunity during the past week to hear Groveure sing, see Pavlova dance, or watch Zybysko wrestle. My mental conflict was terrific, and I compromised finally by working in the laboratory. I'm afraid you'll be shocked at my mentioning Zybysko in the same breath as the "art artists." And while I'm at it, I might as well admit that I attended a prize fight down in Oakland recently— Meehan vs. Gunboat Smith, I think it was. Two things I want to learn: one is boxing, the other the successful *balancing of a cup of tea on my knee and the laying down simultaneously of a barrage of chatter that weighs less than two cents per ton. I figure I will then be in a position to defend myself whatever comes.*

We are amid our rainy season here. I've noticed, though, that the sun shines invariably on the days when your letters reach California. Please don't keep us standing in the rain too long.

Sincerely,

TE Phipps

February 24, 1921
Columbus, Miss.

Dear Mr. Phipps,

The reports of your Weather Bureau are so pleasing that they produce immediate reaction, you see. Your California industries are too important; you have too many vineyards for me to take my responsibility lightly.

You think you will teach next year? You say "after all," and I think I know what that means. I am still teaching "after all." I'll accept your advice about degrees and such, provided you won't be peeved at having to listen to my broad, long, and boresome experience about teaching. There are compensations. The people in a university community are congenial, and there is always the library; I suppose it is about as near the ideal of plain living and high thinking as one can attain.

When I was a senior, the head of the History Department

asked me to do a paper for a bulletin on the North Carolina Journals of Education. I read and I read and I read that mush about the glory and honor and sacred importance of the teacher—only teachers and preachers are important according to some teachers and preachers—until I was sickened by the whole thing. Two weeks before the paper was due, I told the dean that I couldn't write it. I was tongue-tied about it then (don't you wish I still were?) and didn't try to explain, but by some miracle, Mr. Jackson let it pass, though I don't yet see how he managed to.

Then "after all," I taught in a high school, and I found that the children were dear to me, and some of them loved me, and so sentimentally I forgot that I was for tearing sentimentality out of the system. But the public schools require more force than I have, and I fled back to college.

Yet, all things considered, I find life in the University more nearly satisfying than life elsewhere. Have I read too much into your "after all"? Have I rushed in where angels fear to tread?

I won't do the de profundis again, I promise.

When you acquire your blank cartridges for your tea battles, you might share with me. Not to mix metaphors, but as you may recall, I'm short suited there myself. By way of contrast, I'm reading Plato's Republic. I told people who saw me with the book that I had to look up some allusions. It wouldn't do to admit to anyone nearer than California an honest interest in such a book. It would scare people. I'm not joking. It would. I know. But poetry echoing strains of all philosophies as it does, I can't go on forever teaching it without wanting to know what I'm talking about.

Tell me about your dissertations and perversities, whatever the uninitiated can understand of them. I don't know any chemistry, but I think I can follow the gleam, provided it be translated into Mother Goose first. I remember reading a novel years ago, Susan Glaspell's Glory of the Conquered, that gave me a glimpse at least of the romance of science. Is that a paradox?

This is a fearsome letter, but it's all your fault. You shouldn't start subjects that are my own pet hobbies.

Sincerely,

Eleanor Morgan

CHAPTER XV

Columbus, Mississippi

THE PINE TREES were bursting with pollen, little snakes of yellow jessamine here and there curling about the branches, as Eleanor scaled a steep slope deep in nearby Lindamood Woods. Lured by the emergence of stems from wakening roots all around them, Eleanor and her new comrade, Elise, had been gleefully playing at Midsummer Night's Dream together throughout their Sunday ramble.

"I know a bank where the wild thyme blows!" Eleanor called down a slope to Elise.

"Where oxlips grow and violets nod their heads?" Elise called up, one hand on her hat.

"*Quite* overcanopied with luscious woodbine."

This prompted Elise to catch up, despite her heels, and share the sight: a large patch of white violets at the bottom of the other side of the slope, nearing the bank of the Tombigbee River. A chorus of warblers and buntings chattered around them, the screech of hawks far overhead.

"Let's go down and gather up a few," Eleanor said.

Elise wrinkled her nose. "Looks marshy down there."

Although she delighted in Shakespeare and loved to hike, Elise wore heels and makeup and brought along a little vanity case with a powder puff and mirror. She took the unthinkable measure of carrying a pistol over her shoulder as they made their way through the fairyland of Lindamood Woods, punctuating amid the dream a kind of grave reality of how a woman from the crowded ways of New York really felt about the quiet of the small Southern town.

Eleanor stood for a moment, propelled by an urge to touch the violets, to smell them and speak to them. Her own shoes were a small sacrifice. "Let me just try it."

She had a secret thought that she might save some to send in her next letter to Erwin. *Dreams and sighs, wishes and tears, poor fancy's followers.* Despite their growing friendship, there was so much she had not shared in her letters to Erwin: the fallout with Papa over Harrison, her lack of a home, prompting her to spend what little she had to secure a summer spot at Barnard College, her growing discomfort with Columbus and Mr. Carpenter. But Erwin's letters had brought her such joy that she refused to weigh down her own responses with heartache and strife. Meeting his words, with what little joy of her own she could muster, had given her strength, after all. And deep in the woods, she could always be happy.

She carefully made her way down the other side of the slope. A tiny flutter of purplish red caught her eye, way down low next to the white violets. The firm ground under her feet gave way gradually to mud, stirring the rich, vegetative odor of earth and leaf mold.

"Oh, be careful!" Elise shouted from the top.

Eleanor stood in the grassy mud, inching as close as she could without getting wet to see the flutter of the purple flower with dark, spotted leaves. It looked like a fairy in flight. The enchantment sent ripples of excitement to her heart. "I found the love-in-idleness flower!" she shouted.

If only she could engineer a way to squeeze its oils onto Erwin's eyelids as he slept, to be the one he saw when he opened them. To at last have some certainty of reciprocity for what she felt for him, the magnetic qualities of his friendship, which persisted despite her every attempt to squelch it. It felt as though fairy magic had gotten her this far and wouldn't be *real*, she repeatedly thought, unless or until Helen was aware of it.

"Can you reach it? Bring it hither! I want to see too!" Elise said.

Eleanor leaned forward, but the flower was well out of her reach. She took hold of an aspen sapling next to her, resting her weight gently on its lower branches, releasing its resiny smell, bending it to give her leverage to stretch her arm ever forward, gaze fixed on the flower's ethereal petals. She stretched closer until the branch gave way, dumping her unceremoniously into the water.

CHAPTER XVI

Berkeley, California

AFTER SOME SUCCESSFUL tweaking of the stirrer in his apparatus, Erwin was finally able to begin the series of observations that would make up the practical side of his study of conductivity in liquid sodium. He went into spring with the heady expectation of publishing his thesis and graduating in May. He didn't think it practical to muse on what may come after, but he was sure that his groundbreaking study would leave him well positioned for the job market.

He began to put in long days at the lab, going to painstaking lengths to ensure that each of his readings would be sound. Dr. Lewis took to stopping through to oversee Erwin's progress, doubling his own enthusiasm. But on one of his afternoon visits, Dr. Lewis wore a somber expression. He approached Erwin at the bench.

"Some hard luck, I'm afraid," he said.

Erwin's stomach tightened at the words, preparing for the Law of Perversity's punch.

"I've been told, Mr. Phipps, that Dr. Kraus will be publishing his findings in the conductivity of alkali metals in a June issue of the *Journal of the American Chemical Society*."

A punch it was.

Of course he'd been half-expecting to come up against this news all along, assuring himself repeatedly that he wouldn't be defeated if and when it happened. But he was so close to that same finish line. He was more than defeated; he felt acute failure at Dr. Lewis's announcement. As if, in the final quarter of a winning game, he'd fumbled the ball and lost it all.

He crumpled into a nearby chair.

Dr. Lewis nodded sympathetically. "I know that pain, Phipps, and I'm sorry," he said, placing a hand on Erwin's shoulder. "I'd recommend waiting until his findings are published, then incorporating them into your own research. And at *that* point, you'll be in a position to complete your own thesis."

But it wouldn't be a success. His fantasy of laurels dissolved into thin air. It became painfully clear, then, just how much he had depended on the wild hope that this success would be the thing to launch his career as a research chemist, as well as his life with Eleanor. Now he was just another chem student on a well-worn path to a degree.

April 3, 1921
Berkeley, Cal.

Dear Miss Morgan,

I had the unfortunate realization a day or two ago that my thesis work was in too incomplete a state to allow me to finish this month as I had planned, and now it looks as if my arduous labor will continue until July. I was in quite a surly mood over this delay yesterday and tried to dispel the gloom by going poppying in the hills. Before I reached the poppy fields, though, a hailstorm and shower commingled, overtook me, and so it's just a wee little bud that thought it was safe down near the road that I'm sending you. Now that you've seen the gloomy background, maybe you'll be charitable toward my April letter.

I ran across an idea in Middlemarch *not long ago that was so unusual that I made note of it. It seemed really to analyze most successfully the consciousness of the poet of nature. Would you like to hear it?*

For Eliot, the element of tragedy for most people lies in the unusual . . .

"That element which lies in the very fact of its frequency, has not yet wrought itself into the coarse emotion of mankind; and perhaps our frames could hardly bear much of it.

"If we had a keen vision and feeling of all ordinary human life, it would be like hearing the grass grow and the squirrel's heart beat, and we should die of that roar which lies on the other side of silence."

You were kind enough to express interest in my problem, and this is the Mother Goose version as near as I can translate it: I am determining the conductivities of certain "blue" solutions (a most wonderful indigo color they are) which are made by dissolving sodium or potassium (metals) in liquid ammonia. You doubtless know that copper is an excellent conductor of electricity—no! I'm not talking about policemen nor yet about the brass buttoned guy that collects your six cents on the streetcar—I mean copper like the big kettles used to be made out of. Well, these blue solutions, unlike any other solutions at all, conduct the current of electricity, almost as well as copper or aluminum, and it has been my task to devise an apparatus for making these blue solutions in the absence of air and measuring their conductivities at various concentrations. The joker in the problem is that these solutions aren't stable but are constantly "fading" on account of a secondary reaction between the metal and the solvent. A single experiment requires nearly all of one day uninterrupted. It is a most annoying and discouraging problem.

I consider your arraignment of our educational system masterly, and I cheered lustily (from the sidelines) while you were playing havoc with "sentimentality" in education. Atta boy! Hit 'im again, and the rest of it.

I am very much interested in your progress in Plato. Write soon, please.

Yours sincerely,

TE Phipps

April 18, 1921
Columbus, Miss.

Dear Mr. Phipps,

I'm going a-poppying myself someday; I don't know just how I'm to get there, but somehow I'm going. Yet I do know I'll not wear any new hat, French heels, or new vanity case. I know better. I'll wear an old middy suit and the oldest walking shoes in the world and no hat at all. (I can never be quite a lady—hats and gloves are an abomination to my soul.) But go poppying I shall. I begin to suspect that the forty-niners have been maligned all *these years and that they weren't mercenary after all; I believe somebody sent them a red-gold poppy.*

Meantime, I must be content tramping Sunday afternoons now and then with a girl who is here temporarily from Barnard for a rest. She carries a sure-enough cannon strapped over her shoulder, and so we feel safe to go for miles across the hills, through the pine woods. The other girl carries the pistol, you observe. To tell the truth, I believe I shouldn't have thought of it. We've found wild azalea and dogwood and sweet william and woodbine. And last time, we discovered the dogtooth violet. Somebody committed a crime in naming that flower; it's the prettiest thing that grows, not even excepting your glorious poppy. It's so human, I want to pick it up and pet it and "love" it. It just looks at you so. I think it is the real, true blue flower, I do.

And I'm perfectly selfishly good-humored tonight because it poured down rain and I didn't have to go to a stupid reception this afternoon but could stay at home and do as I pleased. Rain is usually only a spoil sport.

You asked about my Platonic progress. Plato and I don't get on with each other very well. Sometimes he is silly, sometimes monstrous, and sometimes wise, sometimes sublime. That is, sometimes he says what I want him to, and sometimes he says the opposite. He never is very sensible. But nothing great is commonsensible, is it? Or Milton wouldn't have put his eyes out, and Bacon wouldn't have caught that bad cold, and Juliet would be living ignobly ever afterward, and Wilson wouldn't be a casualty.

Your problem sounds most dreadfully difficult and mysterious. I think of the alchemists of old. I wish I could see that I'm doing something, could measure my work;

I never know when I'm right and when I'm wrong. If I understand, you're having to do a great deal of patient labor. It isn't all exciting discovery, is it? Please, may I tell you that I'm wishing for splendid success for you?

Sincerely,

Eleanor Morgan

May 23, 1921
Berkeley, Cal.

Dear Miss Morgan,
   Our hills have already lost their freshest green and are beginning to show sunburnt patches of brown. I hope spring hasn't been so evanescent in your pine woods. I'm sure your sweet william is outlasting my poppies.
   I've formed the habit lately, for the sake of exercise and the view, of climbing up daily to the big "C," which is a gigantic concrete letter on the hill that overshadows the campus to the east. From there, one can see the east bay towns, Alameda, Oakland, Berkeley, and Richmond, laid out street by street below, hugging the bay front for a distance of twenty miles or more. On very clear days, it's possible to see the Faralone Islands through the gate, forty miles out to sea.
   There's a grove of eucalyptus trees on the hill above the C, and this morning when I went up, the birds were having some kind of riot there, or else it was a happy, unrehearsed melody. I wished very much for a hatless friend of mine in a middy suit to tell me what they were

saying. It's on, still further up, that the poppies grow, but they're almost gone now.

Next year is still puzzling me. I could teach here in Santa Maria High School at a princely salary (about double, I think, what industrial work would pay initially), or I could go to Illinois University as an instructor at a starvation wage. There may be some other chance. I hope so.

While I'm marking time "on the road that rolls on through the heart of May," I'm hoping that your road is very pleasant too.

Sincerely,

TE Phipps

June 8, 1921
Goldsboro, N.C.

Dear Mr. Phipps,

Your letter made a pleasant interlude during examinations. But exams weren't so bad as they might have been—my girls sandwiched all sorts of little farewell notes through their papers; that relieved the strain. They're wise, do you say? Maybe so, because I know I thought C-, C-, C- straight through one paper, until I got to the end and found a message for myself, and then, well, right or wrong, I couldn't help thinking C. I'd better take a course in anatomy this summer and try to discover just what the right place is for my heart and for my conscience.

It is almost time for me to congratulate the Herr Doktor. You don't mind my saying "Herr Doktor," do you? Since you quote German yourself, though it surprises me when you do, for I remember what your sister used to say about your opinion of things Teutonic. You see, I know your opinions on more subjects than you might suspect—Helen and I, when we roomed together, formed a Brotherly Adoration Society; she talked about you almost as much as I did about my brother, Lawrence. The war made us unduly concerned, I hasten to explain.

I prophecy that you'll take the Illinois place because I fancy you're looking toward the future. "Starvation" isn't bad in good company, I happen to know. Still, a "princely salary" for a few years would help any of us in getting established. You really have reached the place where whatever one does counts definitely; I wish I had gone so far. I'm tired of feeling temporary. But year after next, I'm going to study, and I hope the year after that too.

I hope your summer will be pleasant. I'd like to hear about it, and mail is always forwarded to me if it is addressed just Goldsboro, North Carolina.

Sincerely,

Eleanor Morgan

CHAPTER XVII

New York City

IT WAS DARK by the time the performance let out. Eleanor made her way through the boil of voices and people, into the muggy July night, as she and Elise and Sallie, another instructor of English at MSCW who'd joined them at Barnard College for the summer, tried to reconcile what they'd just seen. They were sharing Elise's three-room flat on 121st Street, and this was the fourth Broadway show they'd seen together that summer.

"I'm still not sure whether Liliom went to heaven or hell at the end," said Sallie. "Which was it? Were we supposed to know?" She had cropped blond curls and soulful, close-set eyes.

"He went to heaven, Sallie, of course," said Elise. "Didn't you see how the scales tipped upward at the end?"

The play, though well done and thoroughly fascinating, had been a character study of a rather objectively bad man, Liliom, selfish and cowardly, who had done nothing to redeem his own destructive actions, despite plentiful opportunity to do so.

"He oughtn't to have been admitted to heaven," said Eleanor. "If he was, it was on the back of a pack mule."

"But his wife wasn't *hurt* when he beat her. She wasn't hurt, because she loved him. So, her love saved him from condemnation,"

Elise explained, as if that notion were perfectly sound. As if it had been some sort of love story.

'*Liliom, Franz Molnar's Comedy of Life*,' the marquee read. Eleanor shuddered. "We should have gone to see *Lightnin'* again instead," she said.

"Oh, let's go dancing," said Sallie, "like we did after *Lightnin'*. That night was so much fun."

"Yes, yes, let's," Elise chimed in.

"No thanks," Eleanor said decisively.

"Not in the mood for fun?" Elise kidded.

"*Liliom* didn't exactly set the stage for it, no. To your pleasures. I am for other than dancing measures."

Elise smiled at the line. "Are you okay getting home by yourself?"

"Always."

As she walked, the fire escapes were populated with residents trying to escape the heat, voices surrounding her, talking, arguing, singing, cursing. No one batted an eye at her, as though she were invisible. She would have found this freeing, had the feeling not also been accompanied by the sense that the thin veil again was enveloping her here in New York, a veil that likely covered everyone, to manage this strange way of living—people stacked on top of each other, life all around without anyone really seeing each other. And along with the progression of hot, crowded, unrelenting days, she had begun to feel claustrophobic in her concrete, treeless neighborhood.

She arrived at their building, collected their mail, and made her way up the stairs to the fifth-floor railroad apartment. A letter from Helen, forwarded from Goldsboro, was among them.

⇠—○—⇢

July 14, 1921
Austin, Tex.

Dear Eleanor,

I've decided to celebrate my birthday this year by writing to some of the friends whom I've been neglecting. I have just reread your very interesting letter, which I have kept since last summer. I feel both conscience-stricken and grieved that it has not been answered before—mostly the latter, for I might have had another a long time ago. Please forgive me and reinstate me by writing me all about your life and current doings. Are you still working among the "columbines"? But I am supposing that you are home for the summer and so am sending the letter there.

There isn't anything very thrilling to write about my life just now—only about the thrills yet to come: in September I am to swap the scenery of Austin for Columbia University in New York. And then each member of my family will be in a different place; Erwin has finished his degree work, and despite Kent's efforts to get him to join him in Mexico, and Peggy's efforts to get him back at Austin, he has taken a position at Illinois University in Urbana. I am worried that it will be lonely for Papa and Peggy, but it really is a wonderful opportunity for him. It is a university of some distinction, and, well, Erwin is happy anywhere.

Now, the next thing to worry over is how to pack my life down into one trunk. My aunt used to say that you always must have at least two worries to lead a well-balanced life, and so I have the two.

Once I get to New York, I will have to "take the veil" and resist the abundance of entertainments, at least until my degree work is over. I will be living on borrowed money and don't think much of it should go that way. But won't *you visit and make me forget that oath? I would love to see you again and would take gleeful exception if you cared to make the trip.*

I hope you are having a lovely summer. Please write and tell me all about it. I do hope that our paths can cross again before <u>too</u> long.

With much love,

Helen

Eleanor looked out her open window onto the city below, feeling as gray as the concrete itself. It had been two months since Erwin's last letter. Helen would be here in September, after Eleanor had already returned to Columbus. Erwin would go to Illinois. Changes had been made in their lives that she had not known about. She wanted to cry, but she laughed instead, to protect herself from the old, familiar hurt, at persistently being at the center of no one's life but her own. And the distance between herself and those whose company she longed for grew by the day, quite against her wishes for it to do otherwise.

For the first time, she understood one of the Japanese tales that Mama used to tell, about a well-to-do young woman named Kiyohime. She'd fallen in love with a monk, who did not reciprocate her strong feelings. The monk left on a journey, falsely promising to return. When he didn't, Kiyohime became so enraged that she left in pursuit of him. And when she found him, he fled, prompting her to transform into a dragon because of her anger at his rejection.

As a young person, never having loved intensely, she couldn't understand Kiyohime's intense reaction. How she could allow that to happen. But after reading Helen's letter, Eleanor was horrified to feel that same twinge of angry despondence at being left behind. That impulse that could lead a woman on such a self-destructive pursuit.

Like Kiyohime, she couldn't force anyone else's hand. But she could protect her own heart. Of course Erwin wouldn't have mentioned to Helen that she was in New York for the summer. He clearly hadn't brought their correspondence up at all, having had a year's time to do so. Would Erwin eventually also share his news with her? Or was she yet again stuck, waiting for a letter that may never arrive? No. No more foolishness. It's not real. Erwin was happy anywhere, as Helen said, with or without her. And she had to accept that.

CHAPTER XVIII

September 20, 1921
Urbana, Ill.

Dear Miss Morgan,
 After the prophecy you made last June, you'll not be surprised to hear from me in Illinois. You may have wondered, though, why some people don't answer other people's letters—at least I hope you didn't forget to wonder, because I think you'd acquit me if you knew how closely I was pressed with work during my concluding weeks at the University of California.
 But before I talk about myself, please tell me about Barnard College. I suppose you "tripped the light fantastic on the sidewalks of New York" in the fashion approved by the famous song. Were you filled with awe? Fired with ambition? Or did you simply smile and enjoy being alive amid it all? I'm very eager to hear of your adventures in the land of the giants, Miss Alice Gulliver. My sister is in New York by now, I hope. Do you know of her plans? After your experiences with New York and Helen, do you candidly think she may manage for nine months to avoid

being run over? I suppose you haven't forgotten her mad method of perambulation with nose in the air and a faraway look in her eye.

I would spare you the following account of my recent struggles and privations, except that you promised to be interested in my summer's doings. I concluded my work in California the beginning of this month, which was the date of my final public examination. One of the members of my subcommittee was Prof. Exum Percival Lewis (a fellow countryman of yours), head of the Physics Department, under whom I had my minor. After signing my thesis, he looked over his specs at me and muttered ominously, "I'll see you again at your public ex." I experienced Brutus's feeling (without his bravado) when he replied to the ghost of his own evil spirit, "Ay, at Philippi." The less said about that ex., the better. There were two hours of it, and the subcommittee experienced great embarrassment in finding subjects on which the candidate could appear semi-intelligent.

I concluded my affairs and left for the Grand Canyon two days later. I declined the mule-back trip down into the canyon and went down on foot with another simpleton. I have a vivid impression of the last 600 feet before one reaches the rim (going up), and I would recommend the mules to all except the extremely young and foolish. I was relieved to find that the coloring of the cliffs and peaks is much less gaudy than most lantern slides indicate. Instead, a purple-pink mist seems to tone down the red sandstone glare, and dark shadows falling here and there in the most fantastic way make the distant view more somber, especially in the late afternoon. And it is in the early morning, I think, when the sense of vastness is most compelling; one can see back into the remote places without being dazzled by the light reflected from nearby cliffs.

One tubby old German started down afoot a little after we did, and toward dark, he wobbled back to the rim vowing that for nothing less than a cask of Pilsner would he undertake to climb out of that Aller Verdammten gulch again.

I spent two days there and then came to Urbana by way of Kansas City and St. Louis. I'm pleased with Urbana and the University. Things are on a tremendous scale. Even California is dwarfed by comparison, and the campus is beautiful. After the glare of Texas and California and the Canyon, I love to rest my eyes by looking at green trees, grass, and robins. Really, my eyes' relief is the most pleasant of all my discoveries in my new haven. And the people are more friendly, and the prices are cheaper, but alas, freshmen are more abundant. As the poet says, "Into each life some rain must fall," so I'm reminded of an eight o'clock tomorrow morning.

Sincerely,

TE Phipps

P.S. Please cancel all prefixes.

October 1, 1921
Columbus, Miss.

Dear Mr. Phipps,

Prefixes <u>are</u> better canceled, aren't they? At least I like my own better so. They give the effect one gets looking through the wrong end of field glasses, stretching the geography beyond recognition. And when a body has known a body almost three whole years, "Miss" becomes rather unnecessary, don't you think so? And "Dr." too formidable for use.

Two friends of mine joined me in New York. We rented rooms in an apartment, kept house, and had a thoroughly good time the whole six weeks. We took an extreme course in New York and barely enough work at Barnard to ease our consciences. We enjoyed the theater more than anything else. Frank Bacon, George Arliss, and Ethel Barrymore were the stars; just seeing them would have made a summer.

Helen did write me of her plans, and I wish I could be with her this winter. But really the main thing I learned during the summer is that I don't want to live in New York for good, ever. I like my own great big front porch too well, my big old magnolia trees, and my neighbors that know everything I have for breakfast, dinner, and supper every day in the week; I do truly.

When there aren't too many eight o'clocks—aren't they the bane of existence, though?—I'd like to hear about the University and your experiences in Illinois. Your sister wrote me a little bit about your success and what a recognition your going to Illinois means; may I not say I'm very glad for you?

Sincerely,

Eleanor

P.S. I didn't "forget to wonder" why you didn't write, but I didn't wonder. I thought I knew that you were very, very hard at work.

October 5, 1921
Goldsboro, N.C.

Eleanor dear,

Mrs. Allen asked that I mail off to you the enclosed invitation to Julia's wedding that is to take place next month here in Goldsboro. She hopes that as Julia's oldest friend, you could make exception to your semester to join her on this happy occasion.

I'm sick about it, for two reasons: She does not know of your expulsion last summer (I cannot bring myself to tell her of it), and my heart just aches that you have not been able to return to your home for an entire year. I do not know what to say, to Papa or to you, but there you have it.

If you wish to return for Julia's wedding and can find accommodation elsewhere, I will not utter a word about it to Papa. I am sorry, dear girl, but I have a notion that the association of your visit with a wedding may be more than he will stomach. He is, at heart, still a kind man, but it's all locked up tight.

And then, please know that we will both be glad to see you for Christmas this year, and I will try to make you as comfortable as possible, under the circumstances.

Please write when you are able.

With all my love,

Mama

October 9, 1921
Urbana, Ill.

Dear Eleanor,

I'm very happy to be included among your old friends, and I'll try not to do or say anything so rash as to cause my expulsion from the circle.

At Illinois, most of the buildings are red brick and built around a large rectangle. Champaign bounds us on the west, and Urbana on the east. Streetcars going to the center of either town pass right by the chem building steps. Champaign is much more of a town than Urbana, boasting several movies and a Junior Orpheum Circuit.

Trees are everywhere, hard maples, sugar maples, hackberries, and "ellums," with a hundred blackbirds, ten robins, and two squirrels to every tree. Squirrels are protected, robins are tolerated, and blackbirds are outlawed.

I am staying with Mrs. Parmelee and have a walk of only three blocks to school every morning. Dr. Parmelee is a professor of ceramics, a department closely allied with chemistry. They are New Jersey people. Mrs. Parmelee is a typical shrewd Easterner who talks fluently and enjoys hearing it. Dr. Parmelee talks less and defers to the madam, who has all interesting information in a more exact and readily available form. They are very kind and thoughtful people and invite me often to join them in the sitting room.

And a description of the Parmelees isn't complete without some reference to Tom, the huge Maltese cat who knocks me over every morning when I open the front door, in his mad attempt to escape the cold and attain his place by the fireside.

My work at the University comes in the morning, and

I have about sixteen hours a week of instruction. I had hoped for work in the Physical Chemistry Department with sophomores or juniors, but I was more or less a crack-filler and had to take the leavins.

I have a neat little pigeonhole up on the third floor with a nice desk, but without a swivel chair, alas! And a swivel chair, for one who must interview freshmen, is an absolute necessity. How can one, sitting straight-backed, without the possibility of squeaking impressive strings, properly awe the tutee? But if I was overlooked in the distribution of swivel chairs, at least I am equipped with one necessity in the form of an immense roller towel at the end next to the door, where I may, with one fell swoop, remove 50 percent or more of the grime of research before making my appearance in a quiz section.

So you've gone over to the Republicans and become a "front porch" enthusiast. I wouldn't have thought it. But the magnolia trees at least don't suggest Harding. My father has always had a wish for a magnolia tree (and a mockingbird) in the yard by the porch and has spent lots of time and worry and Colorado River water trying to defeat nature and nurse a little magnolia tree into health. I'm afraid the tree dreams about Louisiana swamps and pines away despite all my father can do.

Will you choose from among my names the one which sounds least "formidable" to you? And so that you may not be prejudiced, I'll sign myself this time as . . .

Your friend,

Thomas Erwin Phipps

October 16, 1921
Columbus, Miss.

Dear Erwin,

You see, I've always heard you called Erwin. It is nice so, isn't it? For me, it's very pleasant to be assured of a friendship that is so welcome. Just now, it is particularly pleasant, because I'm feeling rather deserted.

My very oldest friend is about to marry and abandon me completely. Julia lived on the next block from mine in the days when she was going to Scotland to live on a mountaintop and write books. And I, practical soul, was torn between a longing to invent a boat with detachable steel runners like a sled—a sort of hydro-sleigh affair, in which I could sail and slide my way to discover the North Pole—and a desire to follow Julia and serve as her admiring audience on the mountaintop. Later, we were going to college together, but we didn't; then, during the war, we were going into the Navy together, and then we were going to teach together, but always something interfered. I went to Oklahoma. Julia followed me. Her family followed her and are living in Muskogee now. Just before they came, I left Oklahoma. And now we never can do anything or plan anything together again. Julia is a foul deserter. And I'm peeved because I can't go to her wedding. Peary beat me to the North Pole, and now Julia won't reserve any mountaintop in Scotland either; at least, there won't be any room for me on it. I'm feeling dreadfully injured.

Columbus, however, is all aflutter, preparing to celebrate its centennial. The town is resplendent in fresh paint and bunting and newly hung lights. Placards are appearing on every hand: The First School in Mississippi

Was Erected on this Site in 1821; Jefferson Davis Spent the Night in This House Once. Tomorrow, Confederate flags will be flying everywhere, and the next day, the band will give us "Tenting Tonight" on the Old Campground. I don't exaggerate. I declare I don't.

To an outsider, the commotion is amusing. But I know better than to express myself to any true Columbiad. Helen calls them columbines, but she doesn't know them; they're Columbiads.

Mr. Carpenter just now says I look like I'm having too good a time, all to myself, scribbling. I am. I have you where you can't escape, and I can chatter all I please. That's the penalty of long-distance friendship; if you were here, you could plead work to do or something very important and run away. And I should see through it and get my feelings hurt, properly. But I'll have a little mercy on both you and Mr. Carpenter this time.

Your friend, sincerely,

Eleanor

CHAPTER XIX

Urbana, Illinois

"**D**IAMOND IS THE hardest substance known to man," Erwin said, standing at his Chem I lecture class. "And graphite is soft, slippery." He held up his pencil, pointing to its tip. "Seemingly opposite things. And yet, both are composed of the same element: carbon."

He enjoyed introducing elements as puzzles—to induce wonder, if only for a moment. He believed that science required imagination, dreaming about the way things really *were*, a crucial aspect that seemed to have been lost in the mad dash toward industrialization. If he could do his part to reinstate it, he could consider his teaching efforts successful.

"The only difference between these two vastly different forms of carbon lies in their atomic bond structures. In Greek, the word *ions,* roughly translated, means 'wanderers,' and there are no ions in diamond." He drew the firm structure of tetrahedral lattice on the chalkboard. "So it does not conduct electricity. Graphite, however," he said, drawing the layered, chicken-wire structure of it, "contains these *free* electrons that can move through the substance, carrying an electric charge from place to place. Bonds are created when two atoms share electrons."

The wind rattled against the windowpanes, drawing the eyes of his students to the swirl of brown leaves outside, and his thoughts flashed to Eleanor, on her letter, which, as had become his custom, was stashed in his breast pocket. And in the stack of letters in his room that he'd received from her, grimy and thumb-worn over the days and months of being read and reread. In her words, he always felt less alone, more positively charged. Some force had always drawn him to Eleanor, over and over, like electrons through the carbon, his heart eager for a sense of a bond between them.

Erwin ended the class, assigning his students to consult the text to discern whether carbon was an element present in their own bodies. And if they could discern that and still had curiosity to spare, find out what role carbon played in fire.

It was his twenty-sixth birthday, a fact that he was content to keep concealed from all fellow Illinois residents. He preferred to be left to his thoughts and collect his well-wishes from afar, from those loved ones scattered across the country who already resided in his heart. The last thing he wanted was for someone here to impose a convivial aspect upon the day; that would only result in his attempt to knock the top rail off the corral and stampede—his accustomed response to social observances, particularly those in his honor.

And although Eleanor didn't realize it, she had given him a gift of sorts in her letter—in choosing to call him Erwin, as his family did. It was to him a key that unlocked something deep inside, something that had been shut tight for years. *If you were here, you could plead work to do or something very important and run away*, she'd written. Oh, if she only knew. He'd put that top rail back on so that he could be corralled next to her forever.

When he arrived that evening back at the Parmelee house, soaked by a cold, thundering rain, he found a small package from Peggy waiting for him on the entry table and a full scuttle of coal next to the little fireplace of his room. His heart warmed instantly. He'd have a gift to open and a fire to heat the room. The idea of this little fireplace had delighted him when he'd arrived in September, and he had yet to make use of it.

With the sting of phosphorous from the match still in his nose, he laid his wet clothes across a chair next to the fireplace, donned his robe, and sat on the footstool, watching as the black of the coal in the grate began to glow orange—the forces of attraction at play between the atoms of carbon and oxygen.

He untied the string around the little package, tearing through its brown paper wrapping, and found a box of chocolates and a jar of pecans from the tree at his family home in Austin. It read, *Happy birthday! Wish you were here. Peggy and Papa.*

It was no mistake that Erwin hadn't stopped in Austin on his way to Illinois. At the time, he rationalized that he needed the time to settle in Urbana before the start of the fall semester. That he would pay his family dues by going home for Christmas in just three months' time. But seeing Peggy's note brought forth the truth of the matter; now that Peggy was on her own with Papa, she would do her level best to campaign for the rest of the family to consider rejoining them there. *Wish you were here.*

He blew gently at the spreading flame, feeling the heat penetrate his skin, popped a pecan into his mouth, and rested his thoughts on Eleanor again. On the plaintive tone of her last letter, now drying on the chair next to him. She'd described a feeling he knew well—the sudden disappearance of hopes, an internal collapse of an identity you slowly built up for yourself and kept waiting in the wings for, but it was not to be. He wanted to fly to her then, whisk her away. The way she saw the world—he had always felt as if he were dreaming and thinking *with* her, wanting what she wanted.

He listened to the drum of the rain on his windowpane and, with his next breath, made a birthday wish: for Eleanor to love him, to be with him, to bring their shared vision, their harmony, back together, finally. It was time to test the connection again, to crack open that door she'd unlocked inside him. He would offer to think up her next adventure. And her reaction, he hoped, would telegraph to him what he needed to know first, to know how to proceed.

⇐—o—⇒

October 31, 1921
Urbana, Ill.

Dear Eleanor,
 Did you survive the centennial? Count yourself lucky that you don't live and move and have your being in Abraham Lincoln's state, or you really would have cause to hang your harp upon the willow and refuse in the strange land to sing "Tenting Tonight." Why, before I can take a book from the library, I have to run the gauntlet of some half dozen busts of Lincoln and finally pass under an ox yoke that purports to be the work of the All-Highest's own hands. Think not, my friend, that the South is alone in its proneness to "lopsided" retrospection.
 Please tell me something good to read. I've been reading here and yonder, hit and miss, catch as catch can, for the last few weeks. In the hour or two a day that I allow myself, I've been reading Thomas Burrough's Under the Apple Trees, a sort of blending of natural history and philosophy, with enough Darwinism to flavor it. I love to read his observations of nature, but I always take a running jump into the middle of the next page when he begins to quote Walt Whitman. For my part, I prefer Baled Hay to Leaves of Grass any old day and would rather look for a needle in a haystack than for the pearl or dew drop

or whatever it is that Walt has hidden somewhere on the lawn.

With both Poles discovered and Mt. Everest almost "clumb," it looks as though all the daring, glorious things have been stolen from you. If you like, though, I'll try to think up some for you soon.

With best wishes, your friend,

Erwin Phipps

November 11, 1921

ON THE USUAL spot at the corner of Green Street and Lincoln Ave, Erwin met his friend and colleague Henry Lochte, and they walked together toward the heart of campustown. In the Chem Department, every Friday was given over to what they loosely called a "staff luncheon," organized for the sharing of ideas, at the Green Teapot Café.

"You shooting on your problem today?" asked Lochte.

Erwin had recently found himself drawn to a new research problem: measuring the conductivity of liquid hydrofluoric acid, which was a notoriously bad actor. The central problem, as best he could wager, was finding a material with which to construct the apparatus—one that wouldn't be attacked by the acid. It was perhaps an impossible problem—but a tantalizing one. He hoped Dr. Kunz, esteemed in the department and just returned from the University of Chicago, might provide some insight.

"I hope to."

"Good thing. It's a wild idea, Phipps. Wild and *dangerous*."

On this particular Friday, their walk featured a number of banners and decorations, commemorating the University's homecoming weekend.

"Is it still homecoming for us if we're from elsewhere?" Lochte said.

"Is that a rhetorical question?"

"I don't know, is it?"

Lochte was a fellow Texan and chemist, a boisterous and imposing young man, one to be taken seriously in scientific matters only, Erwin had long since decided. So, he made a good sparring partner.

"Speaking of homecomings and dangerous things, Phipps, you ought to get yourself married," said Lochte, with a sly sideways grin. "Get yourself a nice woman to come home to."

Erwin's stomach lurched anxiously, as he was still awaiting the results of his "test" with Eleanor. He would never confide in Lochte that the idea of homecoming had put him in mind of the same thing, that coming home to Eleanor was his heart's desire, one he longed, against the odds, to make a reality. But if he so much as hinted at her existence, he'd never hear the end of it, and he didn't want to give Lochte the satisfaction.

"That's a fine bit of advice from a man who's been engaged, what, two years?"

"Three!" said Lochte, followed by an odd sort of chuckle.

"That long-suffering girl," Erwin said. "Are you going home to her for Christmas?"

"Not if I want to finish my research this year." Lochte was a doctoral student, hoping to devise a new way to measure the surface tension of various substances. "You?"

"Yes. I'm overdue, as far as my family is concerned," he said, though some part of him wished there were some way he could spend Christmas with Eleanor instead. But he must be patient, he knew, if that could ever come to pass.

As they neared the Green Teapot, a large banner was on display against the murky sky, featuring a soldier with a bandaged head and outstretched arms, flanked by both a field of cross-shaped headstones and a field of poppies, with the words *Build that Stadium*—the slogan for a campaign to create a new football field in honor of the fallen soldiers.

A shiver went up Erwin's back at the sight of the graves commingled with the poppies, recalling what this day three years ago was to him, how one decision between the right humans changed not only his fate but the course of history.

"Germany Accepts Terms." Major Emmerling had read the headline of the newspaper to his battery after reveille that morning at Camp Jackson, Erwin having just returned from the base hospital after his near-fatal brush with Spanish flu. Then a roaring jubilation, all simple struggles brought to an end. He never had to go overseas. He could continue his life, his studies.

But he was haunted by the thought of the hundred thousand who didn't come home, whose boots had beat out the same rhythms as his. Continuing to thrive in a country that once banked on his own death. A verse of Rupert Brooke's flew into his thoughts:

These laid the world away; poured out the red
Sweet wine of youth; gave up the years to be
Of work and joy, and that unhoped serene,
That men call age; and those who would have been,
Their sons, they gave, their immortality.

Erwin and Lochte went quiet as they walked the last block, for they had both served and chose not to verbalize the particular grief of this weighty day.

The cigarette smoke was thick upon their entrance to the café, and Erwin and Lochte found much of the chem faculty crowded around Dr. Kunz in their customary dining room, listening with expressions of childlike suspense. They hastened forward to catch his words.

"So you see, if this is true, we don't care if coal and gas *do* play out," Kunz said animatedly as they approached. "If this is true, *everything we touch* has unbelievable amounts of energy in it, which we may be able to liberate."

"What have we missed? If *what* is true?" Lochte whispered to Dr. Rodebush, a professor in Physical Chemistry.

"Dr. Anderson at the University of Chicago discharged an electric current through a tungsten wire in a vacuum, producing temperatures of *twenty thousand degrees*," Rodebush said. "He got a big explosion in one or two experiments, but in another, he found the tungsten had actually been decomposed into lighter elements."

Erwin and Lochte both gasped, echoing each other's surprise both at the temperature—hotter than the stars themselves—and at the notion of tungsten of all things being made to decompose into lighter elements. Until now, radium and uranium had been the only elements capable of decomposing this way, and that only ever happened spontaneously. Erwin's imagination became seized by this magical, novel idea.

The waitstaff brought sandwiches and a big bowl of greens with oil and vinegar, and Erwin could only think, *Everything we touch has unbelievable amounts of energy, which may, by spark, be liberated.* Whether he ate or not, he didn't remember. He was a boy of eight again, full of wonder at the world and fascinated by the unexpected, atomic-level truths behind nature's puzzles. And the universe, a storm of beauty, where danger and discovery walked hand in hand.

He made his way back to the Parmelee house in this daze, past a red and black storm flag being raised, and the first snowflakes began to fall—tiny intermittent points of white, like embers. Erwin closed his eyes and inhaled the cold air deeply, longing for a blizzard like he used to as a young boy, recalling the last snowfall he could remember: before his family left Tennessee, and Mamma was alive, inside making stew on the blue flame oil stove. An acute sorrow set in as he wished to again be in the company of those he cared for—and someone else too, sick for a home he'd never seen.

Then images of places he'd been—fields and water and houses—whirled through his head without any sequence or willing, with new and curious and impossible associations of things, as if a heavy mantle had been thrown off, a restless wish for something to change, even if it brought danger. Increase pressure to increase temperature; perhaps he too could liberate this energy inside himself, inside Eleanor, bring equilibrium, combine their fires within.

Upon the Parmelee's entry table, he found a letter from Eleanor—the answer to his test—and, heart gleefully pounding as loud as his footsteps, hastened to his attic room to devour it.

November 8, 1921
Columbus, Miss.

Dear Erwin,

Fritz Lieber has just played here in Hamlet. Unfortunately, he came during our Centennial celebration. The Opera House is on Main Street. A street dance was also on Main Street. And the ban against firecrackers had been lifted.

"To be—" Bang, bang, bang!

"Or not to be—" Applause outside for an encore, followed by the latest jazz racket.

The girl next to me ate popcorn. The freshmen hoped it would be a romance. And thanks to the aesthetic discrimination of the pianist—there was no orchestra—the curtain went down on Ophelia's death to the tune of "Ain't We Got Fun." The distractions made me rather incredulous of the play, for if Hamlet had felt one tiniest fraction as murderous as I, he wouldn't have wasted any time hesitating. Despite all, I enjoyed the performance; can you believe it?

You asked for something good to read, but I haven't found anything in some time. I share your antipathy to Whitman, and I can't read this modern so-called realism with patience. Main Street and the like don't convince me of their superior wisdom, and certainly there is little sweetness and light in them. As a relief from their sordidness, I found W.H. Hudson's beautiful fantasy

Green Mansions *a joy and delight.*

Tantalize me some more with what you're doing and seeing, I like being tantalized so. And don't forget that you're to plan some adventures for me, if I like. I do like. Did you ever have someone tell you to "shut your eyes and open your mouth" and pop a strawberry or some other goody in? My eyes are shut and my mouth open; you must think up a delicious morsel of adventure for me, for sight unseen I solemnly pledge myself to the undertaking.

Sincerely,

Eleanor

Eleanor, with eyes shut, in suspended animation, awaiting the unforeseen. He remembered it with tenderness, from that fateful night, during their game of levitation. Fire ran through him. Every inch of her lying there in the flickering light, lifted clear and still and strange. He'd longed to build his air castles so, when she opened her eyes, he might have a life he could invite her into, to fulfill her hopes and dreams. Instead, his strength had buckled, and he dropped her, crashing to the earth, the perfect moment of infinite possibility crushed underneath them.

His thoughts alighted with the memory of their parting, holding her hand in front of the fire, trying to find the words to tell her he would seek to sustain this connection forever, not finding them; he had just met her, after all, and held his tongue so as not to appear ridiculous.

Everything he wanted to say would have sounded insincere at best, the ravings of a soldier just released from war duty. Suddenly the mad vision he'd wished for that night flashed real. And he wouldn't drop her this time. Before the spark died, he rushed to his desk, toward heat, toward light. He took out paper and pen and found the words for what he'd needed to say ever since.

CHAPTER XX

November 14, 1921

Columbus, Mississippi

ELEANOR'S HEART JUMPED with a shock of excitement when she noticed Erwin's handwriting peeking out from the letters in her PO box, mere days after she'd sent her letter. She had grown accustomed to the weeks, sometimes months, of waiting. But she'd let herself get daringly flirtatious in the last letter, above and beyond anything she might have attempted last year. This time around, they had at least achieved the familiar attitude and dropped the prefixes, so she felt a truer sense of confidence. Regardless of the nature of their relationship, he'd given her the opportunity to make herself known, and despite herself, she took it. So, what could this singular haste in his response mean? Her stomach fluttered at the prospect that it might really contain a morsel of adventure for her.

Once in her life, Eleanor had cried tears of joy. Seven years previously, as a college senior, she was preparing to graduate at the top of her class. The dean of the English Department showed her a letter he'd received from the head of the History Department at the University of Wisconsin, asking him to recommend an instructor. He offered Eleanor the position, extolling her qualifications for it—her prizes, her papers, her amiability, and her scholarship, told her what a splendid opportunity it was, and gave her two weeks to consider it.

Eleanor knew her decision but thought it wise to take the time to deliberate, thanking the dean for the offer. As she left his office, she was giddy. Here was exactly what she'd been hoping and striving for—success and opportunity and adventure all in one breath, offered to her, by her own merits. Warm, thankful tears rolled down her cheeks; she'd never been so happy. Her future had never looked so bright. But it all came abruptly crashing back to Earth when she found a telegram waiting for her: "*Your mother stricken with a grave illness. Doctors working to save her. Will notify when out of danger. Papa.*"

Panic set in, overriding her joy. She finished her last exam in a daze and hurriedly traveled home. Mama was by that time out of immediate danger, but weak and in need of care. As Eleanor tended to her, Papa took her aside to tell her that after graduation, her help was required at home. She told him about the offer provided to her at Wisconsin, in the hope that it would draw pride, but Papa's expression went cold.

"Home is where you're needed now, Eleanor," he said. "Mama probably didn't say anything, but she has been unwell for some time."

Eleanor felt a weight on her chest. Tears of frustration rose to her eyes.

"Brace up and be a support," Papa said. "Not a dead weight like your brother, not now."

Eleanor felt a sting; she'd long sensed that Papa had written Lawrence off as a hapless philanderer, and the duties of parental care would fall to her, but she hadn't imagined it would eclipse her own hopes so soon, so entirely.

She returned to campus for her commencement exercises, which she had hoped to do with honor and glee for the future and support of her loved ones, and accepted her diploma. With a heavy heart, she told the dean that it would be impossible for her to accept his very kind offer. She headed for home—toward family, away from glory—full of the grief of her lost call and deeply unhappy. And the delirious joy she'd known for those short minutes between the offer and Papa's telegram—the happiness of having her life's wish fulfilled—had remained unparalleled. By this pain, she had learned not to let her hopes rise too high; even when her heart's desire waspresented to her, obligation could and did interfere. And she hadn't cried those pure tears of joy since.

Eleanor's colleague, Thelma, tapped her on the shoulder, bringing her back to the moment. If she had been alone at the post office, she would've torn into Erwin's letter immediately, but she was never alone at the post office. On this day, she'd made the trip with Sallie and Thelma, a friend of Sallie's from Jackson who had taken Elise's place at the college. She was tall, with dark, bobbed hair and thin lips, which produced a serious-looking expression.

"Ready?" Thelma said.

Eleanor swallowed hard against a rising tightness in her throat and nodded. It was all she could do to resist the urge to dash away, letter in hand, and make her way home unaccompanied, just for the sake of privacy with which to open Erwin's letter.

As soon as they were outside, Eleanor breathed deeply and matched her steps with Thelma and Sallie, down the sidewalk lined with barren trees and evergreens. She shook her head to clear her thoughts and attempted to put Erwin's letter out of the forefront of her mind, focusing instead on what Sallie was saying.

"Just a card from Nettie today." Sallie tucked her letter in her notebook. "I was half afraid James would go and send me another special *Marry me, Sallie Parkinson*. He simply will not let up. Even when *he* says he will. Do you know he vowed on Saturday night that he was just gonna forget about me, that he was *never* gonna see me again?" she said. "Then what shows up on Sunday morning but a special delivery letter asking me to go for a soda before I catch my train." Sallie laughed brightly, her blond curls moving with the breeze. She had been home to Jackson the previous weekend to attend a wedding and returned with an apparent store of comic tales featuring her longtime beau, James.

"Sallie, stop torturing that poor man," said Thelma. "You're just going to have to say yes or say no!"

"Oh, he thinks I'm just being coy," Sallie said, "and this is all just a game that Southern girls are supposed to play. But I won't say yes, and I won't say no, Thelma, because *I don't know*."

"Well, you have to start *somewhere*," said Thelma. "I told Billy no three times before I finally said yes." Her tone telegraphed that she took a good deal of pride about the matter.

"I don't know. That just doesn't seem sincere. What do you think, Eleanor?"

Eleanor couldn't fathom why tradition developed and sanctioned this sort of pretense in a woman. She couldn't faintly imagine feeling such ambivalence about a man and then consenting to marry him. She would be with Harrison if that was so. She was reminded of Alice's notion that great love stories start out with the principals not liking each other. She just couldn't understand that state of mind. Even if she'd never met Erwin, she'd rather live out her days as a lonely spinster than capitulate and marry for anything less than the great thing: a love that would make it possible to *share*—ideas, dreams, books, nature. The kind of love that would *be* an adventure.

"It seems one *knows*, when one's found the right person to marry and they make the offer," she said. "Is James at least someone you feel you can . . . talk to?"

"Oh, he can talk all right." Sallie laughed. "Whether I can get a word in edgewise is another matter entirely!"

This was how she knew that she'd found something rare and precious with Erwin. With him, she felt a freedom to be who she was, to speak her mind in a way that she couldn't with other people, and to be honored for it. Her heart bounced once more at the thought of his letter.

"Sallie, you do deserve someone you love," Eleanor said.

She shrugged. "Maybe I do, but there he is."

They stopped in front of the elegant brick foursquare where Thelma roomed, operated by the King family. Sallie roomed in the house next door. "Goodness, Eleanor, if you only lived here too, you'd already be home," she teased. "And we wouldn't have to walk you *all* the way to the Carpenter's and back. Just think, closer to the PO. We could also walk together in the mornings—"

"You could bunk with either one of us, Eleanor," Thelma chimed in. "And then after I get married and move out, my room could be all yours."

On any other day, Eleanor would be likely to welcome the offer; Thelma and Sallie were pleasant enough, and Edna was expecting again. She had been thinking about changing up her living situation. Conditions at the Carpenter house were already turbulent at times, with such small children, and one more threatened to be a zoo. But Eleanor's head was currently in Urbana. She just couldn't help it; she was entertaining a small but persistent hope that Erwin's letter might contain an invitation to study there. She hoped, at least, to be studying again *somewhere*, and by next school year, she just might be able to save up enough for it. If. If.

"Maybe," she replied. "Thank you for the offer, Thelma. Let me just consider it."

"*You* won't say yes or no either?"

An urge to flee overtook Eleanor. She couldn't bear the suspense any longer. She knew running would create a mild spectacle, but she didn't care what was in the way of the door to her room this time; she couldn't match her steps with Thelma and Sallie, and she couldn't listen to their tales of ambivalence any longer. She simply had to know what Erwin's letter said.

"No need to walk with me today, ladies. I'll just sprint the rest of the way." And with that, she took off down Second Avenue, in the direction of the Carpenter house.

"Eleanor!" she heard Sallie holler, her footsteps behind her.

"Wait! You can't just go off alone like that!"

She kept up her pace, past the point that she no longer heard Sallie's feet behind her, past the gates to the college, past the porch sitters of Third Street, their eyes on her, judging. For once, she didn't concern herself with her appearance; her hair was coming loose into a mess, but she didn't care. She was thinking of Urbana, of trees and blackbirds and immense chemistry labs and wide-open spaces, where a person could go about as necessary, of just actually being in the same place as Erwin, her small hope growing larger by the block.

She bounded up onto the porch, yanked open the door, bolted up the stairs, ignoring Mr. Carpenter's voice calling hello, her marathon ending in a crash on her bed, where she lifted up Erwin's letter, closed her eyes in anticipation, and held it for a brief moment to her chest; then she tore it open.

November 11, 1921
Urbana, Ill.

Dear Eleanor,
You're peekin'! And your mouth must be ever so much wider open. Eleanor, I want you to be my sweetheart and my wife. I saw you once as you sat in a big armchair, looking at me with sweet, brown eyes, and ever since, I've thought of you most tenderly and wished that all my life I might look into those same kind eyes for encouragement and reproof and for love. But the miles and the years have been so unrelenting, Eleanor, and now an intense longing for companionship with you has urged me to this poor way of pen and paper. I love you very dearly, and though it isn't honeyed over in the daintiest way, I hope you'll find my surprise very sweet at the center.

Your devoted lover,

Erwin

Eleanor put the letter down, her heart racing, and lay for a moment in stunned silence. The world had so thoroughly just spun off its axis, that she half expected Erwin to materialize next to her. The emergent truth that he *loved* her—*had* been in love with her all this time and hungered for her companionship in the same way as she had—opened deep wells of hidden sentiment, flooding her senses, blotting out the years of anguish and doubts and blunders. All those times she'd so desperately wanted to read love in between the lines of Erwin's letters, it really had been there, all along. And now, to her astonishment, he'd come all the way, and all the disappointment had been in preparation for the dawn of something yet to come, something great. She longed to put her arms about him, to kiss him and hold him close, feel his arms about her, his warmth against her. To be able to look into his face, the clean, light look of him. And then she realized that she *would*. One day soon and forever after. Her heart trembled, and she sobbed tears of joy.

She drew a leaf of paper, intending to answer back his heart's call as truly as she could, feeling even so that her pen was no equal to the glow of her heart, nor the deep, encroaching sense of trepidation she felt. Were she to have given way to feeling without thought, she would write of her intense desire to have him fly to her now, to sit by her side, that he might press her close to his heart and put her trembling fear to rest. To whisper the things in their hearts that pens just can't write. To assure her that his love was real, that this fancy was true.

From there, her hopes built swiftly. Her heart went alight with the idea of Erwin finally telling Helen of their friendship and their dearest plans, of them all coming back together in celebration of this happiest turn of events.

It was November. In a month's time, she would return to

Goldsboro for Christmas as an engaged woman, and Erwin would come to her there. Her prize heart. And Papa and Harrison and the XYZ club could finally all go hang.

> *Nov 14, 1921*
> *Columbus, Miss.*
> *Dear,*

She let her pen rest there. For so long, it had been Mr. Phipps, then Erwin, and now, she realized, it could just be what she had always hoped: dear.

> *I love you. From the time I first met you, you have been my ideal. Every letter has brought you closer, and now I am happy in the thought that you love me. To be your sweetheart, to be your wife—yes and yes and yes. Erwin, you make me very happy.*
>
> *We have seen each other only once, yet you know me better than anyone else in the world. You speak of surprises, but when one has hoped, one can't be altogether too surprised. I think my own love made a mirror for itself.*
>
> *Dearest, it has been hard never to see you; yet that very fact, maybe relenting soon, has made our love more beautiful. Not time nor space could hinder it. When it is possible for you to get away from your work—at Christmas, dare I hope?—I shall be at home, and then you will come to me.*
>
> *I love you, dear,*
>
> *Eleanor*

November 16, 1921
Urbana, Ill.

Dearest Eleanor,

After reading your letter, I went out for a long walk, walking toward the moon, forgot that my feet were moving, and wondered as it sailed along past those millions of bright shiny twigs. But it was neither the moon nor the twigs that I thought most of, but that you've really been loving me all the while—which made me just a little bit giddy—and how you're loving me right now, and that brought me to pray that you may always be at least as happy when I'm near, as now when I'm far away. I think you'll be a little ashamed of me when you hear that I've daydreamed so much of you that other kinds of research have been kept waiting.

And really, Eleanor, I think you're a very poor scientist when I reflect how meager must be the data upon which you proceed with this very important "experiment." Now I know you're really brave, and because you trust me so sweetly, your love seems dearer and dearer to me. And did it seem a long, long time, dear, before your love came home to you?

When I wrote you last Friday, the first snow of the winter was falling, the first I've seen in many years. It managed to cover the ground, so I put on my big overcoat and waded around with huge glee as I went to mail your letter. In the afternoon, I went over to the chrysanthemum show and wished a dozen times for you. There were hundreds and hundreds of pots of seedlings in full bloom, no two alike, some double, some single, some with small centers, some with big, and displaying every variation imaginable. And they seemed all the prettier because the wind was howling so cold outside. It's unbelievable that all these beauties were developed from one little straggly weed.

I've been promising Kent and Peggy for more than a year that I'd come home to Austin this Christmas. Kent is still very much a kid and takes such keen delight in the prospect of homecomings. Besides, he thinks he's bigger than I am now, and I'm bound to prove to him that I can still set him on his ear. Do you think I'm cruel to be planning to go in the wrong direction? If only I could see you for one little hour. Will you tell me just what you'd do if you were in my place?

Have you a picture or a snapshot of yourself, Eleanor, that you wouldn't mind my gazing foolishly upon, once in a day?

I love you, dearest.

Erwin

Nov 19, 1921
Columbus, Miss.

Dearest Erwin,

Brave, am I? No. I'm afraid. I was a wee bit afraid even when I answered your very first letter, though I hadn't faced the truth of my own feeling for you. I had consciously been measuring people by you—but I didn't admit to myself the whole truth then. Yet I reassured myself. I remembered you, oh, very well. I was afraid when I answered the letter that told me of your love, more afraid than I had ever been in my life. I am afraid in many ways now. But the answer to my fears is that I trust you.

You are not as other men. I do not want my love shadowed with pretense, and coyness is pretense. Coquetry, I despise. And the man I love is not the man to be toyed with. Therefore, I did not dally with the truth. You and I meet on the level of love as we wish it to be.

Yet I am afraid. Your strength must carry us through. If you love me, I am strong enough. I am afraid of love.

I'm glad you would like to see me during Christmas, and I'm sorry that it looks as if you can't. You couldn't change your plans now without making explanations that would be incomprehensible to anyone else, any *third* person, could you? I see how it is. Much as I would like to have you, I understand. But I want my home too, and so now I think I'll go there.

You have helped me much through trying days this week. I've had some nagging, hateful little problems at school—and there have been moments that hurt, hurt. And then for the first time in my life, I found the meaning of those lines:

"But if the while I think on thee, dear friend,
All losses are restored and sorrows end."

Erwin, would you know my ideal, my belief in how love is with us? I think that it is together that we try the great adventure, with neither loving more than the other, but with equal love and equal responsibility.

And because I love you, I shall have a picture made for you. I have none now. Having a picture made is a frightful ordeal. I insist on your undergoing it too. Do you see how selfish I am?

Devotedly,

Eleanor

P.s. You in overcoat and galoshes, and I in a thin silk dress with short sleeves—it is a fearfully big map.

CHAPTER XXI

Urbana, Ill.

AS LONG AS Erwin could remember, gold held a particular power over him. Something about the shimmer, combined with the strength, the stability. He felt similarly about most metals. Many childhood memories centered around Mama's massive copper kettle in the kitchen, pulled out for the messy work of jams and stews and floor polish, the gleam of the copper impervious to the flame, its shine inviolable by its contents. And Papa's gold coins, brought back from Turkey, hundreds of years old and emblazoned with a script that mystified him, still glowing, untarnished by the centuries. They made a delightful tone when Papa flipped them in the air, high and round and shimmering. The sound and the gleam together possessed him, making him feel radiant also.

And this is very much how he felt upon learning that Eleanor loved him, consenting so wholeheartedly to be his wife. Radiance, from deep within. And it was this feeling, extended over the days, which provided his first notion about how to contain hydrofluoric acid: he would try plating his apparatus in gold. If the gold could withstand the attack of the acid—and he thought there was a good chance that it might—he would have figured out the containment problem on his first run, thanks to the amazing catalytic properties of Eleanor Morgan.

He procured a copper vessel, and as soon as the students

began to clear the campus for Thanksgiving holiday, he began his gold-plating operation. In the evenings, he settled into a reading of *Green Mansions*, picked up from the library at Eleanor's mention. He devoured the tale of the heroic young explorer, Abel, who traveled to Venezuela in the hopes of finding a lost city of gold, only to find a mysterious and enchanting young woman, Rima, who made her home in the jungle. The story mingled in a dreamlike way with his present circumstances—his own experiments of love and conductivity—and he settled further into bright thoughts of the future: sharing these dreamy musings with Eleanor.

The first layer of gold plate turned out beautifully. The vessel shone in a nice, luminous, even coat. But it wouldn't be enough. He needed to thicken it by at least one more coat to stand a chance against the hydrofluoric. In the morning hours of the day before Thanksgiving, he went to the lab to electrolyze the second plating solution. He increased the voltage slightly, in the hopes that he could safely speed up the operation on the second layer, cutting a daylong operation in half, and went to have his picture taken.

Erwin had always hated being in front of a camera. He'd put up with it as a youngster because having a family picture made was an occasion of great importance to Mama, and under her influence, he could always find the patience, the right aspect. Erwin was having the picture done this time for a lovely and noble purpose—*for Eleanor*—yet the familiar restlessness creeped in. He felt the absence, for the first time since his hasty proposal, of guidance. The kind of voice that Mama would surely provide, were she here, a light to show him the right aspect.

Erwin attempted a smile and willed his most radiant thoughts to the forefront of his mind, hoping by extension to appear so to the camera.

The photographer looked displeased. "Try to look cheerful *without* the smile, eh?" he said curtly. "And turn your face just slightly to the left, to balance out those ears."

Erwin's unease flared into irritation. Weren't photographers supposed to put their subjects in a good humor? He tried to get his face straight, but he'd lost his focus.

"There we are." The photographer lifted a very small dark metal bird into the air, appearing more like a lump of coal than a representation of an animal. "Now watch the birdie!"

Erwin squinted at it, trying to make it out clearly, and with his internal discomfort at a peak, the photographer set off the flash.

After he left the photography studio, removing himself from the unpleasant situation, he still felt the irritation, like of a grain of sand. He waded through the slush of melted snow back to the lab, his thoughts drifting to Helen, Peggy, Papa, and going home to Austin when he ought instead to fly to Eleanor. His heart needed communion with her, yet obligation drew him in the opposite direction. His radiance clouded, the pain of distance and uncertainty settled in, and his body trembled against the cold. How should he begin, *really*, to integrate his dearest new plan with his duty to family? Even if he and Eleanor could be as economical as church mice, he wouldn't have enough money to follow through on his plan to help support Helen in her studies. And he swore to do that for her. But how could he say as much to Eleanor now that she was relying so sweetly on his strength? And perhaps, when she had dreams of further study, which he would be unable to support. He wanted to offer her something better than what he could.

He arrived back to the lab to check on the progress of the plating solution. He found his vessel no longer gold but dark caramel, blackening in spots all around. The heightened voltage revealed itself to have been a fatal choice. He lifted it out of the solution, its gold coat now loosely adherent and useless.

On Thanksgiving, he slipped back into the lab to begin his plating operation from the start. *Try, fail, repeat,* his mantra repeated. He studied the copper vessel. He couldn't fail Eleanor. He felt a rising fear, a need for guidance to prevent him from wrecking the precarious beauty of his circumstances. As he watched a cone of blue flame at the base of a burner, his mind drifted to the winter he was eight years old, when Papa brought home a brand-new oil stove.

The flame of the oil stove is blue, Papa explained, and because blue flame is hottest, hotter even than white, it heats instantly. No more stoking a slow coal fire in the kitchen. Mama, for her part, was delighted.

And Erwin was delighted too. He loved to look at the mysterious ring of fire. He knew that flames could be red-hot, orange-hot, even white-hot. *But,* he wondered, *how do they get to blue-hot?* And he was just beginning to brim over with such questions: *Why does a pot of water on the hot stove make bubbles? What are the stars made of, and how far away are they? And what is in between?* But this blue flame threw him into a new state of wonder.

Helen, Peggy, and Foster had grown up and left home, and their departures meant something for everyone in the household. Mama lost Helen's and Peggy's help in the kitchen; Papa lost Foster's help with the fires. And so, Erwin was allowed to make fires in the hearth.

"You and Kent are the men of the house now," Papa said. *Prometheus and Epimethus,* he called them in jest, never specifying which he thought was which, but steeped as they were in Greek mythology, Erwin understood the shorthand he was using: Foresight and Carelessness.

"To bring the fire inside requires great control," he said, "because it is a weighty responsibility. It can be extremely dangerous if you're not very cautious."

And yet Erwin found himself irrepressibly curious to know whether a flame in the hearth could be made to blaze blue. Confident that he was the Prometheus of the mix, he fancied that he was canny enough to conduct the experiment. He fed the fire, stoking it larger and through all its colors—orange to red to white—well past the point to which Papa had instructed him in no uncertain terms to stop. But he had a thrilling sense of being in control of this mighty force. He dragged the old bellows from the kitchen and set upon the experiment: He would give short, forceful blasts directed at the white of the fire, just enough to see if he could get it to blue-hot.

But the first blast from the bellows sent forth a showering of intense sparks from the hearth, hitting his shirt and burning through to his skin, hitting a nearby footstool with Mama's latest handiwork of crochet laid atop, which ignited instantly.

Erwin's heart seized. In quick measure, he dropped the bellows and removed his shirt to tamp out the flaming footstool, which had produced a good deal of smoke. By the time the flame was extinguished, Mama had smelled the smoke and come hurtling down the stairs. They surveyed the aftermath in the same second: the raging hearth fire, the smoking footstool, the red welts on his shirtless skin.

"*Erwin!*" she shrieked. "*What have you done?*"

The bitter pinch of pain and fear rendered him wordless. Tears and ash stung his face. There he was, only able to make sense of this terrible scene in front of him though hindsight. Just as Epimethus would do.

Standing in the lab, grown Erwin knew very well that the blue color wasn't the result of temperature only but the combustion of oil molecules, which he could not have recreated in the fireplace. He'd misplaced his bravery entirely, *foolishly*, and caused pain.

Erwin remembered Papa's long-ago words as he began once more to electrolyze his plating solution: *carelessness can mean pain*. And steadily, his strength returned. This strange door Eleanor had unlocked within, which now cracked open to reveal a luminous new future, mustn't be thrown wide open, much as he would like. He needed to give Eleanor the space for her independence. After such a hasty proposal, here they were without any of the practicalities figured out. Slow and steady, don't let it burn down the house.

My dearest,

All day yesterday, I hoped I'd find a letter from you waiting, and it was there; your very earnestness is what I love most, Eleanor, and your unpretending fearfulness of love came like a sweet breath to my soul. You seem to me like Hudson's Rima would be if she weren't way off in the Green Mansions but with all her fineness translated into the crowded ways.

Shall I tell you about little things again? Books, schools, and people? You won't misunderstand and think I'd rather talk about trifles? But I must stop watching the aeroplane occasionally and watch the leaves dancing around below—to rest my poor neck. Pain comes when I think so long and earnestly of my love, so far away, and instead I chat with you awhile.

I anticipated your wish and went to have my picture taken. As you've said, this was no gala occasion but refined torture. Commands like "turn your chin toward the left," "prick up your left ear," "look cheerful," etc., make me feel like a donkey, and I look mournful and long-faced to match. I'm afraid I shall seem less happy than I feel. I will have the proofs tomorrow.

Illinois won last Saturday in the final game of the season with Ohio, on Ohio's home grounds. I celebrated by eating at Cooper's, Champaign's best cafeteria, where they have brass railings, canary birds, and saxophones, and the cashier has a way of seeing double when she comes to adding up the items on one's tray.

I'm determined to do all I can to be happy, contented, and strong, for that is the only sure way to be happiest with you some sweet day. Tell me that you are happy again, my darling.

Your devoted Erwin

———◇———

Columbus, Miss.

Dearest,

All day long, I've been trying to get away from people to talk to you. But there have been people, people, people, and I couldn't escape.

I am happy. Your letter was what I wanted. Dare I confess what was the realest trouble I had been disturbed over? I didn't know what you were thinking of me. My letters, I was afraid, had seemed . . . too frank. So, you gave me the perfect answer. If I'm ever pettish, won't you do this for me? Suspect that I want you to talk to me as your letter did today. I cherish every word.

I go about wondering, wondering how this great joy came to me. You think of me and Rima—you couldn't say anything sweeter to me. Yet our own story is the more beautiful; we have found each other in a denser forest even than the Green Mansions, *with infinitely greater distractions and difficulties, without glamorous background and in a work-a-day world;* to have heard a voice across a screaming continent is more wonderful than to have listened in a dim, still forest.

Pen and paper are cold and rigid. There are things I cannot write. Love, if only you were here, I might whisper some of them. No, I don't think that you would rather talk about trifles. I, too, know the poignancy that must be silent.

I wore the sophomore colors and saw the freshmen win

the basketball game today. Rather, I had to leave before the game began to keep a dinner arrangement. Mrs. Badger, who held my position in the English Department previously, invited me for the day. We sat on the porch, even uncomfortable warm, and I thought of you in the cold. I'm very absent-minded company—can you imagine why? At a dinner party last week, I caught myself being almost rude.

I'm thinking I'll have your picture soon. You may expect the South to be slower, but I'll have mine ready before long, my dearest one.

Eleanor

Urbana, Ill.

Dearest Eleanor,

I always look like a simp in pictures, but I shouldn't make any further apology here except that the operator was very ugly and the "birdie" very uninteresting.

I'm having the same trouble that you have, Eleanor, to escape from people and things every day when I want to think of you. I do think of you a large share of my leisure hours, and when I look again at the words you've written me and think of you, smiling as your own hand writes these pretty things to me, I wonder if it's really I that has lighted that dancing flame of happy love in your heart. Well, if it's really I, sweetheart, I will be worthy, and you will find an equal love in my heart when you come there some day to rest and to stay. Even now, I can almost hear *your whisper in my ear and feel your light caress. I'm happy as a little squirrel when a bright warm day has waked him from a long nap.*

Won't you talk to me some more like you did last time? And don't fear that anything near your heart will ever offend me. You aren't afraid of just me anymore, are you, dearest?

Goodnight, sweetheart,

Erwin

CHAPTER XXII

Columbus, Miss.

WHEN ELEANOR TOLD Erwin that she had no picture of herself, she hadn't been entirely honest. A portrait of her did exist, one taken early in 1918, as a brand-new professor of poetry at Oklahoma U. On top of the world, in retrospect. It would match with the version of herself Erwin had met that night long ago. She considered writing to Mama, to ask her to send it. But doing so would invite questions she was not yet prepared to answer. How could either of them, really, begin to make explanations to the outside world for all that had passed between them?

She longed to share her happy news with Mama, Lawrence, and Helen, but under the circumstances, she couldn't find an acceptable way. *Dear Mama, I'm engaged to be married! He is a man I met once in passing three years ago. I know it sounds improbable, but he's the only one in the world for me. Can you send my photo for him to remember me by?* Mama, along with the world, would surely say they couldn't possibly know each other well enough for such a thing, couldn't possibly expect their blessing. Because knowing each other hadn't been a matter of years going about together, as would be expected. And she couldn't help being sorely disappointed that her plans with Erwin were now pushed ahead indefinitely. She daily battled her clamorousness; she needed his presence to put her trembling fears to rest.

If he could really see and go about with *this* Eleanor, the one who sat for a new photo in Columbus, on whom the years of teaching and strife had begun to tell, would he still feel the same? What if the veil of time and distance that Erwin had so bemoaned was the cause of the strength of his love, based on a remembered vision that no longer existed?

Her heart growing heavy and her head beginning to ache, she heard the approach of Mr. Carpenter's footsteps up the stairs, slow and steady, halting at her closed door.

He knocked softly. "Eleanor?"

She shut her eyes and took a deep breath. Edna was spending December with her family in Biloxi and had taken the children with her, with the expectation of Mr. Carpenter rejoining them for Christmas. The house was quieter, but Eleanor felt no peace as a result. Rather, Mr. Carpenter's growing attentions filled her with unease. "Yes, Mr. Carpenter."

Her doorknob turned and opened—there was no lock—and Mr. Carpenter freely popped his head in.

"Fancy a walk down to the Tombigbee?" he asked in his accustomed jovial tone. "With Edna gone, I feel as though I must exercise more of my freedoms."

"Thank you for the invitation, but my work beckons. No recreations for me," she said coolly, with none of the discomfort at his intrusion. And none of the roiling jealousy at his freedom to have a simple evening walk to the river when one felt like it simply because one was a man, the morality of strolling with his female faculty not even a question in his mind.

He then slid fully into her room, looking at the floor, as if to gather his thoughts. Eleanor bristled. "Is there something else, Mr. Carpenter?"

"The college board plans to meet before the holiday break to discuss the upcoming summer semester. May I inquire as to your plan? Are you planning to go north to attend Barnard again?"

The heaviness in her chest returned; her temples throbbed. She *planned* to be married, that is, until Erwin's hesitation put their dearer plans in opaque territory. And she had decided to bear up and not ask questions. At present, the only thing she could be sure of was the continued need to support herself. "No, not this summer. I suppose I'd like to be able to stay on in Columbus," she managed, though that wasn't at all what she wanted.

With a pleased expression, he walked over to her desk and put a hand on her shoulder. He smelled of tobacco and hair pomade. "Very good. I will be sure to make your case. With your personality, I'm sure the board will approve." He patted her on the back and made his way out the door, leaving it open as he proceeded, whistling, back down the stairs.

Eleanor felt like crying. She had come to recognize over the last year—ever since Mr. Carpenter's quip about not having men around to rub minds with—that it was this pet notion of "personality" that he valued in her. Not breadth of knowledge, not intellectual capacity nor determination, but "personality." This seemed to extend also to her living situation; here, she was a good sport, a stand-in for Edna when he wanted attention, someone patient and kind with his children. It was a great disappointment to her that he of all people would not regard her as a person of substance but only that shiny surface which she reflected back to him. What she really longed for was her *new* life, her great adventure with Erwin. Not this.

Despair rose in her throat, but she refused to submit to it. No. Erwin had his reasons for putting things off, and she would show herself to be a poor sort if she couldn't trust where she didn't understand. She thought, with some measure of guilt, of the times over the course of years that she'd obstructed Lawrence's love life with her own needs, her own demands. And then the black veil moved painfully at the back of Eleanor's mind: Neuel. It had been years since she'd heard anyone so much as mention her oldest brother's name. She longed to know where he was, *how* he was. Papa forbade her from speaking to him, and now all her memories of him coiled tight in her stomach, like a writhing snake.

No one had known of the deep love that Neuel shared with their cousin, Margaret, until one day—seven years previously—when they announced their intention to be married. Rather than welcome the news with open arms, Papa so sternly objected that he threatened to banish Neuel from the family if they carried through with it. And, choosing love, their decision tore the family apart, to the everlasting anguish of all involved. Eleanor never understood why their love could cause such a rift, but Papa would offer no explanation. "Is it because they are cousins?" she'd asked. Papa only shook his head.

"Marriage is not made up of the same stuff as dreams" was all that Mama cryptically offered, as she sought to soothe her. As Eleanor analyzed the situation over the years, she had come to suspect that, like many other matters she didn't understand, it was a bitter root from before she was born.

You and I meet on the level of love as we wish it to be, she thought, clearing her head and drawing out a leaf of stationery. She got up from her desk, closed her bedroom door, and took another deep breath.

> *My dearest,*
>
> *You said in your last letter that I might discuss with you anything and never fear it would offend you. Erwin, I have been thinking of Christmas, our plans, and how far apart we shall be, feeling quite forlorn at the distance—but I have now come to the conclusion that it will be your letters that will <u>make</u> my Christmas, for it is you I'll be wanting all the time, dear.*
>
> *I've expected too much of my brother to take you from your sisters now. Once, when I was all of fifteen, at the time of the annual Virginia-Carolina baseball game,*

Lawrence wrote me and asked, if he took me to the game that afternoon, would I mind if he called on his best girlfriend at her college that evening. I rose up and replied that if he loved her more than he did me, he was perfectly welcome to go see her. Lawrence came to see <u>me</u>. I'm sorry for my impudence now. I suppose it is too much to ask a girl who has no brother to understand how a brother cares for his sister.

Don't think I trust your love the less because we can't be together this Christmas. I understand. I'm eleven years older than fifteen now, sweetheart.

I know how Helen adores you. Your loyalty to your sisters is part of what I love in you. Enjoy your Christmas, sweetheart, but write to me as often as you have time and tell me every little thing you can. I'll love it all. And in our hearts, we shall both be thinking of our own Christmases together, not the least sweet of all the joys ahead for us.

Eleanor stopped and pushed herself back in her chair. She opened the desk drawer in which she'd stashed Erwin's photograph and took in his dear face, his fine features, his sweet soul. So often, when she roomed with Helen, she'd stolen glances of his bureau-top photo, wondering over him. And now she had a photo of her very own. She longed to display it, to drink in the sight of him at length and over the days. But Mr. Carpenter made that an impossibility.

There's a bit of a look about your brows—is it the work that went into your degree, or is it the picture-agony? I think it is the picture-agony because I remember that Helen's photograph of you, the one she had when I was with her, had more of it than this one, and you yourself hadn't that look at all. But whether it is lasting or momentary, I wish you were here now so that I might smooth it out, ever so lightly. And yet I love it too. I am glad it is there.

Afraid of you, sweetheart? If there's a bit of timidity in me, think of the years of training in reserve that girls are given, and forgive me. It is only that I can't talk easily. My anxiety is that I should be less than you think me. You said once that I had few data. I had all that are important. It isn't that I <u>believe</u> in you; it is that I <u>know</u>. There is something absolute about my knowledge of you, something no more to be argued about than the sunlight.

You are "all to me that I love
For which my soul doth pine
A green isle in the sea, love,
A fountain and a shrine"

These words keep coming back to my heart, love.

Your loving Eleanor

And the next passage of the Poe verse, which hung over this beautiful sentiment like a dark cloud, she sought to shut out:

Ah, dream too bright to last!
Ah, starry Hope! That didst arise
But to be overcast!

CHAPTER XXIII

Urbana, Ill.

THE SIGHT OF a watercolor picture in a shop window stopped Erwin in his tracks. Until that moment, he was fretful, pressed with duties, and working double speed to check off his list before he left for Austin. He'd had some more hard luck—his gold-plating experiment hadn't worked out after all: the acid chewed up the copper vessel at the slightest scratch, doubling his distress. He was back in the dark, and the road ahead was longer and more uncertain.

The little picture that caught his eye was a meadow landscape, white clouds against a blue sky, with a calm, almost golden sense of beauty, striking against the dark, barren winter landscape in which he stood. It put him in mind of Chesterton's words—that the purpose of the artistic life was to dig for the "submerged sunrise of wonder"—so a man sitting in a chair might suddenly realize that he was alive and be happy.

Whether under the spell of the picture or Chesterton's words, he had a powerful vision: Eleanor lounging in an armchair, sitting down low beside her, putting his cheek against her shoulder. And they would read the prettiest books there are to be found, talk to each other, and bring their hearts to each other in a hundred different ways. She would bend over him to whisper softly and draw his head close to her, close against her heart, until his kiss would make her heart beat faster. The kind of moment he wished he could steal into and remain there as long as he wished.

And the promise of it all seemed to be there, in this little watercolor picture, displayed in the window of an art gallery. Having previously been unable to think of a truly meaningful gift—he had been of the mind that he would get Eleanor a little pearl handled pocketknife—he realized it had to be this picture. The sight of it made him wish for her, for their life ahead, together. In this picture, his heart was calm, giving him a vision of stability—something that he had known little of, in the nomadic ways of his family. And this was just the kind of anchor he longed for in his life together with Eleanor. He never could quite find words to tell her how he longed to fill her heart, to bring her joy and deep peace. In his present reality, he had to go to Austin, but he hoped the gift of the picture could convey his heart to Eleanor in his absence.

> *Dearest,*
>
> *I asked Santa Claus what big girls like for Christmas, and he confessed utter ignorance. What a silly he is anyhow! So I'm going to be beforehand with my gift and greetings. I'll not pretend to think it's appropriate or adequate in bringing my heart of love to you, but I'll hope that when you feel tense and beset by trouble or weariness, you may lean back in your chair and look up dreamily at it until a haze of happiness steals over your face, and you smile contentedly.*
>
> *I am glad you're somebody's sister and can understand me so perfectly, but you can't understand entirely until you know how much all the boys in the family owe to them and*

can't ever repay. Helen is the principal justification of our family, and I grow ashamed of myself when I think about how plucky she has always been. I have been thinking that maybe she would be more willing to let me help with another year of study, which she needs for a degree, if she thought I wasn't planning for a home. Eleanor, next to wanting you, I want to make up some of the things Helen has missed and wanted. So you'll know why it is that I'm so impatient with pittances in teaching positions and I have seemed restless and ill-content. Dear, it's very sweet to come to you and whisper what's in my heart, knowing your love leaps far beyond the words.

You don't know Peggy yet, do you? Someday you'll love her too. Can I praise her a word or two now? She's always walking on tiptoes when she's happy and loves people more than anybody I've known, and she twists things to make them funny, to keep them from being sad.

Do you have holly, or must you use red berries and mistletoe as we do in Texas? I'm sure Kent will have everything littered with mistletoe, and Papa will have much too big a fire in honor of the occasion. Then we'll go out and see how much the magnolia and pecan and walnut trees have grown, and there'll be three ripe persimmons on the Japanese persimmon tree, which are carefully kept 'til then.

Sweetheart, I love you all the day.

Erwin

Columbus, Miss.

Dearest,

I wish I could bring to you the glow of happiness you have given me today. Your gift not appropriate, Erwin? Haven't you secretly a thought why it <u>is</u> appropriate? I mean—shall we not look at it together some day, dearest? I want to try to make a place for it, a home for you that will always reflect the loveliness of the picture itself. It is a miniature of the gift of your love; the beauty of its spirit makes me catch my breath with wonder.

And your letter gave me a still deeper joy. I'm very glad that you wrote me as you did. I have known all the time the situation is as you describe; I've been wanting you to tell me.

I believe I have learned how to meet my problems where they can be met, but I am telling you no less than the truth when I tell you that all my life, I have seen tragedy. For myself, I have had all, but no "experience," as the term is so hideously applied, because I have seen so much that is dreadful, and I was determined as early as I can remember, thinking of such things, to have nothing of love in my life unless I could have it gloriously. Helen will tell you, if she remembers, what I used to say: that I had planned my own life with no idea of ever marrying.

I leave for Goldsboro tomorrow. I see that I cannot write to you, but please write to me. My family will think nothing. They are quite sure that I am—oh, well, impervious, sort of.

I love you, Erwin,

Eleanor

CHAPTER XXIV

Goldsboro, N.C.

IN PACKING TO leave Columbus, Eleanor had been at odds with herself as to bringing the watercolor picture with her over Christmas holiday. She didn't want to let it out of her sight; the prospect of being away from it for even a week saddened her. But putting it in harm's way just for the sake of having it with her for such a short time was not the right thing to do, she knew. And so she left it behind in her room, trying her best to carry the golden image in her heart as she traveled home to spend the holidays in Goldsboro.

And by this strategy, she was able to pass the days with cheer, buoyed by the inward image of the beautiful meadow. She helped Mama in her domestic duties—seeing with new eyes the care that she took in her holiday decoration, the tree all dressed up with glittering tinsel, the welcoming wreath on their door—and glowed with thoughts of her own future Christmases. She was surprised by this new enthusiasm for domesticity, which seemed to burst into bloom.

She had tucked Erwin's photograph into her suitcase, and now she looked and looked; he seemed to be meeting her gaze with love and approval, and she was often quite near the bursting point with her happy news. But knowing that this future would not come to pass for another year—the year Helen was at her studies—she thought it prudent to keep it to herself. It would be different, she told herself, if they knew Erwin. Instead, she diverted her energies into baking cornbread, calling on her friends, and knitting a sweater, the occupation of which granted her the space to give her thoughts over to love's musings—with each stitch imagining what homemaking projects she might set herself to once she began, finally, to prepare herself for having a home with Erwin. How different this all was from the adventures she had once imagined for herself, but how infinitely more dear it was to her heart.

CHAPTER XXV

Austin, Tex.

My Dearest Eleanor,
 I'm writing to you now at the end of a long, happy day, and looking at your picture at the end of every line. I know you'll think I had forgotten my promise, but there's been just one chance to write to you before now, and that was in the station at St. Louis where I waited for about an hour, and I'll tell you everything now before I go to bed.
 But before that, I must tell you how I love your picture. Eleanor, it's just the way I remembered you, except that my memory had diminished some of the beauty of your eyes, and now the picture has brought it back to me with a rush of love and sweetness and joy; all that I had dreamed of and tried for so long to recall and make a part of me has now come in all its loveliness. I see in those eyes something that triumphs over tragedy and is serene despite all fate, and I stop and wonder if there's any hope for me to learn that sorely needed lesson there so that we two can be serene and unafraid in the face of all winds blowing. Sweetheart, how can I find words to tell you that you grow lovelier to me every day?
 And now for a little account of my trip and Christmas Day. I arrived in St. Louis Thursday night amid a blizzard and sleet, and I arrived at Muskogee at seven the next

morning. I found my brother and his family all very happy and well and little Foster Jr. quite elated over the arrival of "Unka Tom." I can't tell you all the wise and droll and comical things he says and does, even if I should write you a document instead of a letter, but I seriously think he's too wise and knowing for a little towhead of scarcely five years.

He has a beautiful nursery, and around the window frames are little gold stars, badges of "good" days, with here and there very rare gaps that he is quite sensitive about and conceals from Santa Claus by judiciously placing the Christmas tree so as to shut them from view. He told me some pretty fairy tales, which are composite of the hundreds his mother and grandmother have steeped him in, and we fought the Trojan War over again. He was the wily Ulysses, and his rocking chair horse made a terrific breach in the Trojan's piano-stool-rocking-chair walls. He is so intense in all of his interests that he seems always to resent that meals must come to break his line of thought and shatter his inspiration, and his time is entirely too valuable to squander in sleeping. He told me goodbye at bedtime Friday night, and I continued early Saturday morning upon my journey south.

I rode all day Saturday through a dull, gray sky and was rewarded with a beautiful cloud of purple and scarlet and gold in the west at sunset, reaching home soon after. Kent and Peggy met me at the train. We sat 'til well after twelve, and Papa must tell me of the latest Ku Klux outrages here (we are in the very hotbed of it, I'm ashamed to say), and Kent related some of his hairbreadth escapes in Mexico from machetes and Mexican generals and burning oil wells and gallinippers. The fire was burning merrily just as I told you it would, and we went to bed.

Today, Peggy and I walked to church, and I was happy to see old familiar faces in the old familiar places and realizing that the world in which I once saw myself as so important and essential can scrape along fairly well in my absence. We had just ordinary dinner today. The turkey comes tomorrow, and I am elected to slay and help dress him.

I sat in my chair for five solid hours with my toes to the fire and talked with Papa. Though he has aged considerably, I find that in many ways I am the conservative standpatter, and he the fire-eating radical, which you must know is quite an upsetting of the precedent. He has a most annoying way of eluding me just when I have nailed him in one of his inconsistencies or have convicted him of prejudice, of which he still has a bountiful supply. I declared a truce at nine o'clock tonight and came to write you.

I haven't told Peggy of our engagement yet, Eleanor, but somehow, I feel that I shall before I go, for I know almost that she will understand and help me in my plan for Helen.

Will you send me a kiss with the New Year?

Your devoted Erwin

Kent's voice came with a loud knock to Erwin's door in the early morning. "Wake up! We've got a feisty one this year!"

But Erwin had already been awakened by the yelps of the newly delivered turkey as it struggled inside its crate on their back porch. The Phipps family had always had a live bird for Christmas dinner, and though it was tradition, it always involved the initial unpleasantness that one could never get used to. Papa had long since declared his turkey slaying days to be over, and Peggy and Kent rightly asserted that this year, it was Erwin's turn.

He arose from his bed and steeled himself for the task, hoping that in time the bird would begin to calm itself. A calm bird made all the difference. He also hoped today would be the day to catch a moment with Peggy, to confide in her about Eleanor, finally, and about his plan for Helen. He would be leaving again in two days and didn't want to leave the conversation until she was seeing him off at the train. Observing her over the course of this last day gave him a new impression of Peggy as the principal magnet of the family; there seemed to be something ever more of Mama now in her. And Erwin longed to enlist her support in figuring out this happy new puzzle of his, to have a comrade in his plan. For years, Peggy had recommend him to all the young ladies who she thought suited him, telling him all the while—to his deep chagrin—that one day a great love would come to him. Erwin expected that she would be mighty pleased to know that her prophecy had come true after all. She might even offer up Mama's diamond ring, if she had it.

Erwin reread his Christmas letter, thinking of Eleanor and imagining her in the distance, passing the holiday with her family and their own traditions. He felt a hollow pang, longing for her words now; it brought him a little sadness to realize he wouldn't receive them until his arrival back to Illinois. He folded the letter into its envelope, addressed to her in Goldsboro, tucked it in his pocket, and made his way downstairs to the breakfast table.

"Erwin!" Papa's voice boomed as he entered the kitchen. "That bird will wake the whole block! Put it out of its misery before old Potter gets peevish and starts bothering over property lines again."

"Now, Papa," said Peggy, who was stationed at the stove, "Erwin's only just gotten up. Can we give him and that poor old turkey just a few more moments to get settled?" She put a bowl of scrambled eggs on the table as Kent ambled in. The bird continued its noisy tirade outside.

"You don't know how they now pester me about this property," Papa muttered, shoveling the eggs onto his plate. Their home's lot was three times larger than any other property on the block, which gave their family space for large gardens—Mama's pride and joy—despite being stationed at the very heart of Austin, right across from the Capitol building. As Austin grew up around them, so it seems did interest in the size of the space they occupied. Particularly now that Mama was gone, Papa seemed to grow increasingly defensive about it.

"Woe to those who devise iniquity and plot evil on their beds!" Papa began speaking in Bible verse, over the turkey's cries. "At morning's light, they accomplish it because the power is in their hands. They covet fields, and they seize them."

"It's not as if you've struck oil here, Papa," Kent said as he wolfed down his eggs. He seemed to have a nonchalant way of saying the things that his older siblings were unable to.

"We'd better do the deed, Brother," Peggy said, flashing Erwin a knowing look. She grabbed a spare blanket from the chest. "Let's go murder this turkey."

Relieved for her offer of help and knowing that he would never be able to keep down his breakfast until after it was done anyway, Erwin retrieved the knife from his pocket and followed Peggy out the door.

The morning air was crisp, chilly. The bird startled at their appearance and squawked, trying unsuccessfully to span its wings inside a too-small crate.

"Trust me, if we don't do this now, we're gonna get another sermon from Papa, this time his vitriol about Potter," Peggy said, "and how the Irish are to blame for the bloodiest battles in history, and so Potter just can't help himself but try to encroach on Papa's land."

Erwin's muscles tightened at this notion, which seemed beneath Papa, or at least beneath the image of Papa that he wanted to have. He lifted the crate from the porch floor.

"How is he, Peggy?"

"His sciatica's pretty bad most days." Her voice took on a hard edge. "But he does his best. Mostly." She flashed a small, tight smile.

Erwin carried the crate down the steps to the backyard, under the pecan tree, and set it down carefully on the lawn. Peggy sat next to it and draped the blanket across her lap. "It's okay, big guy," she cooed. "See here? This is Erwin. He's come all the way from Illinois to meet you." She clasped her hands and smiled, as if trying to entertain a child. The bird went quiet, and after a beat, Peggy looked up at Erwin. "You know I summoned you here for the dirty work, right?" she joked, but the strained expression remained behind her smile.

Erwin suddenly felt a stranger as he crouched down. The turkey's feathers rose and lowered with each little stimulus. "I was overdue, I admit," he said.

"Okay, Tommie," Peggy said, using Erwin's boyhood nickname, "are you ready?"

Erwin only nodded. Who could be ready for such a task?

Peggy unlatched the crate. "I'll hold him down for you, but I'll leave you to string him up and dress him. If I don't get our pies in the oven, there won't be any room later for this big guy."

"I need to go to post a letter after I string him up," Erwin said.

"Who for?"

Peggy drew the turkey out of the crate and wrapped it in the blanket. Erwin let the question hang in the air as he ran his hand down the underside of the turkey's neck, smoothing out its downy feathers. It wasn't time to break his news just yet. It had been five years since this job had fallen to him. The deep sadness of Mama's absence that year—she had died only ten days previously—was countered by Foster and Merle's announcement that they were expecting a child. He hoped that his news would land similarly in Peggy's heart, lifting the morning's unpleasantness. He would finish the deed and tell her. He couldn't be sure he'd have another opportunity.

With the turkey calmed under Erwin's touch, Peggy gently put her weight on top to pin it down. His stomach tightened again as he slid the knife across its throat. This was the dreadful part. Peggy closed her eyes and turned her face away as the giant bird thrashed under her, every muscle in its body tense, instinctually fighting against the release of its lifeblood. Erwin held on to the turkey's neck as the blood spilled into a pool on the lawn, still stroking it with his other hand as the thrashing grew weaker and stillness settled in.

Relief and gratitude washed over him after he felt the life drain out of the turkey. Peggy let out a resolute breath and straightened herself. The awkward silence hung between them.

"Sis, your prophecy has come true. I'm engaged to be married," he said, looking up. He meant to convey that the letter in his breast pocket was intended for his future wife and began to tell Peggy all about the odyssey that brought them together. But the eyes that met his were not joyous. Instead, they conveyed shocked despair, a deep sadness, that he hadn't expected at all.

"Sis." He startled to standing. "What is it?"

"You'll make your start together at Illinois then."

"Yes."

Her face wrenched. They stood over the lifeless bird for another moment.

"I can't do this by myself anymore." Peggy closed her eyes and turned her face to the side.

Erwin reached for her shoulder. "I'm here."

She nodded and heaved a small, sad laugh. "Only after I pressed you to come home."

This felt like a punch. He knew he deserved it, but it pained him.

"You've done a beautiful job here, Sis. You have so much to be proud of."

"Have I?" she said, turning to face him again. "Don't you see, Tommie? I smooth things out, make things beautiful for others, but no one does the same for me. You all just dance around my pain, like you always have, striking out without looking back. I only hoped that you were different, Tommie. I hoped you could see." Tears stained her cheeks. "I hoped you would make your start *here*."

But the way Erwin saw it, Peggy's extreme displays of grief had forced him and Helen to downplay theirs, to bring Peggy back to life's cares. Perhaps it had been a dance, but not the one that she now imagined. He remained silent, mulling over whether his saying so would actually help to ameliorate the situation now.

"I'm sorry," Peggy said. "That was unnecessary. And unkind." She drew out her handkerchief. "I blame Papa's influence. But the sentiment is true."

"You'll love Eleanor, Sis. And she'll love you. Already does, I believe. You see, Eleanor roomed with Helen at Norman. So you might consider it gaining a sister rather than losing a brother."

Astonished, Peggy dropped her handkerchief. "Oh! My. What does Helen think of all this?"

"Well, there's a bit of a puzzle involved. I'm keeping it a secret from Helen so that she will let me help pay for her school year. She wouldn't hear of it if she knew."

"Rightly so. But secret engagements are disgraceful, Erwin. I will keep your secret, but you must find a way to tell everyone and clear the path for your future."

CHAPTER XXVI

Goldsboro, N.C.

So came the last day of 1921, and Eleanor had never been happier. Even the arrival of her sister, Clara, and Clara's husband, Frank, for New Year's Eve amusements could not dampen her mood, as it would otherwise surely have done. Clara was Papa's eldest child; she was still very young when her mother died giving birth to brother Neuel, leaving Papa a widower. And even though it was Mama who raised her from that age, Clara seemed always to be exercising some strange propriety over Papa—to the detriment of any real bond that she might have made with Mama and the family that Papa would have with her.

Clara sat at the piano bench, leafing through the music sheets on a nearby stand.

"It's such a pity I never had music lessons, like Cousin Margaret did," she said. "I might have been quite talented. Better, even, than her. Don't you think so, Papa?"

"Yes, Clara, of course," said Papa, half-listening, in his chair next to the fire, going on with Frank about Goldsboro happenings, improvements, openings, the year's tobacco crops—an endless source of North Carolina conversation.

"Yes," Clara repeated, her voice raised slightly too high, "but I suppose Ms. Kate was rather preoccupied with her own children at the time that I might have been properly instructed."

Eleanor sat silently with her knitting. It always upset her to hear Clara call Mama by that name. However, she'd come to expect such insufferable behavior from Clara and raised her defenses accordingly.

"It's never too late for instruction," Eleanor said.

Clara opened the sheet music for "Alice Blue Gown." "Oh, Eleanor," she said dismissively. "I expect that you have plenty of time and energy to spend in such recreations, without a family of your own to tend to. But for some of us, time for such occupation is a luxury." She began haltingly to play the tune, singing rather off-key but with a devilish smile, ending to the applause of Frank and Papa. She bowed her head, and they went back to their conversation.

"Frank," said Clara, in a bid to hold their attention, "did I ever tell you about the time that Eleanor thought she was Joan of Arc?"

Eleanor's heart dropped into her stomach. Not this again.

Frank stopped talking and flashed a bewildered look. He'd always struck Eleanor as something of an oversized baby, both in features and character.

Clara's grin broke into a laugh. "Oh yes! Of course, she probably wasn't more than eight or nine at the time, but she insisted up and down that she'd heard the *saints* calling her!"

"I remember that yarn," said Papa.

"And do you know what that saintly sound turned out to be?" Clara doubled with laughter. Eleanor calmly put down her knitting and made her way across the living room, in the direction of the kitchen.

"It was—it was—the Exum's new dinner gong! Can you imagine? Even so, she wouldn't be convinced! Cousin Margaret tried to make her see that it was all in her head. Lawrence defended her, of course."

"A dinner gong." Frank laughed and clapped his hands. The old humiliation would never die. Clara would forever see to it that the story lived on, past everyone else's memory of it. Even if it meant bringing up Cousin Margaret—whose elopement with Neuel had caused so much strife—in Papa's company. Of course, Papa gave no objection when *Clara* did it. Eleanor left the room amid their peals of laughter.

In the kitchen, Mama was drying the dishes from dinner.

"Once again, I've provided the amusements," Eleanor said and drew up a stool. Their shared glances communicated all.

Mama passed her a bowl of walnuts and a nutcracker. "Well, here you are, Joan," she said playfully.

"Oh, I *was* Joan of Arc, until I told Margaret about it," Eleanor said. And thereafter patently not, apparently. But Mama understood. It was their old pastime of playing at books, indulging in the fanciful side of life. And Clara had never been remotely bookish.

Still, the old hurt sat in her stomach. Her memories of Cousin Margaret now revived: Margaret, who had more musical talent in one of her pinky fingers than Clara possessed in her entire being. How dearly she missed her beautiful études.

In the living room, Clara, still laughing, began a rendition of "Forever Blowing Bubbles."

I'm forever blowing bubbles,
Pretty bubbles in the air,
They fly so high, nearly reach the sky,
Then like my dreams, they fade and die.

"Mama, have you heard anything of Neuel?" Eleanor asked.

The old strain of bitterness welled up in Mama's face at the question, and Eleanor immediately regretted asking. "No," she said quietly.

Eleanor wished she could understand and comfort Mama. But instead, standing there in the kitchen, she now held fast to the secret of her own dearest plans, wondering if it had been like this for Neuel too. As much as she had wanted to, it now felt treasonous somehow to share her secret with Mama. She'd always felt an inevitability around the notion that she was the one Mama counted on to return home someday, to help her when she needed of it. And Eleanor wanted to *be* that person to her, to help maintain the necessary illusion, so that Mama would know that she wasn't alone, that she was loved in return. Clara carried on in the living room.

I'm dreaming dreams, I'm scheming schemes,
I'm building castles high.
They're born anew, their days are few,
Just like a sweet butterfly.

Eleanor heard the slap of mail on the floor of the foyer. Today, she didn't wait for Papa; she flitted instantly from the kitchen to retrieve it. It was New Year's Eve, after all, and she was hoping that a certain person might send her a sweet remembrance of the day, one particular to their own story, in which an errant New Year greeting of three years ago marked the opening chapter of her current joy.

So she was relieved to find a letter from him amid the stack, as if he'd read her need exactly. Just the thing to restore her spirit. She stole into the parlor to read it straight away.

Austin, Tex.

Dearest,

I'm afraid I can't quite do justice to my love tonight. I've had just a little reaction today after the first joy of home. It lingers in my thoughts, and I think you'll want to know. For it worries me to see my father so engrossed with grievances that seem to me petty, thinking thoughts (albeit earnestly) that can't enlarge one's soul but taper it always smaller. And now he seems very much afraid that I shall become a "Yankee." I told him that if Ku Kluxism is to characterize the new South, and if our lawmakers and public men in Texas are always to be ignorant and prejudiced, I shall probably change my "nationality."

But to see Peggy's old-time enthusiasm wane, slipping

into a little groove that always "returns to self-same spot," this is what makes me saddest and makes me long to snatch both Papa and Peggy up and far away—away from themselves if that could be, to begin again and <u>live</u>. How bitter it is to feel despair for those we love! How foolish too, perhaps, when he who despairs may be himself in a desperate plight. Is this tragedy of the kind you know, Eleanor?

But I don't wish to be all gloomy in this letter. I can't be when I think of you. I told Peggy today, Eleanor, and she seemed surprised that I shouldn't have trusted her sooner. Then I told her that one in love doesn't shout it from the housetop, but this was very ill-advised, for she didn't think herself a housetop, "tho' almost as big as the side of a house." And yet despite the banter and lightness with which she treated it, I couldn't help feeling mean and selfish. It must seem to her as though she is being left alone to care for Papa; he is so easily annoyed and often contentious, and Peggy isn't stolid enough to bear up without fretting. And now that Kent is soon to leave, I tremble for her.

I told her my plans for Helen, and she approved of that but said that she didn't approve of long engagements, which let the best years of people's lives slip away. Eleanor, you understand what I'm thinking and experiencing, don't you?

Peggy was very sweet to me; it wasn't anything she said but only what I felt was in her heart to be fought down, and a tear in her eye couldn't be fought down, and that made me feel that I was bringing more cause for mental strife into her life. Her happiness is so utterly dependent upon others and upon the others who understand her.

Please forgive this poor letter, but the conditions really

are very adverse. But I should never have forgiven myself if I hadn't come and seen firsthand.

Your Erwin

Eleanor numbly folded the letter and slid it back into the envelope. *What is he saying? Why did he say that about long engagements without vowing his constancy in the face of it?* Something started swelling inside her, and she couldn't breathe. This fragile, gleaming thing between them now seemed as if it would disappear. *This future with Erwin perhaps isn't real after all.* Her skin went hot. When she emerged from the parlor, she must've looked as though she'd seen a ghost because, when Clara saw her, she stopped playing, and, apparently locating her conscience, apologized for laughing at her.

CHAPTER XXVII

Urbana, Illinois

WHEN ERWIN FINALLY arrived back at the Parmelee house a full eighteen hours after he'd planned to, he was exhausted to a point he hadn't been since his Army camp days. He'd caught a cold on his last day in Austin, and a freight wreck had disrupted his travel, displacing him in Oklahoma, unable to catch his sleeper car connection.

Had his plans not been disturbed, he still would have been cutting it close, hoping for one good night's rest back in Urbana before his first morning lecture. But with the sleepless delay, he had to break straight for the chem building upon his arrival.

As students filtered into his classroom, Erwin was still smoothing the wrinkles in his suit. His memories of the last days ran rampant through his sleep-addled mind: Peggy's parting words and subsequent show of emotion at the station as she saw him off. *Helen wouldn't hear of such a plan, if she knew,* she had said. In taking Peggy into his confidence, he'd hoped at least for confirmation that his plan was the right one, but she'd instead been hurt by his news and worked to convince him of the wrongheadedness of delaying his own wedding so that he could support Helen. But he couldn't listen to that. He owed this to Helen. It was his duty. He shook his head and drew his notes from the textbook, trying to reset his mental state as best he could to deliver his lecture on iron. His throat was scratchy. His body ached.

"Welcome back," he croaked to his students, turning to draw the chemical symbol *Fe* on the chalkboard.

"Iron—*Ferrum*, in Latin—in the form that we are most familiar with it, is a hard, tenacious metal," he said. "The word alone suggests strength."

As much as Erwin was taken with gold as a child, he'd been troubled by iron. A heavy iron coal scuttle had been a fixture of their family home in wintertime, and he could barely lift it. But he noticed, at the start of winter one year, that the bottom had become eaten through with rust. This vexed him, the appearance of this red dust. *How can something so heavy and strong become so brittle? And can the entire heft of the scuttle be reduced to powder?*

"Iron forms the core of the Earth," Erwin continued. "All the way down there, it's solid and strong. But up here on the Earth's crust, it oxidizes into ferrous iron, or rust. To protect it from this corrosion in its production, carbon content is commonly increased, creating steel."

He described the processes by which different steels are created from iron, but by the time he got to the ferrous compounds, his throat was on fire.

"Let's leave it there for next time," he managed and motioned to his throat. "I'm apparently rusted out myself."

With the last of his reserves of strength, he lugged his suitcase home through the frigid landscape. Relieved not to be met at the door by Mrs. Parmelee and her social demands, he found instead a little package from Eleanor, waiting diligently for him on the entry table, along with two letters. The sight was an oasis to his soul; oh, how he'd missed her words. He took the little pile upstairs, started a fire in his grate, and eagerly sat down to read. First, he opened the package, which was postmarked just after Christmas. He unraveled the string and tore through the brown paper, fingertips still numb from the cold.

"To Erwin, Christmas 1921.

Because Green Mansions foreshadows the joy we realize more poignantly in our lives, because you called me 'Rima,' and because on nearer view, you have not thought the less of your earthly Eleanor, I am sending this to you, my dear love."

A green and gold leather-wrapped book emerged. *Little Boy Lost.* A wry smile stretched across his face, awed at Eleanor's ability to run ahead and foreknow him. Of course, on the one hand, it was merely the gift of another W.H. Hudson novel after *Green Mansions*, but the way in which its title also seemed perfectly to punctuate this moment made his heart swell with happiness, providing warmth and healing. Eleanor was not just his catalyst but also his comfort and delight.

The two letters were both postmarked on January 1. His heart dropped at the detail, to realize that they would be in response to his poor follow-up letter of Christmas, the day he told Peggy, the day his cheerful visit turned sour. Eleanor would have seen how lost he really was. She would have seen his inability to rise above his worries and lack of confidence. She would know he was no heroic figure. He held the letters in his hand for a few moments longer, hoping he hadn't lost her faith in him. He drew out her picture from his suitcase for reassurance. *Those lovely, sweet eyes!* It was uncanny how her face always seemed to reflect back his own mood; for now he saw a diffidence in them that helped to set him at ease. He pushed his feet toward the fire, opened the letters, and began to read.

Goldsboro, N.C.

Dearest,
The letter is not happy, sweetheart, but I am glad you

have written to me so. Erwin, I know what you are experiencing. Only, I saw these things before I was old enough to understand and make allowances. My own father is eternally prejudiced on some subjects, even such paltry things as cards and dancing. In my case, I believe he is really very lonely, and I would give much to be able to reach him. But every attempt I make fails, and matters are worse than before. Then, when I try to make my presence negligible, such a course is mistaken too. As for being natural, as if things were all right, that is impossible. All this is a cross to Mama.

But these things are only a part of what I was referring to. I have a half brother and a half sister, and I have Lawrence. When I was away finishing college, my half brother Neuel fell desperately in love with our cousin Margaret. And when they married against Papa's wishes, he disowned them. Sometime after, I heard a man ask my father how many children he had, Papa answered "three." And there are other memories, blacker than that. But this is what I learned that may help us now: I saw love in desperation, and by that agony, I saw, in hope, what love must be in happiness. I look to you for this. And I saw the truism that love is the greatest thing in life. I saw the truth in suffering; you and I will someday realize it in joy.

These circumstances are never mentioned in our home. It has been years since I heard my father call his son's name. We do not know certainly even where he is. I wouldn't have broached the matter, except I believe that from the bitter suffering of others, you and I may make our love more enduring. And I would never want our love to be the cause of such a breakdown in <u>your</u> family. I desire no future that will break the ties of the past, to quote Eliot.

The daily tragedy of decline, do not think I minimize

that. I have grown up with it. All my life, I have lived in fear of a break at home. Except for the hurt to Mama, I am afraid I should not greatly care. <u>Our</u> home must be different from any I have known. Do you understand?

Erwin, your sister's doubts as to a long engagement have not infected you, have they? Tell me. Tell me the whole truth. On my side, there is only this left that you do not know: I can imagine duties developing that would require me at home. For Mama's sake, I wish that I could have been there all this time. For my own sake, I'm glad to have been away from Papa's prejudices.

No matter what happens, I shall have known the beauty of love. Erwin, tell me what you think.

Your devoted Eleanor.

Dearest Erwin,

My letters will make a bewildering stack waiting for you when you get back to Illinois, but I'm not content to let what I wrote you New Year's Eve be the last word you hear from me for days. Tomorrow, I start back to Mississippi, and it will be several days before I can write you again.

Sweetheart, do not let the things I told you distress you. These are old, old troubles I have poured out to you, and my heart has long since learned what calmness it can about them. I would not have burdened you, but it seemed the only way to make my mind open to you.

I do not want you to think me insufferably self-sufficient. I want your love. I want your tenderness. And when the time comes for dear companionship every day, I shall be *very glad.*

I wish that I might be of comfort to you, as you are to me. Your confidence is precious to me. That was all I meant when I said "tell me the whole truth"—that I do not wish to be shielded or shut off from those things that weigh on you. Even if these very same things throw our own future in doubt.

And if they don't, Erwin, Peggy will love me some day, will she not? I know very well how she must feel. And if she loves you as Helen loves you—I know how Helen loves you—no wonder she couldn't keep back the tears.

Your Eleanor

Erwin folded the letters and squeezed his eyes shut. But his mind remained on the image of the iron coal scuttle with the rusted-out bottom. He ought to have flown to her. He ought to have changed his plans. In his blindness, he distressed her. The sleepless delirium returned.

Papa explained, all those years ago, that the fault lay with the thrust of the scoop over the years, which left scratches behind. And those scratches let moisture in, creating rust in their wakes. And now, in his blindness, he'd caused a little scar in Eleanor's heart that let doubt creep in, and he must banish that doubt before rust could follow.

CHAPTER XXVIII

Columbus, Mississippi

> Drive my dead thoughts over the universe
> Like wither'd leaves to quicken a new birth!
> And, by the incantation of this verse,
> Scatter, as from an unextinguish'd hearth
> Ashes and sparks, my words among mankind!
> Be through my lips to unawaken'd earth
> The trumpet of a prophecy! O Wind,
> If Winter comes, can Spring be far behind?
> —Percy Bysshe Shelley

AS ELEANOR LAUNCHED into the second part of her reading of Shelley's thundering poem, sniffles arose from among the girls in her classroom. Without looking, she fleetingly surmised that many of them had caught colds on their journeys over the holidays. But when she'd read to the end of all five parts, she finally looked up. The girls were in tears.

The first few days after their return from holiday break were always particularly trying for the girls of MSCW, and this time Eleanor was no exception. Upon her own return, she found no letter from Erwin waiting in her PO box; she was left with nothing but the despairing tone of the last letter she'd received at Goldsboro, and her heart ached with the uncertainty.

She could scarcely look again at the landscape picture in her room, but she just couldn't take it down. During those first days, she spent as many hours as she could away from her room, away from the reminder of that glorious future of hers that may not come to pass after all.

Among the invitations that she might otherwise have declined was a tea hosted by her former student, Lucy Whittaker. Lucy had taken to bringing her troubles to "Auntie Morgan" and summoned Eleanor and fellow instructor Thelma to her boarding house on College Street.

Lucy was clearly agitated as she greeted Eleanor and Thelma. "I just had a big row with Miss Kern over the spring dance," she said. "I could surely use this diversion."

"And I've just had a whole class erupt in tears over *Ode to the West Wind*," Eleanor said. They all sat down in the parlor.

"Oh, Auntie Morgan," Lucy said, her bright blue eyes flashing recognition. "Every girl I know is reading *If Winter Comes*—you know its title comes from that poem—and having a good old-fashioned cry over it. I suspect your girls were in tears both over Shelley's words and in the fate of that poor Effie Bright."

How clever Lucy was, how clearly she could often see through to the heart of matters. "I haven't yet read the book; shall I ask her fate?" Eleanor asked.

"A poor sacrificial lamb, sorry to say. Ensnared by love and ended up only bringing hardship to those who tried to help her."

A sadness hung in the air. *Why is it that tradition seemed to admire hopeless love in men yet scorn it in women?* Lucy rose and poured three cups of tea from a dainty porcelain teapot, painted with a cartouche of spring flowers. Steam rose from the cups.

"What was this row with Miss Kern?" Thelma asked.

Lucy sat back down; her face tightened. "*Well,*" she huffed. "You see, Miss Kern says that anyone attending the spring dance in

Starkville had better have a letter of permission from their mother first. That she would write them to inquire about it. Because . . . *men* will be there." She put her hand to her chest in dramatic fashion. "So, I told her, Miss Kern, I *would* like to go to the spring dance, I am a senior this year after all, but I have no mother for you to write to." Her voice dropped. Lucy lost her mother at an early age. She sat silently for a moment, sipping her tea, recomposing herself. "And what do you think she told me?" she said, finally. "*I'm sorry, Miss Whittaker, I can not make any exception to the rules.* So, I offered up all the people in my life I thought could give such consent—Father, Aunt Mildred, *you*—but she wouldn't budge. How they expect us to act as grown women when we matriculate from this place is beyond me."

Eleanor shifted uncomfortably in her seat, not knowing what to say. She could see that Lucy was absolutely, infuriatingly right, yet in her capacity as instructor, she could not condemn Miss Kern's actions. And that loyalty to her professional circumstances left her feeling sickeningly hypocritical. Miss Kern's condescending attitude only served to narrow the girls' experience, and hence, their thoughts. Her face grew hot.

Thelma threw an arm around Lucy. "Oh, dearie, I'm sorry. But you know Miss Kern will be at that dance too, with her little measuring stick, making sure nobody comes within six inches of each other." And they laughed together at the ridiculousness of it.

MSCW was just not the place to learn about life. Eleanor wished she could muster the moxie to say so. She imagined Miss Kern with her ruler. In fact, she sometimes wondered if the whole purpose of this place is to keep them from it.

When they were parting, Lucy said, "Goodbye, Auntie Morgan. Goodbye, Miss West!"

Eleanor felt stung by the differentiation. She knew Thelma was Miss West because Thelma was engaged, and she was Auntie Morgan because, as far as Lucy knew, she wasn't. She'd found the name somewhat endearing up until now, when she flashed on a possible future as the spinster aunt that Lucy imagined her to be: accountable to everyone, cherished by no one.

"I think it's perfectly abominable what Miss Kern is doing to Lucy," Eleanor said to Thelma as they made their way to the post office. *And what Columbus is doing to us*, she thought, weighing the notion of asking Thelma about her offer to share her room.

"Rules are rules, Eleanor. We can't begrudge Miss Kern," Thelma said, her tone dismissive. "Lucy will get over it."

Eleanor simmered, the sense of restriction becoming physical, suffocating, like a tightly laced corset she struggled to unloose. "Is it too late to accept your offer to share your room?"

Thelma stopped walking. "Of course not!" she said. "Are you sure?"

"I think so." Eleanor nodded and took a deep breath.

"Well, let's go tell Mr. Carpenter this minute!" Thelma grabbed her hand and moved to change course to the English building.

A tickle of panic ran through her at Thelma's urgency, at the possible consequences of this action. All of a sudden, she feared losing Mr. Carpenter's esteem, and perhaps her job, over such a rash announcement. She did not want to leave little Mary; already, the sense of that impending loss began to engulf her. The reality of the move, she realized, frightened her.

"I'm not ready *this minute*, Thelma. I only meant to ensure the offer was still open, and I'm pleased that it is. I would like to take you up on it, but give me a bit to settle on a timeline."

"Suit yourself!" Thelma said, affecting an indifference.

She retrieved the mail from her PO box, finding a letter from Erwin, finally. But numbness engulfed her. As if she were lost in a cold wood and offered a path, but it was dark, and she didn't yet know where the path led. She pushed the letter inside her notebook and clasped it shut, continuing on with Thelma. She made her way back to her room and sat looking at Erwin's photo for a long time, trying to reconcile the things that might be contained in his letter.

Urbana, Ill.

My dearest,

Your letters were waiting for me here upon my arrival this morning, and I was sorry to think that you'd not find one waiting for you on your return. I tried without success to write to you on trains or at stations, and at home I was the sole attraction, not e pluribus Unum as I had hoped to be. But now that I'm freer again, I want to make up for lost time. Little Boy Lost with the lovely inscription made me very happy.

Forgive me, Eleanor, for such a miserable letter as I lately wrote to you. I should have risen above and found pleasanter ways to say those things. I'm sorry that I seemed to lead you back to old unhappiness. Did it creep into your mind, dearest, that I could ever be estranged from you? It almost sounded so, but if it crept in, it couldn't stay for long, could it? I know how a hurtful thing, often recalled, may leave a scar, and, dear, there mustn't be a scar.

Darling, outside things may buffet us, and the world may bring us tears, but always you and I must know peace and love, and that love, Eleanor, mustn't be the love that clings to unloveliness through pain, for that is tragedy, but a love that knows no regrets and marvels at its own completeness. That isn't too much to hope for, is it, dear? And having looked with anguish upon shipwrecks and havoc, we will never trifle with the shallows and the reefs.

I'm not afraid that you might think me sentimental, Eleanor, for I know that you know dross from gold, however much alike they may appear on the surface. My only fear is that I may seem like a stranger to you when me meet, and you may be loving not me but some heroic, fanciful Erwin. And this is the disappointment I wouldn't *bring to you for all the world.*

I think I now understand better what your trials are when you are at home. And, sweet, since unpleasant memories of my own home have enabled me to understand you better, I can look back with some measure of gladness, for they were just preparing me to help and appreciate and love you as I do. But I wouldn't have you fail to understand what Peggy said about long engagements, Eleanor. She was urging a short engagement, saying that my duty is with you and not with Helen. True as it may be, I just couldn't listen to that. This is something that we have owed to Helen for a long time. You know the whole truth, Eleanor. I'm keeping nothing from you unless it be how madly I love you.

"Dear eyes, dear eyes and rare complete -
Being heavenly-sweet and earthly-sweet,
- I marvel that God made you mine,
For when He frowns, 'tis then ye shine!"

With a little kiss,

Your Erwin

Columbus, Miss.

Dearest Erwin,
I wish I could make you as happy with a letter as you have made me today. You say things I longed to hear, but I am a little afraid that <u>you</u> have idealized <u>me</u>. You need have no fear for yourself. I know that. My reason is that

inexpressible something I have been trying and trying to make expressible. My love, sweetheart, grows with your letters, but it had its beginnings elsewhere, at the time we saw each other. <u>Confidence</u> is as near as I can approach in words how you made me feel. It is that perfect recollection that made it easy for me, that and your letters too, to put my hand in yours. And now I love your picture as much as your letters. The soul of you is in both. It is <u>you</u>, Erwin, that I love.

Then you forget, dearest, that for a long school year, I saw you through Helen's eyes. That is another reason your plan must go through. Peggy is very sweet, but you are right. And we shall be the happier for your carrying things through as you planned.

I did fear estrangement from you, Erwin, but perhaps not in the deadly sense of the word. I did have, and will always have, sudden terror at the notion that fate and time and circumstance would keep us apart. You have given me a vision of happiness I had only dreamed of, hardly even daring to hope that it could ever be mine. You are more than my ideal. You have given a new meaning to the word; you have exalted that ideal. You are "all that to me, love, for which my soul doth pine."

Your loving Eleanor

P.S. *Could you, by any possible chance, have had a reason you didn't tell for quoting Sidney Lanier? I'm wondering if you remember something.*

Urbana, Ill.

My dearest,
   Never fear about yourself, Eleanor. No, you're to me a glorified "I"—what I might be or might have been, if this or that didn't thwart my spirit at the testing times. I see you always just a little higher up the slope than I, telling me of the things that you can see, bidding me to hurry up, and patiently helping me when there is need. (I think I'm only in the lead going downhill). But this is in the spirit, dearest, where I am weak, and where I am stronger and you frailer perchance. There, I shall hope to slip my arm about you, and your feet will only just touch the ground. Have no fear, sweetheart, for though it's only a little part of you that I know, it's <u>you</u>.
   There has been a little skating on Crystal Lake over in Urbana's park, but so far I haven't been over to see it. If I can get up enough courage and convince myself that the time will be well spent, I shall try a round or two with ice skates. I suppose it is a sign of old age that I didn't have skates on and sat on the bank waiting for the ice to get thick enough.
   There are dozens of things happening on campus now. Readings, operatics, basketball matches, wrestling, etc. It's so bewildering that I have stopped altogether. Just "more of the same" doesn't make me happy anymore. Is this a sign of development or just plain ennui? I am forced to remember that Chesterton said once that there are no such things as may be called uninteresting, only people who are uninterested. So I had better step lightly. I hear ice cracking.
   Dear, I love to hear you tell about yourself every day. Maybe you can't believe it, but being so devoid of

imagination, I can't decide whether it's pink or blue or brown scarves that you like the best, whether you like cats, and a hundred other important things.

Oh, I remembered very well, dear. I knew I hadn't dreamed about your most favorite poet. He wrote just for me:

Over the monstrous shambling sea
Over the Caliban sea
Bright Ariel-cloud, thou lingerest,
Wait, oh wait in the warm red West;
Thy Prospero I'll be

I love you, dearest,

Erwin

Columbus, Miss.

Oh Erwin,

I don't know how else to express it: Your love has led me into a new world. Always before I had to think of myself; all my energy had been forced into planning and working and saving so that I could be "independent" and amount to something. What interest remained, I spent on the "number of things" for which we should all be "happy as kings," and to keep human kindness in my heart, I spent affection wherever such affection could be spent. I was not unhappy. But now I know that no number of things can bless the spirit as does the great thing. It is you, love, that turned my face toward the light. It is you who showed me the vision.

And when I'm writing to you, I can almost imagine that you are with me. When I read your letters, I feel your presence. Sometimes I don't see the words very plainly; the happiness in my heart blurs things. Then I read your letter again, and I almost see you. Today, love, it was as though in truth I had reached my haven, in your arms; you seemed so near. So I'll just "play" like you're here with me, and we're enjoying these almonds together. We'll build a big fire in the living room—cozier than the parlor—though the weather doesn't require it, and we'll find a big chair for you and a foot stool for me, and we'll tell each other what we see in the flames.

I've never seen ice-skating. And I've seen precious few snows. Eastern Carolina is very low, flat country, and warm, you know. We're not a very great distance from the Dismal Swamp, where the deer and bears and alligators are still to be found. And so your Southerner will like very much to have snow pictures, when you can send them. But please have somebody else take part of them so you can be in them, can't you? Please. Please, dear.

And so you are ice-skating, maybe, and yesterday I was out with only a light scarf for a wrap. Oh yes, the scarf is brown. Red? Red is taboo, to my regret. Pink is hardly to be risked, and yellow seldom tolerated. For, to my never-ending annoyance, there's too much red in my hair to allow those close shades. Feminine problems are no trivial matters, you observe.

In winter, brown; in summer, light green, lavender, white, or any shade of blue. There's the whole color scheme. It is terribly important. Yes, it is.*

And I wonder whether you like coffee. You like angel food cake, you said once. I don't know how to make it, but

I can learn. And will you like to read to me sometimes in the evening while I labor on some foolish bit of fancywork? With your toes to the fire in an easy chair?

Dearest, you say the sweetest words I can ever hear when you say that I bring you happiness. I can never be to you all that I wish to be. That is my sorrow. I can never truly appreciate your work; I can't follow you in your chosen field. Erwin, will you try to tell me enough about it someday so I can catch the spirit of it, faintly? I would give you sympathy in everything, and here I fail. But, love, you will tell me your aspirations; you will tell me your plans and your hopes, won't you? And when things go wrong, you will tell me?

Love, do you know how it touched me, your remembering about Lanier? I wasn't going to let myself be really disappointed if you didn't remember, it was asking too much, but, dearest, finding that you remember is sweet. I love you more and more.

*And gray. Gray is essential.

Your Eleanor

CHAPTER XXIX

Urbana, Illinois

"Missed you this morning, Phipps," said Lochte, entering the third-floor office of the deserted chem building on a late Sunday morning.

Erwin peeked over the pages of the *Chicago Tribune*, lowering his feet from atop his desk. "I wouldn't wager you really *missed* me," he said.

Lochte plunked down a large canvas bag onto the workbench and unraveled a thick winter scarf from his neck.

"What was the sermon?" Erwin asked.

"Isaiah 55."

That morning, Erwin woke in dread at the thought of sitting in a dim religious light, listening to an organ and the preacher impart the hope of God's promise to man. For much of his life, he wanted to believe in the God of his father's sermons, but always the doubt sat with him, scoffing, arguing, until he'd come to the unhappy conclusion that it was not possible for him to be at once intellectually honest and religious.

But he hadn't expected Isaiah 55, with its lyrical quality, like a verse of Shelley; *You will go out in joy and be led forth in peace; the mountains and hills will burst into song before you, and all the trees of the field will clap their hands.* He'd memorized the verse many years ago, when having recall of Bible passages was a requirement of the family table, and this had been one of his favorites. He began to regret his truant mood of the morning.

"I've been working on my problem," Erwin said. "And Mrs. Parmelee is trying to inveigle me into signing up for the faculty folk-dancing class on Monday. Between the two, I thought it best to avoid all human contact this weekend."

"Then you probably also missed the buzz that was all around the Green Teapot yesterday," Lochte said.

"The buzz? What about?"

Lochte lifted out two pairs of ice skates from the canvas bag. "Fancy a go?"

The bitter cold temperature would have provided him plenty excuse, but Erwin thrilled at the idea of trying a round on the skates. He happily retrieved his overcoat and hat, and after borrowing the Parmelee's folding Kodak, he joined Lochte in an excursion out to Crystal Lake.

"Start out with a marching motion," Lochte said as they sat, lacing up their skates on the frigid bank. "You know, like the old drills. But then work to change those steps into *glides*."

"Easy for you to say." Erwin stood and hobbled toward the slick surface of the ice, breath vaporizing into little clouds in the air. The snow had been cleared into little mounds around the ice's surface, and there were several fellow skaters out, but few in comparison to what he'd seen on his previous visit. He stood on the ice, trying to balance while his blades slipped on the surface, the metal at his feet creating the pressure on the ice, which momentarily undid the expansion of the water. The solid into the fluid. He steadied himself.

Lochte glided by with ease. "Where are you now with your problem?" he asked. "You didn't look so hard at work on it today."

Erwin lifted his knees back and forth, ankles still wobbling. "I'm still trying to conceive of another material that might withstand the acid's attack for long enough to measure its conductivity. I was thinking that perhaps a platinum crucible coated with paraffin might—" His first attempt at a glide threw him off balance, and he fell to the ice. "Oops."

Lochte skated over, arms outstretched, and lifted him back to standing. "Try not to lean forward so much," he said. Erwin lifted his knees again, standing straighter.

"These new artificial amber resins are said to be able to withstand acid's attack," Lochte said. "You know, Formica and Redmanol and the like. I don't know how they would hold up against Miss Hydrofluoric, but I wouldn't be surprised if those companies had a representative at the American Chemical Society meeting next month. Perhaps you could inquire there."

"The American Chemical Society meeting?" Erwin puzzled.

"Ah yes!" Lochte laughed. "That was the buzz about the Green Teapot yesterday. It's to be held in Birmingham this year. All chemists east of the Mississippi ought to be going."

"Birmingham, *Alabama*?" Erwin asked. But his thoughts were not on acids, artificial amber, or ice-skating; they were forming a map of the states, noting that Alabama sat right next to Mississippi. "When?"

"Beginning of March," Lochte said.

Erwin forgot his feet. It would be the start of spring in the South. And he could make up to Eleanor what he failed to do at Christmas; he could come to her. The conference could be the sacrificial anode that would heal the scar.

Erwin's step eased into a glide. Lochte clapped. "Phipps! You've got it! Perhaps you should join up with that folk-dancing class after all!"

Urbana, Ill.

My dearest,

Your "play-like" letter came today and made me very happy. With the weather ranging from zero to ten, as it is here, the big fire was well-timed, and the easy chair was a grateful change. But to have you and your fire-fancies and the light touch of your fingers upon mine is the most joyous, needful thing of all. You shall sit beside me in this "play-like" chair. We can make-believe it's very big and roomy, can't we? And one ear might be against my shoulder and one hand in mine. And if we grow too very happy, you shall recite the poem that hints of tears and rain against the windowpane and quiet memories of far-off things.

Someday, if you like, we'll explore in the nebulas of atoms and molecules, marveling at all the wonder. Unfortunately, there doesn't seem to be much "spirit" in it these days. Scientific development, like a child, goes through stages of growth, and the stage of wonder seems to be almost past, or the wonder is buried under the "I don't know." There's very little "looking up," as Sara Teasdale wrote of "Children's faces looking up, Holding wonder like a cup."

Sweet, it must never be a sorrow to you that you've found joy in a different world than I; it's a great pleasure that you can lead me into your world when I'm weary of mine, that often seems cold and colorless. And you shall make excursions into mine when it seems sunnier to us both—as you'll often make it seem sunnier, I know.

Eleanor, the American Chemical Society has its meeting this year in Birmingham. Several are going from here, but I couldn't go that near to you without seeing you.

Would a short visit be awkward? Oh, Eleanor, if you can consent, I want to bring a ring to you as a token of our engagement. Isn't this one of the sweetest customs, dear? And you will wear it always.

Your Erwin

Inscription on the back of a photo: Crystal Lake and me in my overcoat and "jelly-bean" hat, as Kent calls it. Also, snow-grins

CHAPTER XXX

Columbus, Mississippi

THELMA POPPED HER head into Eleanor's classroom. "What are you smiling about?"

Eleanor casually slid Erwin's letter and snow pictures back in the envelope, a burst of pleasure swelling to the breaking point inside. Erwin would come to her, at last, but she now had to act—and fast. She could never receive him as a visitor if she still roomed at the Carpenter house. She felt an exhilarating tailwind.

"Thelma, I think I'm ready to make the move. Let's go tell Mr. Carpenter."

"It's about time!"

Eleanor couldn't predict the outcome of this action, but she couldn't imagine that it would go well. But more than that, she was filled with a teetering delight, made all the more dizzying by its proximity to potential disaster. She reached out and squeezed Thelma's hand as they made their way down the English building hall to Mr. Carpenter's office. They heard his voice echoing upon their approach, forcefully dramatic. "*Let the great gods, That keep this dreadful pudder o'er our heads, Find out their enemies now. Tremble, thou wretch, That hast within thee undivulged crimes Unwhipp'd of justice.*"

"Lear," Eleanor said. Thelma tapped on the door.

It quickly cracked open, but the face that peered out was that of

Miss Hobbes, the drama teacher. "Ladies?" she whispered, shooing them back into the hall. "Mr. Carpenter is busy preparing for a lecture and recital he's to give on Shakespeare at Millsaps tomorrow. Can you come back?"

"What ho, Miss Hobbes?" came Mr. Carpenter's voice from inside, in comic fashion.

Miss Hobbes, with pursed lips, swung the door open wider so he could see Eleanor and Thelma. He stood in front of his desk, garbed in theater department robes, and bade them inside. "What is it, girls?"

Eleanor's pulse quickened. She couldn't form words. She could only think of Erwin's kiss, this being the only obstacle left between her and it.

"We'll make this quick, Mr. Carpenter," said Thelma. "I've invited Eleanor to room with me at the King house. And she's accepted my offer, so we plan to make arrangements as soon as possible." She sounded so nonchalant, while Eleanor's blood pounded like a drum.

"Is that so, Eleanor?" said Mr. Carpenter, with that unreadable expression. She thought of Miss Kern with her ruler. Miss Hobbes tapped her foot.

"Yes," she heard herself say. "It's purely a matter of convenience, you see. I've felt the need to be closer to the post office for some time, and Thelma was kind enough to offer."

He went quiet, as if carefully gathering his words. "Yes. Yes, I see," he said finally. Then he chortled, in an almost good-natured way. His gaze fixed on Eleanor, he went back to Lear.

"*My wits begin to turn. Poor fool and knave, I have one part in my heart That's sorry yet for thee.*"

Miss Hobbes took her cue and shuttled Eleanor and Thelma back out the door. "A first-class actor was lost to the stage when Mr. Carpenter chose teaching as his profession," Miss Hobbes said fawningly. She closed the door, and he continued with his impersonation. "*O, let me not be mad, not mad, sweet heaven; Keep me in temper: I would not be mad!*"

A confusing rush of anticipation and dread rose in Eleanor as they hurried away. The winds had turned, and she had secured the safety, finally, of Erwin's visit, but she had been made to feel no safer than Cordelia at Mr. Carpenter's Lear.

<hr />

Columbus, Miss.

My dearest one,

Just the faintest hope that I may see you soon is making me radiantly happy. Love, it would not be the least bit awkward for me to see you here, now that a charming girl has just taken me into room with her. Thelma and I have practically the same work, and we are perfectly congenial. Now I'm in a more convenient living situation, and the rest of the year with her promises to be very pleasant.

I long to see you, and your visit will make me very, very happy. Letters don't tell me all, I know; I long to hear your voice, I long to see you, and I want your kiss upon my lips.

My heart hurts, love. Yet we have compensation: we have known each other without the distractions and encumbrances of every day. We know each other better than if our friendship and love had been ordinary.

Oh, Erwin, I do not ask a dream world to be sweeter than just this present is to me. When I think how slender the thread of chance that brought us together, I—it scares me. Only once has chance favored us, and though I have longed to see you, there's something very beautiful to me in that our friendship and love—and there's no division in my thought of friendship and love—has been just as it has been.

Thelma is waiting for me to finish my letter and go with her to buy some fruit. If you'll go with us, we'll show you the "first breath of spring" in full bloom, around the corner and a block away—a Japanese magnolia ready to open.

Hold me very close, dear love. I kiss you, Erwin.

Eleanor

———

Urbana, Ill.

Dearest,

I had quite a talk with Prof. Hopkins about the trip. He and Prof. Beal are going to Birmingham and have asked me to go along with them. I've never attended a National Meeting of the Society, so I have missed out on the inspiration and enthusiasm that comes from such gatherings of chemists of nationwide fame, all overflowing with zeal and eager to learn from each other. For a long time, it's been my wish to attend such a meeting, but I've always been so far from the center of population that going was impossible.

The meeting runs from Wednesday to Friday, the first week of March. It occurred to me that I might slip away on Friday and see you Saturday. Would that be nice? Do you have classes on Saturday? It's about fifteen hours from Urbana to Birmingham. Can you tell me the distance between Birmingham and Columbus? (Dearest, I'm all question marks and eagerness if you do really want me to come). I'm afraid, though, that we must leave a loophole *for disappointment; if too many of the staff want to go, that might mean drawing lots. But I hope this is remote.*

One thing that isn't remote, dear love of mine, is the joy I'm promising myself of soon choosing a ring for you—a beautiful something that will have been touched by lips and fingers of us both, that will seem to you a transplanting of spirit beauty into a tangible, earthly thing. Just a symbol after all, sweetheart, but I shall cherish it. It's a very long, slender finger, isn't it? Could it be lassoed and circumferenced, do you suppose?

We'll fill our hours very full, won't we? After we've gotten breath again from the first breathtaking joy of meeting? We can walk outside if the sky ain't weeping or if there's a moon.

Your Erwin

Columbus, Miss.

Dearest Valentine,

This letter will reach you on the fourteenth, I think. I am remembering that your first letter reached me two years ago that day. You wrote me before that. Do you remember? A New Year card for 1919. I wanted so to answer that card; I treasured it. But I wasn't sure you wanted an answer, so I didn't dare. And when I packed to leave Oklahoma, I burned it; I thought it wasn't "nice" to keep it. You understand, don't you, Erwin? But the remembrance stayed.

And so I was very pleased when your note came two years ago and told me you hadn't forgotten. I'm glad

Valentine's Day is an anniversary of our own particularly; that it belongs to all lovers is an added joy too. But no other lovers know a sweeter happiness than we.

In twenty days, I'll be most gloriously happy. Even if you must draw lots, Erwin, let's hope for good luck. I can't promise not to be disappointed, dear, if you don't come. I'm all impatient for the letter that will tell me whether you have secured your spot.

I'm hoping for at least one beautiful evening all to ourselves—and other hours in the day. It will be all too short. Dearest, we shall not be strange to each other even one little minute?

Columbus is 121 miles from Birmingham, but a 5.5 hour's journey. That ride is the most miserable in all the rides that the Southern railroad affords. You will have to want very much to come before you undertake it.

On Saturday, I have a 10 a.m. class. I would like to cut it, but the comments would be as neither of us wishes; the college is small-townish and old-maidenish. I'll make an arrangement, give quizzes, and thus have all but a few minutes with you. I begrudge every second.

The ring will be lovely. I want it, oh, very much. But, Erwin, I want you to put it on my finger; I want that beautiful time together so we may have the moment's joy the rest of our lives.

They will give you a card for the measurement; I don't know the size. You guessed it pretty well, or do you remember?

I send you a kiss, dear. I love you.

Eleanor

CHAPTER XXXI

Urbana, Illinois

ERWIN PUT THE letter down. *Oh, he remembered.* He'd been rather self-conscious of reminding her of it himself. That night, when he left Norman, he held her hand in front of the fire, still faintly flickering violet and blue and green from the driftwood powder. He had been nearly afraid to look into her eyes again; his heart was so full. As he gazed at her delicate hand, he wondered aloud what her ring size might be. It was the only way he could conceive to impress upon her in some way that intense feeling of his, the feeling of which he did not want to let go.

At the very least, he had hoped that his New Year card would appear to her a bid for continued friendship, that their strange and wonderful parting moment would allow Eleanor to distinguish it differently from the card he'd also sent to Miss Green (who, because he'd also levitated, he felt a polite obligation to remember). Now, knowing that Eleanor longed to respond and didn't, it brought a little ache to his heart. He realized, for the first time, that there had been doubt since the very first, doubt about his feeling. And she proved how very much she cared by first being sure in her own heart that he wanted her letters.

The next day, he entered the jewelry store downtown with these thoughts fresh in his mind: Eleanor's pent-up longing and his own halting approach, both working against what they couldn't have known was a common impulse—to love each other.

He perused a display of gold rings, shining warmly with all manner of design, engraving, and gemstone. In the next case, glints of diamond flashed in the light as he moved. He thought of their atomic structure, the firm tetrahedral lattice, the immovable carbon bonds formed within. He was fascinated by Mama's diamond ring as a child, how it looked like a big, glittering explosion. Ephemeral, somehow, yet absolutely solid. He hadn't gotten up the nerve to ask Peggy about whether she or Helen had it, and it was just as well, he thought, looking at the gorgeous display. A new one would wipe out all his savings, but it would be the aspirational architecture of his love for Eleanor, forming the circuitry of their future together. But the expense of the ring and the trip, he knew, would have to sustain them both for a long time.

"Planning a Valentine's Day proposal?" asked a sales assistant from behind the counter.

"Something like that."

"Congratulations. It's quite a decision," he said. "Have you put any thought into the ring's design or expense? We've many different gemstones that are popular; even turquoise and pearl are making a comeback." The sales assistant moved to the other display case to show an assortment of possibilities, but Erwin did not budge from the glittering case in front of him.

"A diamond, if you please," he said. And his eyes caught onto one in particular and wouldn't let go, its gold band filigreed to give the impression of twisting vines and the single diamond in its center to look like a precious, rare, gleaming flower.

"That one. What's its size?"

"Six, sir." He took the ring out for Erwin to inspect.

He was mesmerized, as if looking into his future, like it portended everything that his heart wished. And it was exactly the size he had guessed.

"It's lovely" was all he could think to convey to the sales assistant. "I'll take it," he said, thinking of the ring and the future.

"She'll be well pleased," he responded.

After the purchase was completed, the sales assistant produced a little black book with 1922 emblazoned on the front. A calendar. "Free with large purchase, and so that you can fix the date," he said.

My bright little Ariel-cloud,

Your Valentine greeting came in good time, and it recalled our first exchange in a very pleasant, sweet way. All along, I dared hope that you cared for me a little more than as just an everyday sort of a friend. Your letters were really all I looked forward to with any great joy, for a long time. But while I was under such strain in my work for a degree, working all hours and often in despair of ever finishing, I couldn't bring myself to speak of love to you, Eleanor. I longed to, many times, but I felt it best to wait. You've understood, haven't you, dear?

And now, darling, my spot in the conference has finally been secured. Prof. Hopkins thinks he will not stay to the end, as Friday and Saturday are principally given to excursions and sightseeing. I will not be sorry if he does leave early, for he would probably plan all sorts of things for me to do at the weekend, and I would have to begin with one accord to make excuse, in the biblical fashion. Imagine me sitting still and listening raptly to an account of the wonderful Bessemer steel converters, when my sweetheart is waiting for me not many miles away.

If Friday had something terribly important scheduled for the morning, I might have to come in the night and see you for just Saturday. But it would have to be something like a successful perpetual motion machine or a new kind of atom or some real Sunday supplement science to keep me there. You can't scare me away, sweetheart, with tales of hardship and woe on the trains of the Southern. I'd ride a camel or a burro that far.

I suppose I should leave Columbus not later than Saturday afternoon at five via Tuscaloosa. That's correct, isn't it? We'll not seem strange to each other when we finally come to our time together, Eleanor. And some sweet day, the strange thing will be the years apart.

Your Erwin

CHAPTER XXXII

Columbus, Mississippi

THE TELEPHONE AT Eleanor's new abode rang often, primarily on account of Mr. and Mrs. King's daughter, Hester. In Eleanor's experience, the telephone was something typically reserved for emergencies, its trill associated with alarm. But for Hester King, the phone was apparently a main mode of communication.

At fourteen, Hester was in what Columbus society affectionately called the "rosebud set": popular and social, very nearly a debutante. And such was the typical commotion of the King household—Hester flitting, comet-like, between the trill of the phone and her social engagements, while Mrs. King arranged endless ladies' society meetings. The upstairs, where Eleanor and Thelma had their room, was a mercifully less dynamic environment but, as Eleanor came to realize, presented its own set of challenges.

At first, Eleanor basked in the newfound camaraderie. With ease, she and Thelma commiserated over the bottomless stacks of essays and themes. They shared and laughed over the periodic blunders—a paper that referred to Juliet as "he" throughout, a persistent and comical confusion among students over the terms "epithet" and "epitaph"—and she liked Thelma immensely, grateful for a living arrangement in which she felt freer to be herself, freer to move about.

But when it came to teaching duties, Eleanor knew her limits. She was always careful to allot herself time to rest, to regenerate for the new day. But Thelma, it increasingly seemed, was not. Instead, she pressed on late through the evening, lamp burning, reading, and grading, the sound of her pen scratching, while Eleanor lay just feet away, trying to sleep despite the distraction.

And so, she was losing sleep as a result, increasingly disoriented and on edge—things she typically worked hard *not* to be—but clung fast to the anticipation of Erwin's visit.

On the season's first warm Saturday, Eleanor and Thelma lounged with their notebooks open on the porch. But Eleanor longed to venture out to the woods and among the first blooms. Clear her head. "Fancy a hike to the hill?" she asked.

Thelma distractedly scribbled on a student essay. "Not today," she said. "Too much to do."

Hester emerged from the house, dressed to look like some sort of confection in a blush-pink gown trimmed in gold, which produced a hoop effect in her apron-style skirt, her chestnut hair upswept in tight curls. Eleanor mused over the curious, comical spectacle of it, pondering the strange threshold from the real to the unreal, the fussy display of artifice, when her own instinct was to go revel in earthiness.

Mrs. King followed shortly. "Miss Violet Armstrong is coming out into society today," she said with an air of soft triumph, as if Eleanor and Thelma knew the Armstrong family, longed for the same type of validation as a debutante party represents. "And such a day for it!" She stepped into the sun and proceeded down the walk, arm in arm with Hester.

"She certainly is at her fluffiest today," Eleanor joked, centering herself back in reality.

"What's the difference between a soldier, a society belle, and a sandwich?" Thelma said.

Eleanor wrinkled her nose, knowing one of Thelma's puns was forthcoming.

"A soldier faces the powder, and a belle powders her face!"

Eleanor groaned. "All right, Thelma, and the sandwich?"

"Why, that was for you to bite on!"

"Oh, I could grind *you* to powder."

And she half meant it, or at least Eleanor found that she was growing peevish with Thelma—perhaps due to lack of sleep, perhaps because there seemed an unreadable calculus to their relations that she hadn't perceived before. Either way, Thelma was so different a roommate than Helen.

Eleanor and Helen had such similar needs, in terms of rest and habits. And they developed a true sense of closeness, freely sharing their deepest emotions as though they were long-lost sisters. She wished it were so with Thelma, but Thelma seemed so very closed off in this way. And now Eleanor was withholding her deepest feelings from Helen.

She shook off her thoughts and drew a leaf of stationery.

Dearest,

Today is the most beautiful day, warm and sunny. Oh, I wish you were here. We would walk down to see the high water, or maybe we would rather climb the hills in the Lindamood Woods. And this evening, if it is as nice as last, we will sit in the swing on the porch and later walk a little way down a beautiful shadowy path, past several rather melancholy old Southern houses. But, love, I doubt whether we should have eyes for the outward glamour. I shall be very happy, dearest, just walking beside you. And when we come back to the house, you will tell me goodnight very tenderly, my lover. My heart rather takes my mind out of what we <u>would</u> do into what we <u>will</u> do, you see, dear.

Erwin, I hope you will not be disappointed in me, the outward me you know only slightly. I am afraid, dear. Long years of teaching betray one, and I have taught since I was nineteen. But you know my heart, and it is my heart that you love. Sweetheart, we can't send each other affection except on paper now, but I know our affection is nonetheless real. To think a kiss is to kiss. But I want your kiss upon my lips too, dear love.

Your Eleanor

Urbana, Ill.

Eleanor,

What a high-sounding name, Lindamood Woods. Are the hills really "knobs"? Or do you call round, steep hills "knobs" in Carolina?

Porch swings, soft air, and moonlight make me think of summer nights I once spent so dreamily on the big front porch at home, when I needed to lie stretched out full-length, swinging endways just a little, look out through a honeysuckle vine, past a tall live oak tree, and divide thoughts with the moon and frogs. I wonder if I could start the same train of thoughts and wonderings off again, if everything surrounding was exactly the same. I'm afraid I couldn't. I sometimes think I can understand what Maggie Tulliver meant when she wished she had died at sixteen, for then everything in the universe was so plain to her. But tangles and riddles wouldn't make me melancholy—of that I'm certain. And with you beside me, Eleanor, I shall see beauties in the night that were never there before. The moon and frogs will be easy to solve. But a curl of hair in the moonlight, a light touch of fingers, and a whisper will be far sweeter riddles—and more wonder-worthy.

The woodpeckers came this morning and beat a tattoo on my roof. There's a little patch of tin up there, and this rattle seems to please them more than wood. They aren't looking for bugs; they are just letting the world know that they are alive and feeling prime. That's what Mrs. Parmelee says, at least. A sure sign of spring, she calls it. I imagine they are just sharpening their axes and getting into practice. But soon I'll smell pine trees and see cardinals and daffodils and something more beautiful than all these: love in my Eleanor's eyes.

I leave tomorrow for the Hotel Bencor in Birmingham, on the morning train. Please be sure to address any letters accordingly. How sweet it is to know that you are waiting for me, my dear Eleanor, with a kiss.

Your own Erwin

Columbus, Miss.

Dearest,

I doubt whether this note will reach you before you leave, but I'm sending it in the hope that it will. I hope you can get here Friday evening; I've been saying "Friday evening" over and over to myself, and I'm almost daring to feel certain that it really will be Friday evening.

I'm wondering whether you find the warm weather uncomfortable, coming to it so suddenly from your recent snow. In Columbus, the wisteria and spirea are blooming *just for you, and roses are budding up. And somebody is waiting for you, longing with all her heart, love.*

Come as soon as you can, dearest. I want you so.

Your devoted Eleanor

Eleanor was dropping off to sleep when the telephone trilled, cutting through the quiet. It was a much later hour than would be acceptable for any social call, even by King family standards, so she was roused to wakefulness by the unease it caused. Thelma sat up in bed. She had acquiesced to conclude her work by 10 p.m. for two nights so Eleanor could finally get some rest ahead of Erwin's visit. Not without some ribbing over the notion of having a visit from a man, but that was a small price to pay for the state of blissful gratitude at having secured the promise of a quiet, dark room all night long.

Mrs. King's voice rose downstairs. Minutes later came the sound of footsteps on the stairs, punctuated by a soft knock on their door.

"Eleanor, Thelma? Are you awake?" Mrs. King called.

Thelma jumped to her feet. "I'll go see what it is," she whispered. "You stay here."

Eleanor was irritated yet fearful that something might've happened with Hester. "No, I'm awake. Let her in."

Thelma opened the door to the dim light of the lantern that Mrs. King carried, the strain on her face evident. "I've had a call from Mr. Carpenter just now," she said. "I'm afraid there's been a disturbance at the college."

"What happened? What kind of disturbance?" said Thelma.

"The girls are all falling terribly ill from something served at dinner. Ptomaine poisoning, he said—at least that's what they think. The infirmary is filling up. He said the college needs all available staff to report to the dormitories immediately."

Eleanor wearily lifted herself out of bed, her plans for rest erased immediately by the news, a hard fist of fear growing in her stomach.

She and Thelma hurriedly dressed and made their way through the college gates. It was nearly midnight.

They arrived at the dormitory to find Miss Hobbes standing with a group of girls outside. One girl lay in the grass with her eyes closed, moaning and clutching her stomach.

"Thelma! Eleanor!" Miss Hobbes waved across the dark. "They're sending a car every fifteen minutes, going to the infirmary. Can you shepherd the next bunch?"

Another girl dropped to her knees, then onto all fours. She began to heave, producing nothing, but already the air carried the scent of sick. More girls were hobbled out of the building. There would be no rest.

The train car's windows were propped open, letting in the earthy smell of the newly plowed Alabama fields, which mingled with the smell of soot from the engine. The early March air was hot and heavy, and Erwin was sweating in his winter suit. He closed his eyes. A faint fragrance of wisteria also swirled in the air, transporting him back to his front porch in Austin.

The older, sixtyish woman in the seat opposite his had been sizing him up for the first hour or so of the ride, in between crochet stitches. Erwin could feel the weight of her gaze. The train lumbered through a succession of extended stops at tiny stations; still, they sat silently, amid the lazy clanging of the bell, the woman's hands working the crochet hook. Erwin brought a short stack of chemical literature, collected over the previous days in Birmingham. But rather than try to sift through it, he left it on the seat next to him, preferring to stay in his thoughts, letting the fresh inspiration of the meeting mingle with the sights and sounds of the atmosphere. The engineer stopped the train next to a grove of trees and got out to pick a handful of blue phlox. Cardinals sang from their perches in the trees. Delight grew in Erwin's heart, thoughts moving to Eleanor and the diamond ring stashed in his breast pocket.

Every day, he had opened the little velvet-lined leather box to look at the ring, playing out the scene in his mind, imagining Eleanor's eyes as she looked at him in that happy moment that he had dreamed of since the night they met. But now he had to stop trying, for it began to put his heart into a commotion. The happy time was nigh, and he just couldn't know how her face would appear. So many things he could not know until then. He longed to talk about the question of religion, Eleanor's hopes and dreams, and whether she was as eager for a family of their own as he was. But these were so close to his heart that he had no idea how he would possibly broach them. The thought of further opening that door inside gave him a deep trepidation.

"Unaccustomed hot today," said his traveling companion, her voice a measured, slow drawl.

Erwin was surprised to feel relief at the interruption, distracting him from his widening fear: that the visit might go wrong or go flat, that in some unforeseen way, he would end up bringing pain instead of joy to Eleanor, a thought he couldn't bear.

"You started out from somewhere up north?" she said, noticing his wool suit.

"Yes," he said. "From Illinois, where the snow is only just melting. It's quite a change."

"I expect so," she said. "And are you on your way home or on your way to somewhere?"

He was delivering a diamond ring to the love of his life, whom he had met only once three years ago. A fiendish flash of delight ran through him. He would welcome a verbal joust, in protection of this delicious frisson of secrecy. The train lurched forward.

"To somewhere." He smiled, settling in for a grilling. "Columbus."

She leaned forward. "I'm going to Columbus as well. That's home for my sister." She studied the stack of chemical literature beside him. "Say, are you investigating the poisoning?"

Erwin straightened at the question. "Poisoning? Has there been a poisoning?"

"Oh!" she said with a wave of the hand. "I only thought, well, pardon my intrusion for noticing your reading; when you said 'Columbus,' I thought I'd just put two and two together, that maybe you were going to investigate the cause of the attack there."

Attack? Erwin's heart beat faster. "No, I've come from a chemical meeting in Birmingham and not read any accounts yet of a poisoning. What happened?" Erwin's fears about himself melted into alarm for Eleanor.

"Those poor girls." She clucked. "Well, as best they can tell, the hot weather tainted something they ate at the women's college. Hundreds of them fell ill with ptomaine poisoning, paper said. Last I knew, they were sending in chemists to get to the bottom of what the source of the problem was."

Erwin knew that ptomaine poisoning could well be fatal. "Did anybody . . ."—he paused—"Is everyone okay?"

"There were several very near cases, last I knew," she said. "But I haven't gotten word whether they're recovered."

Erwin's heart sank. The sudden notion that his visit to Eleanor might be coming too late filled him with anguish. That she might've been in critical pain, unable to reach out. He had to see her, had to know she was okay, that time and circumstance had not robbed them of their fate.

Erwin attempted to restrain his urgency, but there was no time to lose. "Tell me," he said, "do you happen to know the direction from the station to the King house on Second Avenue?"

"I don't know particularly about the King house, but Second Avenue is just one street north of the train depot."

"Thank you."

She went back to her crochet hook, and they fell back into silence.

The final hour of the ride was excruciating. Its slow pace, once dreamy and curious, became agonizing. He wondered if it was this same impotent despair that Helen had felt, at the report of his death, years ago. The old grief rose from his depths as he gazed out the window, the sun lowering in a rosy sky.

The train gave one last long, drawn-out shriek as it backed, finally, into the Columbus station. Erwin grabbed his suitcase and leaped immediately onto the platform, leaving it behind with the porter. And thus, after procuring the street number orientation from the traveler's aid, he sprinted in the direction of the King house.

Eleanor woke from a much-needed nap. She'd dreamed that Friday had come and gone, and although Erwin had arrived in Columbus, he hadn't called on her, though she waited till late at night. She tried to make sense of it, to shake off the unease. And she was in this state of foggy disquiet when Mrs. King's voice called up the stairs that she had a caller at the door. Her heart leaped that it was Erwin, but she still felt that her senses were not yet a thing to put much stock in.

She checked her appearance in the vanity mirror, finding the under-eye circles still there, skin still sallow. What she had been through showed on her face. She had hoped rest would improve these things, but the lack of it—and the long hours tending to the girls—had instead increased their appearance. She thought fleetingly of changing her dress, but she was simply too tired. If it really was Erwin, she would have to trust that he loved the inward Eleanor. She made her way down the stairs, buoying her senses by thinking of the December night years ago in which she descended the stairs at the Brandenburg house, resigned to join the stupid tea party, only to have her fate most wonderfully changed by the surprise visit of Helen's brother, Erwin.

And her heart fluttered to find him once more, standing on the King porch, in a handsome brown suit. Time fell back on itself again.

He was really here, and all the world seemed to drop away. In his face, she saw first the worry look, which gave way to a wistful relief.

"Eleanor." He reached for her.

Her heart raced at the sound of his voice uttering her name. She wanted to leap into his arms, but with Mrs. King behind her, she could only reach out her hand to lead him inside. "You're really here," she said softly. A warming shiver went through her at his touch.

"I am," he said with a velvety warmth. "On the train, I heard the news of poisoning at the college. Are you all right? Was anyone here affected?"

Eleanor saw the worry look flash across his face once more and understood then that he *knew*, and his heart had been hurting with uncertainty at the news. The worry was for her.

Mrs. King said, "Goodness, no. It was limited to the college girls who take their meals at the cafeteria. Eleanor was good enough to provide care to the sufferers throughout the night."

Erwin's gaze shifted to Eleanor. "Is that so?" He smiled. Eleanor's cheeks grew hot.

Mrs. King made a motion toward the parlor. "Of course, my ladies' society congregated to assist, but I'm afraid the crisis had already passed. We were too late to be of any *real* help."

The telephone trilled, and Hester came in a clatter down the stairs. "Hester, please show consideration for our guest," Mrs. King scolded. "This is Mr. Phipps."

"Pleased to meet you, Mr. Phipps!" Hester shouted as she sprinted to the back parlor.

"My daughter, Hester," said Mrs. King. "Pardon her impudence. Now, where were we? Come! Please tell me all about where you're from."

So often, Eleanor had mused over what their reunion would be like, the many ways in which their hearts might find their way to sweet communion. But she had not figured on Mrs. King to commandeer the first precious moments away from them. Dread rose in her that the magic of their reunion would be lost entirely to Mrs. King's banalities. But at present, she found herself off balance, timid, and lost, somehow, in his presence. She wanted to be hospitable to him in her own way, but Mrs. King was making that quite impossible. Eleanor stood firm in the entryway, and Erwin remained by her side. She clasped her hands behind her back, and Erwin brushed her arm with two fingers, sending sparks shooting through her body.

"Illinois. But my family home is in Texas," Erwin said, maintaining a courteous smile.

"Ah!" said Mrs. King, "My sister, Beatrice, has traveled recently to San Antonio. Beautiful country, she says."

"It is. My home is in Austin, a way north of there."

"And what drew you to Illinois?"

"A position at the University. In the Chemistry Department."

From the back parlor, the telephone began to ring again.

"A chemist! Oh! Mr. Phipps, my ladies' society would be so grateful if you give us a little talk before you leave. Won't you please come in? Oh! How long are you staying?"

Eleanor grew pink with indignation at the idea that Mrs. King would attempt to steal away any of their precious little time together.

"Well . . ." Erwin glanced at Eleanor in assembling his response. "Not long, I'm afraid."

"*Mother*," came Hester's voice across the house, "it's Mrs. *Fairchild*!"

"Please excuse me for now, Mr. Phipps. It's so nice to meet you." She drifted toward the back parlor, disappearing across the threshold. For once, Eleanor was glad for the constant interruption of the telephone at the King house.

Erwin looked at Eleanor with a kind, bemused grin, and Eleanor took his hand, thrilling to its touch once more, this time grasping it and holding it, finally stealing away out the door.

"The King house, for all its charms, is rather a gay and confused place," she said once they were outside. "Visitors in the front parlor, telephone calls in the back parlor, back and forth ad infinitum. We're much better off out here." The moon was already rising, large and looming in the sky, and the porch swing gave a silvery creak as they sat.

"You know Everett True, don't you, from the comic page?" Erwin said. "Sometimes I wish I had his disposition and his very useful umbrella—the way he smashes away nobly with it whenever conventions and tiresome people get in his way. I think that if ever I win a million dollars, I will set a regiment of Everett Trues forth to reform the world."

"An admirable plan," Eleanor said. "I could make great use of it here in Columbus."

"You must've had a trying handful of days, tending to the sick ones," Erwin said, understanding glowing as clear as daylight in his eyes. Eleanor's heart warmed at the perfect display of sympathy. *Here is Erwin*, she thought and flushed.

"Thank you. On the whole, the girls were very brave."

"Did they determine the cause yet?"

"Chicken salad, as best anyone can tell. The accepted opinion is that the hot weather affected it, though no one in authority has claimed responsibility."

"Does the college have a refrigerating system?"

"No. Even now, whether they'll be made to see the necessity is another matter entirely. The college has a long-standing habit of cutting expenses where they least ought to be cut."

"And what a pity I couldn't just bring some of my cold weather with me!"

Eleanor laughed. "You must be melting in that suit."

"Yes, well, the sprint from the station didn't help," he said, removing his hat to fan himself, dots of sweat beading his forehead. "I'm so relieved to know that you weren't afflicted." His voice was both earnest and strong.

She wanted so much to touch him, to smooth his brow. "Thank you," she said tenderly.

They sat in comfortable silence for several minutes, the creak of the swing like a frog's voice in the evening air. He closed his eyes and tilted his head upward. "For a while there, when I was at California, my fellow chemiker, Roy, and I—did I ever mention him?—were interested in developing a cheap, simple refrigerating system, one that could operate with a kerosene flame where electricity isn't available. The units on the market now are all electrical and very expensive, and there is a distinct need for it, I think, throughout the South. We worked out the chemical end of it fairly well."

Eleanor warmed at his ease of speaking confidingly, bringing his hopes and fancies to her. "Your idea would also work well for the dairies," she said. "Did you ever see milk wells covered with lattice work and used for keeping the milk and butter? I remember crawling into one when I was very small and venturesome and getting the scare of my life. I don't know what I imagined was inside, but I nearly fell into the water."

A lively current ran through her as they laughed together; she felt more herself than she had in a very long time.

"Now I see how one of those dazzling smiles develops," he said playfully. "I have a fond memory of one during one of our games, was it?"

"You quite saved my life. Or do you remember?"

Ah yes, this was how she felt those years ago too. How silly to have been so worried over appearances when this is what it is to be with Erwin.

Strolling along through the dusky streets of Columbus, Erwin could almost sense a thrumming of energy between them. Eleanor's step was light, her face open and airy. She had a slim, wild kind of beauty—flowerlike—that made his heart race upon seeing her again.

They passed a front garden with a young leafless tree, dotted up with pink blossoms. He'd noticed it during his sprint, and now that the urgency had passed, he could settle into revelry. "The peach trees are in bloom," he said. "It's been years since I remember seeing one."

"Aren't they just beautiful?" Eleanor stopped to admire its delicate blossoms. "When they're just beginning to bloom like this, they remind me of the colorful woodblock prints that Mama brought back with us from Japan."

They moved along in their walk, nodding salutations to those Columbiads who sat stationed on their front porches. Eyes seemed to be everywhere. Never had Erwin been made more aware of propriety, and so he made sure to walk a respectful distance apart.

Some houses looked distinctly different from any he'd seen— rather like wedding cakes. And to complete the romantic atmosphere, purple wisteria drooped down from the trees. The light was soft and gentle, hills still to be seen in the distance.

"Was the chemical meeting as profitable an experience as you hoped?" Eleanor asked.

"Yes, very. And I reconnected with some of the chemical folk I've known over the years. Roy Newton was there too. I hoped he might also find a position at Illinois so we could continue building our air castles."

"Where is he now?" she asked.

"Teaching at a denominational school in Ohio, though rather unhappily, I'm afraid." He would have stopped there in his description of Roy's predicament, but Eleanor looked at him searchingly, encouraging him to continue, and he saw its potential for a gambit. She had such a keen insight, such a breadth of compassion, but on religious matters, they had spoken not at all. And he didn't want to cause her any distress.

"I owe much of my success to him; he's the most brilliant chemist and mathematician for his age. And quite the philosopher, but his unorthodox ideas aren't particularly . . . popular with the sectarians there. He's rather outspoken about his atheism." He paused on the weight of the word, almost afraid to look at Eleanor, but when he did, he saw what he took to be a flash of understanding. Was this only what he wanted to see?

"Does that affect your opinion of him?"

"Only that he perhaps need not be so outspoken about it."

"I think you're right, Erwin." The sound of his name from her lips gave him a shock of pleasure. "One can be foolishly cocksure about *not* knowing as well as about knowing. And one has a right to make allowance for other people's not understanding one's attitude."

Encouraging, but what is her attitude? Outside of the scientific community, he'd often felt as if he were in a dark cave with his doubts, beyond ministration and protected only by silence.

"As for me," he ventured, "I can't bring myself to say or believe that I am standing on the only Rock of Truth, and all others are marked for Destruction." He hesitated. "I hope that this doesn't bring you pain."

"On the contrary." Eleanor stopped walking. "When I was ten years old, I made a sensation among a group of little girls coming out of Sunday school, expressing the rank heresy that I didn't know whether I believed the Bible or not. I would wait until I was grown up and then study and see whether there was any proof of it." She started walking again.

"And, Miss Five Times Five, is there any proof?"

"Still undetermined, I'm afraid," she said. "Erwin, what I mean to say is this: We don't have to blindfold ourselves to be happy. It's my hope that we can talk through these things, the burden of the mystery, together."

His heart swelled at the thought of daylight finally entering his cave. To be with Eleanor, he realized, would mean that his days would be given over to exactly this mutual exploration. In the distance, an owl called overhead, its rich melodic notes filling the night air.

She continued, "I too make serious charges against any conception of God that teaches man to despise one another—and to despise the here and now. This seems to be at the heart of my troubles with Papa when I am at home."

Yes, there was the old unhappiness. But Erwin couldn't bring himself to regret bringing up the subject. They were forging a new, higher path now, together.

They crossed the street at an intersection, walking toward a neighborhood of massive oaks and plantation-style homes.

"If the truth hurts us, we ought to change our philosophy until the truth is beautiful," Eleanor said. "Is this not right? I would think that we should 'taste all of it,' as Browning wrote, and find the beauty in it."

"That sounds *just* right," he said. It was nearly dark by then, the sky shot with the last stray beams of red. They had stopped in front of an overgrown row of hedges, which Erwin could see were meant to be the perimeter of the grounds to a towering mansion.

"Waverly Heights," Eleanor said. "Nearly a hundred years old and unoccupied for decades now. Aristocrats gone to seed."

Across the hedge, another cluster of old peach trees stood, festooned with pink blossoms. Erwin fingered his pocketknife.

"Where does the truth fall when it comes to pulling a few sprays from the peach tree?"

"Wicked. Decidedly so," Eleanor said. She tilted her head. "But, if we don't pull them, they will surely be pillaged by small boys." She returned her gaze to Erwin with a wry smile. "And *we* may have our own peach tree someday, may we not? And then we mustn't fret when its sprays are pulled by some other courting couple."

"Our truth is decided," said Erwin.

He found the path through the hedge and proceeded to cut three stems from the tree, the sweet, hay-like fragrance of its blooms in the air. Swallows swooped and dove around them, chattering against the coming night. The whitewashed brick plantation house loomed, an island set in a sea of giant, overgrown cypress, cascades of wisteria hanging from its façade, reminding him in a small way of his family home.

He presented the stems to Eleanor, his thoughts flashing ahead to the diamond ring and the promise of that particular moment. He could almost know, now, how her eyes would look. She inhaled the fragrance of the blossoms. "And can we also have sweet peas in our yard? And pansies? And violets, beds and beds of violets?" she said, her voice growing light, melodic.

Erwin bowed playfully. "I will happily spade up the ground for your sweet peas, pansies, and violets, when we have our very own home." He loved the sound of that, the promise, just as the buds in Eleanor's arms held the promise of nourishment. *Our very own home.*

"Of course our home would be far smaller, simpler," she said.

Erwin regarded the mansion again, superimposing his thoughts toward what their home might look like, when the time came: a lovely little cottage with its windows and doors wide open. A garden, a hearth, children.

"It's empty, you say?" He looked sideways at Eleanor, then out to the walkway, for any prying eyes.

"Unoccupied," she said. "But I've been told everything inside is just the way they left it."

"Perhaps we should investigate."

The wide, sweeping porch was shadowed with purple and strewn with brown leaves that made a sound like ice cracking as they walked toward the ornate front door, framed all around with circles of red glass.

"Formidable," Eleanor said.

Erwin leaned toward the window in the door's center, peering inside, thinking it looked rather lit up for a place that was unoccupied. He turned the handle. It was unlocked. He knocked, just in case. Finding no answer, he called out a friendly "Hello?" to the inside, the word echoing through its cavernous interior. Satisfied that the lit-up effect did not indicate occupancy, he stepped inside, inviting Eleanor to follow.

They giggled like little children in the vast drawing room of the old mansion and, letting their heads fall back, were treated to the source of all that light. The ceiling went up and up, a circular tower with windows all around, letting in the moonlight. A massive crystal chandelier was anchored in the center of their view, reflecting shimmering bits of light.

"Oh, this is *enchanting*," Eleanor cooed, circling around, head back, cradling the peach sprays. The sight of her moonlit face arrayed around the pink blossoms was jarring, exciting.

He wanted so to take her in his arms, to kiss her, but he was overcome with shyness. Now that concerns of propriety were off the table, he still felt a pull toward restraint. She appeared as something like the first violet of the season, beckoning him with her purple petals. And with the first violet, he was always of two impulses: to hold it gently, carefully, keeping its petals in order, or to tighten his grip and crush its oils, releasing its delicious fragrance. But he needed to be guided by her eyes, and at present, they were still cast toward the outward beauty.

The great room was painted white and sparsely furnished, with an entry table in between two large sweeping staircases and a piano to one side. "It certainly doesn't seem very *lived in*," Erwin said, moving in the direction of the adjoining room. "Not at all the way our home will be."

"Yes," Eleanor said. "Formality often feels so cold, doesn't it?"

"For contrast, you'd laugh to see the way I have my lab all littered up with Mason fruit jars," he said, "each with its lid forested with brass tubes leading in all directions. And there are cakes of paraffin lying all about. You'd think I'd started a cannery and quit being a misguided chemistry researcher. I can't guarantee that our kitchen wouldn't end up in similar fashion."

She walked in his direction. "Is 'lying all about' just the state in which cakes of paraffin are handiest? Or may I come in and pick them up and put them in a box in its regular place?"

"That's a sweet thought," he said tenderly. "But you shouldn't be indulgent to my carelessness. You may have to lay hold of my ear."

"Never fear, dear chemist," she said. "I've a desk of my own, and I know what it is to want my things just as I left them. You may pick up your own paraffin cakes. Though I have to warn you, you're taking a terrible risk. We may have to resort to eating them for our supper."

They found themselves in a dining hall. In the dim light stood a long table, with walnut and cane chairs, and china closets across the far wall reflected the moonlight. On the side was a regal mahogany server, supporting candlesticks and a shimmering brass gong, which immediately called to him. Erwin walked toward it; he was feeling too jovial, he couldn't resist.

"Dinner is served!" he said, picking up the hammer and giving it a crash into the metal surface. Eleanor's face went completely still as the sonorous tones filled the room, as if she'd been startled or frightened. Then, she began to laugh. A giggle at first, erupting into deep peals.

"Have I got a story for you!" she said.

Erwin moved toward her, an unexpected tremor of desire building at the sound of her laughter. He draped an arm lightly about her shoulders, thinking to sweep her up weightlessly into his arms. But as she collected her wits, they heard the sharp bark of a dog outside. Pinched with fear and excitement, Erwin grabbed Eleanor's hand and scurried out the door before they could be rooted out.

And as soon as Erwin could ensure that there wouldn't be a dog in pursuit, they made their way back out to the street, past the English building, and through the college gates, back toward Eleanor's house, gay and relaxed and invincible.

The moon floated above them as they arrived back at the King house, rosy, almost, with a bruise of purple in the sky behind it. The constellations glittered down.

"Do you know how to find your way to the hotel Gilmore?" she asked, stopped at the porch steps, starlight in her hair. She looked magnificent. *And when we have come back to the house, you will tell me good night very tenderly, my lover.*

"Yes. Well, no. But I have to go back to the station and retrieve my suitcase. I'll get direction from there." The terrified shyness enveloped him again. He didn't want to ruin the moment. *But how to approach?* Eleanor seemed a heavenly creature, and his legs felt as though they were made of clay.

"Good night, my darling Rima." He reached for her exquisite, slender hand and raised it to his face. He closed his eyes and pressed his lips to it in a shy, sweet kiss, the perfume of peach blossom about her soft skin.

When he opened his eyes, she placed her hand on his cheek, gazing up at him with a wistful look, beckoning him closer. At this distance, he could see warm flecks of amber and a shock of copper in her eyes. A stray curl fell across her forehead.

"Erwin," she whispered, voice full of tenderness and longing. "My love." Her words like gems in the air between them, he felt a sweeping flare of happiness, like a match being struck. And in her eyes, he could see her need, and he forgot everything except his own yearning to fill it. He took her sweet face in his hands and pushed back her curls, kissing her forehead and eyes and lips. He felt her love rush up to meet him as she lifted herself up on tiptoes and put her arms about his neck, her breath coming in little catches, almost sobs.

He realized, *felt*, how much they really meant to each other, and his arms tightened about her at the thought, kisses growing closer and longer and warmer, like a spreading flame.

"Eleanor," he whispered back, "I love you so." He buried his face in her hair and drew her body up against his, feeling as though his heart was going from his body to hers, a transmutation of strength; the sweet thrill made him tremble with joy.

CHAPTER XXXIII

The face of all the world is changed, I think,
Since first I heard the footsteps of thy soul
Move still, oh, still, beside me, as they stole
Betwixt me and the dreadful outer brink
Of obvious death, where I, who thought to sink,
Was caught up into love, and taught the whole
Of life in a new rhythm. The cup of dole
God gave for baptism, I am fain to drink,
And praise its sweetness, Sweet, with thee anear.
The names of country, heaven, are changed away
For where thou art or shalt be, there or here.

—Elizabeth Barrett Browning

ELEANOR SAT AT the desk in her classroom on Saturday morning, everything around her just the same as it had been a week ago, but she was not the same. It wasn't only the blissful night's sleep she'd just had, lit up with the happy dreams of future gardens, nor the toes that ached from standing so long on their tips; there was a glow of happiness in her heart. She felt transported, her perfect evening with Erwin reminding her that mere living can be a delightful adventure.

It was the first day of scheduled classes after the ptomaine epidemic, and only six girls reported to Eleanor's literature section.

So, she and Sallie and Thelma, each with poorly attended 10 a.m. classes, made the executive decision to combine them into Thelma's classroom and read aloud snatches of springtime poetry.

They had begun with a jolly class rendition of *Sumer Is Icumen In* and wound their way dreamily through the romantics—until Thelma dampened the mood with a long-winded and overblown piece by Walt Whitman. While Thelma was reciting, Eleanor caught a glimpse through the opaque glass panel of the door; it was the shape of a man lingering in the outside hall. Her heart leaped up. Erwin had come early to meet her. Her chest spread with warmth that he would be so eager, but she was trepidatious that his appearance at the English building would be the start of unwanted gossip.

Thelma droned on, reading of the doleful mourning of the ever-returning spring. Eleanor rose to open the door. Erwin met her gaze and made a comic face at the recognition of Whitman's verse. Thinking quickly, she motioned for him to join them in the classroom. It was the only way she could figure to help quelch the start of the rumor mill. It may cause a stir, but she could manage it. The hour was drawing to a close, and Thelma finished with Whitman. Erwin entered.

"Girls, this is Mr. Phipps, on a brief visit from Illinois," Eleanor said.

The girls straightened their backs, turning to look at him.

"Hello," he said, taking off his hat in greeting. The girls tittered.

Sallie looked rather astonished. "Well hello, Mr. Phipps," she said. "This is quite a surprise. Welcome to our rather informal gathering of Saturday English classes. We wouldn't want you to think this was par for the course. But seeing that it is for today, perhaps you have a final poem you'd like to share?"

Cheeky Sallie, Eleanor thought. A small worry grew larger in her; she'd meant only to introduce him to the class, not to put him on the spot. For consideration's sake, as well for the sake of preventing word of his presence spreading to Mr. Carpenter.

"Well," Erwin started, "you'll have to forgive me. I'm a quite lopsided man of science, and there aren't very many poems I know well enough to recite. But there's one very short one that I've read recently that I may be able to do justice to." He pursed his lips and narrowed his eyes in Eleanor's direction, feigning annoyance. But his smile betrayed him.

Humble, just like Erwin, Eleanor thought.

"Please," said Sallie.

Erwin cleared his throat.

"So one in heart and thought, I trow,

That thou might'st press the strings and I might draw the bow

And both would meet in music sweet,

Thou and I, I trow"

Eleanor met his gaze. The electric feeling was almost worth the risk of fumbling her attempt to avoid gossip.

"That's a lovely poem," said Thelma. "Who is it?"

"Sidney Lanier," Eleanor said, smiling.

Mr. Carpenter's voice interrupted the reverie. "What ho, girls?" He had appeared at the open door and peered searchingly across the room. Eleanor's stomach dropped. He'd never actually visited in on her class before. *Why today, of all days?*

"Hello, Mr. Carpenter," said Thelma with measured confidence. "We scraped together our poorly attended sections for a reading day. Monday will find us all more composed, I hope."

"Thank you, girls. That'll be all for today," said Sallie.

Mr. Carpenter nodded toward Thelma and paused as the girls filed out, whispering animatedly to each other. His eyes rested on Erwin, and he frowned quizzically before turning his attentions to the girls leaving the classroom. "I trust you're all feeling much stronger today?" He disappeared with them down the hall.

Eleanor exhaled, trying to release her anxiety—for what Mr. Carpenter might have thought about Erwin's presence and the consequences that might lie ahead as a result. Any whiff of romantic involvement, and she might lose her job. She stood straight, nervously clasping her hands behind her back.

"And what are you two up to today?" Sallie asked slyly.

Erwin walked up behind Eleanor and touched her arm, sending a warming shiver through her, returning the electricity.

"A hike. Lindamood Woods, I believe," Eleanor said, glancing back at Erwin. His smile widened in approval. She longed for another walk with him, to learn to know the feel of his hand in hers along the way. To freely be in his arms, finally.

Just Erwin's presence made Eleanor's heart happy, her step light. In the sun's glare, Erwin's hair was the color of a field of oats, and she realized with a flutter that she had never before seen him in the open light of day. She wanted to drink in the sight of him, but until they could steal away into some semblance of privacy, she could only try to catch as many glances as she could. A procession of automobiles sputtered past them in the street.

"Tell me more about the chemical society meeting," she said. "That is, what you can in Mother Goose. I want to know about everything that touches your life."

"The short version is that it was mostly made up of presentations of papers, some of which were very up-to-the-moment and interesting," he said. "But nearly all were geared toward industrial application rather than research. Then there were those of us who arrived with ideas for problems to solve, looking for ears to bend."

"You're working on a problem! Please, tell me all about it."

"Predictably, measuring conductivity again," he said. "Apparently I haven't had my fill of the Law of Perversity's hand. But this time, I aim to attempt it in liquid hydrofluoric acid. You know, the stuff that etches glass?"

Eleanor nodded.

"That's hydrofluoric. And since it etches glass, I can't use that for my apparatus. But it also chews up lead and copper, so I can't use those either. The question of what material can be used to contain it for long enough to measure conductivity is one that I've not been able to answer. I tried plating a glass vessel in gold, but still the acid was able to attack. I was getting quite discouraged, but thanks to the convention, my hope is renewed. I'm having a vessel made from Redmanol, a sort of synthetic amber, transparent and lustrous."

They were nearing the river and had reached a point in the journey where the pavement of the street gave way to gravel. Erwin held out his hand. Eleanor clasped it as she stepped from the smooth pavement to the grassy shoulder, delighting in his touch.

"Redmanol sounds very pretty," she said. "Shall I be foolishly feminine and say I would like to work with such vessels?"

"Not foolish at all," he said. "Chemistry can be quite pretty."

Eleanor felt a zing between them at his words.

"But speaking of work now, tell me about the Great American Desert of theme papers," Erwin said. "Are there really very few oases? And does your camel go dry lots of times and have to be taken out of the desert and given another drink of red ink?"

Eleanor laughed. "Both red ink and tears flow most freely around exam time, which is thankfully over, at least, for the time being," she said. "But oases between stacks of themes are always few and far between."

An automobile passed them on the gravel road, leaving behind a spray of dust. Eleanor quickened her pace to get past the billows. Erwin matched her steps.

"I have a sneaking suspicion that my letters to you have been freckled over with red ink," he said. "I don't see how you could resist."

She turned toward him and nudged him playfully. "Erwin, we don't write; we just talk. Anyway, red ink isn't nearly so deadly as certain acids; you have a most terrific advantage. And there are plenty of freckles on my own pages—but I'm remembering a line, 'In those freckles live their savors'? Is that it? From *Midsummer Night's Dream*."

"Yes, I know it. That's a favorite of mine."

They had come upon a grove of dogwood trees, all blown with white, set apart aways from the road. The sight reminded Eleanor of the watercolor picture, the promise of their future happiness. Seeing no approaching automobiles, in a ripple of mirth, she clasped Erwin's hand and ran through the grass, aiming for the middle of it.

Together, amid the clouds of white, they found a seat on an arched tree trunk that had fallen in the grove. Erwin gently drew her close, and she leaned lightly into him. He reached out, lacing her fingers with his, and kissed them sweetly.

"I loved the touch of your hand in mine along the way," he whispered. The underlying sensuality of his words made Eleanor tremble. She never dreamed that love could be so beautiful. She'd had an idea of intellectual companionship but didn't know there could be such tenderness. She tilted her face toward him, leaned back into the curve of his arms, and gave her response in a kiss, slow and thoughtful, his lips warm and sweet on hers. Sinking into his embrace, she felt the movement of his breathing and leaned her ear against his chest, listening to his heart.

"You were about to tell me a story yesterday evening before we were so rudely interrupted by the dog outside," he said.

Eleanor's face colored. The sound of the gong had caused her to begin to blurt out her fancy just as it had those many years ago. She knew that she'd be safe in recounting the story to Erwin—he wouldn't humiliate her as her family had done—but still; she had been slightly relieved for the interruption, sparing herself the strain of going into the detail of its telling. She closed her eyes and drew a breath.

"I once fancied that I was Joan of Arc," she said. And for the first time, the old humiliating story made her giggle. "I mistook the sound of my cousin's new dinner gong for the voices of the saints calling to me."

Erwin's mouth curved with tenderness as he looked down at her, his hand caressing her cheek. Eleanor felt lighter. "I truly believed it. For days, I held fast to the notion as a glorious secret. And then I erupted with it when I was at my cousin's house and heard the sound so close. I don't know how I so completely misunderstood. I was nine and full of fancy, but I'm afraid I can't say that much has changed with age, pierced as my spirit was those years ago by the laughter of my loved ones. I suppose it just stopped me from sharing my fancies so readily." Rather than reviving the old strain at this unburdening, she felt as if she were floating—the shadows across her heart gone, a powerful relief filling her in their stead.

"When I was about the same age, I fancied myself Prometheus," he said. "And as a result, I very nearly burned our house down. It was a terrible awakening. I cried bitterly then, and I still cringe now. But then my entire scientific career has since been full of such wild ideas and their inevitable shipwrecks. I suppose it's also too late for me to change."

"I wouldn't have it any other way," she said, bringing her cheek to his. Her heart finally found its haven in the white cloud of blooms, with Erwin in this perfect moment.

"Your love has made all the trials worthwhile, Eleanor, if you knew what strength I draw just from the mere thought of you," he said, a faint tremor in his voice, as though touched by emotion. He sat straight and reached his hand inside his jacket, producing a small leather-wrapped box. He then slipped down onto the ground in front of her.

"Dearest, you're perfect to me. I don't want any happiness upon Earth but the joy of your heart's love."

He opened the box to reveal the daintiest, most exquisite diamond ring Eleanor had ever seen. She gasped in delight. Her breath came in little catches again as she extended a trembling hand toward Erwin, this magnificent man bent before her in this kingly manner, with all of his strength, wisdom, tenderness, and exquisite appreciation—how precious and rare his gifts were to her. And she would give her love to him in its fullest measure, now and always. Her eyes welled. He slipped the ring on her finger.

"Six, just as I suspected," he said teasingly and looked up at her.

"I love you, Erwin," she said. "We will be so very happy." The mere words sounded small and humble against the breadth of what she was feeling.

After climbing the hill, they sat in exalted silence on a rock atop a high bluff overlooking the Tombigbee River, gazing toward the outward beauty. In the distance, the horn of a riverboat sounded, its giant voice pouring out over the water and echoing through the banks; one long blast, then two short, coming in for a landing.

Afternoon was upon them, and Erwin would soon be leaving. Grief rose within her at the thought of parting. Everything seemed different, now that their hearts were beating so close. The beautiful ring was on her finger, the bond between them a tangible thing, their future a reality that couldn't come soon enough; there would be an unbearable pain in doing without him for another year.

Wasn't there something in this harmony that could overcome all obstacles? She quickly reproached herself for thinking of Helen as an obstacle. But perhaps Helen was the only thing keeping them apart. She searched for the words to ask. *How soon can we tell her? When will our sweet time be?* But they wouldn't come. She felt clamorous as a child but strove to be womanly.

Erwin closed his hand over hers and then brought it up gently, gazing down at the ring. "Eleanor," he said, his brows knitting together into the worry look. "I've wondered lots of times if there are some dear hopes of your own that you worry may go unfulfilled if you are to be my wife." He looked searchingly at her. "You'd tell me, wouldn't you?"

Her heart rose in her throat at the thought. "Of course I had plans," she said. "My idea of misery is aimlessness, but these new plans, *our plans*, are incomparably dearer than any I once had." She raised her hand to smooth out his brow.

"We shall strive to the end that both our lives may be filled to the fullest." He brushed a gentle kiss across her hand. For an instant, a wistfulness stole into his expression. He seemed to want to speak further yet couldn't. The wistful look melted poignantly into pain, and he buried his face in his hands, overcome with mute despondency.

Eleanor also felt the wordlessness and yearning, the sweet pain of cracking the shells around their hearts. She wanted to help him, to find the words to speak of their future, to chart a course together toward home.

She reached for the solid strength of his arm and said his name, soft and low. "*My husband*," she added in a whisper. He looked up into her eyes with pent-up longing and kissed her eagerly, openly, sending shivers of delight through her. She brought her arms up around his neck in response, giving herself freely to the passion of his kiss, the explosive currents racing through her.

In the distance, voices of others along the trail rose up, making their way up the hill.

"Darling, I will also work for the happiness of our—that is—do you want . . ." He quickly pulled back, the poignancy returning to his face. "A family. Children," he whispered tenderly, leaning into her ear.

"Yes," she answered quickly over her trembling, beating heart. "Yes, yes."

He pressed his body to hers as his lips seared a path down to her throat, and Eleanor gave a little cry at the new sensation. "Oh, Erwin, I love for you to do that," she said.

The hikers drew nearer, and Erwin and Eleanor giddily rose hand in hand from their rock and sprinted away. Erwin bounded with an earth-sprung, athletic gait. Eleanor sought to keep pace, moving behind him. Halfway down, he stopped to regather himself next to a large tree wreathed up in wisteria. He put a hand on the vines twisted around its trunk and looked upward.

"The effect of the vines is beautiful, but I always wonder whether it harms the tree's growth," he said.

"Probably," she said. "A little." Eleanor knew it was merely an aside, but a new and creeping uneasiness began to form in her heart at his words. In her social culture, adults were divided into leaners and leanees, into oaks, more or less sturdy, and into vines, quite clinging. She found herself worrying that she would become that thing she always dreaded, what she feared her mother had become: the "clinging vine" to his success. That she would hamper him. Erwin regarded her quizzically, as if registering what might've appeared to him as a flutter of pain and not knowing whether to ask. He offered his hand out to her instead, and they continued down the hill. And the further away they walked from that moment, the more Eleanor realized; as much as she wanted her future with Erwin *now*, she couldn't interfere with what he saw as his duty. And if Helen knew, she would surely sacrifice her future happiness for the sake of Erwin's, and that would make coming together less beautiful. No, she wouldn't fail Erwin, and she wouldn't fail Helen. She would be strong.

They walked in the direction of the train station, her grief mounting. He slipped her hand through the crook of his arm and squeezed her to him, his body so near yet soon to be so far.

The conductor called for the passengers to begin boarding, and Erwin encircled her in his arms. She buried her face in his chest, pained at the mere thought of letting go. She felt caught in his gravitational field. Her breath came in catches, and she tried not to cry.

"Tell you what," Erwin said. "I'll come back for another visit in the summer. It'll have to be quick again, but that way the goodbye won't be for so long this time." His voice was calm, his gaze steady, his eyes full of endless warmth.

Eleanor nodded mutely, tears welling in her eyes.

"All aboard!" called the porter.

She gave him one last urgent kiss before he raised himself up to the vestibule at the sound of the whistle. He turned to face her with one last clasp of their hands.

"When you look up at the moon tonight," he said, "remember that its light is only a second-and-a-third away from me. And I will be looking at it too, so we will just be a twinkle apart."

"If we could only travel on a moonbeam," Eleanor said.

"I love you, my darling."

The train lurched forward, their hands still outstretched to each other, even as it carried him away, rushing forward under a widening cloud of smoke, opening an ocean of gray between their two shores, until Eleanor lost sight of him on the other side. As it faded into the landscape, she felt ice spreading through her stomach, the sense of loss so acute that it was a physical pain. Her hand still outstretched, the rich timbre of his voice hung in her heart like a star.

"Ma'am?" she heard a voice behind her and a touch at her elbow.

Eleanor spun around. She'd never been called ma'am before. It was the Traveler's Aide, a short, bunchy woman with a pinched expression.

"I've a group of girls here needing to get to the college; might you chaperone them?"

Eleanor was abruptly shocked back to her old reality. With Erwin now gone, a little panic grew over the ring's telltale abilities and the reminder of what that could mean for her job. And so she shoved her hand in her pocket, reluctantly reassuming her identity as maiden aunt.

"Certainly," she said in as reasonable a voice as she could manage. She tilted her chin upward, wiped her eyes, and walked away.

ACT THREE

Absence is to love what wind is to fire; it extinguishes the small, it inflames the great.

Roger de Bussy-Rabutin

Columbus, Mississippi

Dear love,
  I'm missing you very much today. And you are still on the train somewhere. Do you wish for me too, just a wee bit? I know Southern trains, and I know that the unaccustomed warm weather was hard on you; dearest, I hope that you will get a good night's rest.
  Thelma has gone downtown with Sallie, and I'm by myself, and so I have the ring on my finger. It is so beautiful. I can't write much for stopping to look; the lights in it are lovely. When you were here, Erwin, my thoughts were with your presence so I couldn't look at the ring very much, but now I look and look. The ring is perfect company for me, dear; it is part of you with me all the time. Erwin, Erwin, I love you.
  Sweetheart, I wish I could have entertained you not in

somebody else's house. It looks as if there's to be no real home time for us until we have our own home. Yet the little unpleasantness didn't spoil our evening, did it, my dear? We will cherish the memory of that evening's happiness all our lives long, will we not?

Darling, though I miss you, I am happier than before you came. I know your voice now, and my joy in your words is more than trebled; it is many times more. And when you send me kisses, now I know just how sweet they are. Erwin, are you as happy as I am? Your visit was perfect joy to me, dear. Every word was what I longed to hear, and—oh—I wish you were here to take me in your arms and kiss me now.

Your Eleanor

Urbana, Ill.

Dearest Eleanor,

I returned home Sunday night at the start of a torrential rain that went on for days. And today the postman seemed not to have come, and I began to fear that bridges were washed out or the postman couldn't swim, so I sat in the parlor and waited. Finally, I gave up and started for the lab. Then I thought I'd give one more look in the porch box, and my heart leaped up to see your letter down deep against the side, wet but legible—it had a new sweetness, Eleanor, since our hearts have been so close, and my eagerness now seems to be even greater than before.

Dearest, it was like stepping into fairyland to leave this

bleak country and be among the flowers. But flowers and fairyland aren't what I needed, dear. It was to walk beside you through the beauty, hold your hand, run, and laugh with you. Eleanor, you're so lovely and sweet to me.

There were dozens of expressions on your face, every one dear to me. On the ride home, I tried to recall each change that came over you and each evidence of your love. Am I happy? Oh, sweetheart, I never can tell you how beautifully you have fulfilled my hopes and yearnings.

But I was almost in a trance, Eleanor, and often couldn't say what I wanted to say. But you understood that, my dear; you knew without my speaking in that happiest moment, didn't you? You knew my heart so well. You knew where I was weak and needing comfort. I'm so glad there's no pretense in you, sweetheart, that you love and trust me. I have strength to wait and work, and it came from you as we embraced each other. I saw love in your eyes.

We'll never forget our first sweet hours together, Eleanor. They're written deep upon my memory. It was hard to leave you. But whatever comes to us that we cannot see, the past at least is ours, and our love has come to a lovely bloom, with never a chilling frost, in this sweet March.

Kiss me again, dear Eleanor.

Your adoring Erwin

New York City

Dear Tommie,

Don't faint, do anything rash, or be unduly alarmed at receiving a communication from your reticent sister. I know I have "done you mean" about writing, but I know you understand why, and I also know we are even on that score. Peggy is good about handing the letters around, so I think I have seen all that you have written home, and you have seen most of mine.

Peggy wrote me what you all "done" concocted for me when you got together Christmas; you want to offer a hand in getting me educated. I know nobody had better "folks" than I have, though I am not graceful about expressing appreciation. I had planned to get a position in or about New York next year and work on my thesis as time permitted. After mature deliberation and meditation, I am willing to modify my plan to this extent:

Firstly, any help I accept from any of you is strictly a loan with interest, so you may consider that you are putting it in the savings bank for your old age!

Secondly, I shall work intensively the first semester of next year, with the hope and intention of having my thesis by that time out of the woods.

Write and tell me whether you agree, else there will be <u>nothing doing</u>. See?

Seriously, I will accept only in the way I said and even so am afraid that maybe the lack of a ready capital may stand in your way in some capacity that we can't foresee now. You have done so much more for the home than most young men do, and you deserve the very best the Old World holds. Besides, I don't want you to be an old maid—we have enough in the family! I want you to get a start, and by that time, you, with your good judgment, will doubtless be able to make a wise choice. And for the life of Mike, Tommie, pick a woman with sense! I am tired contemplating brainy men with fluttermill wives.

Have you any notion of coming to New York any time to see the sights? I had a letter from Eleanor Morgan a week or two ago. She had hoped to come back here to Barnard College next year but says she will have to give it up. She is going to stay at MSCW.

I have written all the news in my letter home, which will come to you "in dew time," I suppose. Wisht I could see yuh!

With much love,

Helen

Erwin couldn't help to be pleased by the delicious irony of it all. Helen certainly considered Eleanor a woman of sense. And perhaps it wouldn't be so long after all, as the letter seemed to indicate. If Helen only needed his help for a semester's time, perhaps he would then be able to come to Eleanor even sooner than he hoped. But first, he knew, he had to see it through, to do his duty to his family, and then he would be worthy of Eleanor's love.

CHAPTER XXXIV

Columbus, Mississippi

"I HAVE A SNEAKING suspicion that you going to live in Illinois next year," Sallie said in a jesting tone, pulling up a chair in Eleanor's classroom after the girls had filtered out.

Eleanor colored with surprise at the quip. With a slight air of defiance, she thought devilishly of the diamond ring stashed away in her trunk compartment.

"Whatever gave you that idea?" she said.

Sallie tilted her head and raised an eyebrow, her mouth set in suspicion. "Well," she said, "you're *crazy* if you're not."

Eleanor drew up her books from her desk, her lips curved into a smile. "Let's go."

As they walked toward the door, Thelma appeared, pushing past Sallie.

"Eleanor?" There was a short, brittle silence as Thelma pressed her thin lips together and crossed her arms. "Mr. Carpenter is back from Charlotte. He just took *me* to task for having your beau in my classroom Saturday, as if I were the one having the secret affair," Thelma said in exasperation. "No one even knew you had a sweetheart, and suddenly he's here in Columbus, causing havoc. You'd better go talk to Mr. Carpenter, and hurry up—he's *mad*." She stomped away.

"I'm sorry, Thelma," Eleanor called after her.

The lightning had struck, sending her thoughts swirling. The situation she'd dreaded, had taken pains to avoid, was upon her. And there was no getting around it. But Mr. Carpenter couldn't know of her engagement. Not yet. The prospect that she might now be dismissed struck her with force; if she weren't teaching here, it would mean going home to Goldsboro to sleep on the parlor sofa. She didn't know what was going to happen, but she had to preserve her job. She gathered her thoughts and steeled herself, determined one way or another to straighten the havoc.

Leaning against the door for strength, she flashed Sallie a look of unease and then set off for Mr. Carpenter's office.

"I'm unpleasantly surprised at you, Eleanor," said Mr. Carpenter, in response to her knock at his half-open door, "that is, if what Thelma told me is true. A gentleman caller? *On campus*? You of all people should know how highly inappropriate that is. Any of our girls would be dismissed for such a thing."

"Please accept my apologies, Mr. Carpenter," she said, struggling to maintain an even, conciliatory tone, burying her irritation at the plain fact that she would be made to apologize in the first place. "He was merely an old acquaintance passing through. But you are right, of course. I should have exercised better judgment." To use *merely* in a sentence describing Erwin pained her, almost as much as delivering the lie.

Mr. Carpenter nodded. "Yes, indeed you ought to have," he said. "But no one *passes through* Columbus, Eleanor. Who was this man? A friend from home?"

Her legs began to feel weak. She looked out the window to center herself. The blooms of the spirea bushes flanked Music Hall.

"Only . . . the brother of a friend," she said, hearing the quaver in her voice. She felt that if she revealed any more about Erwin, she would lose her composure. She straightened and cleared her throat, mustering a sense of conviction. "I will apologize to the girls. I wouldn't want them under the impression that he was a beau."

Mr. Carpenter flashed a smile of satisfaction, giving Eleanor the fleeting impression that she was out of the woods. But the relief was short-lived. With a tilt of the head, he slid his eyes toward her. "Is he . . . the fellow from Illinois?" he said.

Her heart seized at the question, remembering in a flash those times Mr. Carpenter had made particular notice of her mail.

What could she say? Mr. Carpenter comprehended more than she had realized, and the charade would no longer serve her. Trapped in her lie, she was defeated. "Yes."

Mr. Carpenter regarded her for a moment in silence, his eyes reproachful. "Well then, he's quite more than an acquaintance if he's the very same who's been writing you all those letters for the last year. And all the while, I thought you were a respectable woman." He pointed his pipe like a pistol. "Now I wonder whether your change in living situation has something to do with all of this as well?"

Eleanor's cheeks burned, flushing her with shame. Did he expect an answer to that? She closed her eyes, stomach churning with anxiety and frustration. Any adult woman ought to be allowed friendships and society, she wanted to say, but she couldn't.

"But please, do tell the girls your fictional tale of mere acquaintanceship with this man," he said, his voice cold and lashing. "And apologize to them for your lack of judgment."

"Yes, Mr. Carpenter." She swallowed hard. "Of course."

She turned to walk away. "And Eleanor," he said.

"Yes?" She stopped, turning her head to the side.

"Under the circumstances, I'm afraid I will have to rescind your recommendation for the summer position and next year's contract. Please find other arrangements."

A black fright swept through her, like a trapdoor under her feet had swung open, her fate cast to the wind. She closed her eyes and lifted her head to catch her bearings so she wouldn't fall.

"Yes, Mr. Carpenter," she whispered and walked out the door.

Urbana, Ill.

Dear sweetheart,
  I've been very much excited since yesterday, setting up the Redmanol apparatus that has just come from Chicago. Imagine two cylindrical vessels about eight inches high, made of amber (synthetic, of course), and you have an idea of how it looks. Lids screw into the tops and tubes of the same material connecting them. There are lots of changes I have to make, and I may have a good lot of trouble yet, but prospects are looking much brighter than they were with the gold-plating of my previous attempt. I've made a preliminary test with the hydrofluoric acid and find no action at all apparent on the Redmanol. It "chews up" glass, copper, and lead right away.
  I chased all over Urbana and Champaign looking for odds and ends necessary to set up the apparatus. I needed a thin sheet of rubber dam to make "washers" for my two vessels and couldn't find it anywhere. Finally, I went to Woolworths five-and-dime and bought a ten-cent ladies bathing cap! Now what do you think of me?
  Throughout this chasing, I looked at hundreds of houses, thinking which I liked and didn't, dreaming of when we should have one and call it home. There's one long street that runs between campus and Urbana, with pretty houses on it. Toward Urbana, they thin out, and some cottages are in evidence, almost dollhouses. They seemed not too far away to covet (which I did).
  I have another plan I'm going to get lots of pleasure from, I think. I will have some of the lumber and building companies send me designs and specifications for cottages and think out all the details of a home for us, sweetheart. Won't that be fun? It won't be entirely "make-believe" and

"castles in the air," will it? Even if it should be a pretty long time till the castle crystallizes, we want to think it out ahead and know just how it will be, don't we?

But what I need most now is a little success and the feeling that I really can begin to unravel some of nature's tangles. And since I've seen you, dearest, I've felt somehow that I can succeed; my spirits have risen very high. I owe very much to your love, Eleanor.

And now I'm trying to picture just what you are doing and thinking, dear. Though it's a hopeless thing, I love to do it. I couldn't do without your letters, Eleanor, though sometimes I think there must be days when circumstances make it pretty hard for you to write, aren't there? I love every word you write me, but I don't want to be an insatiable tyrant. Am I?

Oh, I do love you, Eleanor, my Eleanor. You are always closer to me even than I can hold you, always in my heart.

Erwin

CHAPTER XXXV

Columbus, Mississippi

ELEANOR SHUT HER eyes against the light and the scratching of Thelma's pen, hovering again in that liminal state between sleep and wakefulness, to which she had grown uncomfortably accustomed. Thelma was still sore about the events of the day and consequently wasn't the least bit curious as to Eleanor's fate. It was 11 p.m., and she could only hope to be asleep by midnight. But tonight, her thoughts were a puzzle, and she couldn't stand it any longer—she'd slipped the ring back on to her finger, concealing it under the blanket.

She tried calmly weighing the structure of events: Her job would be gone in two months' time, and yet she couldn't go home; Papa had rented out her room. The promise of a beautiful life—far more so than anything she could have imagined—was waiting for her, still just out of reach. And what had she done to deserve such a fate? Have opinions? Conduct a discerning relationship with a man? She stirred uneasily. She wanted to believe that if Mr. Carpenter knew what he was taking away from her, along with her position, he would feel regret and reinstate her. Their history should at least have afforded her that. It wasn't exactly the power he had over her that angered her so but the recklessness with which he'd chosen to exercise it. But if her tenure at MSCW had taught her anything, it was that the norms of society were always assumed to be constructed with higher intelligence than any individual woman's understanding and experience.

I must make up my mind about which is right—society or I, she thought, twisting the ring. Through strange, sleep-addled association, Erwin's letter had put in her mind those words from Ibsen in *A Doll's House*. They so seemed to encapsulate the struggle in which she often found herself: rebuked by society for that in her heart which she felt to be true and right.

She turned over in her bed to face the wall and drew her hand out just enough for a stray beam of light to fall on her ring. She thought of her home together with Erwin, in which they would each be an individual, above all things, and she would be free from this. Theirs would be no Doll House of Ibsen's. She watched the play of colors in her ring. Yet it would just not be right without first following through with his plan for Helen. She could not lean on Erwin, and she would not allow Mr. Carpenter to interfere with their plan. She would make other arrangements for herself; she would be strong.

She kissed the ring silently and drew it back down under the blanket. She resolved to write to Mr. Brewer back at Oklahoma University in the morning to inquire about the availability of a position for her there. The summer session would start in three months, and there wasn't a moment to lose. If she hadn't a position by then, she'd be forced to be a burden on her family. And that could only be a last resort.

With her mind settled on the matter, she tried to throw off her doubts and fears and get the rest she desperately needed. All the while, the strangest image kept coming back to her—intangible and yet vivid. It seemed as if she wanted to open a door to Erwin's heart, not figuratively, actually, literally, so she could nestle down and stay forever with the door fast shut again. Not quite losing herself inside, for *she* was still there, but inside his heart in literal fact. She drew the covers way up to her neck and fell fast asleep.

Sweetheart,

I am happy, my dear chemist, when you tell me about your work. Tell me all you can, Erwin. And you give me deep joy when you say that I mean ever so little to your success. I'm keenly interested in whether the pretty amber vessels succeed. They should, you know, to prove that beauty is efficiency, efficiency, beauty. (Poor Keats!)

Your word "tyrant"—I'm going to do a dreadful thing. I'm going to mark it in red ink "Ch" (Choice of words). And if you should become satiable in regard to my letters, why you would quite break my heart. Your letters are my great joy, Erwin. I depend on them very earnestly. They are my refuge, dear, from everything that disturbs me; you do send me parcels of strength, by post, you know. I have had somewhat of a struggle these past months—with just tiredness, not with anything of real illness, and your letters have helped me far more than you know. I haven't been getting enough sleep since my move to the King house—Thelma works until the wee hours, every night, and I think it will tell on her before very long too.

Let me forget it, dear, for a little while, in your arms. I want to look into your eyes. Will you kiss away my troubles, love? And let me rest with my head on your shoulder?

Erwin, I wish I could hear your voice. I wish you could kiss me.

Your loving Eleanor

CHAPTER XXXVI

Urbana, Illinois

ERWIN WATCHED THE ammeter's needle closely as it rose. Thanks to the Redmanol, he'd been able to carry out his experiment with the hydrofluoric acid. He could barely breathe as the needle steadied itself and then began to fall, indicating that the conductivity measurement was dropping off. He released his breath in an exasperated sigh. A wave of dread washed over him at the notion that the Redmanol too would mark another failed attempt, drawing him down into a well of disappointment as deep as his hopes had just been high. He stood at the lab bench, propped up on his arms, head down, and resolved to find the root of the problem. Again.

Lochte ambled in, tossing an orange in the air and catching it. "I still can't account for you on those last two conference days, Phipps," he said, launching directly into the day's round of kidding. "You *did* go on the Muscle Shoals excursion? Hopkins doesn't recall seeing you there." He sat down, eyes on his orange, as if carrying on the conversation with it. "Or might you have gone to . . . oh I don't know, Mississippi? I've noticed you have an ardent correspondent there." He shot Erwin one of his barbed, comically clever looks, which neutralized as soon as he registered Erwin's pained expression.

"What's wrong?" Lochte joined him at the bench.

"The run with the Redmanol just failed," Erwin said bitterly. "So much for sailing in on this problem and cleaning up."

"Let's see," Lochte said, squinting through the intricacies. "Miss Hydrofluoric's vapor is attacking the electrodes," he posited.

Erwin groaned in frustration; a heaviness centered in his chest. "Even through the gold-plating," he muttered. "And here I already had the published article written in my head."

The unspoken corollary, he had told himself, was that if this run had been a success, he would take it as a sign to go to Eleanor sooner—that the promise of publication would give him just the boost he needed to make their start together.

"I feel for you, Phipps," Lochte said with a gentle pat to the back. "But don't lose your good ol' scientific equilibrium, eh? At least the Redmanol held its own. Next problem is how better to insulate those electrodes, or maybe how to sweep away the vapor inside the vessel?"

Erwin shook his head. Try, fail, repeat. The road to success grew long and shadowy once more.

"Such are the hazards of working in a closed system. No air in, no air out—there's your rub," Lochte said. He pierced the skin of the orange, the sweet smell of citrus cutting through the lab's accustomed malodorousness.

"You really shouldn't have that in here, Lochte."

He shrugged and put it in his pocket. *So careless.*

Erwin fought his impulse to irritation. "In any event," he said, "you'll be long gone before I can grind this to any sort of conclusion."

"*If* I can decide my next move," Lochte said.

"I thought you were going with the Texas offer."

Lochte was from Texas, after all, and the position seemed perfect: professorship within a stone's throw of his fiancée, his family. An ideal start, one that had aroused jealousy in Erwin when Lochte told him of it.

"I was, but just now I've been accepted for an internship at Yale," he said.

"And you're considering it? Wouldn't *Annie* rather be in Texas?"

"She would," he said hesitatingly. "The internship would only be for a year, maybe two. We've waited this long. What's another year?"

Erwin gave him a look of open incredulity. Here they were, two men with long-distance engagements. Erwin longed for the day that his new married life would begin, and he had assumed the same to be true of Lochte. Particularly so, as Lochte's engagement had gone on for years longer than his own. "And what would you stand to gain by that?" Erwin asked.

Instead of answering, he shrugged. Lochte, of all people, didn't have an answer. "We're so different, Annie and I," he said. "She's already bothering over all the awful details of the thing—do you know what 'At Home' cards are? I do, now." His voice was cynical, nonchalant. Gone was the avuncular jester. And Erwin could see, for the first time, that this was perhaps just another act, that behind his bluster and feigned callousness was fear.

"Okay, I'll bite. What are 'At Home' cards?"

"The little cards you're supposed to mail out with your new, *married* address—so everyone you know can call on you, give you congratulations, I suppose," he said with an odd air of drama. "And her address list is a mile long. I shudder to think."

Mr. and Mrs. Phipps: *At Home*. Erwin couldn't think of anything lovelier or more needful.

"Well, what would you advise?" Lochte asked.

"I advise Texas," he said firmly.

Erwin walked back to the Parmelee house, thoughts fired by Lochte's quandary. Proceeding in a safe and slow manner with Eleanor was not only something Erwin assumed had been the best course of action, but—whether he had realized it or not—he had been further justifying because of Lochte. Now, knowing that Lochte would, in selfish manner, put his plans off for fear of acting had untethered something in Erwin's thinking.

There had been a time that he dreaded the thought of marriage, surmising that the drawing of hearts near to each other would be something fraught with pain and uncertainty. But when he thought back to his time with Eleanor, it hadn't been hard to talk heart to heart with her. She was like-minded and sympathetic, she could be both playful and composed, and her love always rushed in to meet him, answering his heart's need with her own. Speeding things up only intensified the beauty of it all. He didn't have to go safe and slow, but he was now obliged to out of financial considerations. Surely he wasn't *afraid*, like Lochte was, not anymore, was he?

Perhaps, as with Miss Hydrofluoric, he had also been operating in a closed system with Eleanor's love. But what dangers would lie in opening it up?

Dearest Eleanor,

My lab work left me exhausted today. Do you know what it is to have something "hang fire" and fail and fail until you almost dread to think about it? It's a little bit that way now about my hydrofluoric acid problem. I tried a plan this afternoon for which I had great hope, and it was an utter failure.

And so I went over to Carle Park, just a few blocks away, and stretched myself out among the dandelions, looked up into the trees, and just let my wits wander all about. They have a way of always wandering south finally. I have a theory that this is due to the wind that blows in that direction usually, but I'm not entirely satisfied with that theory.

What I thought about was whether you're feeling "at home" with the ring or not, or whether it still seems a little strange and mysterious to you. And how very, very much I would like to hold that dear hand in my own again. I've been feeling homesick for you all day long, Eleanor, and it has seemed harder than ever before to be so far away from you. I think it was because you showed me so beautifully how happy we can be with one another, that now the longing hurts. Do you feel it too, darling? Does looking at the ring bring a little shudder of pain sometimes instead of a smile? If it does, I understand, oh my dear sweetheart. But perhaps the pain is the heart of joy, Eleanor?

Sweetheart, I remember so well that night how you came into my arms, and when I saw your face, it seemed that all the memory of the long days of waiting was in your eyes, and, love, there was pain in them too, wasn't there? My heart went out to you, Eleanor, but I was so fearful. For all that I had loved you so long and dearly, it was strange and wonderful to have you in my arms, and my heart was afraid—of what, I don't know.

I'm sorry, sweet, to learn of the trials you've been through with Thelma. I want to help, and yet I've been so helpless. Oh, I want to take you away from it all now. My heart cries "Now." I wish it could be now, love.

I hope you will always fly to me and tell me when troubles come, dear. Remember that I won't be happy unless I can follow each light and shade that comes to you and rejoice with you and console you. It seems as if my love isn't content with little things any longer, dear, but I want to prove it in some large way.

I must move from the Parmelee house soon; their eldest son, Charles, is coming home. I'll let you know before I make the move. If there's ever any doubt, 353 Chem Lab, Univ. of Illinois will always reach me, sooner even than a street address.

Let me kiss you, sweetheart, in the way that seemed so sweet to you, so doubly sweet to me. Then rest your head upon my heart, dear, and forget all else while I whisper

to you again.
I love you.

Your Erwin

CHAPTER XXXVII

Columbus, Mississippi

"I HARDLY KNOW WHICH end is up today," Eleanor said as she and Sallie walked home after class. Her head and chest felt heavy, like lead, the sounds around her muted and sharp at the same time. And all throughout her classroom lesson on personal narrative, her thoughts had drifted in the strangest manner—sometimes stopping her in the middle of a sentence, as some image would come foremost into her mind, and she forgot entirely what she had been saying. Now, walking with Sallie, she had the image of sweet pea tendrils in her mind, vining all about her just as she fancied as a small girl in Mama's garden.

"What do you say we stop for tea at the Golden Goose?" Sallie said.

Eleanor was fairly exhausted and didn't frequent the campus tearoom, but today, a bracing, hot drink struck her as just what she needed.

"Yes. Let's."

As they made their way, Sallie again carried on about James—she got tired whenever she talked to him, she was saying—but all that Eleanor could think was *I wonder when Mama plants lilies of the valley.*

"Oh, Eleanor," Sallie said, bringing her back to the moment as they approached the Golden Goose. "I tell you, I've lost faith in humanity. You were my Gibraltar, and now I never can go near one of my friends without first checking her left hand."

Eleanor made a sheepish smile, and they walked through the door, finding Thelma waiting at the foremost seating area; a pair of rose-colored couches faced each other, a short table with a tray of tea between them. Thelma waved a pennant made from brown paper: "Illinois."

"*Congratulations*, Eleanor," they said as a server approached with an assortment of cakes on the tea tray.

A little engagement party. As kind a gesture as this was, what Eleanor felt first was a wave of apprehension. Of course Thelma and Sallie didn't know they were the only ones, so far, who knew of her engagement. She couldn't give herself to the excitement of the moment; she worried that a chance word to a chattering friend could now find its way to her family, to Erwin's family, to Helen. She knew it seemed paranoid, but even Erwin didn't yet know that their secret was loose here in Columbus; she could scarcely even respond to his letter until she knew whether she'd secured a place in Oklahoma. She needed a moment to reorient herself. Her stomach churned.

"Thank you, my sweet, sweet friends," she said and smiled, half in gratitude, half in dread, as she sat down on the sofa opposite them. Confiding in Thelma had been an olive branch, a palate cleanse, when it became apparent that Thelma's ire would continue without some sort of peace offering. Eleanor calculated that she had nothing more to lose by telling Thelma, who immediately dropped her scowl, took Eleanor in her arms, and danced about the room. And they both scurried hand in hand next door to tell Sallie.

"We are so happy for you, Eleanor," said Sallie excitedly, pouring the tea. "Oh, I just knew it—from the moment he recited that poem. That *I'd* marry him if you weren't going to!"

"We got you a little notion for your trousseau," Thelma said and drew out a handkerchief-sized box with a little gold ribbon around it.

Eleanor was nearly astonished. "Oh, you really shouldn't have," she said. "I don't have anything like that yet." She couldn't afford to even think about assembling a trousseau. She took the box and placed it on the table in front of her, pondering it, trying to force her confused emotions in order.

"Well it's high time to start if you're getting married! Open it!" Thelma said.

The thing that should have been easy for Eleanor to say was that in fact she wouldn't be getting married anytime soon, that they had to wait at least another year until Erwin had finished funding his sister's education. But she could not say it. To say it would invite the dreadful explanations she was not yet prepared to give, even if she weren't half-dead from exhaustion.

And so she played along, fencing at their questions about Mama and Papa and Erwin's life in Illinois, struggling to keep her bearing stiff and proud. She could hear herself speaking calmly, stretching the truth; all the while, her spirit was in chaos, and the words she really wanted most to say were: *Please help me. This is all very sweet, but what I really need is rest.*

The hot tea brought her to her senses once more, and she reached for the little box, unraveling the gold ribbon. Inside was a dainty white linen case, stitched with the words "Hot rolls make the . . ." Eleanor read the words aloud and blinked up at Sallie and Thelma.

"There you're to embroider a butterfly!" Sallie gestured and shrieked comically, "Get it?"

"Hot rolls make the *butter fly*." Thelma laughed. "That way you'll always remember my delightful puns while you're keeping your dinner rolls warm," she said.

Eleanor was touched. It was a perfect token of their friendship and thrust images of dear home thoughts again into her mind—at her future table, all set with linens, having dinner with Erwin, and thinking back in time on this moment. But now she only felt the bitter edge of the image; this faraway sense of a beautiful beginning filled her with mute sorrow and made her head and chest ache all the more.

The pain is the heart of joy? Eleanor remembered Erwin's words.

"Thank you," she managed and looked down at the linen case, forcing a smile, trying instead to imagine the butterfly there—the butterfly that she would embroider while she waited and waited for her future to begin.

As they got up to leave the tearoom, the hostess was taping a notice to the glass of the front door:

```
CLOSING BAN PUT ON TO STOP FLU
COLUMBUS HEALTH BOARD PROMULGATED ORDER,
          IN EFFECT TOMORROW
```
<u>Schools, Theaters, Carnivals, and Public Gatherings Prohibited to Check Influenza Epidemic</u>

Increased severity of influenza cases, together with the gradually increasing number, caused the Board of Health today to issue a drastic order closing all places where crowds congregate, beginning tomorrow. This order will continue until further notice.

CHAPTER XXXVIII

Urbana, Illinois

THE EVENING BEFORE he was set to shoot on his problem at the Green Teapot luncheon, Erwin was trying without success to summon creases into his trousers. He'd finally secured an audience with Dr. Kunz, who would be bringing along a special guest—Dr. Holleman, a well-published physical chemist visiting from Amsterdam. And so, in addition to the scramble to present his problem with its current difficulty, he found himself under the additional painful necessity of presenting himself, considering the esteemed audience. As for his trousers, they had long been unacquainted with creases, and the under-the-mattress trick he'd learned from Roy Newton hadn't worked convincingly. He needed help. He needed heat.

He found Mrs. Parmelee downstairs in her armchair in the living room, reading through the Urbana Courier. "Mr. Phipps!" she said. "I just read in the notices about a little cottage to let just a few blocks down. Why, it would be nearly ideal, I think, for you. Unless you've already found something?"

"I'm sorry, Mrs. Parmelee. I haven't searched yet," Erwin said. "I've been preoccupied lately," he said and gestured to the pants slung over his arm. "May I trouble you for an iron?"

"A pressing engagement?" Mrs. Parmelee teased.

Erwin chuckled. "Indeed. A presentation tomorrow at the

Green Teapot."

"Very well," she said, put down the newspaper, and rose from her chair. "But Charles is set to leave from California *next week*, Mr. Phipps." Her son had procured a secondhand Ford and would be making the trip over land. "He expects to be here in about a month's time. Of course, I will do my level best in helping you, but we must get something arranged. Mrs. Emmett over on Babcock Street told me recently that she had an attic room to let. That's very near the Chemistry building."

"That sounds promising," he said. "How much?"

Erwin paid twenty a month for his room at the Parmelee house, and he couldn't afford much more than that, as he was planning to begin sending the same amount monthly to Helen, and his investment in the diamond ring had tapped out his reserves.

"I don't know exactly, but I can't imagine it would be much more than what you pay here," said Mrs. Parmelee. "The cottage down the street is being let for fifty-five," she added with an arched smile, studying his response.

Fifty-five was far too steep, but Erwin was enjoying the little spar and displayed equal interest in the idea. "Well now, that sounds nice too," he said.

"And Mr. Kirkpatrick said that there were several private apartments still available in his new building on Busey Avenue," she continued, "though he said that the nicest one on the top floor had just been let to a bride and groom." She cast another sideways glance. Mrs. Parmelee often teased him about Eleanor's letters, which had arrived with such frequency as to be impossible to conceal. Just the week before, they'd found a baby dove inside the house, and she teased him that it must have flown in with one of his letters. He suspected that she had a bet up with Mr. Parmelee as to whether he'd be married within the year, and so Erwin took great delight in keeping it up in the air.

"I see." Erwin maintained his poker face. "Plenty to choose

from, then."

"Well," said Mrs. Parmelee with an air of exasperation, "I'll press the trousers, Mr. Phipps, and leave them at your door."

"Thank you very much, Mrs. Parmelee."

"And perhaps after your presentation is out of the way, you might give me *some* guidance as to which place I might arrange a showing," she added pointedly.

It was only after the joust was over and Erwin had slunk back up to his room that he really faced the reality of the choice in front of him. He simply couldn't stay there much longer. And as much as he hadn't wanted to admit it to Mrs. Parmelee, he liked the idea of a little cottage on California Street. If only there were some way he could make the fifty-five a month. Perhaps, if he could soon manage a little extra research appointment, they could make their start together.

He tried to refocus his thoughts on his presentation but was now full of longing and eager for Eleanor's words—it seemed an unusually long time since he'd sent off his last missive to her. *Don't be a tyrant*, he thought. And he got back to work.

CHAPTER XXXIX

Columbus, Mississippi

IT WAS DARK when Eleanor woke, still dressed. How long had she been asleep? She couldn't tell. She fought through the cobwebs of her strange and disquieting dream, that embroidered butterflies had emerged from her new linen notion and carried off her secret, to throw it like a bombshell onto her family, to Helen. With no net to contain them, she could only watch them fly away out the window, sick to her stomach at the upset it could cause.

She sat straight and lit her bedside lamp. The sickness in her stomach persisted, and her head still throbbed, while she tried to get her confused thoughts straight. The house around her was quiet, Thelma's suitcase gone. The college closed for the week; Thelma and Sallie had taken it as their cue to go home to Jackson. Eleanor felt disoriented, had wanted to run to Erwin, but of course could never manage the expense. Instead, she realized, this happenstance could feed her need perfectly: she would have the room to herself for the week, no teaching duties, and all the rest she needed—an oasis, finally.

On her desk was a letter. Had Thelma brought it, somehow? Or had she gone to the post office? She didn't remember.

Norman, Oklahoma

Dear Miss Morgan,
   I am very pleased to receive your letter and glad to know that you are well. The English Department does currently have one opening left for the summer—teaching Modern Drama—might you be interested? If so, we would love to offer it to you.
   Unfortunately, because of the University's regulation, I would not be able to reinstate you with a permanent position. Much as I would like to, Lawrence will return to his position in the fall, and I am still bound to the rule that no two members of the same family can teach concurrently.

Sincerely,

                             Franklin Brewer

She had the image of a little wilted violet going into a vase of cool water. Everything would be okay. Now, at least for the near-term, she wouldn't have to lean on Erwin, muss up his plan. The strain lifted; she began to feel better. Now she could truly find the strength to get over her exhaustion and in turn give some of that strength to Erwin. She pushed aside all focus on her headache or the nausea that vaguely turned her stomach, moved to her desk, and drew out a leaf of stationery. She shook her head to relieve the persistent faintness and began to write.

Sweetheart,
   Can you tell me more about the new difficulty? Did the Redmanol fail? Erwin, you were tired and exasperated

when you wrote—you certainly had a right to be—and now I think surely you must be more hopeful. And, dear, whether you solve this problem doesn't determine whether you are a success or not. Hasn't every scientist found difficulties he couldn't overcome?

And when I tell you the unlovely things that distress me—Papa, Thelma's owlish ways, and my sleeplessness—it is only because I want your sympathy, dear. I have faced worse things than these, by myself. So you mustn't feel that you want to take me out of all this immediately, dear; don't you know that I couldn't come in just that way? Why, that would make me out a failure, Erwin. And worse, coming to you would be less beautiful. I am not escaping from something too unpleasant for me; I am leaving behind something fairly good for something incomparably better, for a larger, sweeter, greater life, dear love, for you. Would you not rather have me come so?

Love, I want to take you in my arms and hold you close to my heart. I love you, my darling. Don't worry anymore, sweetheart. Please, please don't worry.

Your Eleanor

She finished writing, slipped the letter into an envelope, and stood straight. She could make it to the letter box. And with the quarantine in place, it wouldn't be seen as impropriety to make the trip alone.

She began to walk toward the door. The room, however, spun. And before she knew what was happening, her knees buckled, and she fell into darkness once more.

CHAPTER XL

Urbana, Illinois

THE ATTIC ROOM at the Emmett house was nice enough. Larger and brighter than Erwin's room at the Parmelee's, with a big closet and a view of the pleasant little stream that ran through the campus, which had been given the unfortunate name of Boneyard Creek. Everything he needed was already furnished: a bed, study desk, rocking chair, and little coal stove. And for $18 a month, it was a great bargain. It was the obvious choice, but he'd also acquiesced to Mrs. Parmelee's insistence on arranging a showing of the cottage on California Street. "I simply want you to be able to make an informed decision, dear boy," she had said.

He had to admit to himself that Mrs. Parmelee had pretty good judgment, even if she did also seem to think, at times, that he was a hopeless case. She was partly right about that too. And if she enjoyed thinking she was reforming him and shaping his destiny, why not have a look?

Even so, he knew that he simply couldn't afford it. The luncheon, after all, had not been fruitful of results. The solution suggested by Doctors Kunz and Holleman hadn't seemed practical. Precious stones for insulation? Erwin had never heard of such a thing. He once more was left on his own to struggle through the difficulty of insulation material, which began to feel like an unending task, like separating ants from a picnic lunch. But Dr. Kunz had at least agreed to keep him in mind for additional research work. So Erwin had hope enough in the promise of income for the exercise of window-shopping. But he entertained a devilish hope that the cottage would be wrong anyway, and so it could be easy to make up his mind about it.

A "few" blocks down California Street had turned out to be five, which would lengthen considerably his walk to the chem lab, but it was in that lovely section of town that stretched eastward into the open land, the large, imposing houses nearer to the campus whittling away to sweet little cottages.

Mrs. Parmelee double-checked her notes as she stopped in front of a white, one-story bungalow with green shutters, flanked by spirea bushes just beginning to bloom freckles of pink. A man with a mustache waved to them from the front porch. "Here it is," she said and waved back. "That'll be Mr. Lipton. He's a professor of math."

Mr. Lipton approached and shook Erwin's hand at Mrs. Parmelee's introduction, bidding them into the house. "It's a little topsy-turvy just now, I'm afraid," he said as they stepped onto its front porch, which stretched the entire length of the house. It had a little wraparound section outfitted with a porch swing. The entryway was flanked by two side lights, reminding Erwin in a vague way of those at the plantation home he and Eleanor had snuck into in Columbus.

"Five rooms," said Mr. Lipton as they walked through the front door, "a kitchen, a combined living room and dining room, a bath, and two bedrooms of equal size. I'll only be able to show you one of the bedrooms, though. My youngest is having her nap in the other."

They entered the combined living and dining room, a large, beautiful space, full of light, that stretched to the rear of the house. Erwin surveyed the smartly outfitted room. The large, graceful mantle of the fireplace, flanked with family photos.

"I had this place built six years ago, just before I was married," Mr. Lipton said. "But I'm afraid we're already growing out of it. My wife's people are in Chicago, you see, so we plan to spend our summer there. When we return, her mother will be coming to stay, and well, with two little ones already, we're making plans to have a new, larger house built." He gestured to a small stack of catalogs on the armchair by the fireplace—homebuilding kits from lumber companies.

Erwin went green with envy. The house wasn't at all wrong. Rather, everything about it was just right; it was everything he'd imagined for he and Eleanor to get their start. And he didn't have the money for it.

Outside one of the large back windows, a little girl in a middy suit balanced in the sun along a short brick garden wall. He followed behind Mr. Lipton and Mrs. Parmelee, inspecting the house, all the while trying his best not to think, *Our hearth, our kitchen, our dining room.*

"Oh, this would make for a very nice start indeed," Mrs. Parmelee said to Mr. Lipton, though Erwin knew the remark was likely meant for him. "But if I understand correctly, the house is only to be let for the summer?" she asked.

"Oh, no. When we return, we will let a larger house if our new one's not ready yet. This house is available for as long as you like."

"What do you think, Mr. Phipps?"

He felt obliged to tell the truth. Even if a little boost should come through for him and he could make the fifty-five, he couldn't begin to afford to furnish a place like this. Not yet. And it was no use stringing either of them along.

"Thank you, Mr. Lipton, but I'm afraid it is just out of my price range," he said, unable to mask the disappointment in his voice. "At present, I'm just a freshman instructor, not quite in a 'monied' enough position to make a solid go of it."

"I understand," said Mr. Lipton. "I was the same. We nicknamed this house 'The Diamond' because I couldn't afford one for Mrs. Lipton, not if we were building a cottage!" He laughed. But the banter hit Erwin in a soft spot. He'd chosen differently for Eleanor, and that choice would amount to his taking another year as a roomer while they waited out their own opportunity for a house like this. *A diamond as a house*, he thought, *if only*, the irony twisting inside of him. Then his mind lighted, of all things, on a notion from his luncheon presentation. He could use black diamond—carbonados—as a material to insulate his electrodes. And as his mind raced around the possibility, he realized, the reasons why it had seemed a perfect token of his love—the imperviousness, the cool, glittering explosion of it—could prove the very same reasons why it might be just the thing to protect his electrodes from Miss Hydrofluoric's vapors.

In his excitement, Erwin almost didn't hear what Mr. Lipton added, nearly as an afterthought.

"We all have to make sacrifices, I suppose, to get our starts," Mr. Lipton said. "In case it helps you, Mr. Phipps, the house is to be let fully furnished."

CHAPTER XLI

Columbus, Mississippi

I love thee with the passion put to use
In my old griefs, and with my childhood's faith
I love thee with a love I seemed to lose
With my lost saints, - I love thee with the breath,
Smiles, tears, of all my life! - and, if God choose,
I shall but love thee better after death

—Elizabeth Barrett Browning

ELEANOR STRUGGLED DOWN College Avenue, with a parasol against the scorching winds of summer, hair in her face, the glare of the sun reflecting upward, burning her eyes. Wishing, as she had found herself on many occasions during her time there in Norman, Oklahoma, for a moment's stillness to collect herself. She knew that she was dreaming, but she had a sense of really, physically *being* there again. The wind whistled heavily about her, filling her ears with its screeching, but she could also hear beyond it the faint strain of a song she knew, carried through from a window of one of the houses that lined the old familiar street. *Is that Mrs. Dungan? At her piano?*

Forgotten you?
Well, if forgetting be thinking all the day
How the long hours drag since you left me
Days seem years with you away

Dust clouds whirled in the gusts, stinging her cheeks. She was parched. In the distance, a postman's mailbag was upended, and an envelope flew in her direction. As she caught it in her hand, her parasol took on a strong gust that pulled her upward, into the air. Her feet left the ground, and the world around her dropped away into a starless night. *I have no right to be engaged*, she thought.

Someone shook her awake. It was fully light, and she was on the floor of her bedroom in the King house. A man she'd never seen before, in a white coat, bent over her, stethoscope around his neck. "Come, let's get you to the infirmary," he said with the tone one uses when talking to a child.

"I don't know what's wrong with me," Eleanor managed as he lifted her onto a stretcher. "I feel awful." She turned her head and retched onto the floor.

"I bet you do," he responded calmly, as if they were talking about the weather.

Two orderlies raised up the stretcher, and Mrs. King stood to the side of the doorway, shock on her face. Eleanor felt pierced by her expression, wanted to cry, wanted it to stop.

"I'm sorry," she whispered through the anguish. As they carried her off, she saw that the letter she had written to Erwin lay kicked out of the way, still on the floor, and she panicked: *I have to mail that. Please help me,* she wanted to say, but she retched again instead.

Her body shivered with cold as the orderlies helped her into a bed in the infirmary, which appeared to her as a sea of white. Around her, the walls fell slowly away, and she was in the freezing arctic, alone on her boat.

The doctor again roused her out of her dream, listening to her chest with a stethoscope. "I'm Dr. Greenwood," he said.

"I was almost at the North Pole," she told him and swallowed a spoonful of the medicine he offered.

He nodded politely.

"You don't believe me, do you?" she asked, shivering.

"Oh I believe you," he said. "You must be freezing."

He called for a nurse to bring a hot water bottle for her feet and extra blankets. Eleanor struggled to keep her eyes open, but as soon as her feet and body warmed, the darkness enveloped her again.

Urbana, Illinois

Dearest,

Guess what! I'm "in the market" for another diamond, a black one this time. But you'd never guess what or whom I want it for. You <u>did</u> guess it. It's for Miss Hydrofluoric. I'm feeding her diamonds, trying to get her to behave reasonably.

Diamond has great electrical resistance—unlike carbon and graphite—and the crystal owes its hardness to the fact that its atoms are very densely and symmetrically packed together. So you see, we have a very favorable combination of properties: high insulating power, extreme imperviousness, and unusual chemical inertness. (Better hold on tight to <u>your</u> diamond, sugah, or in my fervor for science (!), I may make a raid on it.)

Now I shall ask the department to "stake me" a diamond

or two. Far-fetched as it may sound, I just know that this will be the end of my troubles with the hydrofluoric. I guess it takes something far-fetched to outwit that stuff.

Love, I'm feeling so happy. Suppose the diamond and the gold should be the right combination in love and conductivity both! Sounds reasonable to you, doesn't it, honey? Love, I slipped up behind you then and kissed you. No fair? Well, now we're face-to-face, and you're smiling and leaning backward in my arms while I gather you close, as close as I can hold you.*

Your Erwin

Eleanor was on an island, a dome of beaten gold and the moon above her. "*I will think in gold, and I will dream in silver.*" She remembered the lines of a long-forgotten poem. *What is the rest?* "*Imagine in marble and in bronze conceive . . .*"

Flames rose from the water surrounding her, and she closed her eyes against the heat, feeling a sharp pain sear through her veins, as if her blood was scorching her from the inside and she was being burned from the inside out.

She screamed and opened her eyes in desperation to find Dr. Greenwood hovering over her with a rather large, empty epidermic needle.

He placed a heavy, pawlike hand on her shoulder. "There, there," he said.

"Don't touch me," she shouted through her pain. "I feel as though I'm on fire."

Dr. Greenwood only smiled understandingly, then turned his head to speak over his shoulder to a shadowy figure behind him. "If she can stay awake for a while now, come back to her senses, she will be out of the woods," he said, "but then she'll need extensive rest."

Eleanor squinted, trying to focus on the dark-haired fellow with the wide frog-like mouth, contorted with anguish and relief: Lawrence.

"It's me, Eleanor," he said and approached the bed. "You're not on fire; you've had influenza. And now Dr. Greenwood seems to think that the worst is over."

Eleanor had been in the infirmary for nearly a week, it turned out, and Lawrence had been in Columbus for two days. He'd already paid a visit to Mr. Carpenter, who released her from the remainder of the semester so she might go home to Goldsboro to recuperate. Lawrence would make the arrangements to get her there safely, he told her gently, holding her hand. He'd been to Mrs. King's to pack her things, and he'd been to the post office to collect her mail and close out her box. Eleanor listened quietly, with no sharp understanding, just the sense of the impossible unfolding around her.

"Why didn't you say anything about losing your job?" he asked, finally. "And who is this man Phipps?" He held up a letter. "There were stacks of these in your trunk. And this one from Mr. Brewer on your desk." He put both letters on her bedside table. "Please tell me what is going on."

Eleanor was jolted to consciousness. Instead of making all sorts of half-explanations while she was still somewhat detached from reality herself, she asked Lawrence to read Erwin's letter aloud to her. And he did, with a quiet, even tone that suggested restraint in his judgment.

Lawrence set the letter down. "*Your* Erwin?" he said with an amused bewilderment. "Your diamond? *Sugah?*"

But for Eleanor, to hear Erwin's words cut clean through her fog all at once like a shot, bringing clarity and hope and longing. Her beautiful life was still waiting for her. She mustered her strength and searched her mind for the simplest explanation. *Start at the beginning*, she thought. *Lawrence will understand.*

"Do you remember Helen Phipps from my rooming house in Norman?"

Lawrence nodded. "Of course."

"Erwin is her brother. We are . . . engaged to be married."

"You?" Lawrence's bewilderment was unchanged. "How—" he began, then stopped. "When—" Again, he paused.

Eleanor felt weak at the effort but struggled to tell him as much as she could—about meeting Erwin, the correspondence during his degree work, the proposal, Erwin's visit, how wonderful he was, and how happy he has made her. How hard it must be for Lawrence to understand—even, at times, for her—but it was like a dream come true, she said, and she hoped that Lawrence trusted her on that. She stopped, exhausted, and waited for his response.

"Does Mama know?" he asked.

Eleanor went silent. She wasn't sure she had the strength to get into her reasoning for the delay.

"No," she said simply.

"Well." Lawrence blinked and shook his head. "You're full of surprises, Eleanor."

He poured her a drink of water. "All this and no word to any of us."

"Do you trust me, Lawrence?"

"My dear sister." Humor returned to his face. "I've always thought you had an extraordinary amount of brains, and intuition or something of the sort, about people," he said. "You are not the kind to enter into anything lightly or without giving it every consideration. Hence my surprise, but yes, I don't see why I shouldn't trust that. Only, you might've told me earlier. You know that, I hope?"

"Of course."

"Good. If you are happy, and you love him—well 'that's that,' as they say in English novels."

Eleanor laughed, her spirits lifted; he was saying everything she wanted him to say, hoped that he would say, for so long.

"Thank you, my dear brother."

"But why a chemist?" he kidded. "They are so irritatingly accurate. You'll have to give him fair warning that if he starts flinging his chemical formulas around me, I'll retaliate by quoting huge passages of Shakespeare and obscure Elizabethan ballads. I might even throw an Old French vowel at him or conjugate a Gothic verb." The teasing laughter was back in his eyes, and Eleanor enjoyed the gentle sparring as much as he did.

"Papa wanted me to marry Harrison Summerlin! Can you imagine? My consideration of him?"

"Oh dear God, conditions were much worse than I thought!" He slapped his hands on his legs. "Well then, when will the happy day be?"

"Next summer," she said, unwilling to shield the truth.

"Why so long when you've no position here any longer?"

Eleanor, a little more recharged, did her best to explain the delay, how Mr. Brewer's letter fit in to all of it.

When she was finished, Lawrence soberly held up both Erwin's and Mr. Brewer's letters and placed them on the bed.

"You've always been able to see through emotion to reason, Sis, and from your account of it all, I think you have acted wisely. But now, the wise thing to do is to tell him all, and give his heart the choice."

CHAPTER XLII

Urbana, Illinois

MRS. PARMELEE WAS waiting for Erwin on the porch with a letter when he arrived home from the lab. It was the end of a fortuitous day. He had secured a new position doing glassblowing work as needed by the department. It would help free up the department's mechanician for more specialized designs, Kunz had said when he made the offer. Such an obvious thing for extra remuneration, one that had been in front of him all along. He just hadn't seen it.

"Your Miss Morgan sent it special delivery this time," Mrs. Parmelee ribbed, handing him the envelope.

"Thank you," he said. "You'll be glad to know I've had some good news today, Mrs. Parmelee. And I've decided to let the Lipton house."

Mrs. Parmelee somehow managed to alloy together a look of both shock and glee.

Erwin smiled broadly. "Might you let Mr. Lipton know?"

"Oh, well!" she exclaimed, the first syllable slow and warm, the second like a hearty slap. "This minute, Mr. Phipps!" She shook his hand and disappeared over the threshold, thoroughly pleased in her completed mission.

He wouldn't ask Eleanor to abandon the plans she had for the next year, but he couldn't wait to spring the news that he would have the nest should Eleanor like to make their start sooner.

As he was putting the happy words together in his mind, he opened her letter.

McKinley Hospital
Columbus, Miss.

Dear Erwin,

We want perfect understanding, and I ought not to conceal anything in my love. I would not have you hide your heart from me—I could not bear to think that you would not tell me about your pain, and thus I know that I must keep nothing from you.

Erwin, I've lost my next year's position at MSCW. I will not say anything more about the matter now other than to say that I know I'm in the right and Mr. Carpenter has behaved abominably.

But the strain of it, combined with my exhaustion over so many sleepless nights, left me vulnerable to this horrid influenza virus—there has been an epidemic of it in the town, and this time I was not spared.

Oh Erwin, I'm ashamed of the state I reached—I believe I'm coming out of it now, in the infirmary here, but it seems to me one's duty to take better care of one's health. Circumstances simply got the better of me. Should I have told you sooner, darling? I was afraid you would be unhappy in your plan for Helen, that you would come to me anyway. You see, dear, I couldn't tell you. I couldn't. But now I must.

Mr. Brewer, who is the head of the English Department back in Norman, has offered me a place there again for the summer. The offer is only for summer school, as Lawrence will return to the department next academic year. And I've had my pride about not spending summers at home. You understand that, don't you, dearest? Except for the happiest of all changes in my plans, I should not hesitate about accepting this offer—even though it comes at the expense of travel, hot weather, and a lonesome time.

Won't you tell me what you think about the matter? My heart aches, and I wish I could rest in your arms, love. I wish you could be here with me now. But, dear, I don't want to be importunate. I know that it is a long and tiresome and expensive trip, and I know that you and I must be practical, sweetheart, even if it hurts.

Your Eleanor

Erwin put the letter down. His legs turned to clay, and the foundations of living suddenly slipped. He floundered in an agonizing maelstrom of thoughts: Eleanor ill and all alone, Mr. Carpenter's sharp gaze that morning in her classroom, her position at the mercy of his whims . . . and this was only from what she told. Things may well be worse than that. Fearful images built in his mind, and for once, he was absolutely sure of himself and his rightful place in the universe; it was at Eleanor's side, in this moment. It was clear to him now that Eleanor had sacrificed all, and very nearly her life, to protect his plan for Helen. He couldn't stand the distance between them any longer. He needed to act. And he needed to act *fast*.

He sat down to get onto paper the things he felt needed expression, in this moment, to shore himself up, nagged by the image of clay, how it turns to slip with the dispersion of water.

Urbana, Ill.

Oh my dearest Eleanor,

When I think of your dear arms reaching out for me and not finding me, oh, love, I know that I must run straight to you. I want you now.

Eleanor, you never have failed me when I needed you. You always come with such sweet love and sympathy. My heart is satisfied, thoroughly. What a poor word "satisfied" is. My heart is exultant, love, if exultant can mean humble too. When our hearts were so near to each other, it was almost as if two drops of water were touching each other, wanting to make one big drop together, wasn't it, dear? No love, we belong to each other, and there can't ever be any parting of our hearts, any more than the big drop could be separated again into the same two little drops. They never could be the same, could they?

Kiss me, darling Eleanor, and smile one of those big, brilliant smiles. I love you with all my strength—I'm coming to you, treasure. And I hope you have a calendar, honey, because have I got a surprise for you.

Your devoted Erwin

He addressed the letter to McKinley Hospital and put it in his breast pocket. He reasoned out how soon it would reach her, the slipping feeling persisting inside. It was Friday, so it would probably arrive Monday, unless he sent it special delivery. Then he realized he might be able to get there faster, even, than the letter. With a sure sense that there was no time to lose, he threw a few things into his suitcase and made a break for the postal box. He was finished with the day's duties. Could he be back by Monday lecture? He dropped the letter in the box and headed straight for the train station to find out.

CHAPTER XLIII

Columbus, Mississippi

ELEANOR HADN'T REALIZED that she'd nodded off. It was still happening with frequency, even though she was feeling stronger by the day. Dr. Greenwood said she would be released in a matter of days, and her heart rippled with the faraway wish that Erwin might be compelled to come to her before then. But the fancy also mingled with fear, at what such a visit would cost them both. If he didn't come, she consoled herself, it would be for the best. And she would understand.

The last thing she remembered before falling asleep that afternoon was Lawrence reading aloud from Hawthorne's "Twice-Told Tales"—for the second time, he joked, for the apt reason that they'd read the story collection together once when they were much younger.

As her mind slowly gathered itself back to consciousness, she could still hear Lawrence's voice next to her—he would often continue reading aloud after she'd fallen asleep—and tried to catch the thread of the story once again.

"So physics and poetry aren't entirely distant," Lawrence said. "Only, the poet says something is true, and it's wonderful. But the physicist says something is true, and it is merely a matter of such and such effect."

She tried to make sense of it. This didn't sound like Hawthorne anymore.

He continued, "Reminds of that Wordsworth line: 'One impulse from a vernal wood may teach you more of man, Of moral evil and good, Than all the sages can.'"

"But I'm afraid that still doesn't get us to the fountain of youth," said a laughing voice.

The room had grown dusky with the approaching sunset, but Eleanor didn't need any light to know who Lawrence was talking to. She felt a lurch of excitement within her.

"*Erwin.*" She sat up and turned to find him there, seated next to Lawrence, in a smart gray suit with a bright blue tie that matched his eyes. At the sight of her sitting up, he leaped to his feet, his smooth features bunched into a look that mingled anguish and tenderness.

"Are you really here?" she said with a measure, still, of incredulity. But as soon as her reaching fingers touched the warmth of his outstretched hand, she was sure. Erwin had come.

"In the flesh," he said. And with one forward motion, he took her into his arms. She pressed her cheek to his shoulder, breathing in his scent of cedar and sweat.

"How long have you been here?"

"Long enough that you missed a great ramble about relativity and shooting off into space and reversing time," Lawrence said. "But I can blame Hawthorne and his Dr. Heidegger for that. He started it, anyway." Lawrence lifted the book from his lap. "But your Mr. Phipps had some interesting notions of his own."

Eleanor moved back from their embrace to look into Erwin's eyes, his gaze soft as a caress. She had only barely glanced into a mirror in a week. She might've been horrified by how wretched she looked after what she'd been through, but in the mirror of Erwin's eyes, she felt beautiful.

"Well, I opened my eyes, and there you were. I heartily approve of relativity when it operates in that manner," she said.

"Lawrence has been excellent company," he said. "But first thing's first. How are you feeling?"

"Much better now," she said, "and stronger by the day. Dr. Greenwood is to release me soon, and then Lawrence is to take me home to Goldsboro. But I'm not sure yet how I feel about that." She turned to look at Lawrence, who pursed his lips knowingly. "In any event, Mr. Carpenter has released me from my teaching duties, and I can't say I'm disappointed on that account."

"What happened, Eleanor?" he asked.

She didn't want to say more about Mr. Carpenter. She worried that if Erwin knew the circumstances, he would think himself to blame for her termination, but the problem wasn't Erwin; the problem was Columbus. "I'll tell you about it at a different time, if you don't mind."

"Mr. Carpenter is a man who seems not to recognize women as sovereign beings," Lawrence said.

Eleanor acquiesced. "At least, there seems to be no place here for such an intractable disposition as mine. I'm afraid that my termination here was an inevitability from the beginning, now that I have the hindsight to see it."

"An unfortunate circumstance," Erwin said. "Darling, you should never stay where your sovereignty isn't honored."

"Indeed," Lawrence said. "And you shouldn't stay at Goldsboro too long either, or you'll end up in the asylum." His eyes jumped toward Erwin with an unspoken corollary: *Well, what now?*

"You two have a lot to discuss," Lawrence said. "I'll take my third wheel and be off. See you in the morning, Eleanor." He moved to make his leave. He offered his hand to Erwin. "My pleasure to meet you, Mr. Phipps, and for better or worse, welcome to the family," he said. A jolt of pleasure rose to Eleanor's cheeks at the sight of the two of them together, recalling their bureau-top photos back in Norman.

After Lawrence's departure, Erwin sat back down in the chair next to Eleanor's bed. "Your brother has quite a keen investigative mind. Must be a family trait," he said and nodded toward a little vase of hothouse flowers on Eleanor's side table, from Sallie, with a note:

> *Get well soon, dear Eleanor, and don't forget us one little bit.*
> *P.s.—I told him NO.*

Eleanor met the broad smile that Erwin offered, but upon the feel of his strong hand around hers, the warm glow faded. The thought of postponing their plans as a consequence of her joy scissored through her, giving way to despair.

"Oh, Erwin, the time and expense it took to get here . . . it's certainly more than we can afford." She drew him back into an embrace. "You don't mind my saying 'we' already, do you, dear?"

Eleanor felt a tremble, almost a shudder, pass through Erwin. She closed her eyes. She was in his heart then. She wanted to shut the door fast and stay there forever.

"I had to come, didn't I?" Erwin whispered, his face buried in her hair. "To tell you what I think about the matter with Mr. Brewer and Oklahoma?" He kissed her forehead. "Our time *is* short, though, I'm afraid, and I must be on the train in the morning to make it back in time for my Monday's lecture class."

She nodded and pulled back, her mind still alight with that mixture of hope and fear. Could there be a way for them to be together? That seemed too much to dare hope for, and she didn't want the bitter disappointment of a dashed dream to interfere with the glorious *now*: the powerful relief of Erwin's presence by her side.

Erwin sat for a moment in silence, as if to gather his thoughts.

"My train ride was agony at the thought that I might've lost you, that you were in danger, that our happy days together might never come." His voice broke. "I was more relieved than I've ever been in my life to arrive and find your health restored," he said, the timbre of his voice slowly returning. "To find you in Lawrence's care. And my conversation with him got me thinking further, so excuse my mind for being clouded over with ions and molecules, but Eleanor . . ." He took her hand in his once more. "Our bodies are made out of the elements of the earth, and matter never obeys ideal laws—perpetual motion is only a dream—one doesn't expect even a god to bring *perfect* happiness to creatures that are clay."

There was a tingling in the pit of her stomach. She tried to understand his meaning. She could only remember Mama's bitter words: *Marriage is not made up of the same stuff as dreams.* She'd had time to think over these things too, and that phrase had been coming back to her, in a haunting way. This is what Erwin was trying to tell her too, that they ought to stop confusing the two. They might dream of being together now, but they must be realistic. Despite her efforts to bear up, she felt the nauseating sinking of despair.

Erwin looked down at her hand and caressed her fingers. "Yet," he said, "perpetual motion *is* a stupendous reality in the bodies of the universe. So, Eleanor, maybe in a larger sense, in a way we can't vaguely understand, there is a perfection somewhere. And I think we've found it together, dear, as close as we're able to, just as though our hearts were lock and key."

The air around her went electric at his words; amid the despair, a catch of delight came to her heart, and she brought her hand up to Erwin's cheek.

"I can't let you go again," he whispered and clasped her hand, pressing a kiss into her palm, then drew in a sharp breath. "Here's what I mean to say: Go home to Goldsboro. Get rest. Gather your strength. But please, don't go back to Oklahoma. I will come to you. Let's make, as you said, the happiest of all changes in your plans. We've only to choose a day, and it ought to be soon, right? No time in the asylum for you."

Shock flew through her. "But what about Helen? Oh, after all this, we can't end up sacrificing her happiness, Erwin."

"Darling, I put Helen in front of you and very nearly paid the ultimate price for it. That is what I am sorriest for. I want *you*, more than anything in the world, and I've already got it worked out so we don't have to wait any longer."

Had Helen found out? And refused his help? She tried to throttle the rising current inside.

"How?"

"Helen told me she only needs my help for one semester, and I'll have money for both, Eleanor. I've arranged to have extra income from glassblowing, starting next week. You won't mind my coming home to you with the extra grime and dirt of the job, will you? And if I'm lucky, I'll also have something worth publishing about Miss Hydrofluoric very soon. But in any event, we can live as economically as church mice if need be, can't we, dear?"

Her heart sang with the delightful surprise of it all. "Of course," she said. "Does Helen know about us?"

"No, not yet," Erwin said, "but I will compose the happiest of letters to her on the train ride home. But then she might decide not to accept our help—you don't mind my saying 'our' help, do you dear?" he said affectionately. "And we will have to accept that."

Eleanor felt then as though she'd crossed a great divide into someplace she'd never been before, a gate to which she'd drawn close but not ever entered, passing from a state of conceiving to that of fulfillment. She wouldn't have to wait any longer; she would be going home with Erwin.

"Now then," Erwin said. He reached into his suitcase and produced the little black book with 1922 emblazoned on the front. "Today is April 22. Have you thought about which day would be nicest?"

She hadn't a thought as to a day. She'd never let her imaginings wander that far into reality. "To be married? Oh Erwin, any day with you would be the nicest."

Pleasure lit his eyes, and he flipped through the pages. "I think that Valentine's Day would be most apropos. Pity it's so far away. That won't do at all."

Eleanor's dormant wits renewed at the notion that special days bring back special memories for them. "Or Armistice Day," she chimed in. "I'd be in the asylum by then."

"Right. What's nearer down the pike?" He flipped back to May.

"Memorial Day?" Eleanor said, though that didn't seem quite right. "July Fourth? Fireworks in our honor?"

"Bastille day! *Vive la révolution!*" Erwin said.

Eleanor laughed. "I like that! But oh, even July now seems so far away. I'm far too clamorous for our beginning. And don't forget, hereafter, we will be together for all our celebrations."

He raised an eyebrow. "I've got it. The first day of summer. June 21?"

"The solstice. Oh Erwin, that *is* perfection."

"A Midsummer Day's Dream? Will you have all of your strength by then?"

"Yes. And then some. But what shall I do in the meantime if you forget me and go to sleep?" she kidded, her eyes lighting on the vase of flowers.

"Forget you?" Erwin said. "No, Titania, you'll not have to conspire with Puck. Your Bottom already has magic juice on his eyelids. And it was applied with all manner of incantations said over it, so there's no changing of the charm."

He pressed his lips to hers, and she melted into the velvety warmth of his kiss. Raising his mouth from hers, he looked into her eyes. "I hope the 'fair, large ears' will always delight my fairy queen."

A nurse made the rounds through the room with the day's last mail delivery, reminding them both that visiting hours were to end in fifteen minutes.

"Oh yes, I nearly forgot. A letter of mine ought to be arriving to you on Monday," he said.

"What does it say?"

"Everything that I needed to tell you."

"Yet you came. Why?"

"Are you really so surprised? Darling, I had to. You needed me."

"I do. I need you, Erwin." And saying that out loud was as if another weight had lifted. "I've needed you ever since you first wrote your love, but I couldn't let myself believe you really would come to me. You understand that about me, don't you, dearest? I couldn't express it."

His hand tightened around hers in response. A line of Sara Teasdale popped into her mind: *I shall not let a sorrow die Until I find the heart of it.*

"Do you see now, love, what I meant back then when I wrote that I was afraid? Afraid of love, but also afraid to ask you for what I needed?"

"I do. And, dearest, for me, it was the old, old habit that had ground itself into me of shutting out love for what seemed to be duty. I didn't realize how very different things were after you had said 'yes' to me. Now I know, darling, duty and love are one, and it is a precious, precious thought. Even so, I should have come. And because you hid your heart's keen disappointment, I went on and didn't realize how very hard it was for you. And there has since been that little bitterness? That I could have come and didn't?" His brow bunched into the worry look.

Eleanor lifted her hand to caress it away. "No, Erwin, there hasn't been a moment of bitterness." She paused. "At first, there was bewilderment. Even so, I knew that you were doing what you believed to be your duty and that someday I would understand. I *do* understand. Erwin. If duty did not mean as much to you as it does, you wouldn't be the Erwin I love. You couldn't have seen things any differently from the way you did see them. Because you didn't know. Because I didn't tell you."

Erwin put his arms around her and drew her close. "Darling," he whispered, kissing her forehead. "This is my duty now. When I brought my love to you, I know I was right, and your love has been the sweetest inspiration to my heart ever since. The only ruin that I recognize now is to be without you."

A strange tremor came over Eleanor, as if he was holding her heart in his hand and gently, gently enclosed it with his fingers and quickly opened them again.

"Can I ever make up to you, Eleanor, for that shadowy time?" he said.

But the shadows across her heart, whatever was left of them, were gone. And only a glow from within, like gold, in their stead. Even if there was anything to make up for, he'd done exactly that by coming to her now.

"Soon there will be sweeter joys for you, Eleanor," Erwin said. "I hope there will be such happiness that you will clear forget I ever wrote you any letters. Let's store them all away, and then someday maybe you will rediscover them and read some of them with a smile. But I hope when that time comes, honey, that you will be able to say to yourself, 'Sweet, so sweet—but Erwin could do much better *now* than that.'"

The nurse reappeared to clear the room of visitors.

"Your alchemist power means only happiness for me." Eleanor said. Her breath came in catches. "I have been trying for words to tell you this all the time. I have known this about you from the first moment I looked into your eyes; whether it was to be for me or not, I have known the fineness of your soul. I did not give my heart carelessly; I was very sure."

With a wistful look and a last lingering kiss, he planted a folded piece of stationery in her hand. "Dear, there's one more thing I must tell you about that's not in the letter," he said. Then he disappeared out the door. Eleanor was alone once more, but this time with a date in her heart: June 21—her fancy made real, her plans. Her life. She had never before gotten what she wanted most, she now realized; in the past, she had only been forced to learn how to live without it.

She unfolded the leaf of paper to find a little sketch of a floor plan that Erwin had drawn: "300 W. California St. Urbana," it read, showing all the rooms of a little house, with a backyard garden, a wrapped porch with a swing, and a hearth, with bookcases next to it. *One of the bedrooms now is a nursery,* he had written at the bottom. *Shall we keep it that way?*

New York, NY

Dear Eleanor,

Erwin has just written me the happy news of your engagement. I am just as pleased as can be and so happy with the prospect of having <u>you</u> as my third sister! I have often wondered if you and Erwin cared for each other—but there seems to have been a conspiracy of silence!

He said he has been keeping it as a happy surprise to me. I could hardly believe that he wrote that letter—it sounded so delirious! I almost envy both of you! I have just written to him and told him how lucky he is. Ever since the days of our Brotherly Adoration Society during the war, I felt that you two were made for each other. But then neither ever mentioned the other after you'd met. In my sweet innocence, I asked Erwin in one of my letters whether he ever heard from you, but he did not answer! I have about concluded that he wanted to help me through with my wild scheme of educating myself and was afraid I would not let him if I knew of his own hopes and plans. It would be just like the dear boy. And he was right!

He told me all about his visit to Columbus and raved some more about <u>you</u>. He is so happy, Eleanor dear, and I am happy for you both.

With much love,

Helen

The Goldsboro Daily Argus

Sunday, June 11, 1922, Goldsboro, North Carolina

ENGAGEMENT PARTY

Miss Georgia Freeman entertains in honor of bride-elect Eleanor Morgan

Miss Georgia Freeman was hostess at her home on North Williams Street yesterday evening in honor of a popular Goldsboro bride-elect, Miss Eleanor Morgan, who is to be married this month on the 21st to Dr. Thomas Erwin Phipps.

The home was beautifully decorated in the color scheme of pink and white, with vases of larkspur and sweet pea blossoms gracing the tables, and light from numerous white candles glowed among the happy guests. The place cards were red and heart-shaped, painted with silver arrows.

Strawberry ice cream, cake, and punch were served by the hostess, assisted by Miss Alice Freeman, childhood friend of Miss Morgan. The bride-elect was strikingly pretty in a trousseau gown of floral georgette, and there was much merriment over the cutting of the cake, which revealed the next bride-elect, Miss

Sarah Kornegay, who found the ring in her slice, instantly proving the prophesy true, as Miss Kornegay herself is set to be wed on the 28th of this month.

CHAPTER XLIV

Goldsboro, North Carolina

June 21, 1922

AS THE TRAIN whistle blew, Erwin lifted Eleanor up onto the vestibule of the Carolina Special, the white lace skirt of her dress swirling. The sun was high in the sky, and together they were giddy, reminding Erwin of their shared laughter on the night they met those years ago. The night he lifted her up, into the air, into his thoughts and his dreams, but then dropped her. And so the moment had finally come, this moment his heart had hungered for the most, all along. They were going home, together.

"All aboard!" shouted the porter. "This car for Asheville!" The bell rang as they turned back to face the wedding party on the platform—a teary Mama and smiling Papa, Lawrence, Clara, Frank, the girls of her old XYZ club—leaving behind Eleanor's known world for the great adventure. Leaving behind the pain of the years of longing and vague surmisings for the beauties and joys that lay ahead, forging a new pilgrim's script of the journey they would from this day forward write together.

"What fools we mortals be," Eleanor said with an arched smile, her eyes glowing. It was all there in her face—all that his heart worshipped. *Together, we are platinum*, he thought. *A noble metal, very dense and very strong, and lustrous as gold.*

For a moment, his mind flashed back once more to another train ride, years ago, when the war just ended, remembering the hope embedded deep down in that time of unknown, so fraught with loneliness and doubt that he would ever have his chance at joy. Little could he have known that the train taking him then to see Helen in Norman would blow the stuff of life toward him that could knit together this moment so beautifully; to begin to know Eleanor, the magic of her catalysis—the daintiness and color in her soul—would so richly paint his own scant dreams. And to find in her a wondrous, deep earnestness would sweep her being into his. And here she stood next to him now, looking more ethereal than ever, her corsage of sweet pea blossoms perfuming the air between them, her wild, slim beauty: his wife. With a heart overflowing, he clasped her hand and raised it, waving their goodbyes as the train began its lurch forward.

As it gathered speed, the wedding party shrank away behind them into the horizon. Eleanor lowered her hand and looked to him with a flashing glance of eager affection. "I love you so," she said, "*my husband.*"

Something intense flared through Erwin, and he pulled Eleanor close, holding her with all his strength. A surge of wildness came over his heart at the closeness and warm nearness of hers, thinking ahead to the yet-undreamed precious ways that heart would continue to awaken heart. He felt her chest rise and fall in little breaths, as her arms found their way around his neck.

"Take your seats!" the porter shouted from inside the car.

"Oh how *will* we manage to ride all day without a kiss," he whispered tenderly into her ear, heart beating like a centaur's hoof. "Is there a tunnel somewhere between here and Asheville? And does the horrid porter light the lamps?"

Mr. & Mrs. Thomas Erwin Phipps
At Home
300 W. California St.
Urbana, Ill.

Here the ancient battle ends,
Joining two astonished friends,
Who the kiss can give and take
With more warmth than in that world
Where the tiger claws the snake . . .
—George Meredith

THE END

ACKNOWLEDGMENTS

This book is a work of fiction, based on a real correspondence between Eleanor Morgan and Thomas Erwin Phipps, 1918-1923. Their courtship consisted of hundreds of letters and only a precious few meetings. The spark they shared over the course of one day went on, over time, to light a fire between them, and that fire lit up my own heart, 100 years later, inspiring this novel. The real Eleanor and Erwin married in 1923 and remained so until the end of their lives.

I owe a huge debt of gratitude to Mary, Katie, and Don Clegg for introducing me to the world of the Phipps family. To Tom Phipps Jr., for sharing and entrusting me with your parents' story. And to Erin Lindsay McCabe, for your consistent insight and unflagging cheer through the writing wilderness. This story would not exist without each of you.

Special thanks to Adele Suslick and Leslie Edmondson for sharing your portions of the correspondence. To Laurie Martin and Amanda Danowitz for your early enthusiasm. To my patient readers of the premature drafts, Amy Hassinger, Ann Thomas, Joy Garling Prud'homme, and Graciela Andresen.

Thank you to the team at Koehler Books for giving this story a chance in the world. To Miranda Dillon, for working her editorial magic on the prose, and Catherine Herold for creating such a beautiful package for it.

Big love to my parents, John and Lynn Tuohy, for supporting and encouraging all of my wild endeavors and shaping my world with your appreciation of the arts. Love to my mom and brother, Kurt Tuohy, for being enthusiastic early readers and the best cheerleaders.

And to my husband, Marco, and sons, Mario and Nico, you inspire me every day. I love and admire you all so so much.

And finally, my heartfelt gratitude to my readers, for spending your time in the pages of this story.

www.ingramcontent.com/pod-product-compliance
Lightning Source LLC
LaVergne TN
LVHW091621070526
838199LV00044B/891